ACKNOWLEDGEMENTS

Grateful thanks are due to:
1. E. M. Nicholson, CB, lately Director-General of the Nature Conservancy, who first brought the work of the BSCS to my attention;
2. Dr Bentley Glass, Chairman of the BSCS Steering Committee, and Dr Arnold Grobman, First Director of the BSCS, who introduced me to the work of this project;
3. The Nature Conservancy, the University of Keele and the Staffordshire Education Authority for financial assistance which enabled me to carry out the research and development work which was an important preliminary to the adaptation;
4. The University of Stirling for financial assistance which made the work of adaptation possible;
5. The Director and Staff of the Biological Sciences Curriculum Study, Colorado, and through them all the teachers and biologists whose co-operative efforts produced the original 'Green Version'. Their names appear in the publications of the BSCS;
6. Denys Baker, artist for John Murray (Publishers) Ltd, Ronald Stewart, Chief Technician and Miss Margaret Crawford, Illustrator/Technician, both of the Education Department, University of Stirling;
7. Kenneth Pinnock, Howard Jay and Patricia Winter of John Murray (Publishers) Ltd, to whom the adaptation team offer most sincere thanks for their guidance and help.
8. Finally we are particularly grateful for the forbearance and hard work of Peggy Shatwell and Mary Allan who translated the team's handwriting into legible typescript.

E. PERROTT
Director – British Adaptation

Thanks are also due to the following for permission to reproduce copyright photographs: American Museum of Natural History, cover; Linda Hall Library, 1.1; R. D. Allen and S. R. Taub, 1.2; Herbert F. Helander, 1.4; Gene Cox, 1.5 A, B, C, 1.12 A, B, C, D, 1.16 A, B, C; J. D. Robertson, 1.6; W. G. Whaley, H. H. Mollenhauer and J. Kephart, 1.7; Harold V. Green, 1.16 D; Martin H. Zimmerman, 1.16 E; University of Stirling (Ronald Boyd Stewart), 2.18, 2.25, 3.1, 3.8, 3.16, 3.30, 4.16, 4.19, 5.1; A. D. Greenwood, 2.19; Popperfotos, 3.12 (*left*), 5.9; Heather Angel, 3.12 (*right*), 3.15; Robert J. Rodin, 3.19; U.S. Department of Agriculture, Beltsville, Md., 3.27; Zoological Society of London, 4.2; University of Edinburgh (James Paul), 4.6, 4.28 A, B; Radio Times Hulton Picture Library, 4.12; Bert Kempers, 5.2; Paul Knipping, 5.4 (*both*), 5.23; Bruce Coleman (S. C. Porter), 5.17; Gordon S. Smith, 5.19; Douglas P. Wilson, 5.22; Bruce Coleman (Donald Paterson), 5.24. *Colour plates*: University of Stirling (Ronald Boyd Stewart), I, II, V, IX; Heather Angel, IV, VI, VIII; Gene Cox, VII A–F.

HIGH SCHOOL BIOLOGY
© The Regents of the University of Colorado
on behalf of the Biological Sciences Curriculum Study 1968.
This adaptation © the University of Stirling 1972

All rights reserved. No part of this publication may be reproduced, stored in a retrieval system, or transmitted, in any form or by any means, electronic, mechanical, photocopying, recording or otherwise, without the prior permission of John Murray (Publishers) Ltd, 50 Albemarle Street, London, W1X 4BD

Printed in Great Britain by Jarrold and Sons Ltd, Norwich

Limp 0 7195 2263 3   Cased 0 7195 2264 1

BIOLOGY: AN ENVIRONMENTAL APPROACH

A series of five books adapted from *High School Biology* (the 'Green Version') by permission of Biological Sciences Curriculum Study, Boulder, Colorado

Adaptation Team

Director

Elizabeth Perrott MSc, PhD, DipEd, FLS, FIBiol
Professor of Education, University of Stirling

Team Members

Eric A. H. Martin BSc, DipEd, MEd
Principal Biology Teacher, Marr College, Troon
(*Formerly* Research Fellow, Department of Education, University of Stirling)

Janet Watson BSc
Teacher of Biology, Alva Academy, Clackmannanshire
(*Formerly* Research Student, Departments of Education and Biology, University of Stirling)

David Hughes-Evans BSc
Lecturer and Head of Biology Section, Farnborough Technical College

Ian D. Campbell BSc, DipEd, MIBiol
Research Fellow, Department of Education, University of Stirling
(*Formerly* Teacher of Biology, Johnstone High School, Renfrewshire)

J. Keri Davies BSc, DipEd, MEd, FZS, MIBiol
Lecturer in Biological Education, University of Stirling

LOOKING INTO ORGANISMS

BIOLOGICAL SCIENCES CURRICULUM STUDY

JOHN MURRAY ALBEMARLE STREET LONDON

FOREWORD

When the costs and benefits of the race to explore outer space are debated it would probably occur to few to count in on the credit side the revolutionary modernization of school biology teaching over a large part of the world. Yet it is to the painful shock created by the first Russian sputnik and to the blinding recognition of the inadequacy of American science teaching that we owe the massive, outstanding and sustained effort during the 1960s to design a new contemporary basis for enabling the new generation of Americans to learn what science is about and how it tackles its problems.

Prominent within this broad effort was the Biological Sciences Curriculum Study, which came to be centred on the University of Colorado under the direction of Dr. Arnold Grobman and the chairmanship of Dr. Bentley Glass. About the same time that the American Institute of Biological Sciences first launched this enterprise those concerned with ecology and conservation in Great Britain became seriously concerned at the erosion of status and resources facing biological teaching in schools, and the exaggerated fashion for decrying in particular the pursuit of field studies and for diverting man-power and resources predominantly towards molecular biology. With strong backing from the British Broadcasting Corporation as well as from the Nature Conservancy, an informal study group was set up under my chairmanship to review the situation and to examine what could be done about it. In preparing our report, which was published in 1963 under the title *Science out of Doors*, I picked up the trail of Dr. Glass and through his good offices I was fortunate enough to be given the opportunity in July 1962 to see Dr. Grobman's busy workshop at the University of Colorado. Here teachers, educators and biologists had come together in a dedicated team to put into shape a wholly new and brilliant set of methods and media for modern biological instruction.

The high calibre of this team, the depth and thoroughness of its approach and the evidently immense significance of its work made a deep impression on me. I felt like someone who had happened to drop in on Lancelot Andrewes and his colleagues around 1610 and shared with them for a moment the experience of producing the Authorized Version of the Bible. As a keen convert, I was delighted on my return to Britain to find that my indefatigable colleague on the Study Group, Dr. Elizabeth Perrott, was turning her thoughts in the same direction. With her customary resolution and thoroughness, she made it her business to go to Boulder and see for herself the work in progress. As a result, she developed a personal and sustained participation in the task, of which this long-awaited British version is the outcome.

Among the many wise decisions of the American team, two call for special mention here. The first was not to take the easy course of putting out a single compromise approach to the diverse content of biology but to produce three alternative versions, all with a common nucleus but with different emphasis, the Blue Version, for example, stressing the molecular aspect, the Yellow Version stressing the cellular, while the Green Version (here presented in terms of the British environment) gave more attention to ecology and ways of living.

The second wise decision was neither to pursue a narrow nationalism nor to dictate and disseminate an arbitrary pattern for other countries, but to facilitate and encourage as many as so desired to use this invaluable array of material for producing versions suited and tuned to their own circumstances. Thanks to the generosity and wisdom of the American sponsors, more than 29 countries have already availed themselves of this opportunity, and, as a result, future biologists will more than ever speak the same language.

In Britain, inappropriate approaches to biological teaching in the past have done much to prevent biology from taking its rightful place among the sciences and in national affairs. Nowhere has this been more tellingly stated than in the Ministry of Education Pamphlet No. 38, issued officially in 1960 under the title *Science in Secondary Schools*. It said:

> 'The place which is occupied by advanced biological studies in schools, especially boys' schools, at present, is unfortunately that of vocational training rather than of an instrument of education.' Of the human anatomy section, it added that 'it makes inordinate demands on the memory and very little indeed upon reasoning . . . the contribution which the study makes to the pupil's education is so small that it is doubtful whether such a subject ought to find a place in a school at all'.

Despite the remedial efforts of agencies, such as the Nuffield Foundation, the Association for Science Education and the Schools Council, up to the moment there is no complete course available to British secondary schools in which biology is presented from an ecological viewpoint and in which the new and growing awareness of man and his environment receives due emphasis. This series of books, *Biology – an Environmental Approach*, provides such a course, and I commend these books most strongly to all who believe in the role of biology in our affairs, and to all who carry responsibility for the capacity of our future citizens to cope with the world they will have to live in.

Max Nicholson

September 1971

CONTENTS

1 THE CELL

SOME HISTORY	1
CELL STRUCTURE	3
Investigation 1.1. Diversity in cell structure	7
SOME CELL PHYSIOLOGY	9
Investigation 1.2. Diffusion through a membrane	11
CELL DUPLICATION	15
Investigation 1.3. Process of cell division: onion cells	19
DIFFERENTIATION	21
AGEING	23

2 BIOENERGETICS

LIFE, ENERGY AND CELLS	29
Investigation 2.1. Bioenergetics: an introductory view	30
ENERGY RELEASING PROCESSES	32
Investigation 2.2. Cells: biochemical reactions	33
Investigation 2.3. Fermentation	42
SYNTHESES	43
PHOTOSYNTHESIS	48
Investigation 2.4. Separation of leaf pigments	50
Investigation 2.5. Photosynthetic rate	58

3 THE FUNCTIONING PLANT

PLANTS AS ORGANISMS	63
VASCULAR PLANTS	63
Investigation 3.1. Transpiration	68
Investigation 3.2. Stomata and photosynthesis	70

	Investigation 3.3. Rate of growth: leaves	90
	NON-VASCULAR PLANTS	91
4	**THE FUNCTIONING ANIMAL**	
	Investigation 4.1. Animal structure and function	96
	ACQUIRING ENERGY AND MATERIALS	100
	Investigation 4.2. The action of a digestive enzyme	108
	TRANSPORTING MATERIALS IN THE BODY	112
	Investigation 4.3. A heart at work	120
	REMOVING MATERIALS FROM THE BODY	122
	MAINTAINING A STEADY STATE	128
	Investigation 4.4. Chemoreceptors in man	142
5	**BEHAVIOUR**	
	THE STUDY OF BEHAVIOUR	149
	LEVELS OF BEHAVIOUR	153
	Investigation 5.1. Tropic responses in plants	156
	Investigation 5.2. Behaviour of an invertebrate animal	167
	SOME PATTERNS OF ANIMAL BEHAVIOUR	170
	Investigation 5.3. Social behaviour in fish	175
	INDEX	187

COLOUR PLATES

I. Diffusion of ions through water	*facing page*	56
II. Burning of glucose		56
III. Energy absorption of chlorophylls		57
IV. Chromatogram of leaf pigments		57
V. Chlorophyll: transmitted and reflected light		57
VI. Variegated leaves		57
VII. Some aspects of plant structure		88
VIII. 'Following' instinct in ducklings		89
IX. Seeing in colour and black and white		89

INTRODUCTION

In the other books of this series, individual organisms are taken as the basic biological units of study. Irrespective of their size, they are treated as equal units, as individuals interacting with other individuals and with the abiotic environment.

In this book we shall move from the outside view of the organism to the inside view by posing the question: What activities within the organism produce the activities that can be observed from the outside as behaviour?

To understand these internal activities of an organism we must examine its parts. This raises another question: Is there any basic internal unit from which the parts of an organism are constructed?

The term 'Internal activities' implies that there is an energy source, otherwise the activity would be impossible. We are all aware, probably, of how energy is passed from the sun to organisms, and from one organism to another. However, what happens to this energy within the individual organism?

How does an organism function?

CHAPTER

1

THE CELL

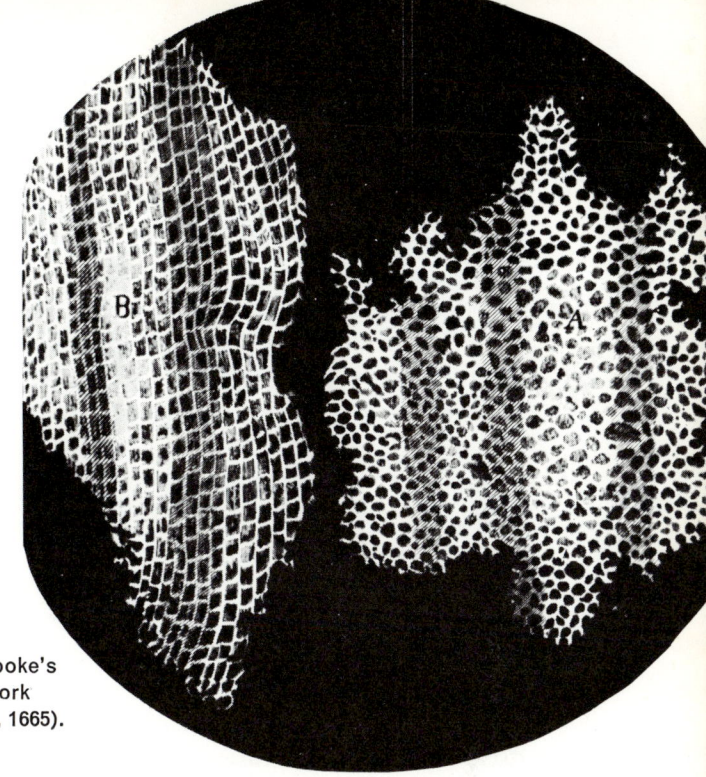

Figure 1.1 Hooke's drawings of cork (*Micrographia*, 1665).

SOME HISTORY

If we examine a fairly large organism, yourself perhaps, we can easily identify a number of parts. Externally there are eyes, arms and hair; inwardly are teeth and tongue; and after a bit of dissection (imaginary, of course!) we find the heart, liver, stomach and other organs. Proceeding in this way, we find smaller and smaller parts. In the case of the human body, investigation of structure through dissection – the study of human anatomy – had almost reached the limits of macroscopic vision by the sixteenth century. When, in 1543, Andreas Vesalius published his great work, *De Humani Corporis Fabrica* ('Concerning the Structure of the Human Body'), many persons no doubt considered the subject complete.

DISCOVERY OF CELLS

Today Vesalius' work appears to have begun, rather than ended, the scientific study of human structure, because in the next century the microscope was developed.

In that turbulent seventeenth century Leeuwenhoek was not the only curious observer, though none had lenses as fine as his. Some fifteen years before Leeuwenhoek's first letter to the Royal Society of London, an Italian, Marcello Malpighi, had seen small, thin-walled blood vessels, later named capillaries. Then in 1665 Robert Hooke, a secretary of the Royal Society, found interesting microscopic structures in cork (the bark of a Mediterranean oak) and in stems of various plants. In cork he observed neat rows of thick-walled compartments that reminded him of honeycomb. Because of this, he called the compartments 'cells'.

The story of Hooke's cells closely parallels the story of Leeuwenhoek's 'little animals'. During the following century and a half many men saw both cells and 'little animals', but no one fully understood their significance.

Hooke himself found that in many living materials (the cork, of course, was dead) the cells were filled with a liquid substance. Gradually attention shifted to this liquid. In 1809 the Frenchman Jean Baptiste de Lamarck wrote: 'Every living body is essentially a mass of cellular tissue in which more or less complex fluids move more or less rapidly.'

Lamarck was a bold originator of generalizations, but he was not good at seeking out facts to support them. His statement did not receive support until 1824, when Henri Dutrochet wrote that 'the cell is truly the fundamental part of the living organism'. Because the boundaries of plant cells are easier to see than those of animals cells, this idea was at first more acceptable to botanists than to zoologists; but by 1839 the generalization was fully developed with respect to both animals and plants. Two Germans, Matthias Schleiden, a botanist, and Theodor Schwann, a zoologist, did much to convince their co-workers of its usefulness. As Schwann wrote, 'We have thrown down a great barrier of separation between the animal and vegetable kingdoms.'

In so doing they began the joining of botany and zoology into the unified science of all life – into biology. The work itself had already been originated in its French form by Lamarck in 1802.

THE CELL THEORY

Thus 'cell', which once referred to an empty space, came to mean a unit of living matter. Leeuwenhoek's 'little animals' were interpreted as the least possible degree of cellular organization – that is, single cells. All other organisms could then be regarded as aggregations (groupings) of cells – very highly organized and differentiated aggregations, to be sure, but nevertheless reducible to cell units.

The cell theory did not lead immediately to a great new era of research. Despite the microscope's usefulness, detailed studies of cells had to await another technological development – dyes that could make cellular structures more clearly visible. This came with a great spurt in chemical knowledge in the 1850s and 1860s. Soon thereafter every life process was being associated with one type of cell or another. The cell quickly came to be regarded as not only the unit of structure but the unit of function as well.

Already, in the decade after Schleiden and Schwann, investigators had begun to find that cells normally and regularly come into being through the division of parent cells. Soon the ideas were established that since the beginning of life there has been no break in the descent of living cells from other cells of the past and that all of heredity and all of evolution must be embodied in cells.

Today the cell theory may be summarized as three main ideas: (1) The cell is the unit of structure of living organisms. (2) The cell is the unit of function in living organisms. (3) All cells come from pre-existing cells.

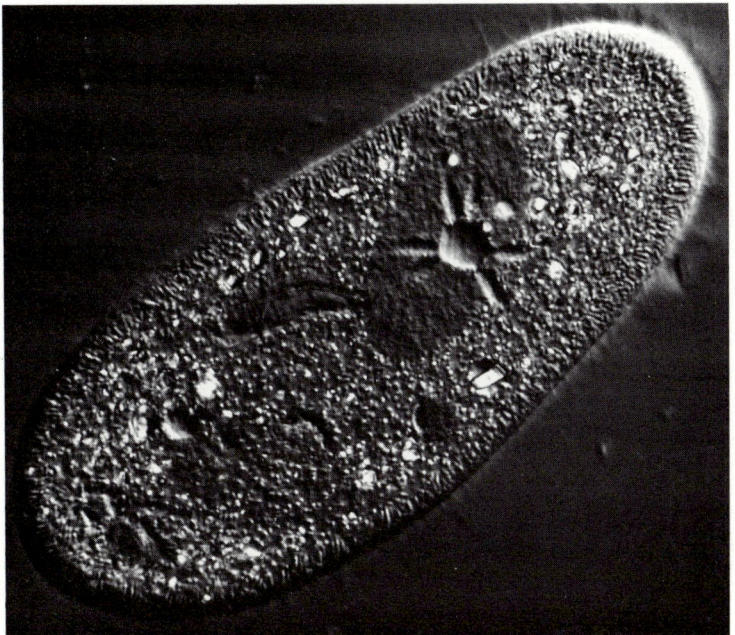

Figure 1.2 Paramecium. The complex structure of this protist has led some biologists to regard it not as a single cell but as an organism that has lost cellular structure.

X 500

CELL STRUCTURE

Differences among cells are great, in size, shape and internal structure. When you study Figure 1.3, do not assume that all the structures shown are to be found in all cells or that all structures known to occur in cells are included. The diagram is intended only to assist you in remembering some of the principal structures of cells. Therefore, some structures that you may encounter in more advanced studies have been omitted. It would be impossible to find any cell that, in every way, looks like the diagram.

Nearly every cell contains at least one *nucleus* (plural, 'nuclei'). Under the microscope the nuclei of living cells are usually difficult to see, but they are readily visible when stained with various kinds of dyes. Compared with the rest of the cell, nuclear substances react differently to stains or take up different amounts of them. This causes a contrast between the nucleus and the surrounding parts of the cell. Unfortunately, most stains kill the cell; but a development in microscopy of the last thirty years – the phase-contrast microscope – allows nuclei to be seen in unstained living cells.

Within the nucleus are one or more small bodies that usually stain even more deeply than the nucleus itself. These are the *nucleoli* (singular, 'nucleolus'). In almost all animal cells, in most protist cells, but in rather few plant cells, a small structure, the *centrosome*, is found just outside (but in a few cases, just inside) the nuclear membrane. Nucleoli and centrosomes will be discussed later in relation to cell division.

The body of the cell outside the nuclear membrane is known as the *cytoplast*. The cytoplast surrounds the nucleus, although the position of the nucleus varies in different kinds of cells; sometimes it is near the centre, sometimes far to one side. With the staining methods most commonly used, the cytoplast as a whole absorbs less stain than the nucleus, so it appears lighter.

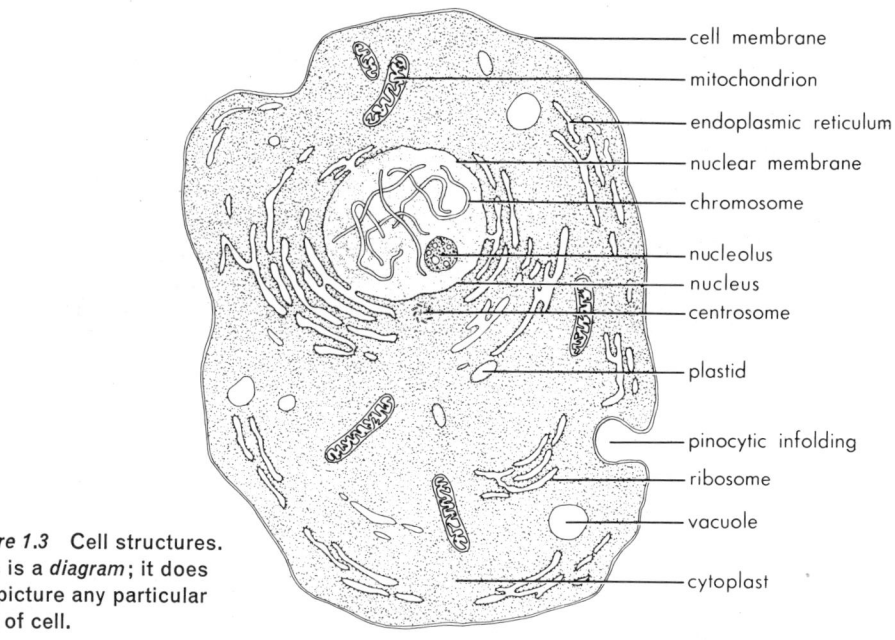

Figure 1.3 Cell structures. This is a *diagram*; it does not picture any particular kind of cell.

Within the cytoplast are various kinds of small structures (*organelles*) that can be made visible with special staining methods. Even without stains it is easy to see the *plastids*, for most of them are naturally coloured by pigments. Plastids are found in cells of plants and some protists. Among the variety of plastids, *chloroplasts*, containing green pigments (chlorophylls), are of major concern to us, because they are involved in photosynthesis. The chromoplasts, plastids containing red and yellow pigments (carotenes and xanthophylls), are of less importance to us. They are found, for example, in the cells of carrots and tomatoes.

Under a light microscope *mitochondria* (singular, 'mitochondrion') appear only as very tiny, rod-shaped bodies that may either be scattered throughout

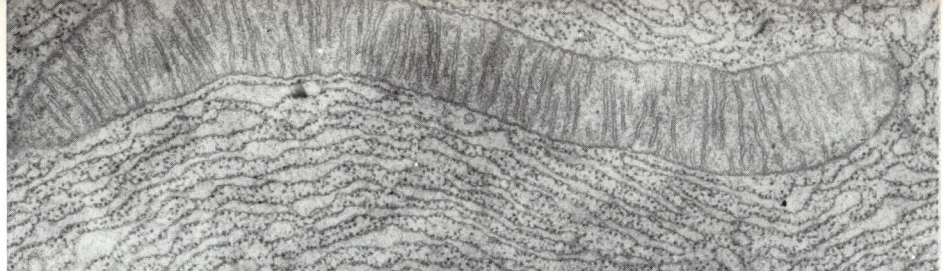

Figure 1.4 A single mitochondrion from zymogen cell of mouse fundic gland. The mitochondrial wall is double in places, and the central cavity is seen to be sub-divided by many transverse 'cristae'. X 29 000

the cytoplast or concentrated in certain places; but under an electron microscope each mitochondrion shows up as a somewhat sausage-shaped body containing parallel infolded layers of membranes (Figure 1.4).

The boundary between the cell and its environment is the *cell membrane*. Under a light microscope the membrane appears merely as the outer surface

A Human blood cells   X 2000

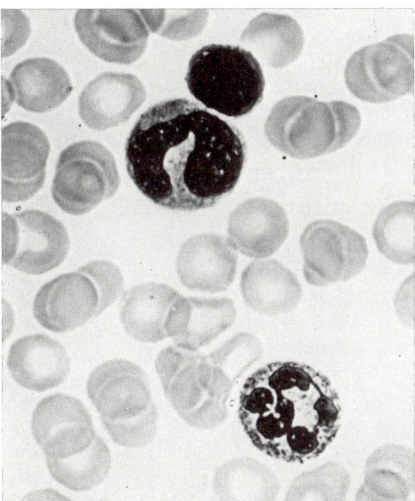

B Bacteria   X 2000

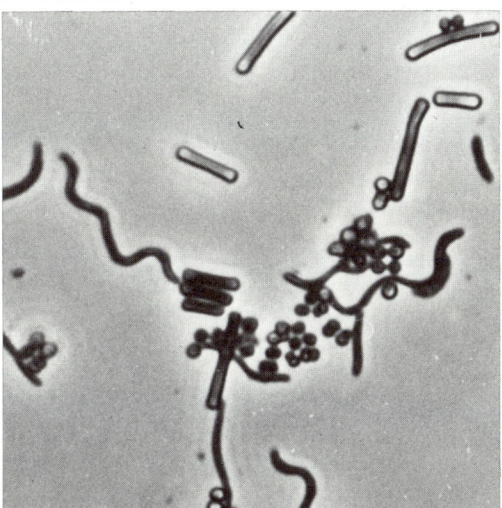

Figure 1.5 Diversity among cells.

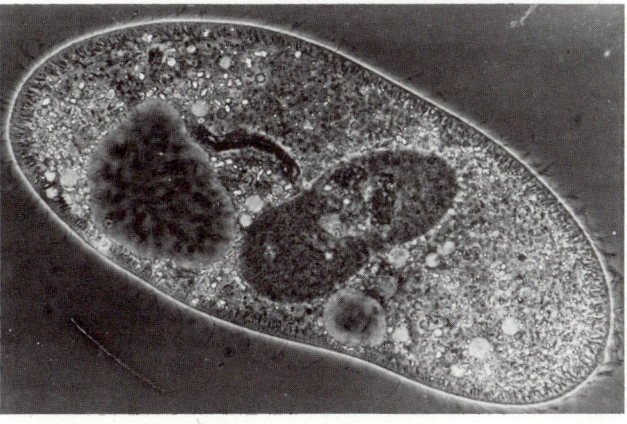

X 370

C *Paramecium*, a protist

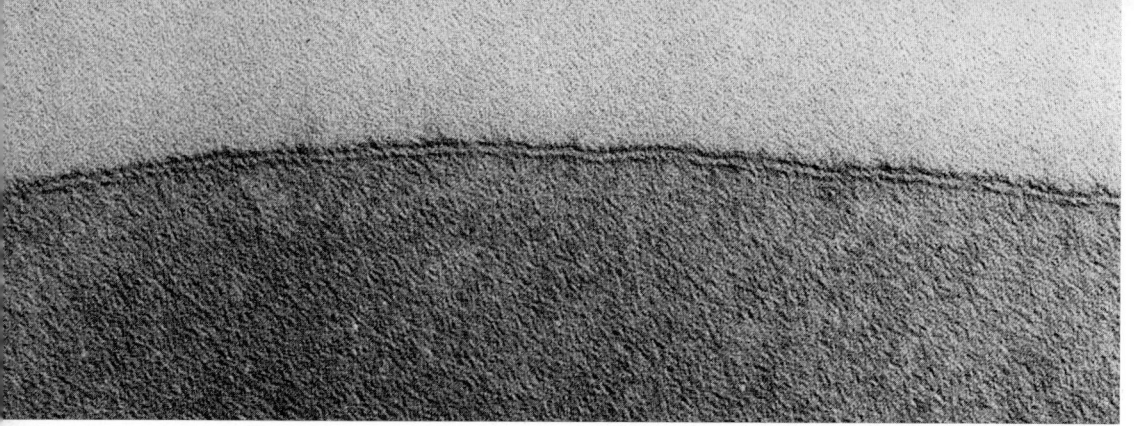

Figure 1.6 Cell membrane of a red blood cell. X 270 000

of the cytoplast, but under an electron microscope it clearly has a two-layered structure (Figure 1.6). Chemical investigations show that the cell membrane is composed of protein and fat-like substances. Possibly it is made up of two protein layers with a layer of fat-like substance between, which would account for the double appearance of the membrane. The membrane that surrounds the nucleus has a similar structure.

The electron microscope reveals within the cytoplast a membranous network called the *endoplasmic reticulum*. This network branches throughout the cytoplast and appears to connect the cell membrane with the nuclear membrane. Adhering to the endoplasmic reticulum are organelles called *ribosomes*. Other ribosomes are found floating within the cytoplast.

Figure 1.7 The endoplasmic reticulum appears below the paler nuclear membrane. Note its connections across this membrane. X 20 000

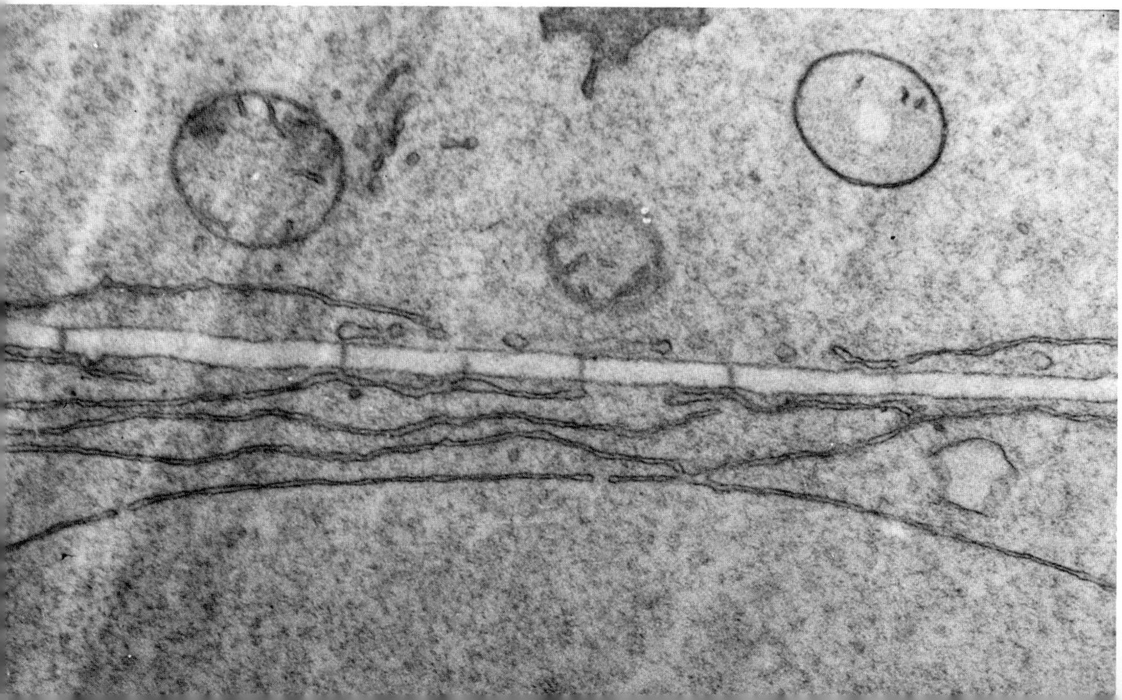

The substance of the cytoplast is a complex and constantly changing mixture of a great variety of organic, and some inorganic, substances in water. Some of these substances clump together to form granular bodies that are sometimes visible under high magnification of a light microscope. Both animal and plant cells contain droplets of liquid (sometimes containing solid particles) that are called *vacuoles*. Vacuoles, usually small and few in the cells of animals and protists, are frequently large and numerous in plant cells.

In addition to cell membranes, the cells of plants and some protists are surrounded by non-living cell walls. Cell walls are not replacements for cell membranes, but in a living cell the two structures are pressed so closely together that they are frequently difficult to distinguish from one another.

INVESTIGATION 1.1

DIVERSITY IN CELL STRUCTURE

PURPOSE
This is an observational exercise in which you will compare the structures of several different kinds of living cells – as far as these structures can be seen with a light microscope.

MATERIALS AND EQUIPMENT
(each pupil or pair of pupils)

Onion, cut into pieces about 1 cm²
Forceps (fine pointed)
Microscope slide
Droppers, 3
Cover slips
Monocular microscope
Iodine–potassium iodide solution
Paper tissues
Elodea leaves
Toothpicks (sterile)
Physiological saline solution
Methylene blue solution
Dissecting needles, 2
Frog blood
Frog skin

PROCEDURE
Onion skin
1. Take a piece of onion and peel off the skin (epidermis) from the inner concave surface.
2. Place a small piece (smaller than a cover slip) on to a slide, avoiding overlapping or wrinkling.
3. Add one or two drops of water and a cover slip.
4. Examine under the low power of your microscope.
5. Draw a small section of the field of view to show how the cells are arranged.
6. Place a drop of iodine–potassium iodide stain along one edge of the cover slip and draw it under the cover slip by placing a piece of paper tissue at the other edge.
7. Record any changes that occur as the stain spreads across the onion epidermis.
8. Switch to high power and draw a single cell including as much detail as you can see.
9. Label all the parts which you can identify. Even with the high power of your microscope you will be able to see only a few of the parts known to occur in cells.

Note: Be sure to clean the slide thoroughly with water and paper tissues before placing another kind of material on it.

***Elodea* leaf**
1. With forceps, remove a young leaf from near the tip of an *Elodea* plant.

2. Place on a clean slide, add a drop of water and cover with a cover slip.
3. Examine under the low power. Slowly turn the fine adjustment back and forth and determine the number of cell layers in the leaf.
4. Turn to high power. Select an average cell of the midrib and focus upon it carefully.

Is there any evidence that the cell is living? If so, what is the evidence?

5. Make a drawing of the cell including as much detail as you can see. Label all the parts which you can identify.

Cheek cells

1. Using the blunt end of a sterile toothpick, scrape the inside surface of your cheek. DO NOT DIG A HOLE IN YOUR CHEEK.
2. You should obtain a barely visible mass of material. Rub the material on a clean slide.
3. Add a drop of physiological saline solution and stir thoroughly with the toothpick.
4. Examine under low power. By carefully using the fine adjustment, try to observe the three-dimensional shape of the cells.

How would you describe them: (*a*) spherical, (*b*) pear shaped, or (*c*) neither?

5. Add a drop of methylene blue and a cover slip.
6. Find several cells well separated from the others. Draw one or two of them including as much detail as you can see.
7. Label all the parts which you can identify.

Frog's blood

1. Place a drop of diluted frog's blood on a clean slide. Add a drop of methylene blue and a cover slip.
2. Examine under low power. Most of the cells seen will be red blood cells.
3. Find an area where the cells are neither too crowded nor too scarce, and centre it in the field of view.
4. Turn to high power and draw one or two cells, labelling all the parts which you can identify.

Frog's skin

1. Place scrapings from a frog's skin on a clean slide. Add a drop of physiological saline, a drop or two of methylene blue and a cover slip.
2. Locate cells with the low power and then switch to high power.
3. Draw one or two cells and label all the parts which you can identify.

SUMMARY

Draw a table like the one shown below and, using your drawings and notes, complete it for each type of cell examined. Put a cross beneath the name of each cell structure observed.

A. Does the lack of a cross indicate that the structure was not present in the cells observed? Give reasons for your answers.
B. On the basis of your observations, which kind of cell (plant or animal) seems to have (*a*) more angular a shape, (*b*) more rounded a shape?
C. What type of cell has the more clearly defined boundaries?
D. What cell structure may be involved in the characteristics discussed in B and C?

Source of cell	Cell wall	Cytoplasm	Nucleus	etc.
Onion epidermis				
Elodea leaf				
etc.				

SOME CELL PHYSIOLOGY

We might study the parts of a clock and still not understand how the clock works, but it is certain that we could never understand how a clock works without studying its parts. Investigation of a mechanism's structure is chiefly aimed at learning how it operates. We have been studying some of the visible parts of cells – the structure of cells. Now we can try to understand how a cell works – how it operates, how it functions. This study of biological function – of biological activity – is called *physiology*.

METABOLISM

The activities of organisms require energy changes. Since cells are the basic functional units of organisms, it follows that these energy changes must take place within cells. For example, you can move your arm because muscle cells can change chemical energy into the mechanical energy that shortens muscles. In one way or another, all activities or functions of organisms basically involve energy changes and chemical reactions. The resulting very large number of continuing chemical reactions in cells are collectively known as *metabolism*.

In obtaining energy for its activities a cell constantly uses up energy-rich molecules, converting them into energy-poor molecules that are useless for metabolism. One of the cell's most striking characteristics is its always shifting but, on the average, constant composition – its steady state. Maintaining this steady state, while the stock of useful energy-rich substances is always being reduced and the burden of energy-poor substances is always being added to, obviously demands that substances continually enter and leave a cell.

TRANSPORT IN CELLS

A cell, then, is an open system. Yet there is a definite boundary, the cell membrane, between a cell and its environment. While the cell membrane acts as a barrier between the living substance and the environment, it must also allow various substances to pass through it. Furthermore, there are internal membranes – the nuclear and mitochondrial ones, for example – through which substances must pass, and substances must move from one part of the cell to another. All this adds up to a complex physiological problem: How do substances move into cells, out of cells, and within cells?

Diffusion. The biologist must constantly make use of the concepts developed by physicists and chemists. At this point we need to use one such concept – the molecular theory of matter. This theory states that all matter is made up of tiny particles called *molecules*, which are in continuous motion. The higher the temperature, the faster the molecules move. In solids, the motion of each molecule occurs round one point; it is a vibration. In liquids and gases and in dissolved solids, the molecules vibrate, too, but they also move easily from one place to another. The direction of these movements appears to be accidental. One molecule bumps another, and both go off in new directions. Such accidental, disordered motion can be described as *random* movement.

If you place a coloured, soluble solid in a test-tube of water, you observe that over a period of days the colour gradually spreads throughout the water. According to the molecular theory, as the coloured substance dissolves, its molecules begin to move in a random manner. This random movement gradually carries them from a place where they are more abundant per unit volume (that is, where their concentration is greater) to places where they are less abundant per unit volume (that is, where their concentration is less). This process is called *diffusion*. Diffusion continues until the molecules of the coloured substances are evenly distributed throughout the water in the test-tube.

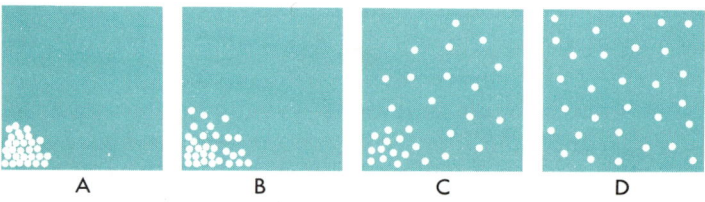

Figure 1.8 Diagram of stages in diffusion. In (D) the particles continue to move; but because each moves randomly, they remain evenly distributed in the available space.

At the same time that the molecules of coloured substance are diffusing, the water molecules are also diffusing. Originally there was *low concentration of water molecules* where the concentration of the coloured substance was low. The molecular theory, of course, applies to the water molecules as well as to the molecules dissolved in the water.

After the solution is completely uniform, collisions and rebounds continue, but for every molecule that moves from right to left there is another that moves from left to right. Thus the movement is continuous among the molecules without a net change in their distribution – and therefore there is no more diffusion.

Now of course all this movement of molecules implies energy. Where does this energy come from? The energy used in diffusion is the heat of the solution itself. Within cells the energy for diffusion is the cell's heat. Because this heat energy is unavailable for other work by the cell, diffusion does not 'cost' the cell any energy.

INVESTIGATION 1.2

DIFFUSION THROUGH A MEMBRANE

PURPOSE
In this investigation you will explore the diffusion of substances that are separated from one another by a membrane.

MATERIALS AND EQUIPMENT
(for each group)
Cellulose tubing, 20-cm lengths, 2
Soluble starch solution
Rubber bands, 2
Glucose solution
Iodine solution
Beakers, 600 cm^3 or 1000 cm^3, 2
Wax pencil
Tes-Tape or piece of Clinitest tablet in a test-tube

PROCEDURE
1. Open the cellulose tubing by moistening it and then rubbing it between the thumb and forefinger.
2. Tie a knot about 1 cm from one end of each piece of tubing.
3. Into one tube pour soluble starch solution to within about 5 cm of the top.
4. Pinch the top of the tube tightly together and rinse the tube under running water to remove any starch on the outside.
5. Fasten the top of the tube with a rubber band and place the tube in a beaker of water (Figure 1.9).
6. Mark the beaker Beaker A, and add enough iodine solution to give the water a distinct yellowish colour.
7. Into the second tube pour glucose solution to within about 5 cm of the top and repeat Instructions 4 and 5.
8. Mark the beaker Beaker B.
9. Allow the tubes to stand for about twenty minutes.
10. Dip a piece of Tes-Tape into the water in Beaker B (alternatively pour a small quantity of the water into a test-tube containing a fragment of a Clinitest tablet).
11. Record the colour in your lab-book.
12. Observe the tube in Beaker A. Record any colour change in either the tube or the water in the beaker.
13. Allow Beaker B to stand overnight and test again the next day. Record any change.

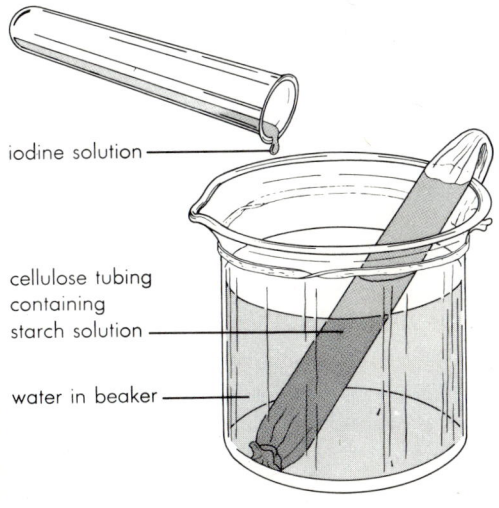

Figure 1.9

STUDYING THE DATA
A. On the basis of the chemical test for starch, what must have happened to the iodine molecules in set-up A?
B. On the basis of the chemical test for glucose, what must have happened to the glucose molecules in set-up B?
C. From the evidence obtained by allowing set-up B to stand overnight, what other substance must have passed through the membrane?
D. Which material did not pass through the membrane? How do you know?

CONCLUSIONS

Physicists can show that the molecules of any one substance are all about the same size but that the molecules of different substances are different in size. Measurements show that iodine molecules and water molecules are very small, glucose molecules are considerably larger, and starch molecules (synthesized from many glucose molecules – page 35) are very large.

A. On this basis, suggest a hypothesis to account for the observations made in this investigation.
B. In your hypothesis what assumption must you make about the structure of the membrane?

The cell membrane. The contents of cells are basically solutions or suspensions of materials in water; all active (that is, not dormant) living cells exist in a water environment. Cells of the human body are no exception. Every one of our living cells (cells of the outer skin are dead) is surrounded by moisture. Therefore, an active living cell is a mixture of things in water, separated by its cell membrane from another mixture of things in water, its environment. The cell membrane is the boundary that separates this unit of living materials from the rest of the universe. Within the cell membrane occur all the activities that, taken together, make up what we mean by 'life'. (Actually, the membrane is living, too, so the word 'within' must be thought of as including the membrane itself.) Through the cell membrane, then, must pass everything that the cell obtains from the environment, and through it must pass also everything that the cell returns to the environment.

Diffusion through membranes. A paper bag will hold potatoes, but it will not hold water very long. A plastic bag will hold water, but oxygen will pass through the plastic fast enough to keep a goldfish alive in the water (but not fast enough to keep *you* alive – you need more oxygen than a goldfish does). The paper bag is *permeable* to water but not to potatoes; the plastic bag is permeable to oxygen but not to water. A membrane that is permeable to some substances and not to others is said to be *differentially* permeable.

Among molecules that diffuse easily through cell membranes are those of water, carbon dioxide and oxygen. Many ions of inorganic substances also diffuse easily, but the molecules of many compounds that are dissolved or suspended inside the cell are too large to pass through the cell membrane by diffusion.

The *direction* in which any given kind of molecule diffuses is determined, as we have discussed above, by the concentration. If the concentration is greater outside the cell, the direction of diffusion is into the cell. The direction is outward if the concentration is higher within the cell.

Differential permeability is of special importance when we consider the water-diffusion relationships of a cell. Let us assume that Compound X, whose molecules are too large to diffuse through the cell membrane, is found in a relatively high concentration within a cell but does not occur in the fluid outside the cell.

First, *imagine* that the cell has no membrane. The tendency for the solution to become uniform results in the diffusion of the molecules of X from the area of their higher concentration to the area of their lower concentration (Figure 1.8). Also (and this is very important) water molecules diffuse from the area of their higher concentration (which is where the concentration of X is lower) to the area of their lower concentration (which is where the concentration of X is higher). This, of course, is the situation that was described earlier (pages 9–10).

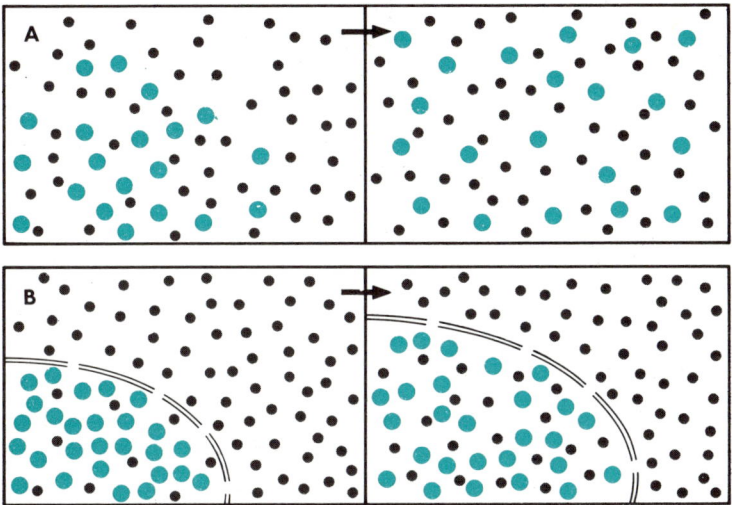

Figure 1.10 Diagram of diffusion: without a differentially permeable membrane (A), and with such a membrane (B). Black dots represent water molecules; coloured dots represent molecules of a substance dissolved in water.

Now consider the *real* situation. The high and low concentrations of X are separated by the differentially permeable cell membrane. Obviously only *one* of the two movements of molecules can occur – the movement of water molecules through the cell membrane into the cell (Figure 1.10). Therefore water accumulates inside the cell. This creates pressure on the membrane from the inside. The pressure may even be sufficient to burst the membrane.

Paramecium lives in a fresh-water environment. Within this organism there is much higher concentration of molecules unable to diffuse through its cell membrane than there is outside. Just as in Figure 1.10, water diffuses from the environment into the *Paramecium* because the concentration of the *water* is higher outside the *Paramecium* than it is inside. In the *Paramecium*, however, the excess water is continuously accumulated in a vacuole and periodically expelled to the exterior. The *Paramecium* must constantly 'pump' water out or it will be 'flooded'. This, of course, is work – it requires energy.

As you saw in Investigation 1.2, substances other than water diffuse through cell membranes. Some relatively large molecules of kinds that are soluble in fat or oil can diffuse through quite freely. This is probably because they easily enter into solution in the fatty part of the cell membrane.

All of this sounds as though cell membranes and non-living membranes function alike. To some extent this is true, but unlike non-living membranes, cell membranes have constantly changing permeabilities. Substances that pass readily through a living membrane at one time may not pass through at other times. Such changes in permeability are frequently observed by biologists, but they are difficult to explain.

Active transport. Not all movements of substances through cell membranes can be explained by diffusion. For example, in most cells the concentration of potassium ions is many times greater inside the cell than it is outside. It can be demonstrated that potassium ions readily pass through cell membranes by diffusion. Then how is it possible for a cell to retain a high concentration of potassium ions when there is a low concentration in the environment? Why is it that these ions do not leave the cell by diffusion?

In fact, there *is* a constant diffusion of potassium ions from the cell. Careful investigation has shown, however, that the cell has a mechanism that moves potassium ions from the environmental fluid into the cell at a rate at least as great as the rate at which they are lost by diffusion. This inward movement of potassium can be called an 'uphill' movement, because it is opposite to the natural direction taken by the diffusion of the ions. Cell physiologists use the term 'ion pumps' for mechanisms that move ions 'uphill' from a region of low concentration to one of high concentration. Of course these are not mechanical devices, but their action requires the expenditure of energy – work – just as it is necessary to use energy to operate a water pump or an air pump.

In addition to ions, many other things are now known to be moved from lower to higher concentrations. This occurs not only through external cell membranes but also through the membranes of mitochondria and nuclei. Any such movement is called *active transport*.

Pinocytosis. Materials that pass through cell membranes by diffusion and active transport are in the form of relatively small molecules and ions. However, very large molecules, even large aggregations of molecules, and volumes of liquid can also pass through cell membranes. Just how the cell accomplishes this is not thoroughly understood, but electronmicrography has been very helpful in picturing the process. At present it seems that a mass of solid or liquid matter lying adjacent to the cell is surrounded by extensions of the membrane. When the mass is completely enclosed, it may move off as a vacuole into the cytoplast. Although separate terms have been applied to such intake of solid and liquid substances, here we refer to both by the single term *pinocytosis*.

Many cells form large molecules that are then passed through their cell membranes into the environment. Often this transfer involves the accumulation of the molecules in granules that are surrounded by membranes similar in appearance to cell membranes. The granules then move to the cell surface so that the membrane of a granule comes in contact with the cell membrane. The fused membranes rupture, permitting the granule to escape. If we consider the granule as approximately equivalent to a vacuole, this process is somewhat similar to pinocytosis except that it moves material in the opposite direction through the cell membrane. In any case, like pinocytosis, it requires expenditure of energy by the cell.

Cyclosis. In most cells diffusion probably accounts for the distribution of substances within the cytoplast. In many kinds of cells, however, substances are carried about by the motion of the matter making up the cytoplast. Especially in plants and protists it is possible to observe this 'streaming', called *cyclosis*, with the high power of an ordinary laboratory microscope. Although the exact way in which cyclosis occurs is not known, it is clear that it requires the expenditure of energy, just as do active transport and pinocytosis.

CELL DUPLICATION

The third major idea in the cell theory is that all cells are produced by pre-existing cells. Why and when does one cell become two? Biologists are not at all sure. Indirectly such cell duplication is probably related to the maximum size that a *given kind* of cell can manage to maintain. Among cells of different kinds there is an enormous variation in size. For example, the yolk of an ostrich egg (a single cell) is about 300 000 times larger than a rickettsial cell. But for a given kind of cell there may be a maximum limit to the size it can maintain. If so, then for the cell to continue growing, it must divide, even though attainment of a certain size is not the direct cause of division.

Whatever the cause, cells *do* divide; and when one cell has divided into two, cell reproduction has taken place. Usually the nucleus and cytoplast divide almost simultaneously, but sometimes they behave differently. The nucleus may divide, but not the cytoplast; such division, if repeated, will give rise to a multinucleate structure like the hypha of *Rhizopus nigricans* (Figure 1.11). Or the nucleus may divide, with division of the cytoplast occurring at some later time, as in spore formation by ascomycetes.

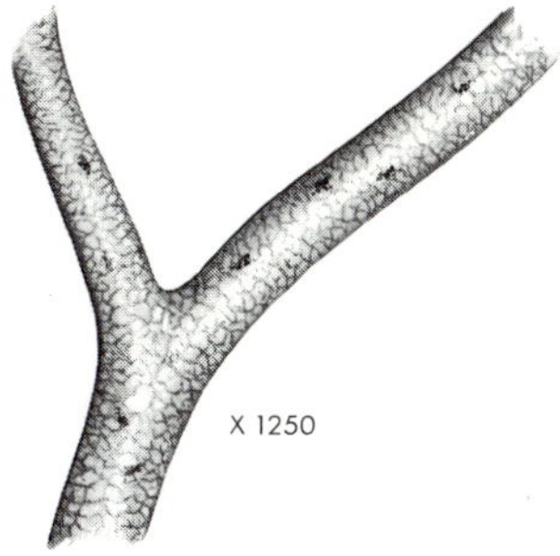

X 1250

Figure 1.11 Hypha of black bread mould (*Rhizopus nigricans*).

MITOSIS

Division of the nuclear substances seems to be a very important part of cellular reproduction. Mature human red blood cells, which have no nuclei, never divide; instead, they survive a short time (about 110 days) and then disintegrate. On the other hand, the cells of blue-green algae divide even though they have no definitely organized nuclei. However, special staining methods have shown that the same substances that characterize nuclei in other organisms occur in blue-green algae.

In the great majority of cells there *is* a definite nucleus, and nuclear division is observable as a clear sequence of events. So much attention has been concentrated on this sequence that the name for it, *mitosis*, is sometimes incorrectly applied to the whole process of cell division.

Mitosis is a remarkably uniform process. There are, however, some slight differences between the ways it occurs in most plant cells and in most animal cells. We shall describe and illustrate mitosis of animal cells and then, in the laboratory, investigate mitosis in plant cells.

Mitosis is a *continuous* process. Therefore, it can be illustrated adequately only in motion pictures. In studying the illustrations in this book and your microscope slides, use your imagination to fill in between the 'still pictures'.

CELL DIVISION IN ANIMALS

The first observable event in animal mitosis is the division of the centrosome. The two portions of the centrosome separate and begin to move around the nucleus. (Refer to Figure 1.12 as you read on.) Fibre-like structures develop around them, radiating from each half-centrosome like the spokes of a wheel. As the two portions of the centrosome continue to move away from each other, the fibres between them lengthen, forming a structure called a *spindle*. While these events are occurring, the nucleolus diminishes in size and disappears. The nuclear membrane disintegrates and also disappears.

At the time that the parts of the centrosome are moving, the nuclear material increases in stainability. This enables an observer to see a set of thread-like parts, called *chromosomes*, in the nucleus. Close examination shows that each chromosome is double from the time it can first be seen. Each strand of a chromosome is called a *chromatid*. The chromatids are attached to each other at a single point, the *centromere* (a synonym is 'kinetochore'). Gradually the chromosomes become shorter, thicker and more distinct. Under high magnification it becomes clear that this is due to coiling, just as a long, thin wire can be coiled into a shorter and thicker spring.

By the time the spindle is complete – that is, when the centrosome halves are 180° apart on the circumference of the nucleus – the chromosomes are fully coiled. If we call the positions of the centrosome halves the 'poles' of the spindle, then we can imagine a disc across the centre of the spindle and equidistant from the poles. This we call the *equatorial plate*. (Because of high

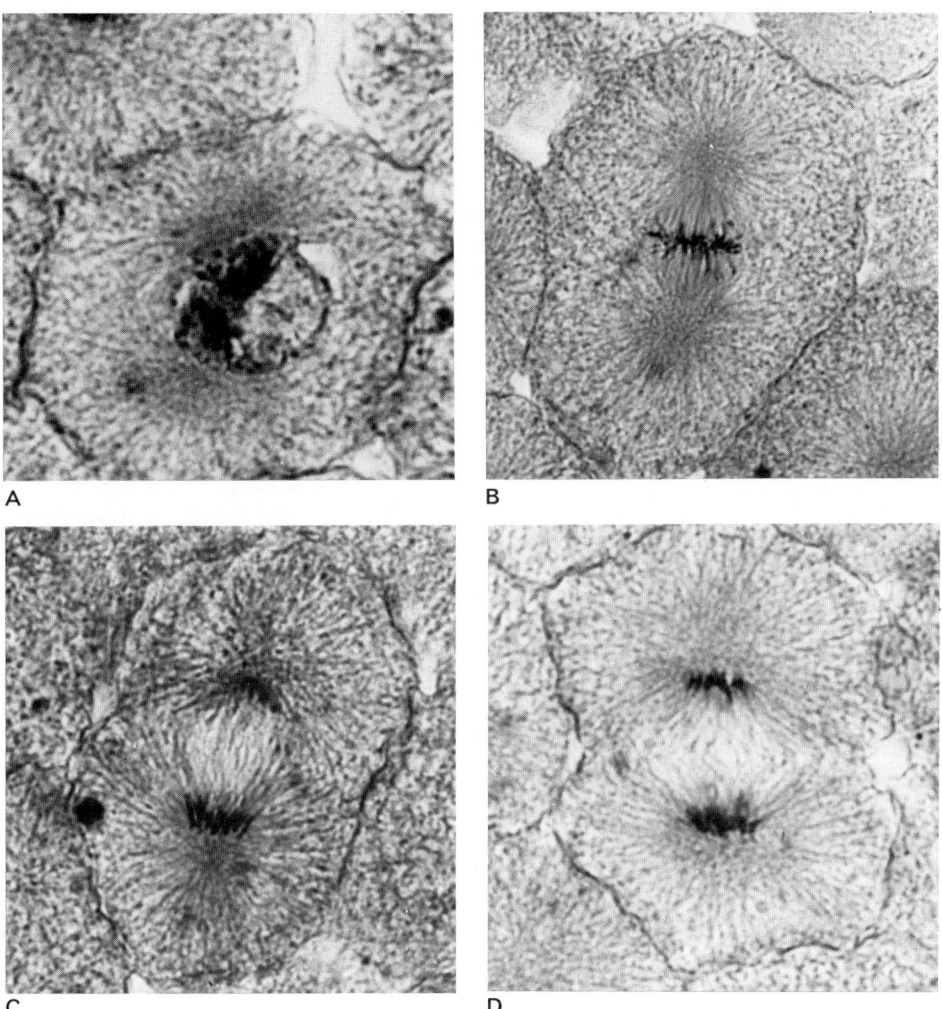

Figure 1.12 Four photographs of mitosis in the cells of an embryonic whitefish. The process is just beginning in (A), and in (D) it is nearly completed. The times between photographs are not equal. How many cell parts can you identify?   X 1000

magnification, the cells in the photographs appear two-dimensional, so the equatorial plate seems to be a line rather than a plane.) The chromosomes move towards the equatorial plate, and their centromeres become attached to spindle fibres. The centromere of each chromosome now divides, so the paired chromatids separate from one another; however, each centromere remains attached to a fibre of the spindle.

The chromatids from each chromosome move apart. Once separated from its former partner, each chromatid of a pair is referred to as a chromosome. One member of each pair moves away from the equatorial plate and towards one pole of the spindle; the second moves towards the other pole. Each centromere leads the way as though pulled by a shortening of the spindle fibres; the rest of the new chromosome trails behind.

Now the fibres of the spindle begin to fade and the chromosomes start to uncoil. At each pole a new nuclear membrane forms around the group of chromosomes, leaving the centrosome outside. A nucleolus appears within each new nuclear membrane. At some time before the next nuclear division occurs, the chromosomes become double (with two chromatids) again; but this cannot be seen. The formation of new nuclei ends mitosis.

Usually division of the cytoplast begins as new chromosomes approach the poles. A furrow forms around the cytoplast in the equatorial plate and deepens until the original cell is cut in two. Because they cluster near the equatorial plate, the mitochondria in the cytoplast are distributed more or less equally between the two new cells. The division of the cytoplast, unlike that of the nucleus, is not always equal, but its completion ends cell division.

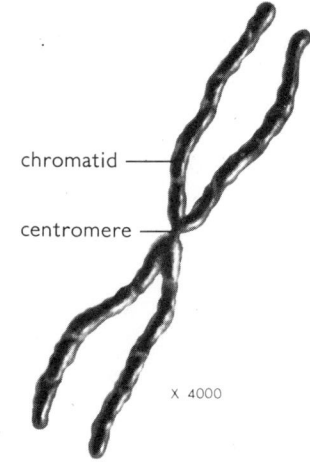

Figure 1.13 A chromosome before separation of chromatids.

THE SIGNIFICANCE OF MITOSIS

Nuclei were discovered and named by Robert Brown, the Scottish botanist (1773–1858), who first reported seeing small bodies within plant cells as they divided. How little he understood the importance of his discovery is shown by the fact that he merely mentioned it in a footnote. Because the unstained nucleus is difficult to see with ordinary microscopes, practially nothing was learnt about it until stains came into use. Thus, the behaviour of the nucleus during mitosis was first described less than a hundred years ago. Even before the discovery of nuclei biologists had begun to ask questions to which mitosis is clearly related: Why does each 'daughter cell' have the characteristics of the 'parent cell'? What determines the characteristics of a cell? How are activities of a cell controlled?

The elaborate sequence of events in mitosis appears to be a device to ensure exact, equal division of the nuclear material, which suggests that this substance is very important. Research during the past eight decades has amply supported this idea. Abundant evidence shows that complex nuclear substances regulate the activities of a cell and that the characteristics of a cell, both structural and functional, are expressions of these activities. Thus, maintaining characteristics from one cell generation to the next depends upon the duplication and separation of the chromosomes in the parent cell, with full, identical sets being transmitted to the daughter cells. Apparently each bit of chromosome material is duplicated before the chromosomes become visible in mitosis. Thus the chromatids in a pair are exact duplicates throughout their length. Then the events of mitosis provide that one chromatid of each pair ends up in each new cell.

INVESTIGATION 1.3

PROCESS OF CELL DIVISION: ONION CELLS

PURPOSE
In this investigation you will learn how to prepare plant cells for microscopic examination of mitosis and cell division and will compare your observations with illustrations of mitosis as seen in animal cells.

BACKGROUND INFORMATION
If an onion is placed with its base in water and kept dark for several days, slender white roots will sprout from it and grow into the water (Figure 1.14). This growth occurs partly by multiplications of cells. Thus, if the end of a root is cut off, mounted in water, and examined under the microscope you might expect to see cell division and mitosis. In fact, very few of the steps in these processes can be observed as there are simply too many cells closely packed together to permit much to be seen.

Root tips can be prepared in two ways: (a) by making a squash preparation in which the cells are separated and stained, or (b) by making a prepared section.

In the second way the root is stained and then gradually saturated with a supporting substance such as paraffin wax. It is cut into a series of very thin slices with a microtome and the slices are mounted on slides. The mounting medium is one which hardens and this makes a permanent preparation.

In this investigation you will prepare cells using method (a) and examine them, and also examine cells prepared using method (b).

MATERIALS AND EQUIPMENT
(for each group)
Solution of one part concentrated hydrochloric acid and one part 95 per cent ethanol solution
Solid watch glasses, 2
Forceps, fine-pointed
Onion roots, in 70 per cent ethanol
Carnoy's fluid (with chloroform)
Microscope slide
Scalpel or razor blade
Aceto-orcein solution
Cover slip
Cleansing tissue
Monocular microscope
Prepared slide, longitudinal sections of onion root tip

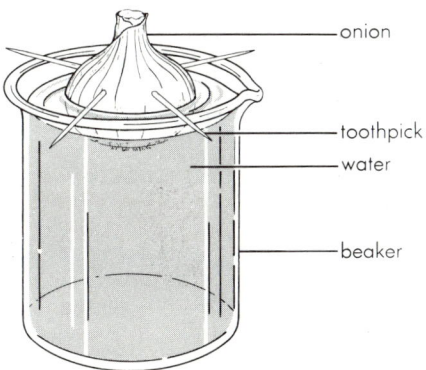

Figure 1.14 Set-up for growing onion root tips.

PROCEDURE
1. Pour the hydrochloric acid – 95 per cent ethanol solution into a solid watch glass to a depth of about 3 mm.
2. Using forceps, pick up a root that has been fixed in 70 per cent

ethanol. PICK UP AT THE CUT END. In all later operations handle the root by the cut end only.

3. Place the root in the watch glass and allow it to remain in the solution for five minutes. This treatment breaks down the cementing material which holds the cells together.
4. Shortly before the five minutes is up, pour Carnoy's fluid (with chloroform) into a second watch glass to a depth of 3 mm.
5. Using forceps, transfer the root to the second watch glass and allow it to remain there for three minutes. This treatment hardens the material which has been softened by the acid treatment and reduces damage to the cells in subsequent procedures.
6. Transfer the root to a clean slide.
7. Take a scalpel or razor blade and cut off the tip of the root, i.e. the last 2 mm or less.
8. Discard all but the tip.
9. Add one or two drops of aceto-orcein solution and cut the tip into small pieces and allow them to remain in the solution for five minutes. Do not let the preparation dry up; if it appears to be doing so, add another drop of the solution. This solution stains certain cell structures including nuclei and chromosomes.
10. Place a clean cover slip over the pieces of root tip and tap lightly on the cover slip with the point of a pencil held vertically. This will separate the cells and spread them out under the cover slip.
11. Fold a paper tissue several times until it is the same shape as the slide, though slightly larger. Make a final fold in the tissue, bringing its ends together.
12. Place the tissue on the table and insert the part of the slide where the cover slip is located into the final fold, making a 'sandwich' with several layers of tissue under the slide and several on top of the cover slip (Figure 1.15).
13. With the 'sandwich' resting flat on the table, press vertically down with your thumb on the upper layer of tissue. Be careful to apply pressure without twisting so that the cover slip is not moved laterally in relation to the slide. This will further spread the cells and flatten them.
14. Remove the slide from the tissue. You have made your 'squash' preparation.

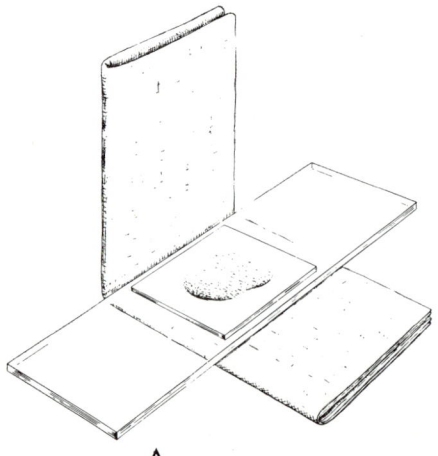

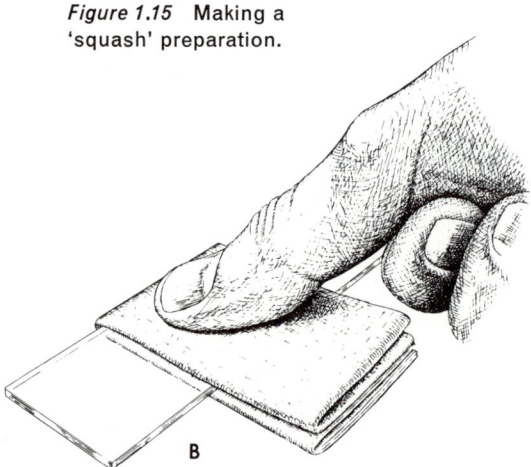

Figure 1.15 Making a 'squash' preparation.

OBSERVATIONS

1. Examine the slide under low power. Scan the entire area under the cover slip. Look for cells in which the nucleus appears to be made up of distinct thread-like parts. Such cells were undergoing mitosis at the time they were killed.
2. Locate an area where cells in various stages of mitosis are numerous and switch to high power.
3. Examine the area carefully, adjusting the iris diaphragm of your microscope if necessary.
4. Draw at least five entire cells, each in a different stage of mitosis.
5. Number your drawings in the order in which you think the stages occurred during mitosis. Use the illustrations of animal-cell mitosis on page 17 as a guide.
6. Now examine the prepared slide containing longitudinal sections of onion root tip. Study each section first under low power and then under high power.

A. In what regions of the root tip are most of the cells which are undergoing mitosis?
B. How does the shape of cells undergoing mitosis compare with that of cells located in other parts of the section?

7. Study a number of cells in different stages of mitosis plus several which do not appear to be dividing.

C. Are any structures visible in these cells on the prepared slide that you could not see in the 'squash' preparation? If so, draw one or more cells showing their structures.

8. Refer to the illustrations of dividing animal cells on page 17.

D. What difference, if any, can you find in the ways mitosis and cell division occur in animal cells and in plant cells?

FOR FURTHER INVESTIGATION

1. If you were attempting to determine the number of chromosomes present in cells of a bean root, would it be better to use 'squash' preparations or sections of the root?
2. Suppose you suspected that frequency of mitosis in onion roots varied with the time of day. How would you go about getting data to confirm or refute your suspicion?
3. Do all the events in mitosis take about the same time, or do some of them occur faster than others? How would you proceed experimentally to obtain information (evidence) to answer this question?

DIFFERENTIATION

After cell division one of two things may follow: either the daughter cells separate or the daughter cells remain together. In the first case there are two unicellular individuals – cell duplication is identical with the reproduction of the individual. In the second case repeated cell divisions result in groups of connected cells. If the cells in the group remain approximately alike, the group is a colony, but if the cells come to differ from each other in various ways, the group becomes a multicellular individual. Because cells usually increase in size between divisions, repeated cell divisions usually result in the growth of a colony or multicellular individual.

A PUZZLE

Buried in the last paragraph is a paradox. If the mechanism of mitosis ensures that both daughter cells will have the *same characteristics*, then how can any of the cells in a group derived from the same parent cell come to *differ* from the others? Differ they do, as you know from observing blood and skin cells of the frog; both of these descended from a single cell. Indeed, every multicellular organism – an oak tree, a cow, a man – develops from a single cell; yet the adult contains cells of a great many kinds.

What is known about this process of *differentiation*? In the past seventy years a multitude of ingenious experiments have provided biologists with information about the mechanisms. It is clear that the cell's final differentiation involves (1) selective use of information stored in the chromosomes, (2) ways in which adjacent cells affect each other in a developing organism, and (3) factors in the environment. Yet the fundamental question – How does differentiation occur? – remains unanswered.

RESULTS OF DIFFERENTIATION

Differentiation is an orderly process. Cells do not become endlessly different; they become different in limited and predictable ways. Further, they become different in groups rather than individually. Microscopic examination of a multicellular organism therefore may reveal the same basic structural characteristics in each member of a particular group of cells. In another group all cells may be similar among themselves but differ from those in the first mass. Groups in which all cells have similar structural and functional characteristics are called *tissues*.

A tissue might be considered a population of similar cells, just as a species is a population of similar individuals. In both cases one population is surrounded by other populations; in the first case, by other kinds of cells, in the second by other kinds of individuals. In both cases the population has many close and necessary relations with adjacent populations. Just as we can artificially remove a portion of a population of individual organisms – a mouse colony, for example – from its ecosystem and keep it in a laboratory, we can also remove a population of similar cells – muscle tissue, perhaps – and cultivate it in a test-tube. In such laboratory situations many valuable things can be learned about tissues, and the structure and function of the whole organism. However, under natural conditions neither a mouse colony nor a muscle tissue lives alone.

Some multicellular organisms, such as sponges and some algae, seem to have no organization other than that of tissues, but most have different tissues grouped into body parts that perform one or more functions for the whole organism. Such a body part, a leaf or a heart for example, is called an *organ*. Organs, like tissues, can be removed from the organism and tended artificially, but this is not done as often as with tissues.

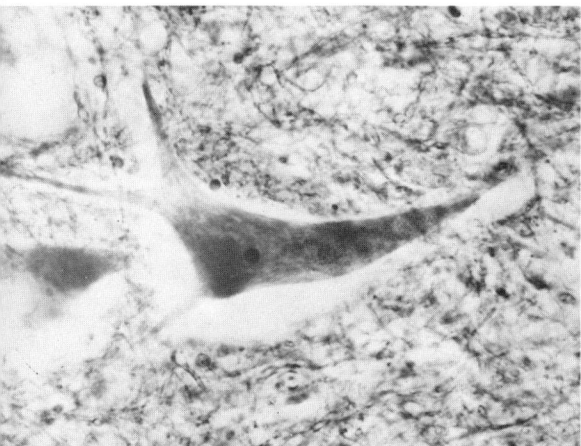

A Nervous tissue   X 500

Figure 1.16   Diversity among tissues.

B Cartilage   X 60

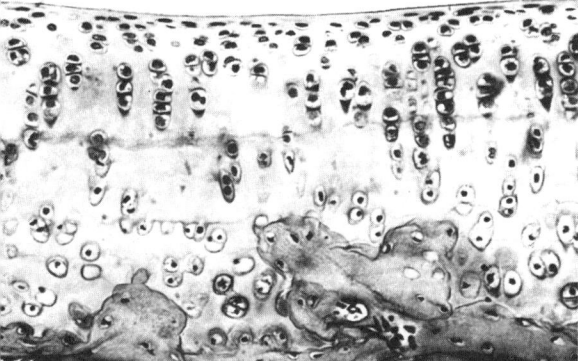

E Pith from a grape stem   X 60

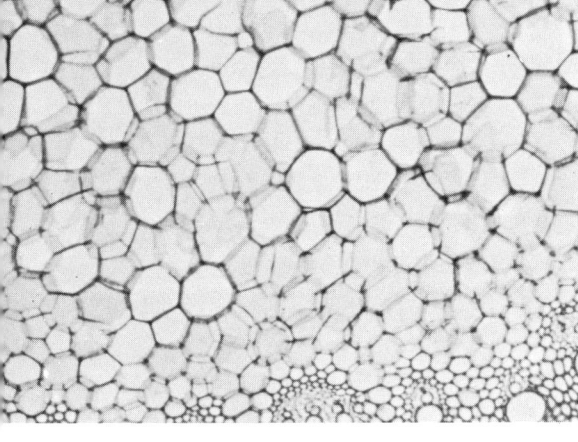

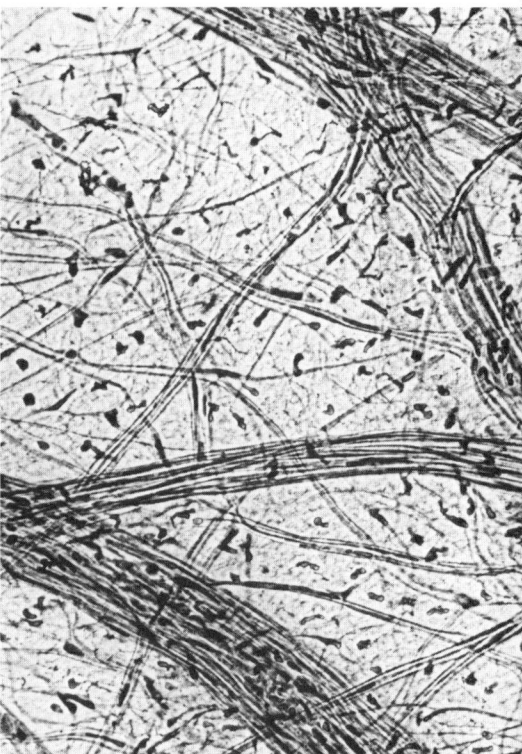

C Areolar connective tissue   X 400

D Wood   X 35

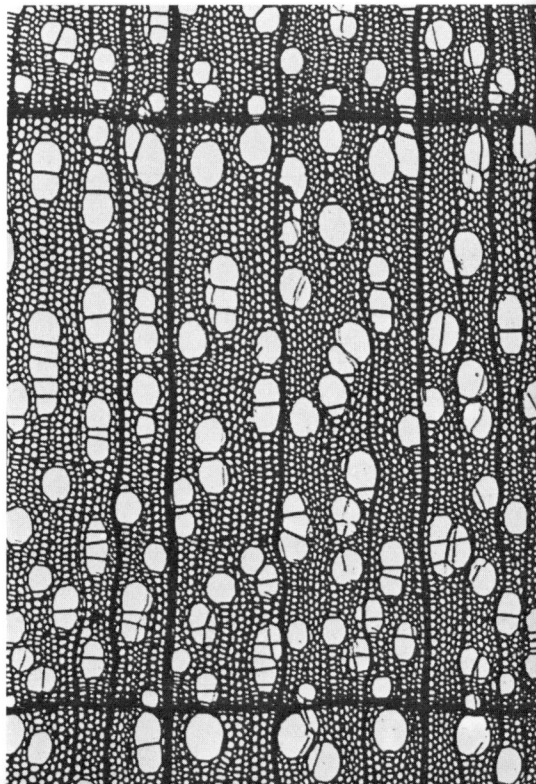

Finally, organs may be considered as parts of groups that perform some large function – circulation, for instance. Such a group of organs is called an *organ system*. In the plant kingdom this term has little meaning, and even in the animal kingdom an organ system is a less definite thing than an organ or a tissue.

AGEING

No cell lives for ever. It either divides to form new cells or dies. Many years ago August Weismann suggested that unicellular organisms are potentially immortal – that is, unless they die because of unfavourable environmental effects (lack of food, accumulation of poisonous wastes, being eaten by other organisms, etc.), they produce enormous numbers of cell generations. This appears to be a valid generalization, but to be really certain it would be necessary to maintain such organisms for very long periods of time in environments containing no unfavourable factors.

Weismann further suggested that in multicellular animals only reproductive cells – those that give rise to new individuals – are potentially immortal. They are passed essentially without change from one generation to the next. In differentiating, the other cells, the 'body cells', lose the ability to give rise to new individuals; so when the organism in which they occur dies, they die without descendants. One difficulty with this idea arose when zoologists found that during the early part of an animal's development they could not always clearly trace the origin of the reproductive cells. However, in the main, Weismann's generalization is probably valid.

Like so many generalizations in biology, this one raises further questions. Why do body cells age and die? Do ageing and death in body cells, as in micro-organisms, result from harmful

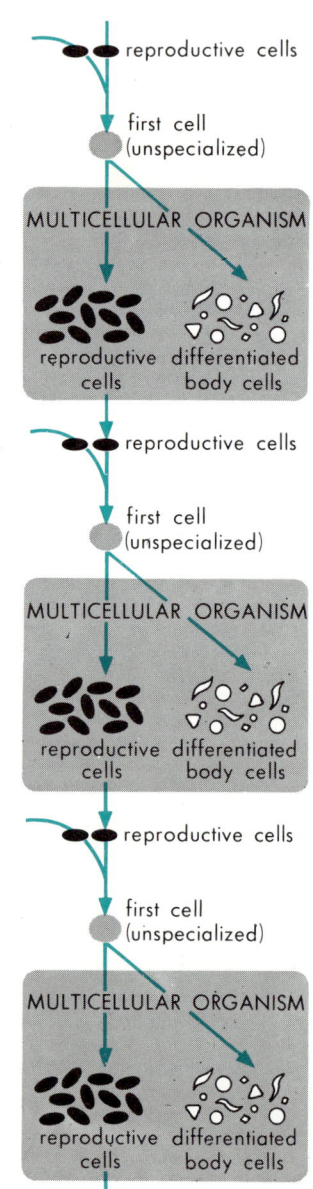

Figure 1.17 Weismann's concept of the continuity of cells in successive generations of multicellular organisms.

environmental effects? Or do they result from internal changes that are caused by differentiation?

Perhaps there is no single answer that holds for all kinds of cells. It seems clear that in many vertebrates the cells of the outer layer of skin and of the lining of the intestine die as a result of unfavourable environmental conditions. On the other hand an internal cause – lack of nuclei – has been suggested as the cause of the early death of red blood cells of mammals; but the red blood cells of birds, which *do* contain nuclei, also have a short life-span.

There is some evidence that hereditary changes occur early in the differentiation of some kinds of cells. Some of these changes may be harmful to the metabolic processes. In recent years some biologists have come to believe that the accumulation of such harmful changes may 'slow down' a cell and result in what we call ageing. Why do not such changes also occur and accumulate in reproductive cells and in unicellular organisms?

Many kinds of cells that are grown in tissue cultures in the laboratory, where they are maintained in an excellent environment, survive and go through cell division almost indefinitely. This suggests that ageing, failure to divide and death may be caused by the cellular environment within the body. Differentiation of cells is itself, at least in part, dependent on that internal environment. In many respects, therefore, tissue-culture cells may not be 'normally' differentiated, so we cannot have complete confidence in such evidence.

Like the problem of differentiation, the problems of ageing and death of cells are complex. Perhaps we shall understand more when we are able to think about the entire life history of a cell as a continuous process rather than about division, differentiation, ageing and death as separate processes.

The concept covered by the word 'cell' has changed greatly since cells were discovered. Today the cell is regarded as the unit of structure, of function and of reproduction in living things. Even in its present state, however, the cell theory cannot be perfectly applied to all organisms.

Cells differ greatly in size, shape and kinds of parts. In general, the cell consists of a nucleus and a cytoplast which can be distinguished by differences in reaction to stains. Within the cytoplast are organelles that carry on special cell functions. Separating the cell from its environment is a membrane; through it must pass inward all the materials the cell uses, and outward, all the materials the cell discards. Diffusion, active transport and pinocytosis account for much of this inflow and outflow and also for the passage of substances through membranes within the cell. Diffusion and cyclosis move substances within the cytoplast itself. The energy used for various cell activities comes from chemical reactions within the cell. The sum of these chemical reactions is metabolism.

In one-celled organisms, duplication of cells results in new individuals. In multicellular organisms, cell duplication results in increase of the number of cells within the individual. Mitosis, the series of nuclear changes that occurs during cell duplication, is remarkably similar in all cells. Mitosis provides each new cell with a set of chromosomes which is a duplicate of the set in the parent cell.

Although cells tend to produce daughter cells like themselves, the daughter cells differentiate during the development of multicellular organisms. In multicellular organisms, groups of cells that are similar in structure and function are called tissues. Different tissues may be organized into organs. Finally, in studying the larger animals it is convenient to consider organs that together perform some major function as parts of an organ system.

GUIDE QUESTIONS

1. How has the meaning of the word 'cell' changed since Hooke's time?
2. What is the cell theory? Why do you think it is called a 'theory'?
3. How are staining techniques useful in the study of cells?
4. Contrast cells of plants, animals and protists, using the principal cell structures as the basis for distinguishing them. Is the distinction clear-cut?
5. What is meant by the metabolism of a cell?
6. What are the *facts* of diffusion? How does the molecular theory explain them?
7. Molecules of different sizes can pass back and forth through a cell's membrane, yet the substance of the cell remains easily distinguishable from the substance of its environment. Explain.
8. If water molecules are less concentrated outside a cell membrane than they are within the membrane, what will be the direction of water diffusion?
9. What observations by cell physiologists support the theory of active transport?
10. How do particles that pass through cell membranes by pinocytosis differ from particles moved by diffusion and active transport?
11. Which of the processes by which substances move into and out of cells require the use of a cell's energy?
12. The terms 'mitosis' and 'cell division' are not synonymous. Explain.
13. In your own words describe the principal events that occur during mitosis.
14. What seems to be the biological meaning of mitosis?
15. How does cell differentiation seem to contradict this meaning?
16. Distinguish between cells, tissues, organs and systems.

17. When cells differentiate, which of their abilities often declines?
18. Why do cells age?

PROBLEMS

1. During the late nineteenth century most knowledge of detailed cell structure was gained by studying stained dead cells. Some biologists objected to many conclusions drawn from such observation, arguing that the processes of killing, staining and mounting cells on slides might cause cell structure to appear very different from cell structure in life. What kinds of evidence are now available to meet at least some of these objections?
2. Examine various kinds of cells from multicellular organisms, either under the microscope or by means of photomicrographs in books. Discuss the relationships between the structural forms of the cells and their functions.
3. Working in a police laboratory, you are given a tiny sample of material and asked to identify it as either plant or animal matter. How could you decide which it is?
4. On the basis of your understanding of the diffusion of water, describe what would happen to (a) a marine jellyfish placed in a fresh-water stream, and (b) a frog placed in ocean water. Some fish (for example, salmon) annually swim from the ocean into fresh-water rivers and back. How are they able to do this?
5. In this chapter mitosis in cells that have a single, well-defined nucleus was described. Investigate what is known about the behaviour of nuclear material (chromatin) during the division in (a) a 'cell' that has more than one nucleus – *Paramecium*, for example, and (b) a 'cell' that lacks a nucleus – a blue-green alga.
6. Much of the money available for cancer research goes into studies of cell differentiation. Why?
7. In what ways are cells of multicellular organisms held together?
8. The living substance of cells is often called 'protoplasm'. Many biologists object to the use of the term. Find out why.
9. Much of the modern understanding of cell structure has resulted from invention of new optical instruments. What kinds of information have been provided by means of electron microscopes? By means of phase-contrast microscopes?

SUGGESTED READING

(See also books by Mercer, and Loewy and Siekevitz, listed at the end of the next chapter.)

COULT, D. A. *Molecules and Cells*. Longmans, Green, 1966. (An up-to-date account of the cell aimed at A-level students.)

FISCHBERG, M. and A. W. BLACKLER. 'How Cells Specialize', *Scientific American* offprint. W. H. Freeman, 1961.

GREEN, D. E. 'The Mitochondrion', *Scientific American*. January 1964. Pp. 63–66+.

HOLTER, H. 'How Things Get into Cells', *Scientific American*, September 1961. Pp. 167–74+.

HURRY, S. W. *The Microstructure of Cells*. John Murray, 1965. (Excellent diagrams and electronmicrographs.)

MAZIA, D. *Cell Division* (BSCS Pamphlet 14). George G. Harrap & Co., 1964. (Emphasis on the details of mitosis and the problems that cell biologists are exploring.)

——. 'How Cells Divide', *Scientific American* offprint. W. H. Freeman, 1961.

ROBERTSON, J. D. 'The Membrane of the Living Cell', *Scientific American*, April 1962. Pp. 64–72.

SOLOMON, A. L. 'Pumps in the Living Cell', *Scientific American*, August 1962. Pp. 100–8.

SWANSON, C. P. *The Cell*. 2nd edn. Prentice-Hall, 1964. (Deals with the structure of the cell as revealed by the electron microsope.)

WADDINGTON, C. H. 'How do Cells Differentiate?', *Scientific American* offprint. W. H. Freeman, 1953.

CHAPTER
2

BIOENERGETICS

LIFE, ENERGY AND CELLS

You can hold a single acorn in the palm of your hand, and yet, when planted in a favourable environment, it may develop into a towering organism perhaps almost 35 m high with a circumference of more than 4 m. Where does the energy to build the kilogrammes of organic compounds in leaf, stem and root come from?

You walk along the shore of a pond: frogs leap from the bank; ducks dabble in the shallows; swallows fly through the air. What is the source of the energy for all this muscular activity?

It cannot be over-emphasized that wherever there is life, energy must be involved. Throughout the biosphere there exist complex pathways, such that energy can pass from one organism to another. We are now to investigate the chemical means by which living things perform the various kinds of energy changes involved in this flow.

According to the cell theory a cell is the functional unit in any organism. We have begun to discuss cellular function – cellular physiology; now we continue the discussion, centring our attention upon the biochemistry of energy transformations – *bioenergetics*.

If a cell has a pigment that can trap radiant energy, it stores the energy in chemical form (food) by the process of photosynthesis. If a cell does not have such pigment (or if it has the pigment but lacks a supply of radiant energy) it must obtain energy from food. In any case, energy to carry on moment-to-moment cell processes comes from food, whether the food be made within the cell or taken in from the environment.

An oak tree is a producer organism, but many cells in its roots, its trunk, its branches – all those cells that do not contain chlorophyll – function like the cells in a consumer. Even its green cells, when they are not supplied with light, depend upon energy-containing carbon compounds to sustain life until they are again exposed to sunlight. The release of energy from food occurs in all cells at all times, as long as they are alive. It is appropriate, therefore, to begin the consideration of bioenergetics with the energy-releasing processes of cells.

INVESTIGATION 2.1

BIOENERGETICS: AN INTRODUCTORY VIEW

PURPOSE
In this investigation you will measure the effects of some biochemical reactions.

MATERIALS AND EQUIPMENT
For each group
  Pea seeds, 80
  Beakers, 50 cm³, 2
  Volumeter
  Graduated cylinder, 100 cm³
  Glass beads, a volume of about 100 cm³
  Paper tissues
  Glass rod
  Non-absorbent cotton wool
  Spatula, porcelain
  Caustic potash, about 3 cm³
  Dropper
  Water coloured with eosin

For special group
  Pea seeds, a volume of about 400 cm³
  Beakers, 400 cm³, 2
  Vacuum flasks, 2
  Non-absorbent cotton wool
  1-hole rubber stoppers to fit vacuum bottles, 2
  Thermometers (−10 °C to +110 °C), 2
  Glycerine

A. What effect should soaking have on the dormant embryos within the seeds?

3. Watch your teacher demonstrate the volumeter and when you understand how it works, assemble a volumeter as shown in Figure 2.1.

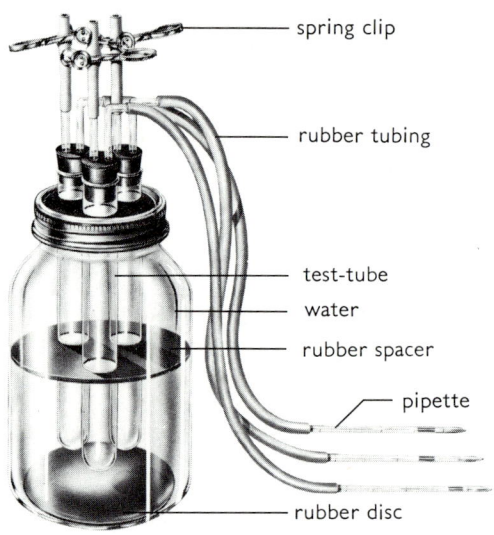

Figure 2.1 Volumeter.

PROCEDURE
1. Twenty-four hours before you wish to begin the experiment each group should set up the peas as follows.
   (a) Place 40 seeds in a small beaker and add water until the peas are well covered.
   (b) Place 40 seeds in a small beaker and leave aside. Do *not* add water.
2. One group in each class should place two additional lots of peas (each having a volume of about 200 cm³) in beakers and add water to cover the seeds in one beaker, leaving the other dry.
3.
4. Remove the stoppers from the volumeter tubes. Measure 50 cm³ of water into a 100-cm³ graduated cylinder and add the 40 soaked seeds to the cylinder. Record the level of the water in the cylinder.
5. Remove the soaked seeds and place them in one of the volumeter tubes.
6. Measure 50 cm³ of water into the cylinder and add the 40 dry seeds. Add glass beads until the level reaches the level recorded for the soaked seeds.

7. Remove the seeds and beads and dry them on a paper tissue. Place them in a second tube of the volumeter.
8. Measure 50 cm³ of water into the cylinder and add glass beads until the level reaches that recorded for the soaked seeds.
9. Remove the beads, dry them and put them in the third tube of the volumeter.

B. What is the role of this third tube in the experimental design?
C. What is the purpose of the glass beads?

10. Using a glass rod, loosely pack cotton wool to a depth of 1 cm over the material in each tube.
11. With the spatula add 1 cm³ of the caustic potash to each tube, taking care not to get it on your skin or clothes.
12. Replace the stoppers and place the tubes in the volumeter.
13. Arrange the volumeter pipettes so that they are level on the table.
14. Using a dropper, place a drop of coloured water in the end of each pipette.
15. To adjust the position of the drop, proceed as follows. Open the clamp at the top of the tube to which the pipette is attached, and, using the dropper, draw or push air through the system.
16. In each of the two pipettes containing peas, adjust the drop to a position near the outer end. In the third pipette, adjust the drop to a position near the middle.
17. Leave the apparatus for 5 minutes and during this time select three of the group to read the pipettes and the fourth to time the readings.
18. At zero time record the position of each drop. Record the position of each drop at two-minute intervals for a total of twenty minutes.
19. The special group should proceed as follows. Mark two vacuum flasks A and B.
20. Place a layer of moist cotton wool in the base of Flask A and add the 200 cm³ of soaked seeds.
21. Place a layer of dry cotton wool in the base of Flask B and add the 200 cm³ of dry seeds.
22. Take two thermometers and lubricate them with glycerine and insert them into the one-holed stoppers.
23. Place the stoppers in the vacuum flasks so that the thermometer bulb is among the peas yet the mercury level is visible.
24. Wait 5 minutes before reading both thermometers. Record the readings.
25. Place both flasks aside for 24 hours and then read the thermometers once more. Record the readings.

STUDYING THE DATA

1. For each tube of the volumeter subtract the reading at zero time from each of the subsequent readings.

A. What does a positive number indicate about the volume of air in the tube pipette system?
B. What does a negative number indicate?

2. Graph the derived data (i.e. that obtained after subtraction), using different colours to represent the different tubes.

C. Which line represents change in a tube not associated with living things?

3. Compare the other two lines with this one.

D. Which one most resembles it?
E. State a hypothesis to account for any difference you found between the data from the tube with the dry peas and the data from the tube with the soaked peas.
F. If you found changes in the position of the marked drops, which of the gases in the system do you think changed in amount?

G. Why was caustic potash – a substance which absorbs carbon dioxide – included in the system?

CONCLUSIONS
A. What evidence does this investigation provide for the hypothesis that physiological activity involves chemical change?
B. What evidence does it provide for the hypothesis that physiological activity involves energy change?

FOR FURTHER INVESTIGATION
You can use the volumeter to investigate these problems.

1. How do advancing stages of seed germination affect the rate of the biochemical processes measured by the apparatus?

2. Do small animals, when placed in the volumeter, produce results similar to those that you obtained with the seeds?

ENERGY-RELEASING PROCESSES

Energy to carry on cell processes comes from foods. The ways in which energy is released from foods are remarkably similar among the most diverse kinds of cells, but the details are extremely complex, so biochemists still have many unsolved problems to investigate.

SOME BASIC POINTS

Foods are carbon compounds that contain hydrogen, oxygen, and often other elements as well. Chemically foods are somewhat like the fuels burned in stoves and furnaces. Indeed, furnace fuels such as wood, coal and oil are carbon compounds derived from dead cells. They serve as fuels because they contain chemical energy. During the chemical reactions of burning, which reduce them to simpler compounds, this energy is released in the forms of heat and light.

Chemical energy in foods is likewise released by chemical reactions, but in cells the chemical reactions are quite different from those in stoves. Only a relatively small amount of the energy appears as heat and light.

Energy units. Energy is commonly measured in units called calories. A *calorie* is defined as the amount of heat energy required to raise 1 g of water by 1 degree C. Thus by definition, a calorie is a unit of heat energy. But since all forms of energy are interchangeable, the calorie can be used as a unit of measure for energy of all kinds. However, different types of scientist measure energy in different ways, e.g. mechanical engineers use foot-poundals, electrical engineers use kilowatt-hours and biochemists generally use the 'big' Calorie (with a capital C), which is equal to 1000 'small' calories. But now by international agreement, there is to be only one unit – the *joule*. This latter unit is defined as that unit of energy which is given to a body when a force of 1 newton is exerted on it for a distance of 1 m in the direction of the force. (One calorie is equivalent to 4.186 joules.)

Catalysis and enzymes. In stoves, release of energy from fuel occurs only at high temperatures. But temperature in living cells is never high enough for such energy-releasing chemical reactions. So how can they occur? By *catalysis*.

Chemists discovered long ago that small quantities of certain substances can greatly speed up some chemical reactions without being used up in the reactions. For instance, a small quantity of finely powdered platinum will cause some gases that normally do not react together to react with explosive rapidity; yet the quantity of platinum does not change. Platinum catalyses the reaction. In cells, also, catalysts regulate chemical reactions. Cell catalysts, however, are different from such catalysts as powdered platinum; they are organic compounds made by living cells. Because they differ so widely from inorganic catalysts, they have a special name – *enzymes*.

Returning to the evidence that biochemists have at present, each enzyme in a living cell catalyses just *one* chemical reaction; that is, enzymes are *specific* in their actions. Though many chemical reactions *could* take place among the hundreds of compounds in a living cell, only those reactions *do* occur for which there are appropriate enzymes. Moreover, these reactions are orderly. Their timing depends in part on the location of the enzymes in the cell. One reaction, catalysed by a certain enzyme, occurs at one place and the products of this reaction pass on to another place where another enzyme catalyses a second reaction. Thus the chemical changes in a cell are controlled as to order and sequence as well as to kind.

INVESTIGATION 2.2

CELLS: BIOCHEMICAL REACTIONS

PURPOSE
In this investigation you find out how hydrogen peroxide is disposed of within living cells.

BACKGROUND INFORMATION
Hydrogen peroxide is a highly toxic chemical that is often used for bleaching and is usually sold as a 3 per cent solution in water. Within living cells hydrogen peroxide is thought to be formed continually, as a by-product of biochemical processes. As it is poisonous, it would soon kill the cell if it were not removed or broken down immediately.

MATERIALS AND EQUIPMENT
(for each group)
Test-tubes, 12 mm × 100 mm, 10
Wax pencil
Test-tube rack
Graduated cylinder, 10 cm^3
100 cm^3 of 3 per cent hydrogen peroxide solution
Scalpel
Manganese dioxide powder
Forceps
Fresh liver 6 mm in diameter, 3 pieces
Fine sand
Mortar and pestle
Bunsen burner
Ring stand
Beaker
Fresh potato

PROCEDURE

1. Arrange nine of the test-tubes in a rack and number them 1 to 9.
2. Put 2 cm³ of water into Tube 1.
3. Put 2 cm³ of hydrogen peroxide into Tubes 2 to 9.
4. After each of the following steps record your observations, comparing observations on different tubes where you think necessary.
5. *Tube 1.* Add a small amount of manganese dioxide (about as much as you can get on a scalpel blade).

   Tube 2. As Tube 1.

   Tube 3. Add a piece of liver; use the forceps.

   Tube 4. Add a little sand, about a scalpel-blade full.

   Tube 5. Take the mortar and pestle. Add a piece of liver and some sand. Grind together and add to Tube 5.

   Tube 6. Place a piece of liver in boiling water for 3 minutes; then add it to Tube 6.

   Tube 7. Take the remaining test-tube: add 2 cm³ of water and a scalpel-blade full of manganese dioxide. Place in a beaker of boiling water for 3 minutes. Add to Tube 7.

   Tube 8. Using the scalpel, cut two cubes of potato about the same size as the liver. Place one cube in Tube 8.

   Tube 9. Wash the mortar and pestle thoroughly. Grind a potato cube with sand and add to Tube 9.

DISCUSSION AND CONCLUSIONS

A. What was the purpose of Tube 1 in this investigation?
B. Do you have any evidence that manganese dioxide catalyses the breakdown of hydrogen peroxide rather than reacting with it?
C. What additional steps in the procedure would be needed to confirm this?
D. Definite experimental evidence exists to show that manganese dioxide is indeed a catalyst in this reaction. Consider the formula of hydrogen peroxide (H_2O_2) and the kind of reaction you observed in Tube 2. What are the most likely products of the breakdown of hydrogen peroxide?
E. How might you confirm your answer?
F. How do you explain the difference in activity between the whole piece of liver and the ground liver?
G. Why is Tube 4 necessary for this explanation?
H. How do you explain the difference in activity between fresh and boiled liver?
I. Suppose that someone comparing Tubes 2 and 3 concluded that liver contained manganese dioxide. What evidence do you have either for or against this conclusion?
J. If you cannot support the conclusion, explain the reaction in Tube 3.
K. What additional information do the results from Tubes 8 and 9 provide?

CELLULAR RESPIRATION

The energy-releasing process in cells can be given several names. 'Burning', the term used when making comparisons, is misleading, because it implies high temperatures, as in the non-living world. Sometimes, the more general chemical term 'oxidation' is used. Among biologists it is customary to speak of the main kind of energy-releasing process as *cellular respiration*. Breathing, the ordinary meaning of the term 'respiration', is related to cellular respiration but is not directly a form of it.

In the burning of fuels, energy is released as light and heat. In cellular respiration, however, the chemical energy released is transformed into motion (on a large scale, as in muscle, or on a small scale, as in the movement of molecules or ions by active transport); or it energizes reactions to form new chemical compounds. To a very small extent, it may be transformed into light (as in glow-worms). Some heat is also released, but this is lost energy as far as cell processes are concerned.

Glucose. One of the principal carbon compounds broken down when energy is released in cells is glucose. Almost all other multicarbon compounds in cells can be converted to glucose, so it is by way of glucose that energy release can best be explained. A glucose molecule contains a series of six linked carbon atoms with oxygen and hydrogen atoms attached. Its formula is $C_6H_{12}O_6$. Biochemists also write it as shown in Figure 2.2A. This diagram is known as a *structural formula*; such a formula is useful because the same numbers and kinds of atoms can be arranged in many patterns, each pattern having its own characteristics and thus representing a distinct chemical compound. Of course, atoms in a molecule seldom occur in the flat shape of a formula on paper. To show the three-dimensional shapes of molecules, chemists use models, as in Figure 2.2B.

Figure 2.2 Glucose.

(A) Structural formula.

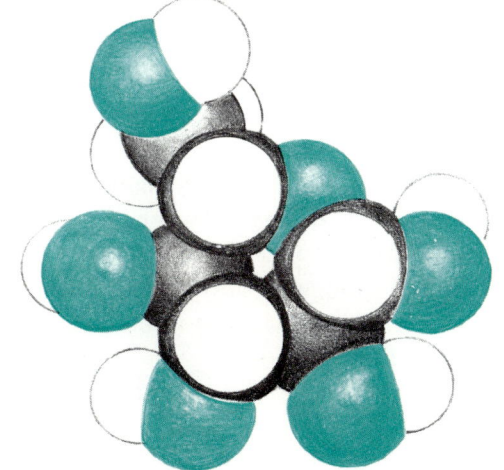

(B) Model. Here atoms are shown as spheres, each kind in a separate diagrammatic shade. Try to find in the model the atoms shown by symbols in the formula.

Energy in small packets. Heat energy released by the burning of petrol can be channelled to move the piston of an engine and the wheels of a car. But the use of energy by a cell is not simple and immediate; it does not occur in great bursts followed by long periods of idleness, as in a petrol engine. It is gradual and continuous.

If you had a ten-pound note, you might find it difficult to use in making day-to-day purchases – a cup of tea, a pad of writing paper, a comb. It would be much easier to use if exchanged for ten one-pound notes. So, too, with energy in the cell. The bigger bursts of energy from glucose are put into 'small change'. This 'small change' is the chemical energy in what are called 'energy-transfer compounds'. The most important is a complex substance known as *adenosine triphosphate*, usually abbreviated ATP.

Each molecule of this substance includes a main section which we shall symbolize as A. Attached to this section are three identical groups of atoms called phosphate groups. We will symbolize each phosphate group as ⓟ. ATP may thus be written A—ⓟ~ⓟ~ⓟ. Each wavy line indicates the attachment of a phosphate group whose removal is accompanied by the release, or transfer, of a small amount of energy.

No matter where energy is required in the cell, ATP or some other energy-transfer compound is the usual source. Each ATP molecule releases a bit of energy whenever the terminal phosphate group breaks off, leaving A—ⓟ~ⓟ. This molecule, with only two phosphate groups, is called adenosine diphosphate – ADP. We can show its formation from ATP as follows:

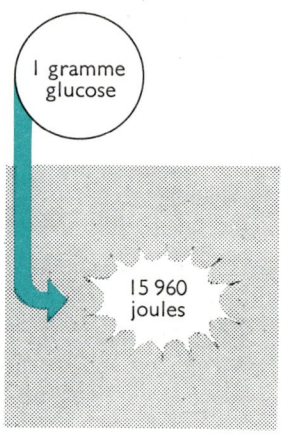

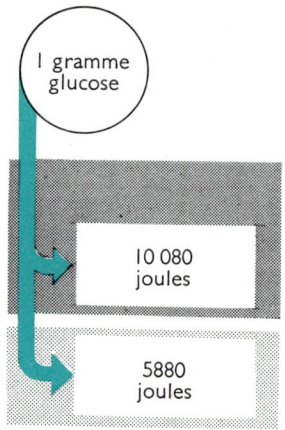

Figure 2.3 Does the amount of energy obtained from a food depend upon the way it is released?

$$A—ⓟ~ⓟ~ⓟ \rightarrow A—ⓟ~ⓟ + ⓟ$$
$$\downarrow$$
$$energy$$

You cannot keep on spending money from your pocket without eventually facing the necessity of putting money in again. Likewise, the cell cannot continually 'spend' its ATP and carry on the above reaction without also continually rebuilding some ADP back into ATP:

$$energy$$
$$\downarrow$$
$$ⓟ + A—ⓟ~ⓟ \rightarrow A—ⓟ~ⓟ~ⓟ$$

Thus there is a continual ADP–ATP cycle.

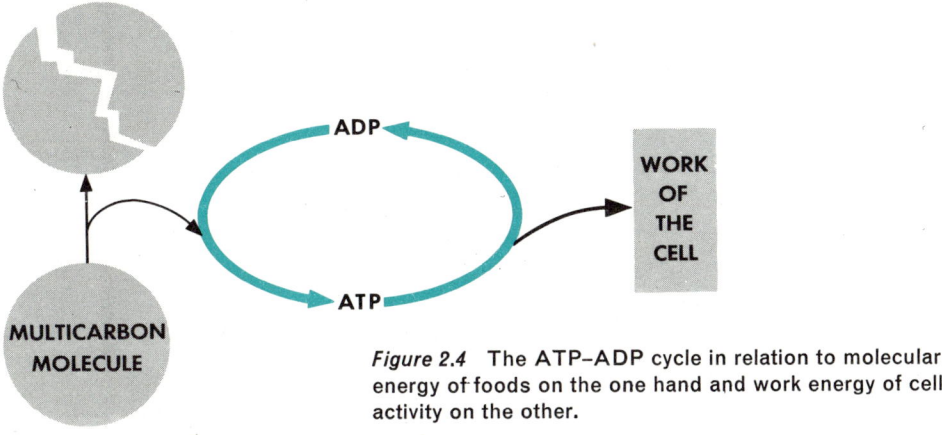

Figure 2.4 The ATP–ADP cycle in relation to molecular energy of foods on the one hand and work energy of cell activity on the other.

From glucose to carbon dioxide and water. Now let us look a little further into cellular respiration, through which energy is made available for ATP formation. A step-by-step breakdown of glucose molecules occurs. In the middle of this breakdown hydrogen is removed from the components of the glucose molecule. Each hydrogen atom becomes a hydrogen ion and a high-energy electron, an electron that carries some of the energy that was in the glucose. Eventually all the hydrogen is stripped away. The whole process can be considered in two major sets of reactions: *glycolysis* and the *Krebs-cycle system*. (Refer to Figure 2.5 as you study the rest of this section.)

Glycolysis consists of a series of reactions, each catalysed by its own specific

Figure 2.5 A diagram of cellular respiration.

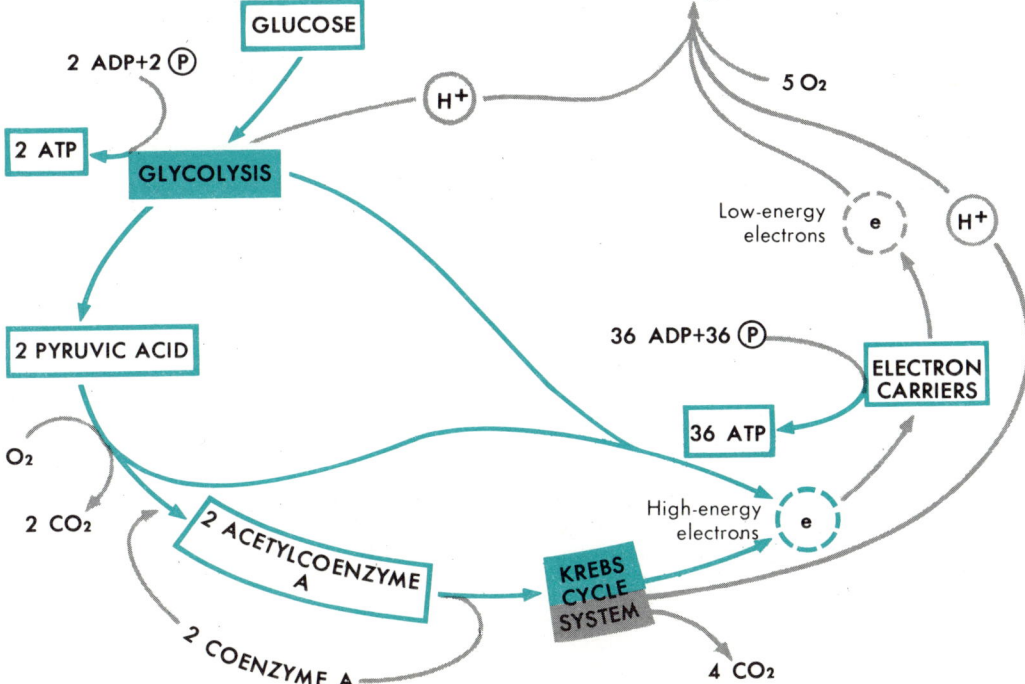

enzyme. As a result of these reactions energy is released, and each six-carbon molecule of glucose is changed to two molecules of a three-carbon compound, *pyruvic acid*. Each of the two pyruvic acid molecules, by removal of a molecule of carbon dioxide, is converted to a molecule of a two-carbon compound, *acetic acid*, releasing still more energy. The acetic acid molecules never really exist by themselves; rather, they are immediately attached to a molecule of *coenzyme A*, forming *acetyl coenzyme A*. Coenzyme A is formed from one of the B vitamins. If this vitamin is lacking in the diet of an animal, coenzyme A cannot be formed and the process of cellular respiration is blocked.

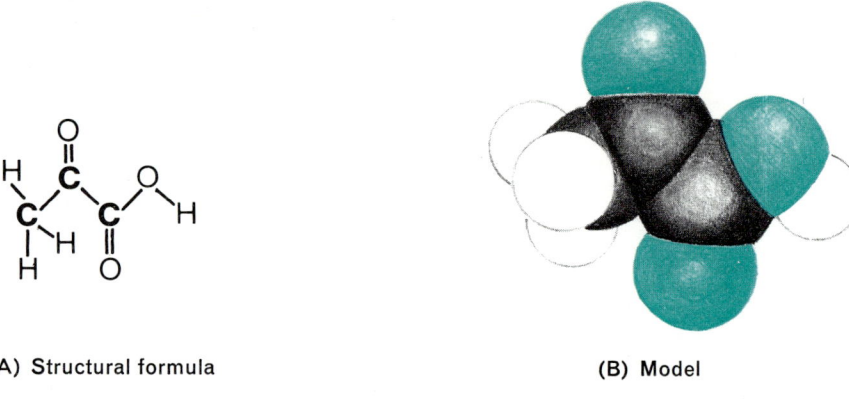

(A) Structural formula (B) Model

Figure 2.6 Pyruvic acid.

(A) Structural formula (B) Model

Figure 2.7 Acetic acid.

After the formation of acetyl coenzyme A, the second part of cellular respiration, the Krebs cycle, begins. The first step is the transfer of acetic acid from acetyl coenzyme A to a molecule of a four-carbon compound, *oxaloacetic acid*. This forms a six-carbon compound, *citric acid*. Then, through a series of reactions (each reaction catalysed by its own enzyme), hydrogen, high-energy electrons, and two carbon atoms (each forming a molecule of CO_2) are removed from the citric acid molecule. Left over is a molecule of the four-carbon oxaloacetic acid. This molecule is now available to start the Krebs cycle again by receiving acetic acid from another acetyl coenzyme A.

Each glucose molecule yields *two* molecules of acetyl coenzyme A, and two molecules of carbon dioxide are formed from each one of acetyl coenzyme A. Therefore, the Krebs-cycle system produces *four* CO_2 molecules from the breakdown of one glucose molecule.

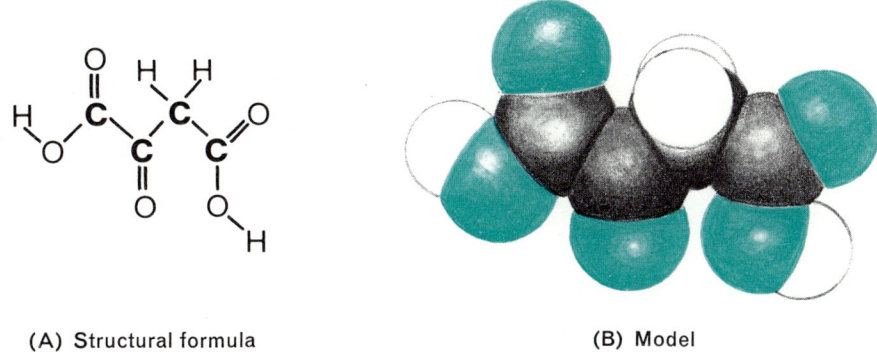

(A) Structural formula   (B) Model

Figure 2.8   Oxaloacetic acid.

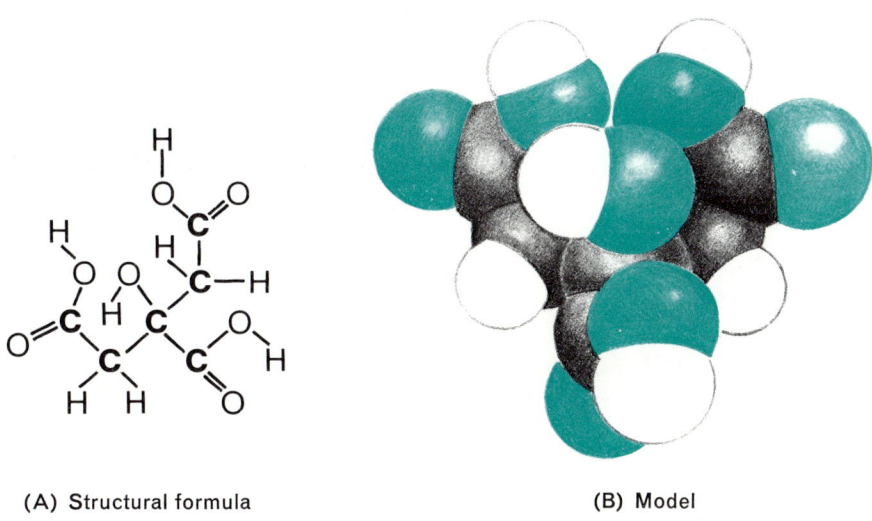

(A) Structural formula   (B) Model

Figure 2.9   Citric acid.

The high-energy electrons resulting from glycolysis and the Krebs cycle are passed to a series of substances we may call 'electron carriers'. In going from one carrier to another, the electrons give up energy, which is used to form ATP molecules. Depleted of much of their energy, the electrons are finally united with hydrogen ions and oxygen to form water. It is only for this last part of cellular respiration that a cell requires an outside source of oxygen.

We can now summarize cellular respiration in the following chemical expression:

$$C_6H_{12}O_6 + 6O_2 \xrightarrow{\text{enzymes}} 6CO_2 + 6H_2O$$
$$\downarrow$$
$$\text{energy to ATP}$$

The many enzymes catalysing cellular respiration are not distributed evenly throughout a cell. Those concerned with the reactions of glycolysis are in the cytoplast. Those concerned with the Krebs-cycle and electron-carrier systems are in the mitochondria. Since most of the energy is released in the mitochondria, they are sometimes called the 'powerhouses' of a cell.

Figure 2.10 The relationship of respiration to cell activities. Into what form does all food energy eventually go?

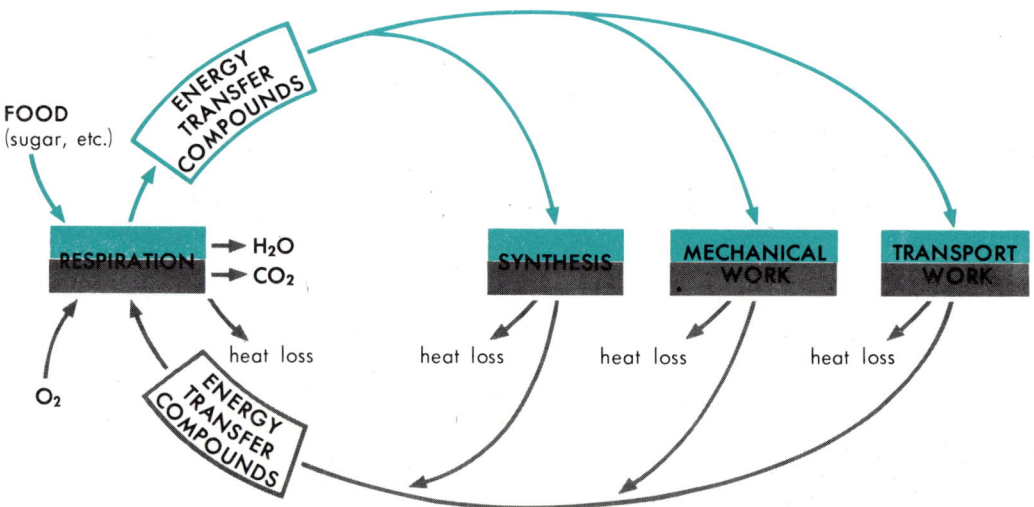

OTHER PATHWAYS OF ENERGY RELEASE

What happens if a cell does not have a supply of oxygen to complete the process of cellular respiration? In our own bodies, for example, muscular exercise may require that energy be supplied faster than it can be released by cellular respiration. The necessary oxygen cannot travel from lungs through blood vessels through cell membranes into muscle cells fast enough. During hard exercise we cannot even breathe fast enough to meet the demand for oxygen. Do the muscle cells die?

No. Under such circumstances glucose is partially broken down by *fermentation*. This is a general term for anaerobic pathways of energy release.

Various anaerobic pathways differ in the end products that are formed but they are alike in releasing only a small fraction of the energy in a glucose molecule. Some biochemists estimate that in cellular respiration as much as 60 per cent of the energy in a glucose molecule may be transferred to ATP. (Figure 2.3 shows that cellular respiration traps in ATP about 10 000 of the 15 960 joules in a gramme of glucose – that is $10\,000/15\,960 \simeq 0.6$, or 60 per cent.) If you now contrast Figure 2.11 with Figure 2.5, you will see that fermentation produces only two ATP molecules per glucose molecule, as compared with thirty-eight produced by cellular respiration. So in fermentation only about $2/38 \times 60$ per cent, or 3.2 per cent of glucose energy is released. Thus fermentation is somewhat like a faulty furnace that allows unburnt coal to pass through with the ashes.

Figure 2.11 Fermentation. In mammalian muscle cells anaerobic energy release leads to lactic acid. Another pathway leads to ethanol.

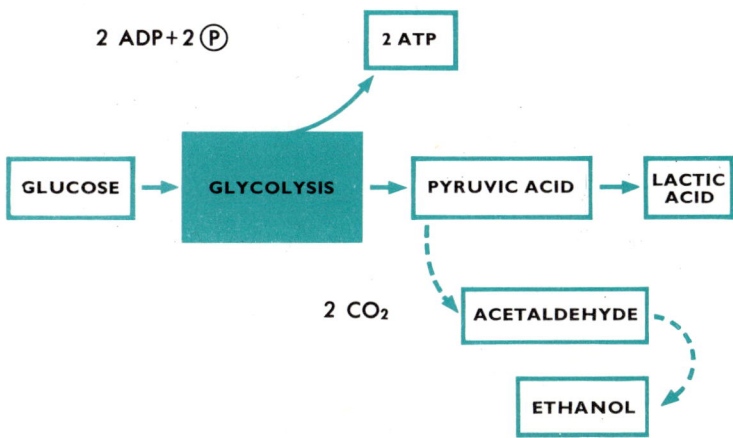

The cells of man and other animals can release energy by fermentation for a time. Eventually they must have oxygen to continue into the more efficient cellular respiration. However, some organisms – for example *Clostridium tetani*, the bacterium of lockjaw – exist entirely by inefficient fermentation. Others, such as yeasts, can exist very well anaerobically, but if oxygen is available they change to the more efficient method, aerobic respiration.

Some of the waste products of fermentation in other organisms are very useful to man. For example, under anaerobic conditions yeasts convert pyruvic acid to ethanol (C_2H_5OH), a waste product. The lactic acid formed by some bacteria curdles milk during cheese-making. And the distinctive flavours of many cheeses are the result of substances left over from the energy-releasing processes of still other micro-organisms.

42 Looking into Organisms

INVESTIGATION 2.3

FERMENTATION

PURPOSE
To study fermentation and compare it with respiration.

MATERIALS AND EQUIPMENT
(for each group)
Vacuum bottles, 2
Stoppers, 2-hole, to fit bottles, 2
Glass tubes about 8 cm long, 2
Thermometers, 2
Glycerine
Rubber tubing, 2 lengths of about 35 cm
Beakers, 250 cm^3, 2
Limewater, 300 cm^3
Treacle, 25 per cent solution in water, 400 cm^3
Dry yeast, about a quarter of a packet
Drinking straw

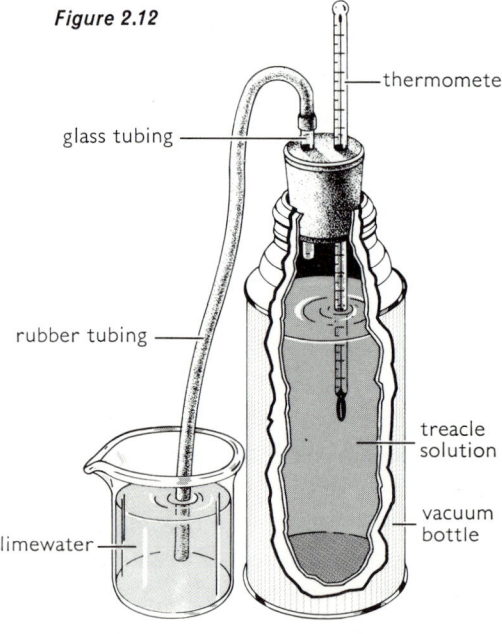

Figure 2.12

PROCEDURE
1. Take two vacuum bottles. Label one A, the other B.
2. Three-quarters fill each with the 25 per cent treacle solution.
3. Lubricate thermometers and glass tubing and insert them into the stoppers as shown in Figure 2.12.
4. Complete the two sets of apparatus as shown in the figure.
5. Remove the stopper from Bottle A and add a quarter of a packet of dry yeast.
6. Mix the yeast and treacle by gently swirling the bottle. Replace the stopper.
7. Set the bottles aside for 5 minutes and during this time place a little limewater in a beaker and blow into it through a straw. Record the result.
8. Record the temperature in each bottle and the time.
9. During the next 48 hours, record the temperatures in each bottle, noting the time of each reading. Record the appearance of the limewater.
10. After 48 hours remove the stoppers from each bottle and compare the smell.

STUDYING THE DATA
1. Graph your data. Use blue to plot Bottle A and red for Bottle B.

A. What evidence do you have that chemical reactions have occurred during the period of your observations?
B. Did reactions occur in Bottle A, Bottle B or both? If both, was there any difference in the amount of reaction?
C. Are conditions within the bottle aerobic or anaerobic? Explain your answer.
D. What evidence have you that a gas was produced in the bottles?
E. Was it produced in both bottles? If not, in which one was it produced?
F. In what way does the gas resemble the gas in exhaled breath?
G. Did the contents of the bottles

smell alike at the end of the experiment? If not, how did they differ?

CONCLUSIONS
A. What variable in the set-up accounts for any difference you may have obtained between results in Bottle A and Bottle B?
B. In what ways does fermentation seem to resemble respiration as observed in Investigation 2.1?
C. In what ways does fermentation seem to differ from respiration?

FOR FURTHER INVESTIGATION
1. If you can obtain some unpasteurized milk, you can use the above apparatus to investigate another kind of fermentation. Compare the two types.

2. The amount of gas produced by yeasts can be used as a measure of fermentation. Devise an apparatus to measure the gas and investigate the effects of environment variables on fermentation (e.g. food, temperature, light).

SYNTHESES

The release of chemical energy from compounds in the cell involves the breaking down of large molecules into smaller ones. You might suppose, therefore, that the building up of large molecules from smaller ones would require energy – and this is actually the case. Any such process is a *synthesis* (plural, 'syntheses'). The energy for *photo*synthesis comes from the sun. In other biological syntheses, the energy to build up large molecules comes from the breakdown of other molecules in the ways discussed before.

You probably know something about three groups of chemical compounds called carbohydrates, fats and proteins. These are ordinarily thought of as foods. They also make up much of the substance of cells. A hungry lion can make use of the fat and protein and carbohydrate of your cells as food, and you can do the same with the cells of a bean. In addition to these compounds (and the ever-present water), it has been discovered within the past forty years that another group makes up a considerable portion – sometimes a very large portion – of cells. These compounds are called *nucleic acids*.

Thus, in studying the chemistry of synthesis in the cell, we are studying the way in which cell substances are produced; and since growth usually involves an increase in the numbers of cells, in a long-range view we are studying how we grow.

CARBOHYDRATES

Carbohydrates contain only the elements carbon, hydrogen and oxygen, with the ratio of hydrogen atoms to oxygen atoms usually 2 to 1, as in water. Sugars, starches and cellulose are familiar carbohydrates.

The structural formula of glucose is shown in Figure 2.2. This is one of the *simple sugars* – which means that it is a sugar containing 3 to 7 carbon atoms. The glucose molecule can be changed in many ways, and the synthesis of many cell substances may be thought of as beginning with glucose.

The most familiar of all sugars is sucrose, or 'table sugar'. The formula of sucrose is $C_{12}H_{22}O_{11}$. This looks like the result of adding together two glucose molecules $(C_6H_{12}O_6)$, except that two hydrogen atoms and one oxygen atom are missing. The chemistry of the matter is rather more complicated than this suggests. In the first place, the atoms in a molecule of a simple 6-carbon sugar called *fructose* are rearranged, forming a molecule of glucose. Then the newly made glucose molecule is combined with a molecule of fructose to form a molecule of sucrose. In the process two hydrogen atoms and an oxygen atom are split off. Enzymes and a small amount of energy from ATP are needed to bring about this synthesis. The process can be summarized as follows:

$$\underset{\text{(glucose)}}{C_6H_{12}O_6} + \underset{\text{(fructose)}}{C_6H_{12}O_6} \xrightarrow[\text{enzymes}]{\text{energy from ATP}} \underset{\text{(sucrose)}}{C_{12}H_{22}O_{11}} + H_2O$$

Such a synthesis is termed a *dehydration synthesis* because water is produced during the reaction.

Sucrose is called a disaccharide, because it is built with *two* simple-sugar units. Maltose (glucose+glucose) and lactose (glucose+galactose) are two other disaccharides we shall encounter later in a discussion of digestion. Also by dehydration synthesis we can obtain *trisaccharides*, made from three simple sugars, and *polysaccharides* made from many simple sugars. In these syntheses, one water molecule is split off for each sugar-to-sugar link. Starch and cellulose are familiar polysaccharides.

FATS

Like carbohydrates, fats are composed of carbon, hydrogen and oxygen atoms only, but in fats the ratio of hydrogen to oxygen atoms is always *greater* than 2 to 1. Weight for weight, fats contain more chemical energy than do carbohydrates. A gramme of fat contains about 38 000 joules of chemical energy; a gramme of carbohydrate contains only about 16 000 joules. The word 'oil' is used for fats that are in the liquid state at room temperatures (about 20 °C).

Fats are built up from *glycerol* and *fatty acids*. Glycerol (glycerine) is perhaps best known to you as an ingredient of cough medicine. Glycerol is a 3-carbon molecule which can be formed from glucose. The simplest fatty acid is acetic acid (Figure 2.7); it is the acid in vinegar. Other fatty acids are built up from acetic acid, so they usually have even numbers of carbon atoms. The ones most commonly used in building fats have from 14 to 18 carbon atoms. Because the —COOH group of atoms is characteristic of the molecular structure of the organic acids, we can symbolize any fatty acid as R—COOH: here R stands for rest of the molecule.

The —COOH group of a fatty acid can react with the —OH groups of glycerol in the manner shown in Figure 2.13. Note that three molecules of fatty acid react with one molecule of glycerol. The three acid molecules may

Bioenergetics 45

Figure 2.13 Formation of a fat.

all be the same kind of fatty acid, or they may be different kinds. As in the synthesis of carbohydrates, water molecules are split off in the process; it is a dehydration synthesis. Both energy and specific enzymes are required for the reaction.

Fats are only one group within a broader chemical group, *lipids*. All lipids are formed from organic acids, but not necessarily in combination with glycerol. Many fatty acids produce various non-fat lipids. The plant wax carnauba, which is used as a floor and car polish, is an example.

PROTEINS

Molecules of fat are large, and those of polysaccharides larger still; but generally much larger and more complex than these are protein molecules. Ordinarily, protein molecules contain thousands of atoms – sometimes tens of thousands. Proteins occur in bewildering variety. Undoubtedly every species of organism has characteristic proteins shared by no others, and it is even possible that every individual organism has proteins found in no other individual.

The basic building units of protein molecules are *amino acids*. Amino acids always contain at least four kinds of atoms. These are the three kinds of atoms that glucose contains: carbon, hydrogen and oxygen – plus a fourth kind, nitrogen.

Figure 2.14 The simplest amino acid, glycine.

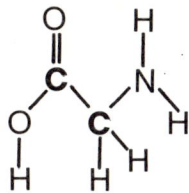

(A) Structural formula   (B) Model

Other amino acids are more complex. Some contain sulphur in addition to C, H, O and N. As in the case of the fatty acids, *R* may be used to represent all the variable parts of an amino acid; thus any amino acid may be symbolized as in Figure 2.15.

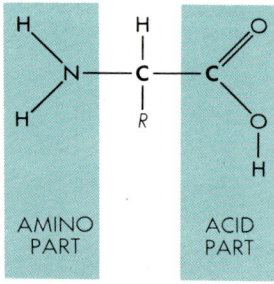

AMINO PART   ACID PART

Figure 2.15 Basic structure of an amino acid. In the glycine molecule what is the *R*?

Approximately twenty different amino acids occur in proteins. Apparently most green plants and some bacteria can synthesize all of these from simple materials. Animals, on the other hand, must obtain amino acids ready-made in their food, though many animals can change one kind to another within their bodies. Our own cells can transform about ten amino acids in this manner.

Once the necessary amino acids are made or obtained, the synthesis of proteins is a matter of linking the amino acids together. When a bond between amino acids is made, a water molecule is split off (another case of dehydration synthesis) and energy from ATP is used. This can be illustrated in the combining of three amino-acid units (Figure 2.16). The resulting molecule is called a *tripeptide*. A longer chain would be a *polypeptide*. The name 'protein' is used when the chain, coiled up like a spring, becomes about a hundred units long or more.

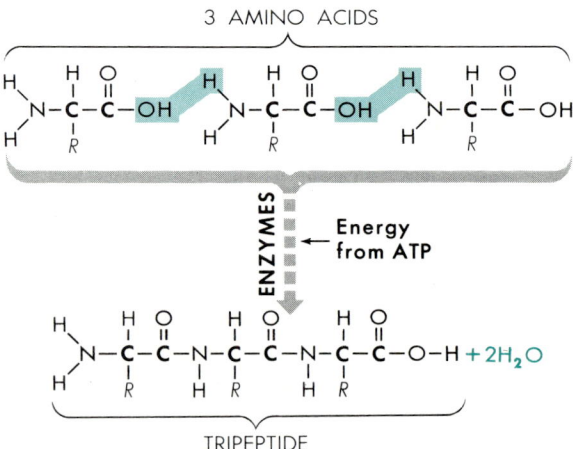

Figure 2.16 Formation of a tripeptide.

The number of ways in which more than twenty different amino-acid units can be combined into hundred – or thousand – unit structures is almost beyond imagination. Thus, the number of possible kinds of protein is practically without limit.

NUCLEIC ACIDS

In the 1920s it became clear that much of the darkly staining material in the nucleus of a cell is composed of a class of substances called nucleic acids. At times nucleic acids may make up more than 50 per cent of a cell's dry weight. Therefore, in discussing the synthesis of cell substances, it is necessary to consider nucleic acids along with carbohydrates, lipids and proteins.

There are two different series of nucleic acids: *ribose* nucleic acids (RNA) and *deoxyribose* nucleic acids (DNA). The RNA series is built from units which contain ribose, a 5-carbon sugar; the DNA series is built from units containing deoxyribose, another 5-carbon sugar that differs from ribose in having one less atom of oxygen. In the units from which nucleic acids are synthesized, ribose or deoxyribose is attached, at one point, to a phosphate group ($-PO_4$) and, on the other, to one of five different kinds of carbon–nitrogen structures called *bases*:

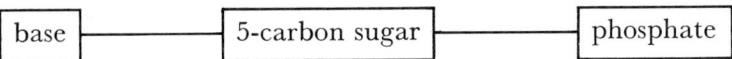

Such a molecule is called a *nucleotide*. In addition to being the units from which nucleic acids are built, nucleotides have other functions in biochemistry. Figure 2.17, for example, shows how a nucleotide, adenosine monophosphate (AMP) is chemically related to ATP and ADP.

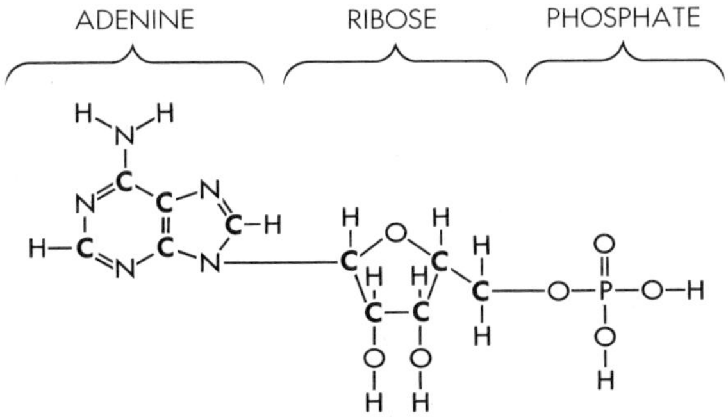

Figure 2.17 Structural formula of a nucleotide, adenosine monophosphate. Addition of a phosphate group would make this ADP; addition of two phosphate groups would make it ATP. Adenine is one of the bases.

The ribose nucleic acids (RNA) are found throughout cells. They participate in the synthesis of proteins. In most cells, deoxyribose nucleic acids (DNA) occur mainly in the nuclei; but in blue-green algae, whose cells have no organized nuclei, they are distributed throughout. DNA molecules are concerned with the transmission of characteristics from one generation to the next – that is, with heredity.

PHOTOSYNTHESIS

All living cells release energy; all living cells put energy into synthesizing new cell molecules. For this reason we discussed these processes first in considering bioenergetics; but in the long run all living cells (except a few bacteria) are dependent upon solar energy. Only certain specialized cells of plants and of a few protists can trap this solar energy. Thus photosynthesis, though last to be discussed here, is the first bioenergetic process when we view the biosphere as a whole.

In 1772 Joseph Priestley placed a shoot of a mint plant in a container of water and inverted a glass jar over it so that air could not enter. Much to his surprise, the shoot remained alive for several months. In another experiment he noted that a burning candle was quickly extinguished when covered with a jar. Then Priestley placed a shoot of mint under the jar, and in a few days the candle when lighted, burned again for a short time. The 'restored' air was, as he phrased it, 'not at all inconvenient to a mouse which I put into it'. Other investigators, however, were unsuccessful when they attempted to repeat Priestley's experiments. As a matter of fact, he himself failed when he tried again six years later.

The reason for this failure became clear in 1779, when Jan Ingen-Housz showed that plants act in the manner described by Priestley only when they are exposed to sunlight. He found, moreover, that only the green tissues take part in this process. Soon it became apparent that these results could be traced to the release of oxygen by plants. Then in 1782 Jean Senebier discovered that illuminated plants absorb carbon dioxide. In 1804 Nicolas de Saussure showed that the increase in plant weight after exposure to sunlight is greater than the weight of the carbon dioxide taken in. He concluded that growth in plants results from the intake of both carbon dioxide and water.

By 1845, Julius Robert Mayer was able to recognize that the essential steps in photosynthesis are the absorption of the energy in the form of light and the transformation of this light energy into chemical energy, which is then stored in compounds manufactured by the plant. Thus more than a century ago, scientists in western Europe had already discovered the basic scheme of photosynthesis.

MACHINERY OF PHOTOSYNTHESIS

It is a characteristic of scientists to be unsatisfied. The Mayer scheme for photosynthesis was clear, but there were many questions that could be asked about it. If you are developing some scientific understanding, you should be able to list several. One certainly would be: Does photosynthesis occur everywhere in a cell or only at certain places?

Botanists long observed that oxygen is produced in photosynthesizing cells only in the vicinity of chloroplasts. To demonstrate clearly that

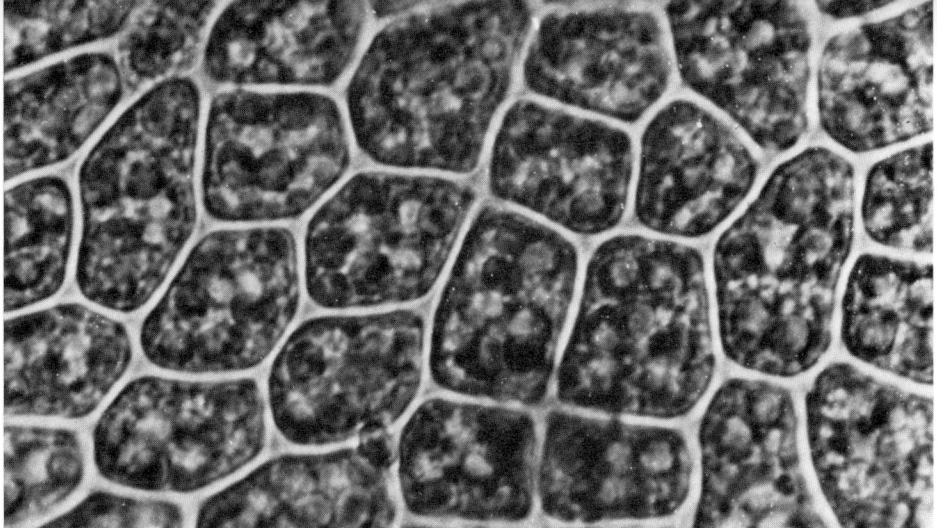

Figure 2.18 Chloroplasts in cells of a moss. X 700

photosynthesis occurs only in the chloroplasts, it is necessary to remove chloroplasts from the rest of the cell. Removal of chloroplasts was accomplished by Robin Hill of the University of Cambridge in 1937, but at first he could not secure convincing evidence of photosynthesis in these isolated chloroplasts. Then, in 1954, Daniel Arnon, of the University of California, and his co-workers were able to demonstrate that chloroplasts, separated from all other parts of the cell, can carry on the entire process of photosynthesis: carbon dioxide and water were combined by the illuminated chloroplasts and both oxygen and carbohydrates were formed.

Chloroplasts. For a long time little was known about the internal structure of chloroplasts. During the past twenty-five years, however, improved microscopic techniques have made it possible to show that many chloroplasts contain small disc-shaped bodies called *grana* (singular, 'granum'). If very thin slices of chloroplasts are examined under an electron microscope each granum is found to be made up of a number of flat plates. Each plate is composed of layers of chlorophyll, protein and lipid molecules.

There is considerable diversity in the details of this structure. For example,

Figure 2.19 Electronmicrograph of a single chloroplast from a bean plant. X 20 000

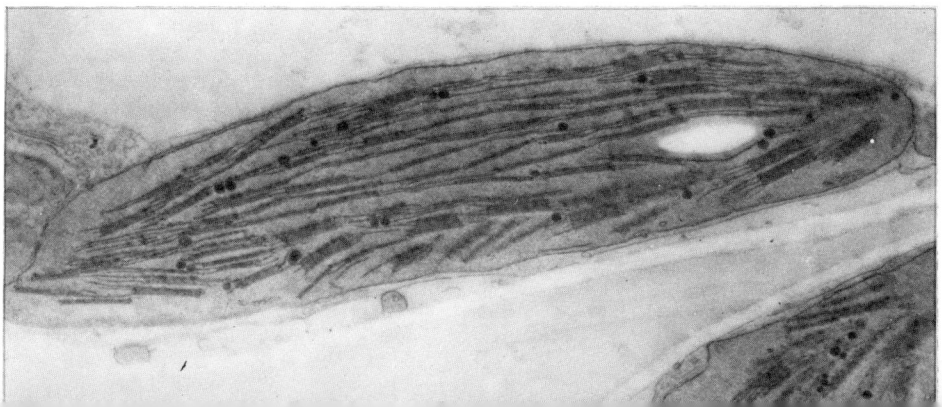

in members of the grass family, some of the plates extend out into the colourless material in which the grana are embedded, forming continuous connecting layers between grana. In the blue-green algae, which lack chloroplasts, the plate-like structures form a network or a series of parallel layers within the cell substance.

The layered structure of the grana allows maximum exposure of chlorophyll molecules to light. It also brings chlorophyll in contact with the protein layers, in which the enzymes required for photosynthesis are located.

Chlorophylls. Four different kinds of chlorophyll are known and identified as *a*, *b*, *c* and *d*. Chlorophyll *a* is believed to be present in all photosynthetic plants. In green algae, bryophytes and tracheophytes, there is also some chlorophyll *b*; in the diatoms and brown algae, chlorophyll *c* occurs instead of *b*; in the red algae, chlorophyll *d* is present instead of *b*.

Chlorophyll molecules are quite complex; the formula for chlorophyll *a*, for example, is $C_{55}H_{72}O_5N_4Mg$. Although the structural formulae of the chlorophyll molecules are known, very little is yet understood about how organisms can form them. It is known, however, that they are produced in the chloroplasts (except, of course, in the case of the blue-green algae, which have no chloroplasts) and that relatively few are formed in the absence of light.

INVESTIGATION 2.4

SEPARATION OF LEAF PIGMENTS

PURPOSE
Here we shall use the simplest kind of chromatography to separate some of the pigments that occur in leaves.

BACKGROUND INFORMATION
How does the biochemist know that the green colour of leaves is the result of a mixture of several kinds of pigments? Obviously he cannot know unless he has some method of separating the pigments from the leaves and from each other. The separation from one another of the multitude of substances found in protoplasm is the first step in any biochemical study. Many methods are used to accomplish this. Substances that are soluble in water (sugars, for example) are easily separated from substances that are insoluble in water (fats, for example), but many substances found in organisms are so much alike that the usual methods of separation employed by chemists fail.

In the late nineteenth century chromatography was discovered by a Russian chemist. At first this method was used (as its name implies) only to separate substances that have *colour* pigments. By the 1930s, however, ways of applying chromatography to the separation of colourless substances had been developed. To the original technique, which involved separation on paper, had been added techniques involving separation on other materials. Many new lines of investigation have been opened to biochemists by the development of the chromatographic techniques.

MATERIALS AND EQUIPMENT
(for each group)

Test-tube, 25 mm × 200 mm, with a cork
Several strips of filter or chromatography paper
Paper clip
Scissors
Wax pencil
Developing solution (8 per cent acetone, 92 per cent petroleum ether)
Test-tube rack
Spinach leaves
Fine sand
Acetone
Mortar and pestle
Cheesecloth
Cleansing tissue
Funnel, long-stemmed
Funnel support
Test-tube, 19 mm × 150 mm
Pencils, 2
Pipette, with a very fine tip

PROCEDURE

1. Take the cork and paper clip and assemble a hook as shown in Figure 2.20.
2. Take a strip of the chromatography paper. Handle it with care as oil and moisture from your fingers can spoil the results. Cut the paper so that when it hangs on the hook it is one centimetre from the base of the tube.
3. Remove the paper and mark lightly a line 2 cm from the bottom.
4. Place the paper across two pencils, each 1 cm from the line.
5. Pour the developing solution into the test-tube to a depth of 2.5 cm.
6. Replace the cork and place the tube in the test-tube rack.
7. Place two or three spinach leaves, a little fine sand and about 5 cm³ of acetone in a mortar. Grind thoroughly.
8. Place a layer of cheesecloth in a funnel and add a layer of cleansing tissue.
9. Take the small test-tube and place it under the funnel: pour the contents of the mortar into the funnel

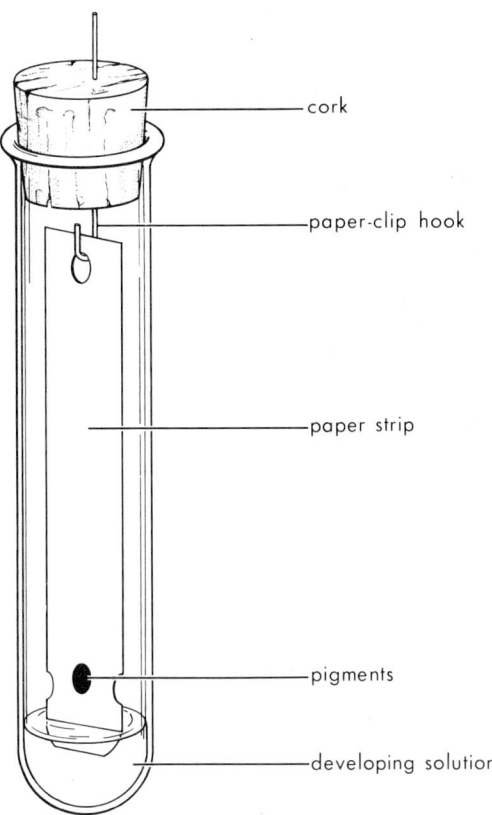

Figure 2.20

and collect the filtrate, i.e. acetone and extracted pigments.

A. What is the colour of the filtrate? Is there any evidence that more than one pigment is dissolved in the acetone?

10. Using a fine-pointed pipette, place a drop of the filtrate at the centre of the line drawn on the chromatography paper.
11. Allow it to dry and then add another drop on top of the first.
12. Repeat until at least four drops have been placed on the paper.
13. When the final drop has dried, remove the cork from the large test-tube and hang the strip on the hook.
14. Insert the cork with the paper strip

attached, making sure that the pigment spot does not touch the developing solution.
15. Make sure that the cork is tight and allow the developing solution to rise up the paper until it almost reaches the hook. Remove the cork and hold it until the paper has dried.

STUDYING THE DATA

A. Examine the *chromatogram*. How many bands of colour can you see?
B. How many of the bands may be made up of chlorophylls?
C. What other colours can you see in the chromatogram?
D. Why are you not able to see these pigments in the leaf?
E. Do you think that all the leaf pigments were soluble in acetone? Give reasons for your answer.
F. Suggest a hypothesis to explain the change of colour that often occurs when leaves die.
G. Consider the process by which the pigments were separated. From what point did all the pigments start as the solvent began to rise?
H. What can you say about the time during which the pigments were moving? Was it the same for each pigment?
I. In what characteristic must the pigments have differed in order for the separation to have occurred?

FOR FURTHER INVESTIGATION

1. Why were the pigments studied in this investigation extracted with acetone? Why was water not used? What liquids besides acetone can be used to extract these pigments from the leaf?

2. Are there any leaf pigments that are not extracted by acetone? If so, what are they, and how can they be extracted?

3. What effect does the kind of developer have on the success of chromatography? Try 100 per cent acetone, 100 per cent petroleum ether, different mixtures of these two, 100 per cent ethanol, and various mixtures of the following: petroleum ether, acetone, ethanol. Does the nature of the pigments you are trying to separate affect the success of chromatography? Using some of the developers listed above, try separating other pigments, such as those in the inks of ball-point pens.

THE BIOCHEMISTRY OF PHOTOSYNTHESIS

During the nineteenth century and the early part of the twentieth, many measurements were made of the amounts of CO_2 and H_2O taken in by illuminated, chlorophyll-bearing cells and of the amounts of oxygen and energy-rich carbon compounds formed there. Although we now know that a large number of different energy-rich compounds are formed during photosynthesis, the kinds identified and measured at that time were simple sugars (such as glucose) or the insoluble starch synthesized from them. The results of these investigations can be summarized in the following equation:

$$6CO_2 + 6H_2O \xrightarrow[\text{enzymes}]{\text{light energy}} C_6H_{12}O_6 + 6O_2$$

If this equation were written with the arrows pointing in the opposite directions, you would recognize it as the one given for cellular respiration. Of course, such equations indicate merely the beginning and the end of a process. It is now known that many of the intermediate steps are not the same in photosynthesis and respiration.

Long before the end of the nineteenth century, many chemists and biologists attempted, without success, to identify some of the intermediate substances that must be produced before glucose is formed. Events occur so rapidly in photosynthesis that identification of the substances involved seemed impossible. By 1905, however, experimental evidence had revealed that photosynthesis takes place in two distinct sets of reactions. One set, called the 'light reactions', occurs only while a chlorophyll-bearing cell is exposed to light. This is immediately followed by a set of 'dark reactions', for which light is not required.

The source of oxygen. Basic to further understanding of photosynthesis was another problem: Where did the oxygen come from? For many years CO_2 was considered the most likely source, but the problem could not be solved until a way was found to distinguish between oxygen derived from H_2O and oxygen derived from CO_2.

An atom of ordinary oxygen is 16 times heavier than a hydrogen atom, but there is an *isotope* of oxygen – another form of the oxygen atom – with an atomic weight 18 times that of hydrogen. This isotope, O^{18}, can be distinguished from O^{16} with an instrument called the mass spectrometer. In 1941, Samuel Ruben and Martin Kamen, working at the University of California, exposed plants to carbon dioxide that contained O^{18}. The mass spectrometer showed that all the oxygen given off by the photosynthesizing plant was O^{18}. Ruben and Kamen exposed other plants to ordinary CO_2 but supplied them with water containing O^{18}. With the mass spectrometer the oxygen given off by these plants was identified as O^{18}. Clearly, the oxygen came only from the water, not from the carbon dioxide.

During the past twenty years much more has been learned about the biochemistry of photosynthesis. Let us now look at the present state of knowledge.

The 'light reactions'. In the first phase of photosynthesis, light energy absorbed by the chlorophyll is transformed into chemical energy and temporarily stored in two compounds. One of these, ATP, has already been discussed. The second is reduced *nicotinamide adenine dinucleotide phosphate*, abbreviated $NADPH_2$.

Experimental evidence now available indicates that ATP is formed in two different ways within chloroplasts. In the first, a cyclic set of reactions (Figure 2.21), light energy is absorbed by a molecule of chlorophyll, causing an electron to be expelled from the molecule. This high-energy electron is passed along a series of electron carriers. As the electron moves along this series, its energy is transferred to enzyme systems that catalyse the change of

ADP to ATP. Before the electron returns to a chlorophyll molecule, two or more molecules of ATP have been formed.

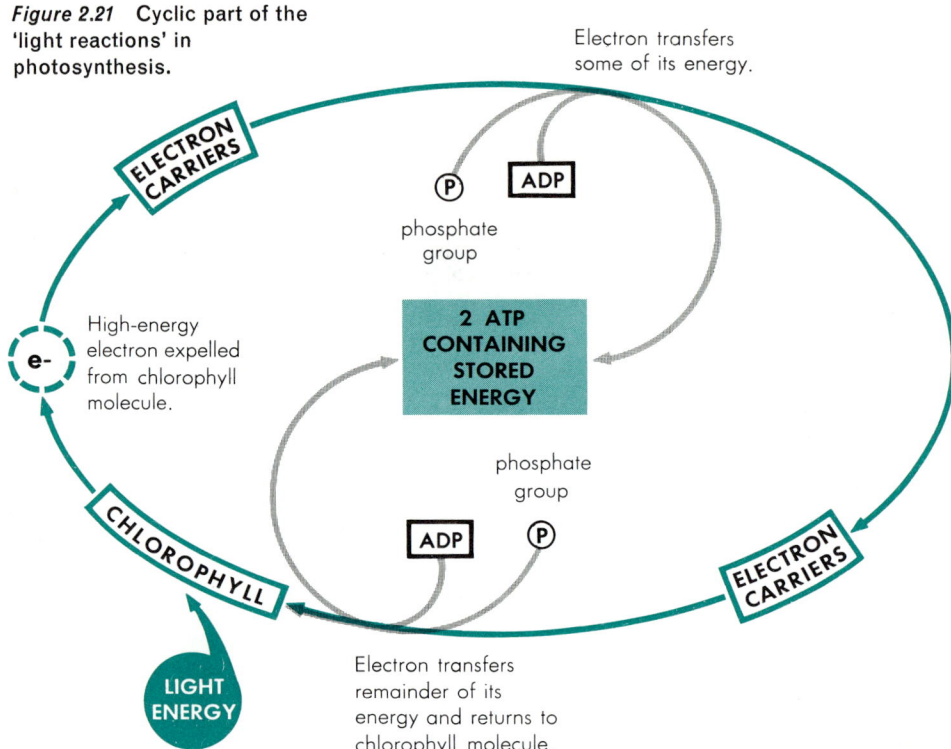

Figure 2.21 Cyclic part of the 'light reactions' in photosynthesis.

In the second way, a non-cyclic set of reactions (Figure 2.22), both ATP and $NADPH_2$ are formed. Water is involved in this set of reactions; it supplies the hydrogen that combines with NADP (oxidized nicotinamide adenine dinucleotide phosphate) to form $NADPH_2$ again.

Light absorbed by some as yet unidentified pigment molecule causes a high-energy electron to be expelled. The pigment is probably either chlorophyll *b* or one of the yellow pigments present in chloroplasts. Biochemists now think that as the electron leaves the pigment molecule, it is replaced by an electron from a hydroxyl ion (OH^-) obtained from the ionization of water. The high-energy electron from the pigment is picked up by electron carriers. Light is absorbed at the same time by a chlorophyll *a* molecule, and a second high-energy electron is expelled. Electron carriers then transfer the first high-energy electron to this chlorophyll molecule. As the electron moves to the chlorophyll molecule, its energy goes into the formation of an ATP molecule from ADP. Notice that in this chain of reactions, light energy is absorbed at one point by the pigment molecule and at a second point by the chlorophyll *a* molecule. Two high-energy electrons, expelled from chlorophyll molecules, and two hydrogen ions (H^+), from ionized water, join a molecule

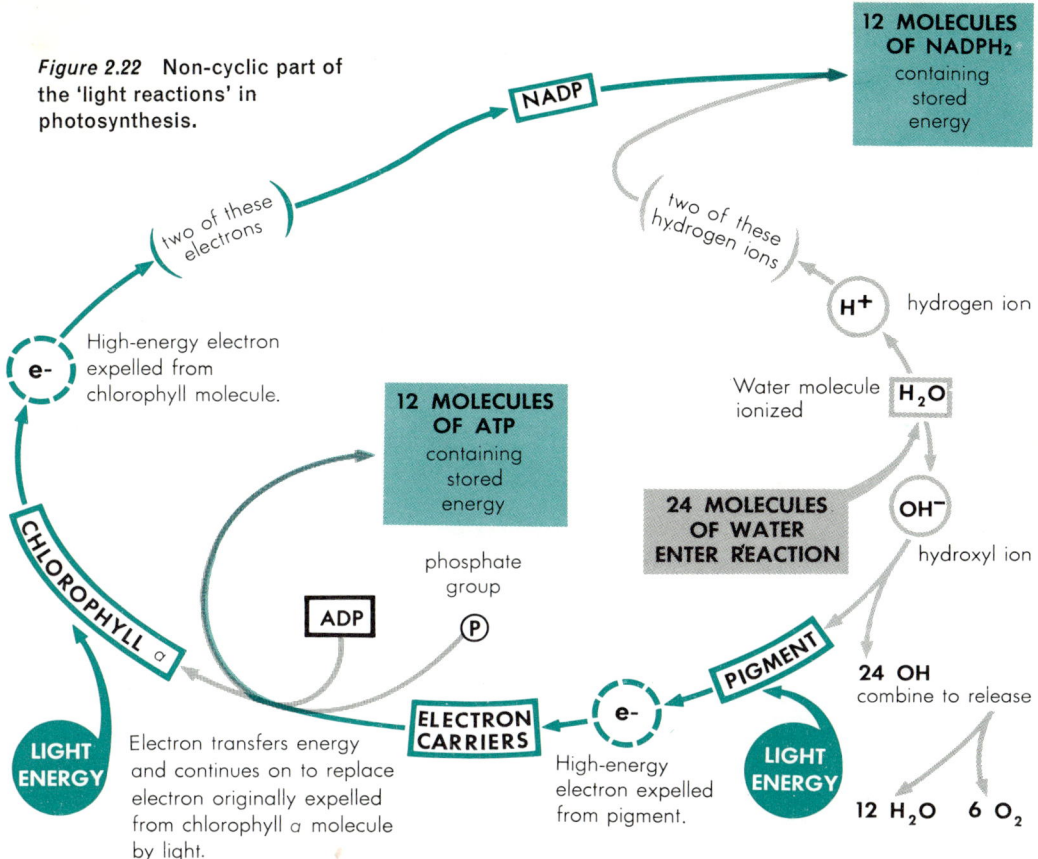

Figure 2.22 Non-cyclic part of the 'light reactions' in photosynthesis.

of NADP; thus an energy-rich molecule of $NADPH_2$ is formed. The light energy absorbed by the chlorophyll molecules has now been transferred to the $NADPH_2$. For every 24 molecules of water entering this non-cyclic set of reactions, 12 molecules of ATP and 12 molecules of $NADPH_2$ are formed.

One important detail remains to be considered. When each of the OH^- ions derived from the water loses an electron, it becomes an OH *radical* – a chemical term for a group of atoms that is neither an independent molecule nor an atom. Twenty-four of these radicals combine to form 12 molecules of water and 6 molecules of oxygen – the oxygen that is given off by photosynthesizing organisms.

The 'dark reactions'. The basic result of this phase of photosynthesis is the formation of multicarbon molecules containing chemical energy that can be used later by the cell. Through many years of ingenious investigations Melvin Calvin and his colleagues at the University of California have worked out many of the details of the more than twenty reactions involved. For these investigations Calvin was awarded a Nobel Prize in 1961.

The carbon source in the 'dark reactions' is carbon dioxide. In a series of steps, carbon dioxide is combined with the complex molecule *ribulose*

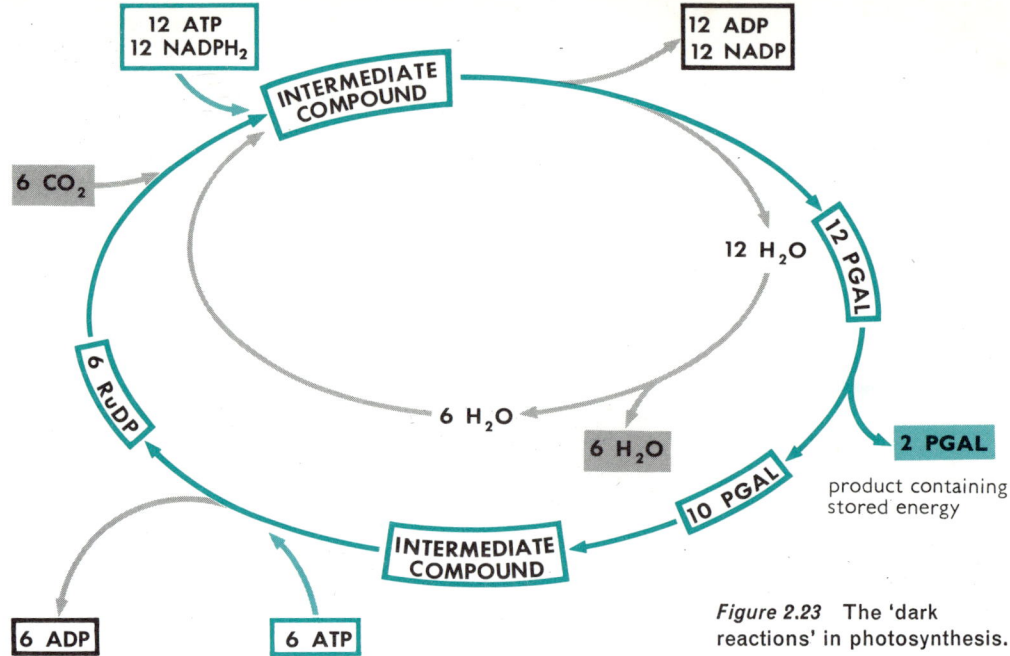

Figure 2.23 The 'dark reactions' in photosynthesis.

diphosphate (RuDP); this eventually results in a 3-carbon molecule, *phosphoglyceraldehyde* (PGAL). For every 6 molecules of CO_2 taken up by the cell, 12 molecules of PGAL are formed. Ten of these are cycled back into the series of reactions that produce RuDP; only 2 molecules of PGAL are left to form carbohydrates, for example glucose, and eventually all the other multicarbon compounds in cells.

To accomplish all this, a supply of energy must be available. It comes from the compounds formed during the light phase – ATP and $NADPH_2$. As the energy is released from ATP, ADP is formed. This ADP is then available for conversion into ATP during the 'light reaction'. Likewise as energy is released from $NADPH_2$, NADP is formed. This is also available for conversion into $NADPH_2$ during the 'light reaction'. Thus, ATP and $NADPH_2$ act as carriers of energy.

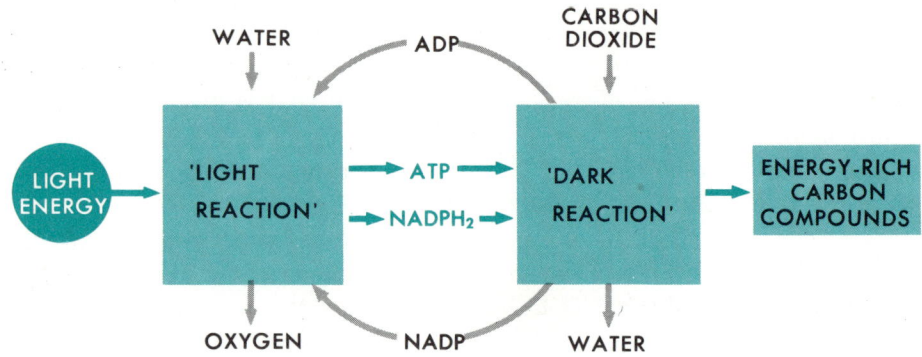

Figure 2.24 Summary of photosynthesis.

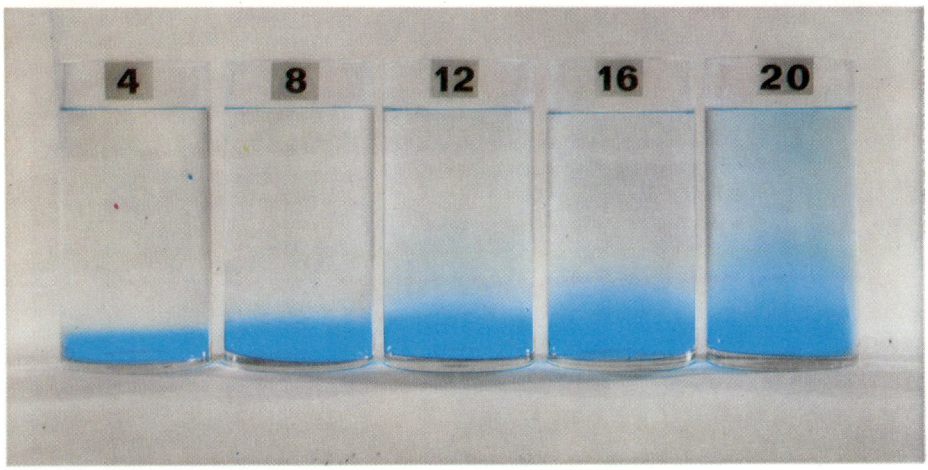

Plate I It takes at least 20 days for copper ions to diffuse through water in the jars. In what way is there a speeding up of the rate at which mineral ions enter plant roots?

Plate II Glucose burns very rapidly in oxygen. How do living things control the rate at which glucose 'burns'?

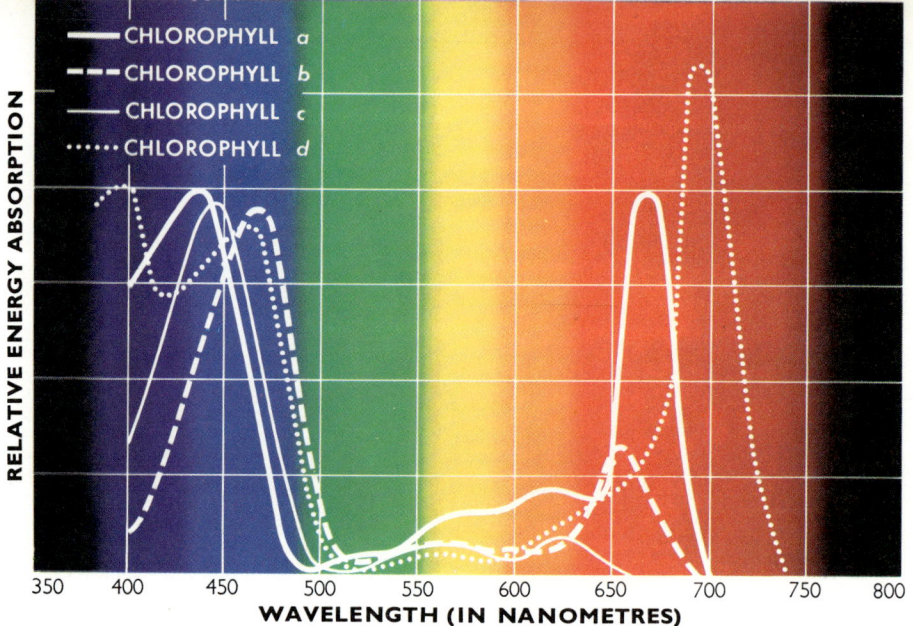

Plate III Patterns of energy absorption of the chlorophylls. The background shows the appearance of the wavelengths to our eyes. What wavelengths (colours) do chlorophylls absorb least?

Plate IV Chromatogram of nettle leaf. The yellow pigments (carotene and xanthophyll) have a quicker diffusion rate than green chlorophyll.

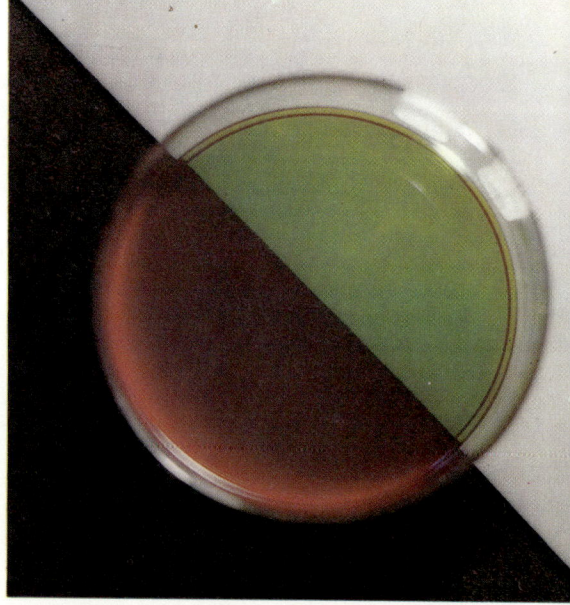

Plate V An extract of chlorophyll appears green when light is passed through it, but red when light is reflected from it. This red 'fluorescence' is caused by re-radiation of some of the light energy absorbed by the chlorophyll.

Plate VI Some of the leaves on this Japanese maple do not have chlorophyll. Why do you think it is uncommon for such leaves to occur in nature?

METHODS OF INVESTIGATION

Much of the complicated picture of photosynthesis presented here was unknown even twenty years ago. How has it been possible to discover so much in such a brief period?

Several experimental techniques have been of great importance in permitting this rapid progress. One has been the use of isolated chloroplasts. Respiration moves in a direction opposite to that of photosynthesis – though the individual steps are not opposites. All the substances that are involved in respiration are present in a cell with all the substances involved in photosynthesis. Even when all these substances are separated and identified, how can the biochemist decide which are respiration substances, which are photosynthesis substances and which are, perhaps, part of both processes? In chloroplasts only the substances of photosynthesis occur. Thus, the study of isolated chloroplasts has greatly simplified the tracing of the steps in the photosynthetic process by removing from the picture the steps by which multicarbon compounds are broken down.

You read how isotopes of oxygen were used in solving one of the problems involved in photosynthesis. You saw how chromatography can be used to separate a mixture of substances. A combination of methods involving isotopes and chromatography has been especially useful in the study of the 'dark reactions' of photosynthesis. In one procedure carbon dioxide that contains carbon-14 (C^{14}), a radioactive isotope of carbon, is supplied to

Figure 2.25 As the biochemist attacks more complex problems, he develops more complex tools. The apparatus shown increases the speed with which chromatographic records can be obtained.

single-celled algae. Shortly afterwards, the algae are killed and the substances in them removed. These substances are then separated by chromatography, and the ones that have taken up C^{14} can be detected by a device sensitive to radioactivity (a Geiger counter, for example). By killing some of the algae every few fractions of a second, the investigator can determine the order in which the substances containing C^{14} are formed. From this information, diagrams such as Figure 2.23 can be constructed.

INVESTIGATION 2.5

PHOTOSYNTHETIC RATE

PURPOSE
In this investigation you will study the effect of light intensity on the rate of photosynthesis in a living plant.

BACKGROUND INFORMATION
The rate of oxygen production can be used as an indication of the rate at which a plant is carrying on photosynthesis. As oxygen is not very soluble in water, visible bubbles of oxygen may be formed by a photosynthesizing aquatic plant. If the bubbles are of uniform size, the number of bubbles formed per unit time indicates the photosynthetic rate, provided all other factors are kept constant.

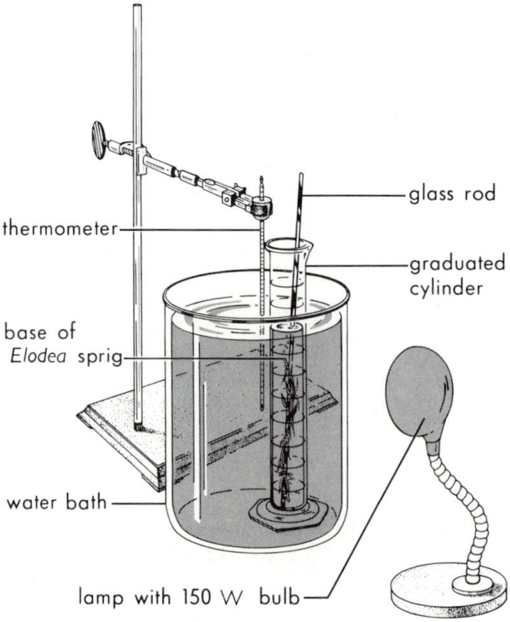

MATERIALS AND EQUIPMENT
(for each group)
Sprig of *Elodea*
Glass rod
Thread
250 cm³ graduated cylinder
250 cm³ sodium hydrogen carbonate solution (0.25 per cent in pond or aquarium water)
Battery jar or small aquarium
Thermometer
Ring stand with clamp
Lamp with reflector and 150-watt bulb
Razor blade
Forceps
Watch with second hand

PROCEDURE
1. Read through the instructions given and construct a hypothesis for the experiment.
2. Examine Figure 2.26 and set up the apparatus as follows.
3. Cut a healthy sprig of *Elodea* and tie it along the glass rod so that the cut end of the sprig is at about the middle of the rod. Use the thread to tie the *Elodea*.
4. Place the rod and twig in the graduated cylinder so that the tip of the sprig is at the bottom of the cylinder.

Figure 2.26

5. Fill the cylinder with the 0.25 per cent sodium hydrogen carbonate solution until it is 5 cm above the level of the cut shoot.
6. Place the cylinder into a battery jar or small aquarium filled with water at room temperature.
7. Suspend a thermometer in the water by means of a stand and clamp.
8. Place the lamp 10 cm from the *Elodea* sprig and switch it on.
9. After several minutes small bubbles will appear and rise through the sodium hydrogen carbonate solution at regular intervals. If bubbles do not appear, lift the rod out of the cylinder and, using the razor blade, cut a short piece off the end of the sprig. Immediately return the rod to the cylinder.
10. If bubbles are large and slow to rise, crush the base of the sprig with a pair of forceps.
11. When the rate of bubble formation becomes fairly uniform, count the number of bubbles formed during 10 one-minute intervals allowing 10 seconds between counts. Check the temperature of the water in the water bath and if it rises by more than 2 °C, add ice or cold water until it is reduced to room temperature.
12. Calculate the average number of bubbles per minute interval.
13. Increase the distance of the lamp to 20 cm from the sprig. Wait two minutes and then count and average as before.
14. Increase the lamp distance to 40 cm from the sprig. Wait two minutes, and count and average.

DISCUSSION

Plot a graph of the data, showing the distance between lamp and sprig on the horizontal axis and the average number of bubbles per minute on the vertical axis.

A. What is the general direction of the slope of the line?
B. How is the change in distance of lamp from plant related to the change in light intensity received by the plant?
C. What, then, is the relationship between light intensity and photosynthetic rate as indicated by your data?
D. What other environmental factors may affect photosynthetic rate?
E. In the design of the experiment, which of these factors was controlled? Explain your answer.
F. Are any factors uncontrolled? If so, how might you change the design of the experiment in order to control them?

FOR FURTHER INVESTIGATION

1. Plan and carry out an experiment in which light intensity is held constant and some other factor affecting photosynthetic rate is varied.
2. In terms of exchange of gases, what process in living organisms is the opposite of photosynthesis? How does this process affect any attempt to measure photosynthetic rate with a high degree of accuracy? Using measurements of gaseous exchange as a basis, plan and carry out an experiment designed to eliminate errors introduced by this process.

All energy for the activities of living things comes from multicarbon compounds that either directly or indirectly come from photosynthesis.

Several biochemical pathways are involved in the release and transfer of energy in cells. Reactions along these pathways go on continuously in all cells. Two series of reactions are of particular importance: glycolysis, which breaks down glucose to pyruvic acid; and the Krebs cycle which oxidizes acetic acid (coming from breakdown of carbohydrates, fats, or proteins) to carbon dioxide and water. Other, less important pathways end with other products.

All these pathways result in the transfer of energy to energy-transfer compounds, the most common being ATP. The breakdown of ATP to ADP releases energy in small amounts. Such energy may be used for the synthesis of large molecules (such as fat or protein) from smaller molecules, for contraction of muscles, for beating of cilia, for active transport of ions or molecules, or for any other activity performed by the cell.

Eventually, after many reactions all the chemical energy that becomes available to organisms through photosynthesis becomes heat and is lost to the biosphere.

GUIDE QUESTIONS

1. Why is the study of energy in living things – bioenergetics – of basic importance to an understanding of biology?
2. What experimental evidence do we have for the idea that living things lose energy to their environments?
3. How are many chemical reactions brought about in living things at relatively low temperatures?
4. How can chemical energy in a substance be measured?
5. How is cellular respiration different from burning?
6. What part does ATP play in the use of energy by cells?
7. What are the main steps in the breakdown of a glucose molecule to carbon dioxide and water?
8. What chemical processes occur in mitochondria?
9. In what ways does fermentation differ from cellular respiration?
10. Where does a cell obtain energy for syntheses?
11. From what chemical units are polysaccharides synthesized?
12. How do fats differ from other lipids?
13. From what chemical units are polypeptides synthesized?
14. How does a protein differ from a polypeptide?
15. How is ATP related chemically to the nucleic acids?
16. List the conditions necessary for photosynthesis.
17. Describe the structure of a chloroplast. How is its structure related to its function?
18. How can the acetone-soluble pigments in leaves be separated? How many chlorophylls usually occur in leaves?
19. In what general ways are photosynthesis and cellular respiration similar? How do they differ?
20. What seems to be the effect of light energy on chlorophyll molecules?
21. How do water molecules enter into the light phase of photosynthesis?
22. How does the light phase of photosynthesis prepare for the dark phase?
23. How have isotopes of chemical elements played a part in the investigation of photosynthesis?

PROBLEMS

1. Find out how biochemists picture the way in which enzymes act in metabolic reactions. Then use this model to explain enzyme specificity.
2. A certain chemical substance is known to increase the activity of an enzyme called nitrate reductase. This enzyme reduces nitrate ions to nitrite ions, which are then used in the synthesis of amino acids. What practical use might be made of this information?
3. Calculate the surface area and volume of ten spheres having diameters of 1 mm, 2 mm, 3 mm, and so on to 10 mm. Plot the two sets of results on the same grid, allowing the vertical axis to represent both mm^2 and mm^3. Keeping in mind the requirements of all living cells for energy and materials from which energy is released, comment on the meaning of your graph. How might cells grow large while avoiding the biological consequences of large size?
4. As you are running in a race your rate of breathing increases. When the race is over, your breathing rate continues to be high for a considerable period. Explain this, using your knowledge of cellular physiology.
5. Proteins in the cells of a wheat plant differ from the proteins in your cells. How can the differences be explained? What must happen when you use wheat as a nutrient for the formation of your protein?
6. Experiments with photosynthesizing tracheophytes have shown that when they are grown in an atmosphere without oxygen they take up carbon dioxide at $1\frac{1}{2}$ times the rate in natural atmosphere, which is about 20 per cent oxygen. (a) What does this information indicate about the relationship between photosynthesis and cellular respiration? (b) How might this relationship affect the composition of the Earth's atmosphere?
7. Many botanists believe that the concentration of carbon dioxide in the air was much greater during the Carboniferous period, when most of the large coal deposits were being formed, than it is at present. What might be the basis for their belief? Is there any reason to suppose that the concentration of carbon dioxide in the air has increased during the last 150 years?
8. Some biochemists have argued that the formation of carbon compounds from carbon dioxide should not be considered a part of photosynthesis. How might this viewpoint be defended?
9. According to one theory of the origin of life, energy for the first living things must have come from chemical compounds formed by the heat and electrical energy in the Earth's atmosphere at that time. Later some organisms apparently began to use energy from sunlight to build up foods. How might this have happened?
10. Gather whatever information you can find about conditions on the surface of Mars and Venus. Then, using your knowledge of cell metabolism, comment on the possibility of life existing on these planets. What life-supporting equipment would probably be desirable for astronauts planning trips to these planets?

SUGGESTED READING

ALLFREY, V. G. and A. E. MIRSKY. 'How Cells Make Molecules', *Scientific American*, September 1961. Pp. 74–82.

ARNON, D. I. 'The Role of Light in Photosynthesis', *Scientific American*, November 1960. Pp. 104–9.

ASIMOV, I. *The Chemicals of Life*. Bell, 1963. (Very easy reading with some useful analogies.)

BAKER, J. J. W. and G. E. ALLEN. *Matter, Energy and Life*. Addison-Wesley, 1965. (A very useful introduction to the chemical and physical aspects of living systems. No previous knowledge of physics or chemistry is assumed.)

BASSHAM, J. A. 'The Path of Carbon in Photosynthesis', *Scientific American*, June 1962. Pp. 88–100.

GAFFRON, H. *Photosynthesis* (BSCS Pamphlet 24). George G. Harrap & Co., 1964.

GAMOW, G. and M. YCAS. *Mr. Tompkins Inside Himself*. Allen & Unwin, 1967.

LEHNINGER, A. L. 'How Cells Transform Energy', *Scientific American*, September 1961. Pp. 62–73.

LOEWY, A. and P. SIEKEVITZ. *Cell Structure and Function*. Holt, Rinehart & Winston, 1963.

McELROY, W. D. *Cellular Physiology and Biochemistry*. Prentice-Hall, 1964. (Contains excellent diagrams of biochemical processes and many structural formulae. Advanced.)

MERCER, E. H. *Cells and Cell Structure*. 2nd edn. Hutchinson, 1961. (Gives a good account of present theories. Fairly advanced reading.)

RABINOWITCH, E. I. and GOVINDJEE. 'The Role of Chlorophyll in Photosynthesis', *Scientific American*, July 1965. Pp. 74–83.

RIEGEL, J. A. *Energy, Life and Animal Organisation*. English Universities Press, 1965. (Covers the subject well, but on the advanced side.)

ROSE, S. *The Chemistry of Life*. Pelican, 1966.

SIMPSON, G. G. and W. S. BECK. *Life: An Introduction to Biology*. 2nd edn. Routledge & Kegan Paul, 1965.

CHAPTER
3

THE FUNCTIONING PLANT

PLANTS AS ORGANISMS

As producers, green plants are of primary importance to other organisms in the web of life. But plants carry on many activities other than photosynthesis – they use nutrients, grow, reproduce, and so forth. We have already discussed photosynthesis; here you will consider some of the other processes that go on in plants.

VASCULAR PLANTS

An estimated 80 per cent of the photosynthetic activity on Earth occurs in the seas, mostly in single-celled plants and protists. We are land animals and so far have made only small use of the sea's productivity. By and large our food is obtained, directly or indirectly, from land plants.

Moreover, land plants are the plants with which we are most familiar, the plants with which we most like to surround ourselves, even in hot, dry houses and dim, stuffy hotel corridors. It seems reasonable, therefore, to use the tracheophytes – the group to which almost all familar land plants belong – as the chief examples in continuing this discussion of plant physiology.

LEAVES

The first tracheophytes, in the Paleozoic era, probably had chlorophyll in most of the cells that were exposed to light. Very early in the history of land plants, flat, green structures appeared that were exposed more or less perpendicularly to the sun's rays. These organs – leaves – were well developed on plants long before the end of the Paleozoic era, and they are characteristic of almost all tracheophytes today.

In general, botanists consider leaves as organs of photosynthesis. To call a leaf an 'organ' may seem somewhat strange. In the human body, organs are usually one of a kind or, in the case of eyes and lungs, two; on the other hand, a large land plant may have thousands of leaves. However, a leaf is an organ, a structure composed of a number of tissues and performing some general function in the life of an organism.

Figure 3.1 Variation in leaves taken from a single sycamore tree.

External view. Variability in appearance is one of the most characteristic features of leaves. Examine the leaves on any one plant. No two leaves are exactly alike. Shapes and sizes vary according to the age of the plant, amount of light received, and other factors. Yet for any particular species of plant, leaf shape is usually distinctive and constant enough to be used as a basis for identification.

A leaf may or may not have a *petiole* (stalk) connecting the *blade* (broader part) to the plant stem. In the needle-like leaves of many conifers there is neither blade nor petiole. In most leaves the blade is in one piece, but in some leaves it is divided into separate parts or leaflets. Leaves may be so highly modified that they no longer function in photosynthesis – *spines* of cactus, for example. Whatever the form, however, there is no doubt that the primary function of most leaves is photosynthesis.

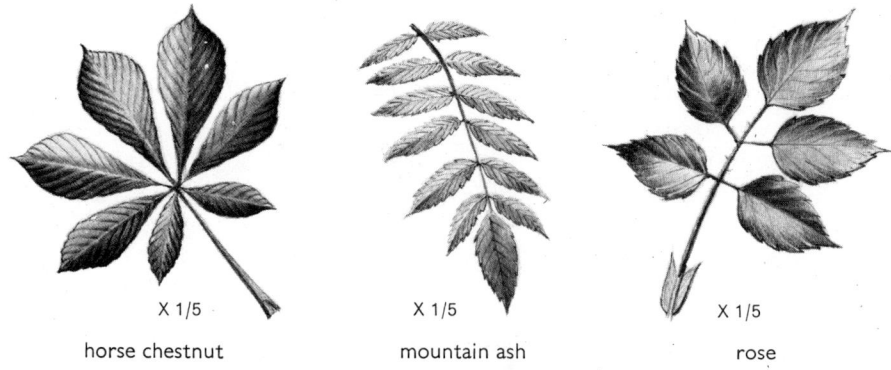

Figure 3.2 In these three compound leaves each blade is divided into separate parts. What other plants with compound leaves can you name?

Inside leaves. Figure 3.10 (p. 75) shows in three dimensions the cellular structure of a photosynthesizing leaf – from a geranium, a blackberry bush, or a poplar, perhaps. Because only a small section can be seen with a microscope at any one time, this kind of drawing must be constructed by the artist from the study of a great many different microscopic views.

Several different tissues can be distinguished in the figure. With your knowledge of photosynthesis, you can set up a number of hypotheses about the functions of these tissues, basing this action on a generalization we have used: that structure and function go together. As cells in a multicellular organism differentiate in structure, they usually acquire special functions in the life of the organism; they become *specialized*.

Photosynthesis requires chlorophyll, and chlorophyll usually occurs in chloroplasts. Since the *mesophyll* cells contain chloroplasts, you can confidently hypothesize that the mesophyll is the specialized tissue in which photosynthesis occurs. You might suspect that more photosynthetic activity takes place in the closely packed upper layers of mesophyll, since the upper leaf surface usually gets the most light. (The upper *epidermal* tissue covers the leaf but allows light to pass through.)

Figure 3.3 Leaves vary internally as well as externally. Sections through two leaves from one privet plant: *(above)* a leaf that was exposed to full sun; *(below)* a leaf that was shaded most of the day. How many structural differences can you see?

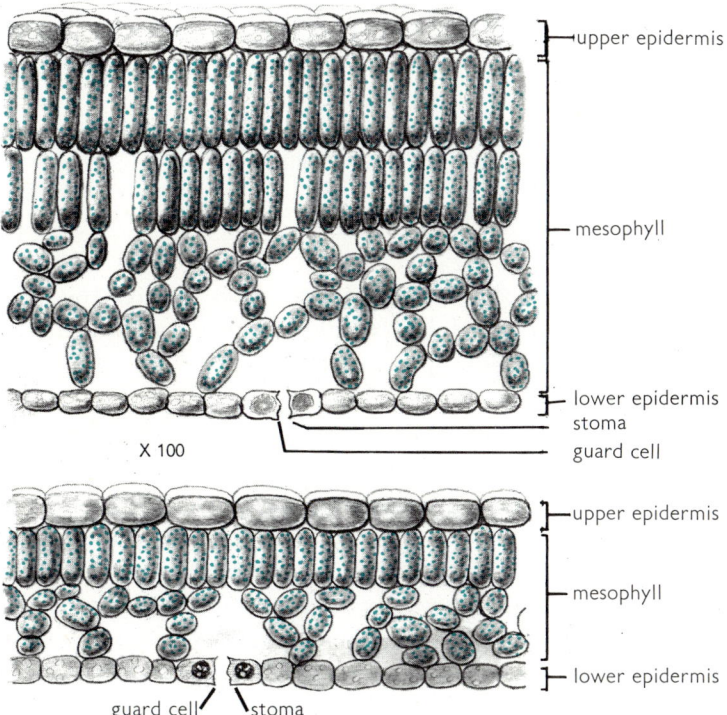

Both of the raw materials of photosynthesis – H_2O and CO_2 – are present in air, but the water molecules used in photosynthesis do not come directly from the atmosphere. The amount of water vapour varies a great deal, and water molecules are not as abundant in air as in the cytoplast of leaf cells. Thus, according to the principle of diffusion, leaves should lose H_2O to the air. The amount of CO_2 in the air does not normally vary much, but it does vary within chlorophyll-bearing cells. CO_2, therefore, might either be given off or taken in by them. An exchange of gases between inner leaf cells and the air is further suggested by the air spaces between the cells of the lower mesophyll. Indeed, Figure 3.10 does show that numerous slit-like pores, *stomata* (singular, 'stoma'), lead from the outside of the leaf through the leaf's epidermis and into the air spaces of the mesophyll. Therefore, you might hypothesize that gas exchange occurs through these pores.

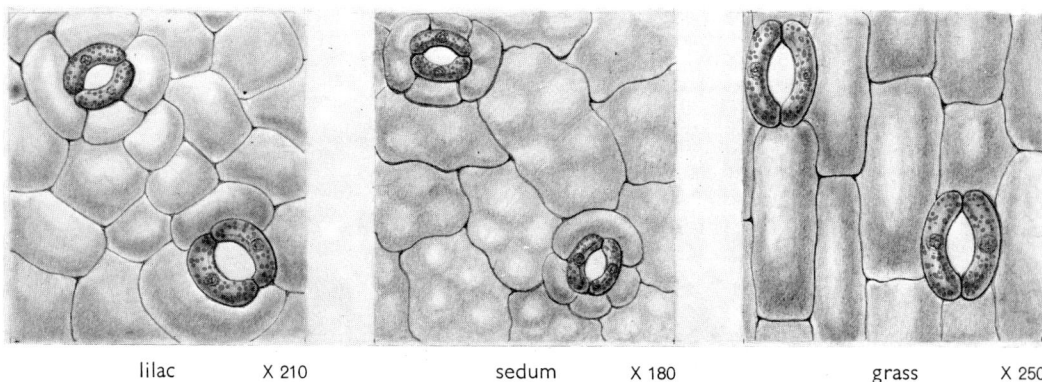

| lilac | X 210 | sedum | X 180 | grass | X 250 |

Figure 3.4 Lower leaf epidermis from three kinds of plants. Which cells contain chlorophyll?

If water is lost through these stomata, how does it enter the leaf? In the figure we see tubular structures labelled *veins*. As these evidently are structures through which liquids can flow, you might hypothesize that water comes to the leaf from other parts of the plant by way of these veins.

Through years of experimentation, mostly during the nineteenth century, plant physiologists have confirmed these hypotheses. Now we shall go a little beyond the hypotheses and discuss matters that are not quite so obvious.

Loss of water from leaves. Air contains less water than cells do. As air moves among mesophyll cells, water must diffuse into the air; the plant loses water. The drier the air, the more rapidly the water is lost. Each stoma that lets air in and out of the mesophyll is surrounded by a pair of specialized cells, *guard cells*. The inner walls of the guard cells are thickened. Thus, when their water content increases, the cells bend outward and this opens the stoma, as shown in Figure 3.5. When the water content decreases, the stoma is closed (closed in a relative sense – never tightly closed). We might hypothesize that this is a mechanism for opening stomata when the air is moist and closing them when the air is dry.

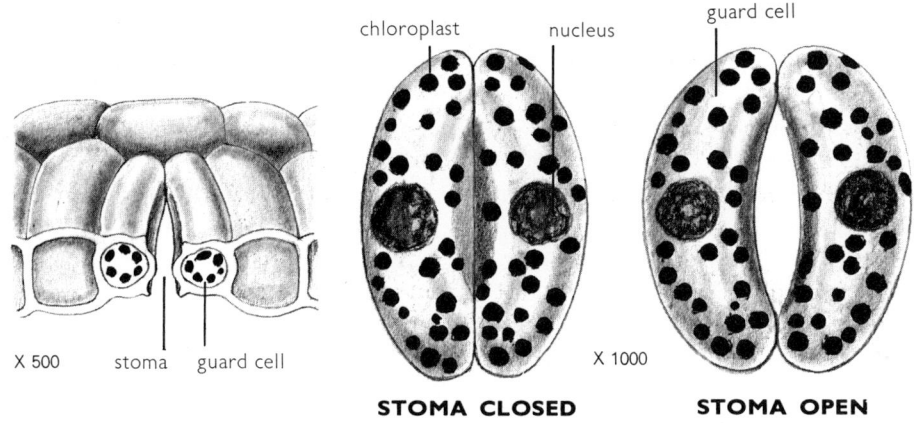

Figure 3.5 Action of stomata: (*left*) a section through an open stoma; (*right*) the changes in guard-cell shape that regulate the stoma.

This hypothesis, however, is not confirmed by observation. In most land plants the stomata are open during daylight hours, when the water content of the air is usually relatively low, and closed at night, when the water content is usually higher. Moreover, experiments have shown that changes in the shape of guard cells are related not to the water content of the air, but to the amount of carbon dioxide dissolved in the cell substance. Therefore, the action of guard cells seems to be associated more with the supply of CO_2 than with the control of water loss. However, this still does not explain another observation of plant physiologists: that stomata of potato plants are closed for only about three hours after sunset. Biologists still have much to learn about stomata.

Regardless of the action of guard cells, land plants lose much water through the stomata of their leaves. They also lose some water directly through their epidermal cells – not only through the leaf epidermis but through the surface of the whole plant. This loss is reduced, but never completely stopped, by the *cuticle*, which covers the outer surface of epidermal cells. Cuticle is composed mostly of a waxy material – a lipid. It is very thin in some cases, as on lettuce leaves, and quite thick on others, as on pine leaves.

All loss of water vapour from plants, both through the stomata and through the epidermal surface, is called *transpiration*. Plant physiologists have made many measurements of transpiration rates. Blackberry bushes lose water through their leaves at the rate of 3.8 cm³ per cm² of leaf surface per day. Put in a different way: mature apple trees have been shown to lose water at the rate of 15 litres per tree per hour. In still another way: a single maize plant has been found to transpire 200 kg of water during a growing season. Such data clearly indicate the large amounts of water that land plants require.

Much of the rigidity of leaves results from the pressure of cytoplasts against the cell walls. When water is lost from the cytoplasts, pressure against the walls decreases. When the internal pressure decreases, a leaf loses its rigidity; we say it wilts. Because water is continually being lost from leaf cells, the rigidity of leaves can be maintained only by continuous replacement of water. This is one function of veins in leaves – they bring water from other parts of the plant body.

INVESTIGATION 3.1

TRANSPIRATION

PURPOSE
Here you will investigate the effect of one environmental factor on transpiration from a leafy shoot.

MATERIALS AND EQUIPMENT
(for each group)

Erlenmeyer flask, 500 cm³
Two-hole stopper (to fit flask)
Glass tubing, bent to a right angle
Rubber tubing, about 20 cm long
Large battery jar or bowl
Leafy potted plant (all groups but one)
Solid glass rod (one group only)
Scalpel
Water at room temperature
Petroleum jelly or warm paraffin wax
Pipette, 1 cm³
Cork (with hole to fit pipette)
Burette clamp
Ring stand
Watch
Plastic bag
String
Graph paper, 1 sheet per pupil
Pencils, 3 colours

PROCEDURE
1. Read through the instructions and state a hypothesis appropriate to the design of the experiment.
2. Examine Figure 3.6 and set up the apparatus as follows.
3. Into one hole of the stopper insert the length of glass tubing bent to a right angle.
4. Attach a length of rubber tubing to the glass tubing.
5. Take the potted plant and immerse the pot in a large container of water until the base of the plant is covered to a height of 5 cm.
6. Cut the stem at a point well under the water level.
7. Keeping the cut end of the shoot under water, insert it in the other hole of the stopper. (Note that one group of pupils should use a solid glass rod in place of the leafy shoot.)
8. Have the flask filled to the brim with water at room temperature. Remove any books or papers from around the flask and then quickly transfer the stopper into the flask. Water will thus be forced up into the tubing.
9. Seal the apparatus – especially where the stem and stopper are joined – with petroleum jelly or warm paraffin wax.

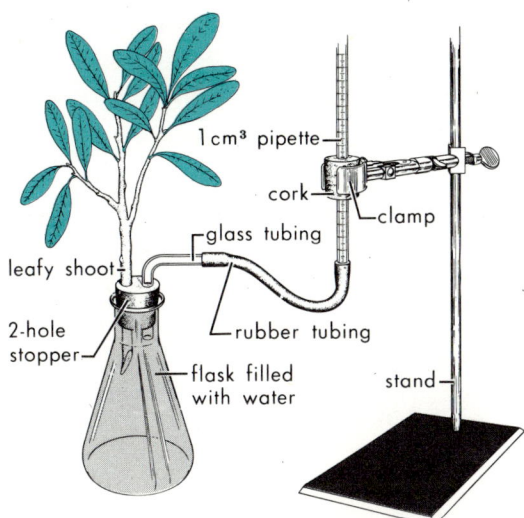

Figure 3.6

10. Insert a pipette through a cork and fill it with water.
11. Hold your index finger over the end of the pipette and insert the lower end into the rubber tubing.
12. Seal the joint with petroleum jelly or paraffin wax.
13. Clamp the cork containing the pipette to a stand for support.
14. Note the position of water level in the pipette. Record its position and the time.
15. Take readings every two minutes for 10 minutes.
16. After the fifth reading, one member of the group should begin to fan the plant.
17. Take readings at two-minute intervals until five readings have been taken. Members of the group should take turns at fanning.
18. After the fifth reading has been taken (tenth since the beginning), cover the shoot loosely with a plastic bag. Gather the bag together at the mouth and tie it shut around the base of the stem.
19. At two-minute intervals, record the position of the water column in the pipette until five more readings have been made.

STUDYING THE DATA

A. Where may water have been lost from the apparatus?
B. Compare the results from the experimental set-ups with the result from the control set-up. What do you think has happened to the water in the experimental set-ups?
C. Do the results obtained from the use of the plastic bags provide any confirmation of this? Give reasons for your answer.
D. How can you determine the amount of water lost from the apparatus? Express your data in graphical form. Plot time along the horizontal axis and pipette readings along the vertical axis. Connect the points, using a different colour for each of the three segments that represent the three conditions of the leafy shoot.
E. What is the variable in this set of data?
F. How do you account for any changes in the slope of your graph line?

CONCLUSIONS

Do your data confirm your hypothesis? Give reasons for your answer.

Looking into Organisms

INVESTIGATION 3.2

STOMATA AND PHOTOSYNTHESIS

PURPOSE

Part A. Here you will observe the appearance and abundance of stomata and the behaviour of their guard cells.

Part B. In this part you will experiment to find a relationship between stomata and photosynthesis.

MATERIALS AND EQUIPMENT
(for each group)

For Part A
Fresh leaves (several kinds)
Microscope
Slides
Cover slips
Forceps
Razor blades
Droppers

For Part B
Potted plants, 2
Scissors
Beakers, 400 cm^3, 3
Forceps
Hot plate
Beaker, 1 litre
Ethanol
Petri dishes, 4
Iodine solution
Test-tubes, 4
Petroleum jelly
Paper tissues
Absorbent cotton
Petrol

PROCEDURE. PART A

1. Hold a leaf with the lower surface upwards. Tear the leaf at an angle. The tearing action should peel off portions of the lower epidermis which will appear as a narrow colourless zone extending beyond the green part of the leaf.
2. Immediately place a small piece of the epidermis in a drop of water on to the slide. Quickly add a cover slip before the fragment dries out.
3. Examine under the low power and locate a group of stomata. Turn to high power and make a drawing of a stomatal region showing the guard cells and a few adjacent cells.
4. Count the number of stomata in ten different high power fields and average your result.
5. Calculate the area of the high power field and, using your figure, find the average number of stomata per square mm of the leaf's surface.
6. Prepare a slide with the upper epidermis of the same leaf on it and count as before. Express your answer as the number of stomata per square mm.
7. Repeat the above procedures for as many leaves as possible and compare the number of stomata per square mm for the upper and lower surfaces of each kind of leaf.

STUDYING THE DATA

A. Did you find exactly the same number of stomata per square mm in different areas of a piece of leaf epidermis?
B. If you wished to compare the number of stomata per square mm for two species of plant, what steps should you take to ensure a reliable comparison?
C. What variations are there in the degree of opening of the stomata you have observed? Can you explain the variation?

PROCEDURE. PART B

Here we will test the hypothesis that carbon dioxide enters the leaf via the stomata.

1. Select two healthy plants of the same species (one of the species you have previously studied).
2. Place one where it will receive no

sunlight and the other where it will be exposed to sunlight.
3. After three days, remove a leaf from each plant, identifying the illuminated one by placing a small notch in its margin.
4. Drop the leaves into a beaker of boiling water and when they are limp, transfer them to a beaker half full of ethanol.
5. Place the beaker in an electrically heated water bath. DO NOT HEAT ETHANOL OVER AN OPEN FLAME, OR ALLOW ITS VAPOUR TO COME INTO CONTACT WITH AN OPEN FLAME.

Heated ethanol slowly extracts chlorophyll from leaves; it also makes them brittle as most of their water is removed.
6. After 10 minutes, remove the leaves from the ethanol and place them into a beaker of water at room temperature.
7. When the leaves become soft, remove them and spread each leaf out in a petri dish. Cover with iodine solution and leave for 3 minutes.
8. Rinse the leaves in water and spread them out in petri dishes containing water and place upon a white piece of paper.
9. Record the colour of each leaf.
10. Take the plant that had been kept in the dark and treat it as follows *without* removing the leaves from the plant.
11. *Leaf 1.* Thoroughly coat the upper surface of this leaf with petroleum jelly, and cut one notch in its margin.
    Leaf 2. Coat the lower surface of the leaf, and cut two notches in its margin.
    Leaf 3. Coat both surfaces of the leaf, and cut three notches in its margin.
    Leaf 4. Do not coat this leaf; simply cut four notches in its margin.

The petroleum jelly forms a highly effective transparent barrier across which many gases (including carbon dioxide) cannot pass.

A. In what ways will the petroleum jelly alter the leaf's normal pattern of gaseous exchange with the air?

12. Place the plant where it will be exposed to sunlight.
13. After three days remove all four leaves, place them on paper tissues, and remove the petroleum jelly by gently rubbing the leaves with absorbent cotton saturated with petrol.
14. Use the iodine test on each leaf.
15. Devise a scheme for comparing the colour reactions of the four leaves, and record your observations.

STUDYING THE DATA

A. In the design of this experiment, what was the purpose of the first set of iodine tests?
B. If you use this test as an indication of photosynthetic activity, what assumption are you making?
C. In the design of the experiment what was the purpose of the leaf marked with four notches?
D. In which of the leaves does photosynthetic activity appear to have been greatest?
E. In which of the leaves does photosynthetic activity appear to have been least?

CONCLUSION

Use your observations from Part A and the results from Part B to justify the claim that carbon dioxide enters the leaf via the stomata and not by some other means.

ROOTS

Water is lost by terrestrial tracheophytes principally through their leaves. Except for epiphytes, terrestrial plants obtain their water from the soil through their roots. With the water they absorb mineral nutrients. Roots have three additional functions: anchorage, storage of food, and the transportation of absorbed water and dissolved minerals. This last function will be discussed later in connection with stems.

Anchorage. Anyone who has weeded a garden or removed dandelions from a lawn is well aware that the roots of a plant anchor it firmly in the soil. In some species the lower end of the uprooted plant is a tough network of roots. This is a *fibrous* root system, and it is characteristic of maize, beans and clover, for example. In other species the plant is anchored by a long, tapering root with only a few small branches. This is a *taproot* system, found in dandelions and young oak trees.

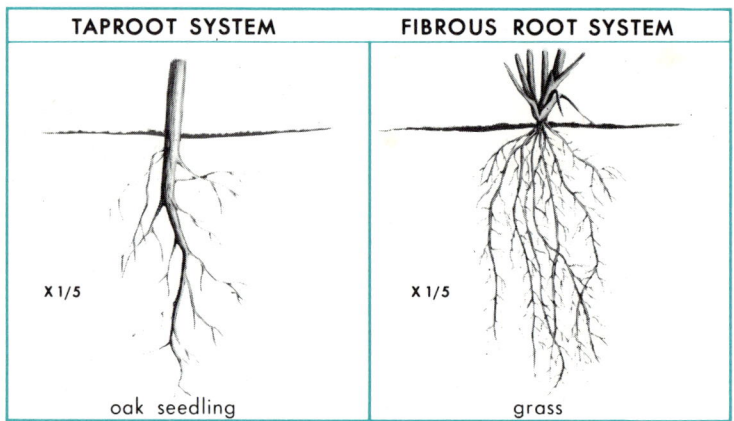

Figure 3.7 Kinds of root systems.

Much of a root system remains in the soil when a plant is pulled up. If a stream of water is used to gently wash away the soil the smaller branch roots remain undamaged and the root system can be seen more completely. When carefully exposed in this way, the root system of a rye plant less than 60 cm in height was estimated to have a total length of about 480 km and a total surface area of more than 600 m². No wonder most land plants are so firmly anchored in the soil!

Absorption. If radish seeds are allowed to germinate in a moist petri dish, the structure of the young root can be seen without the hindrance of soil and entirely undamaged. The tip of such a young root is pointed and bare. Just behind the tip is a region that appears (in a macroscopic view) to be covered with a fuzzy white growth. Observed over a period of several days, this fuzzy band seems to move in the direction of growth as the root lengthens.

The fuzzy region owes its appearance to the presence of numerous *root hairs*. Each root hair is an extended part of an epidermal cell that has a thin cell wall. The central part of a root-hair cell is occupied by a large vacuole; this is filled with water in which sugars, salts and a variety of other compounds are dissolved. Root hairs penetrate the spaces between soil particles and are in contact with soil water. It is principally through these specialized cells that the water required by a plant is obtained.

Figure 3.8 A radish seedling. What part of the plant was first to emerge from the seed coat?

X 8

The substances dissolved in soil water are seldom as concentrated as the substances dissolved in the cytoplast and vacuole of the root hair. Dissolved substances usually pass freely through cell walls; but because cell membranes are differentially permeable, many substances inside root-hair cells cannot pass out through the membranes. Such conditions make possible an inward diffusion of water.

Thus, we can explain the entry into land plants of the two materials required for photosynthesis: carbon dioxide enters chiefly through leaf cells by way of stomata; water enters chiefly through the root hairs.

A plant requires substances in addition to CO_2 and H_2O – mineral nutrients. It requires nitrogen and phosphorus to synthesize proteins and nucleic acids. It requires magnesium to synthesize chlorophyll molecules. A rather long list of additional elements is needed by plants of one kind or another. All of these elements are obtained from soil water in the chemical form of dissolved compounds. Roots take in nitrogen, for example, in the form of ammonium ions or nitrate ions. Because the mineral nutrients are continually used by the synthetic metabolic activities of a plant, they are usually less concentrated inside root-hair cells than in the surrounding water. Usually, therefore, they pass into root hairs by diffusion.

Frequently, however, mineral substances needed by a plant are *less* concentrated in soil water than in the root-hair cells. Under these circumstances, diffusion would carry the substances *from* the cells *into* soil water. Nevertheless, experiments have shown that plants can absorb substances that exist only in low concentrations in soil water. Hans Burström of Sweden grew some barley seedlings in a solution containing 20 parts of a potassium compound per million parts of solution (0.002 per cent). Then he cut off the tops of the plants and collected the sap that welled up out of them. The sap was found to contain 32 parts of the potassium compound per million.

Further experiments have confirmed the conclusion that root hairs and other plant cells can move substances in solution in a direction opposite to that of diffusion. If diffusion alone accounted for such movement, ions would be most concentrated in the soil water, less concentrated in the root hairs, and progressively less concentrated the further a cell is from the root hairs. In certain tissues in roots, minerals accumulate at even higher concentrations than in root hairs themselves. Also, when cells are moving dissolved substances in a direction opposite to that of diffusion, cell respiration speeds up. Clearly, absorption of mineral nutrients involves active transport as well as diffusion.

Root hairs are the usual points of entry for water and mineral nutrients. On their inner sides these special epidermal cells are in contact with other root cells (Figure 3.9). Absorbed substances move deeper into the root by diffusion or active transport from one layer of cells to another. Eventually they reach the conducting tissues, through which they move upwards to the stem and leaves.

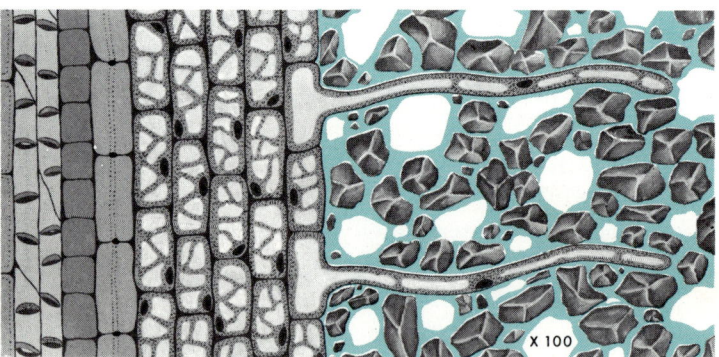

Figure 3.9 Root hairs penetrating into soil. On the left are conducting tissues of the root; soil is shown on the right.

Storage. The *cortex* (Figure 3.10) of a young root may be sloughed off as the root grows older, or it may form part of the bark around the root. Sometimes the plant stores food in the cortex and sometimes in modified cells of the conducting tissues. The food is usually stored as insoluble starch, but sometimes as sugars.

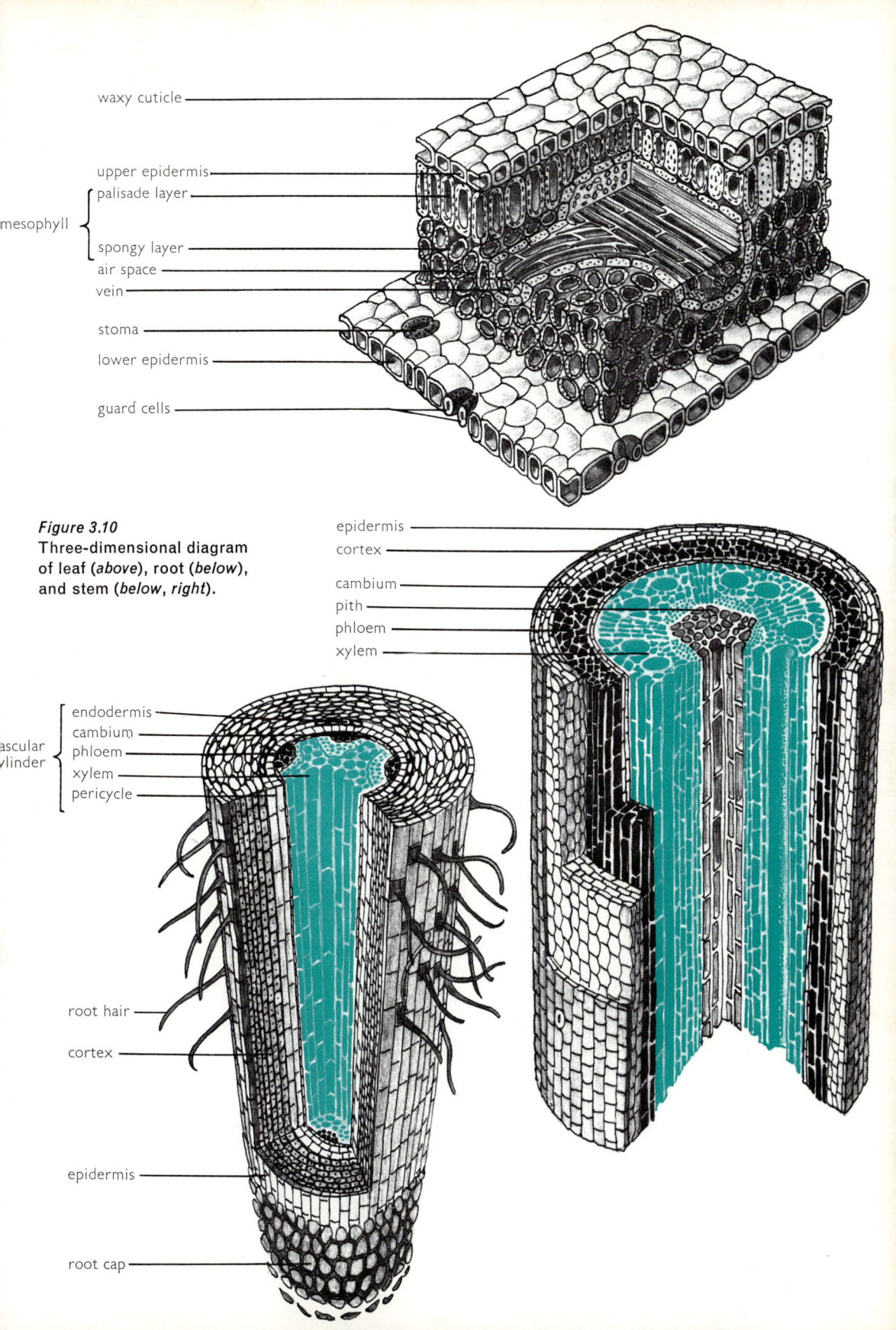

Figure 3.10
Three-dimensional diagram of leaf (*above*), root (*below*), and stem (*below, right*).

Both taproot and fibrous-root systems may have parts where food storage is concentrated. In polar regions, the middle latitudes and those tropical biomes with dry seasons, perennial plants always store a considerable amount of food in roots. Plants that live through only one growing season, however, rarely store much food, except in seeds.

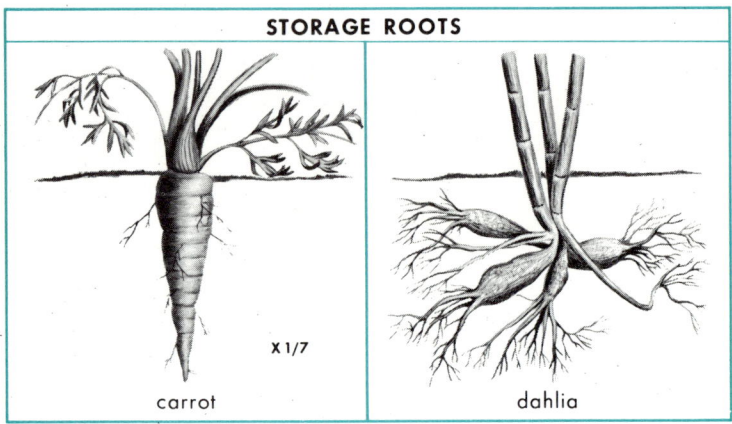

Figure 3.11 When large quantities of food are stored, both taproots (*left*) and fibrous roots (*right*) may be thickened.

STEMS

It is possible and sometimes useful to think of a tracheophyte as consisting of two parts: a root system (ordinarily below ground) and a shoot system (ordinarily above ground).

For botanists the distinction between a root and a stem (the latter usually the principal part of a shoot) has nothing to do with position above or below ground level; it is based on the arrangement of tissues in these structures and

Figure 3.12 Horse chestnut bud (*left*); after opening (*right*).   X 1

on the way the structures originate in the embryo within the seed. The easiest way to make the distinction is to look for buds. A potato has buds ('eyes') and is therefore an example of an underground stem. Most stems, however, grow above ground, supporting leaves and reproductive organs in light and air.

Figure 3.13 In some plants, roots sprout from stems, grow downwards, and penetrate into the soil. This banyan tree grows near the state capital of Hawaii.

Macroscopic structure. Stems differ greatly in structure. The only way to appreciate their diversity is to examine a number of stems. It is convenient to use a portion of a woody twig from a deciduous plant as a starting point in discussing stem structure.

Such a twig, when the leaves have fallen, usually bears conspicuous *buds* A bud is a miniature shoot, consisting of a short length of stem, tiny leaves, and (sometimes) flowers. Growth from a *terminal* bud lengthens the twig; growth from a *lateral* bud starts a new branch. A bud may or may not be covered with protective *scales* (modified leaves); when growth is resumed in the spring, the scales leave scars on the twig. For a few years, old scale scars may remain visible, and from their positions growth in different years can be compared. The places where the petioles of fallen leaves were attached to the twig are also marked by scars. *Lenticels* are simply openings in the bark through which atmospheric gases diffuse into and out of the living cells.

Older woody stems, tree trunks, for example, are best viewed in cross-section. A rather thick bark is characteristic of both older stems and older roots. The bark surrounds the wood. Wood usually shows annual growth rings. Wood *rays* extend radially from the centre outwards towards the bark; these are routes along which liquids move laterally.

Only the tissues of the inner bark and the outer part of the wood are alive; the rest of the wood and bark is composed of dead cell walls such as Hooke saw in cork. Most of the plant liquids (sap) move up and down stems through dead cells – upwards through wood, downwards through bark. Wood through which sap moves upwards is called *sapwood*. The central wood loses its conducting function; it is then called heartwood. It may serve to support the upper parts of a tree; but this is not always important, for many trees stand erect and live for years after the heartwood has rotted away.

Microscopic structure. Figure 3.10 shows in three dimensions the microscopic structure of a young stem. This is a stem from a dicotyledonous plant. By examining several stems through a microscope you will find, as with roots and leaves, that there are many variations.

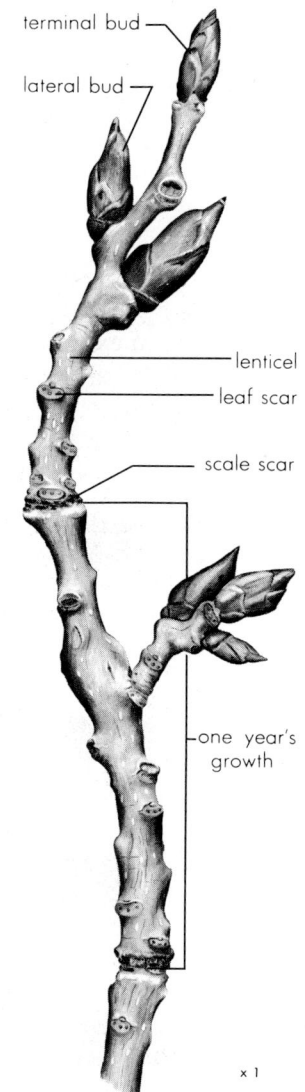

Figure 3.14 A dormant woody twig.

Pith is a tissue characteristic of young stems; it may be large or small; in older plants of many species it does not persist as an organized tissue. The *cambium* tissue consists of cells that divide and form new tissues of other kinds. It separates the bark from the rest of the stem. Because *xylem* cells are continually being formed along the inner margin of the cambium most of the stem eventually consists of xylem tissue; this is the wood of an old stem. *Phloem* tissue is continually being formed along the outer margin of the

Figure 3.15 Logs of larches. Can you decide which was the youngest tree?

cambium; it makes up much of the inner bark of an old stem. Among the xylem and phloem cells are the vascular tissues. Mixed in with the vascular tissues are *fibre* cells, forming a tissue that strengthens the stem. Sometimes fibres and vascular tissues occur in bundles. These *fibrovascular bundles* scattered in pith tissue can be seen macroscopically in maize stems.

Within xylem are found *tracheids* and *vessels*. Tracheids develop from elongated single cells that develop thick walls and then die. Pits occur at many points in the walls of these dead cells. In most cases these pits are so closely paired on adjacent cells that only a thin layer of cell wall separates two adjoining tracheids. At these points water and dissolved materials can easily pass from one tracheid into another.

Vessels are made up of elongated, thick-walled cells joined end to end. When a vessel cell is fully formed, a hole develops in the wall at each end of the cell; then, as in the tracheids, the living

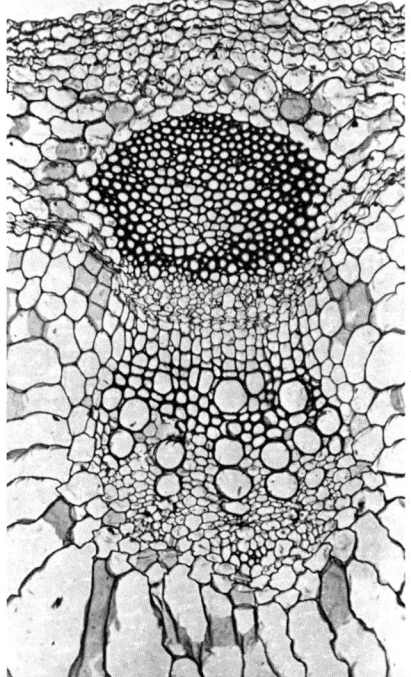

Figure 3.16 Fibrovascular bundle of a sunflower stem in cross-section. The dark outer tissue is fibrous; within it are the smaller cells of phloem; inside that, regular rows of cells, including large ones, of the xylem.   X 100

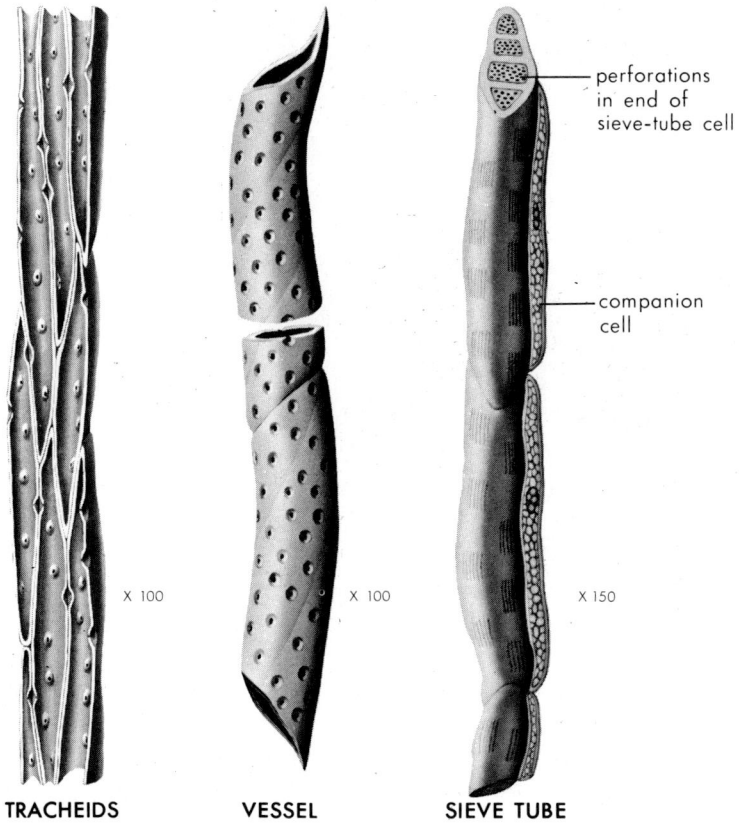

Figure 3.17 Cells from conducting tissues of tracheophytes.

substance dies and disappears. Thus tiny, elongated pipes are formed, extending through the stem. Because water and salts can pass from one end of a vessel to the other without having to pass through pits, vessels would seem to be more efficient for transporting sap than tracheids.

Long lines of phloem cells make up structures called *sieve tubes*. As the cells of a sieve tube develop, small holes form in their end walls. Through these holes the cytoplast of one cell connects with the cytoplast of adjacent cells, making a continuous cell-to-cell system. As a sieve tube matures, the nuclei in the cells disintegrate, but the sieve tube continues to function as long as the cytoplasts remain alive. Located beside each sieve-tube cell are one or two smaller *companion cells*. These *do* have nuclei and are believed to regulate the activity of the adjacent sieve-tube cells.

Conduction. Through the two series of vascular tissues – xylem and phloem – moves sap, a complex mixture of minerals, foods and other materials in solution. Unlike the blood in your vascular system, the sap in a plant is not moved by the pumping action of a heart. How, then, do liquids move in a plant?

To date, all the observations of biologists do not add up to an entirely satisfactory answer. Many experiments show that water from the root rises through xylem – from root xylem to stem xylem, to xylem in the veins of leaves. Even in the tallest trees, water moves against the force of gravity, from the roots to the topmost leaves. Let us consider this upward movement.

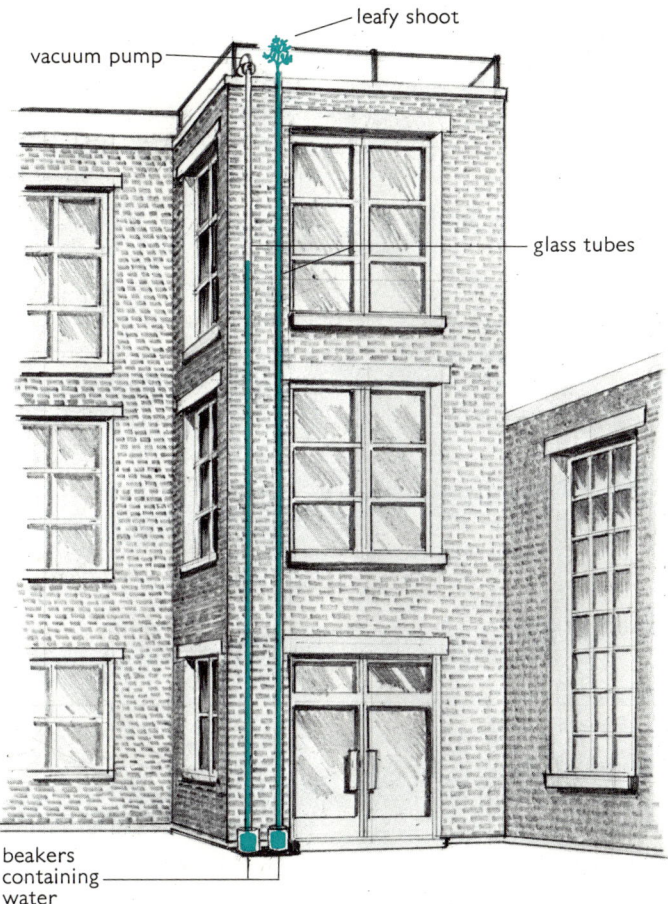

Figure 3.18 **An experiment on rise of liquids in stems.**

Suppose you have a bottle of ginger beer. You place a straw in the liquid, apply your lips to its upper end, and suck. Immediately you are rewarded: the liquid rises to your mouth through the straw. Now let us look at a similar but less familiar situation. A beaker of water is placed on the ground next to a school building. You climb up to the third floor, 13 m above the ground, and, using a long piece of glass tubing you attempt to draw the water up from the beaker. Try as you may, you never succeed. Being stubborn, you borrow a vacuum pump from the physics lab, connect it to the tubing, and turn the pump on. This is also unsuccessful. If the school is near sea level, the water will rise about 10.3 m above the beaker, but no further. At an altitude of 1609 m the water in the tube can be raised only to a height of about 8.4 m, but in some trees water rises to a much greater height.

Now a new experiment – one involving a living plant. Suppose we hold a leafy shoot under water and cut off the top 20 cm with a sharp knife. We insert this cut tip into a short piece of rubber tubing. We then connect the other end of the tubing to a 14-m length of slender (less than 0.5 mm internal diameter) glass tubing that is filled with water. We make certain that there are no leaks in the system. Now we place the lower end of the glass tube in a beaker of boiled water containing a dye so that it can be easily seen. (Boiling removes dissolved air that could form bubbles in the tube.) The entire set-up makes a continuous, water-filled system extending from the mesophyll cells in the leaves down through the xylem tissue of the stem into the rubber tubing and long glass tube, ending in the container on the ground. Gradually the dyed water from the container begins to rise – first 3 m, then 6, 9, and finally to the tip of the shoot – more than 14 m (that is, 3.7 m above the limit reached with a vacuum pump). How is this possible?

Knowledge of an important property of water is basic to understanding the movement in this system. Under certain conditions a column of water has remarkable *tensile strength* (resistance to breaking when pulled lengthwise). Here are the conditions: (1) the water must be contained in tubes of very small diameter; (2) the walls of the tubes must be made of a material to which water molecules will adhere; (3) the water must not contain gas bubbles that break the column of water. Under these conditions, as water molecules are lost by evaporation from the upper end of the column (the leaves), their *cohesion* (attraction for adjoining water molecules) results in a pull, which is transmitted throughout the length of the system. This causes more water to move up into the tube from below. In this way, water can be moved upwards in columns many times higher than 10.3 m. The water column is pulled up just as a wire would be pulled, rather than being pushed up by atmospheric pressure, as it is in a vacuum-pump system.

In 1915 these physical facts were used by H. H. Dixon to develop the 'transpiration-tension' theory for explaining the rise of liquids in plant stems. According to this theory, in a living tree the system of vessels in the xylem corresponds to the slender glass tubing, and soil water in contact with root surfaces corresponds to the dyed water in the container. Sugars produced by photosynthesis are contained within the mesophyll cells. As water evaporates from the mesophyll tissue and passes out through the stomata (transpiration), the concentration of dissolved materials increases. Water molecules then pass into these mesophyll cells from the xylem vessels and tracheids by osmosis. As they move into the mesophyll, cohesion between these water molecules and water molecules in the xylem tissues develops a force that pulls more liquid up the stem.

However, some experimental results do not fit this theory. If the shoot of a well-watered grape-vine is cut off and a vertical glass tube is sealed to the rooted stump, sap will rise in the tube. In this situation one condition assumed in the transpiration-tension theory is not present – there is no transpiration. Here it seems that the rise of the sap must come about through a push from below rather than a pull from above. This push has been called *root pressure*. Measurements of the force of root pressure have indicated that water could be pushed to a height of 90 m under some conditions.

In spite of these measurements, plant physiologists believe that root pressure is not an important factor in the rise of liquids in plants. For one thing, not all plants develop root pressure when their shoots are cut, and some that do not are tall trees. Secondly, in plants that do develop root pressure, the pressure is lowest in the summer, when the plants are moving the most liquid. Moreover, root pressure is simply a name for an observed fact; it is not an explanation. As yet no biologist has fully explained where the force of root pressure comes from. So Dixon's theory still remains the most reasonable *single* explanation for the rise of liquids in plant stems.

Now consider the phloem. Liquids moving through phloem contain much dissolved food, in contrast to the inorganic nutrients that are usually the principal contents of xylem liquids. In general, movement in the phloem is *from* the leaves, where foods are produced by photosynthesis, downwards through stems to roots, where much of the food is stored. This is not always so; occasionally, movement in the phloem is reversed.

We might think the downward movement in the phloem is easily explained; gravity alone might be the cause. But the sieve cells of the phloem are not mere empty tubes; they contain living cytoplasts, through which the moving liquids must pass. Of course, substances can diffuse through cytoplasts, but the rate at which the food-rich liquids move through the phloem is known to be thousands of times faster than diffusion could account for. In many cases the direction of movement is from lesser concentration to greater concentration – opposite to that of diffusion. Some kind of active transport must be involved.

Other stem functions. Conduction of liquids is the more usual function of stems, but in many plants stems perform other functions also. Some stems may carry on photosynthesis. In most herbaceous plants photosynthesis occurs in chlorophyll-bearing cells just beneath the epidermis of stems. Even in woody plants young twigs frequently contain photosynthetic tissues. Some plants have no leaves; in these all photosynthesis occurs in stems.

In most modern plants, however, the functions of stems in food production are supplying water by conduction and supporting leaves where they may be exposed to sunlight. In forests, sturdy trunks hold leaves of trees far above the surface of the ground; plants with weaker stems are left in the shade below, where they must adapt to the reduced light that filters down, or perish. Some plants are almost stemless. The leaves of dandelions, for example, spread out on the surface of the ground, appearing to grow directly from the top of the

84 Looking into Organisms

Figure 3.19 Storage stem of a South African plant. In this environment what do you think might be the chief substance stored?

root. Some such 'stemless' plants are shade-tolerant; others (such as dandelions) grow mostly in places where there are few taller neighbouring plants to cut off solar radiation.

In many plants stems serve as storage organs. Sugar-beet plants store sucrose in their stems. Great quantities of water as well as food are stored in cactus stems. When the storage function of stems is highly developed, other functions may be less evident or absent. The best-known examples of food storage occur in underground stems that have no other important function.

GROWTH

You may be still growing, but you know that a time will come when you will cease to grow – at least in height. Mammals, birds and arthropods have definite limits to growth, but most other animals and all multicellular plants continue to grow throughout their lives, usually at a gradually slowing rate. Nevertheless, there is a fundamental difference between growth in animals and growth in multicellular plants.

Meristems. Growth in multicellular organisms occurs primarily by means of the addition of new cells, followed by enlargement of these cells. In animals these new cells are added in all directions. As you grow, your proportions change; but most of the time growth occurs throughout your body. This is so because most kinds of animal cells retain the ability to reproduce, even though they differentiate in other respects.

In vascular plants, cells that have differentiated – into xylem, phloem and mesophyll, for example – generally lose the ability to divide. Each cell of such tissues is formed from another kind of tissue, an undifferentiated tissue that continues mitosis and cell division as long as the plant lives. This tissue, no matter where it occurs in the plant, is called a *meristem*.

In root tips meristematic tissue is located just behind a *root cap* (Figure 3.10). This meristem forms root-cap cells on the side towards the tip. These cells do not accumulate because they are constantly worn away as the root pushes through the soil. To the rear, this meristem forms cells that differentiate into root tissues, each with a specialized function. Only these become a permanent part of the root.

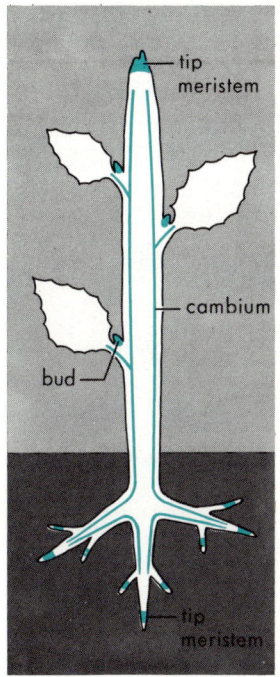

Figure 3.20 Location of principal meristems – a diagram.

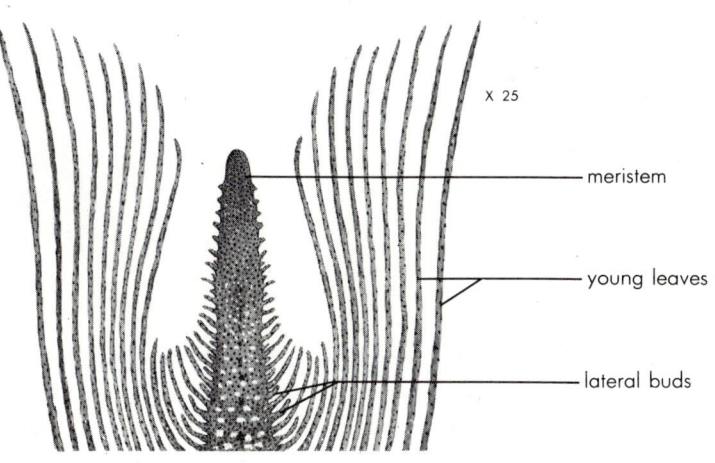

Figure 3.21 Tip of an *Elodea* shoot.

The tips of stems also contain meristems. As a stem lengthens, the tissue at its tip remains meristematic. Small masses of meristem are also left behind, and from them branches and leaves develop. Each branch has a meristem at its tip. In most leaves, however, all the cells differentiate into xylem, phloem, mesophyll, etc. This differentiation takes place at an early stage in leaf formation. For example, in deciduous woody plants, leaves for the following year are fully formed within a bud before the end of the growing season. The cells, though, are quite small. In spring, leaves expand by the enlargement of these small cells without the addition of new cells. Leaves of grasses and some other plants are an exception: in them a meristem remains at the base of the leaf, and the leaf can increase in length even after most of the blade has been cut off by a grazing animal or a lawn mower.

Not all the cells left behind along a lengthening root or stem branch off or differentiate. Except in monocots, the layer of meristem called the cambium remains along the length of each stem and

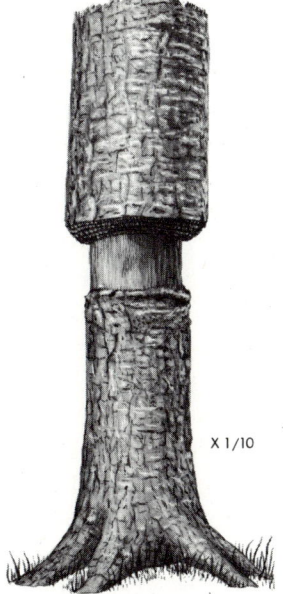

Figure 3.22 Bark and cambium were removed from a strip around the trunk of this tree a year before the top was cut off. Can you explain this result?

root. From cambium new xylem and phloem are formed, increasing the stems and roots in diameter. Cambium remains as a boundary between the central core of wood (xylem) and the outer layer of bark (phloem). Bark can usually be peeled from a tree trunk rather easily because the walls of the cambium cells are thin and easily broken.

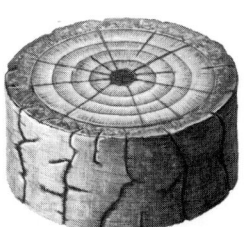 

Figure 3.23 What are the principal changes that a year has made in these stems?

four-year-old stem   five-year-old stem

×3

Chemical control of growth. For a long time it has been known that most green plants grow towards light – a response often called phototropism. This is easily observed in plants growing on window-sills, where almost all the light comes from one side. Nearly ninety years ago, Charles Darwin and his son, Francis, investigated the mechanism of this response. From previous studies the Darwins knew that several zones can be distinguished in a developing plant stem. At the tip is the meristem; just behind it is a zone of elongation, in which the newly formed cells enlarge lengthwise; behind this is a zone in which the cells become xylem, phloem, fibres and other tissues.

The Darwins observed that the bending towards the light occurs not at the very tip, but in the zone of elongation, a few millimetres behind it. They experimented with very young seedlings of grasses and oats, which have a covering called the *coleoptile* over the first leaves. When they placed a tiny metal cap over the tips of the coleoptiles, the zones of elongation no longer bent. Somehow, light shining on the tip affected the cells in the zone of elongation below it. The Darwins concluded that 'when seedlings are freely exposed to a lateral light some influence is transmitted from the upper to the lower part, causing the latter to bend.'

What was this 'influence'? In later years this investigation was pursued by others. In 1910 Boysen-Jensen performed an experiment based on the hypothesis that the 'influence' carried from the tip to the cells in the region of elongation was a chemical substance. He placed oat seedlings in a container that provided light from only one side. He cut off the coleoptile tips of some and left others intact. The intact seedlings bent towards the light source; the tipless seedlings grew straight upwards. Then he used gelatin to fasten the tips to the stumps of the tipless coleoptiles. These seedlings now began to bend towards the light in the same way as the controls (intact plants). Something had evidently passed from the tip through the non-living gelatin to the stumps – most probably a chemical substance.

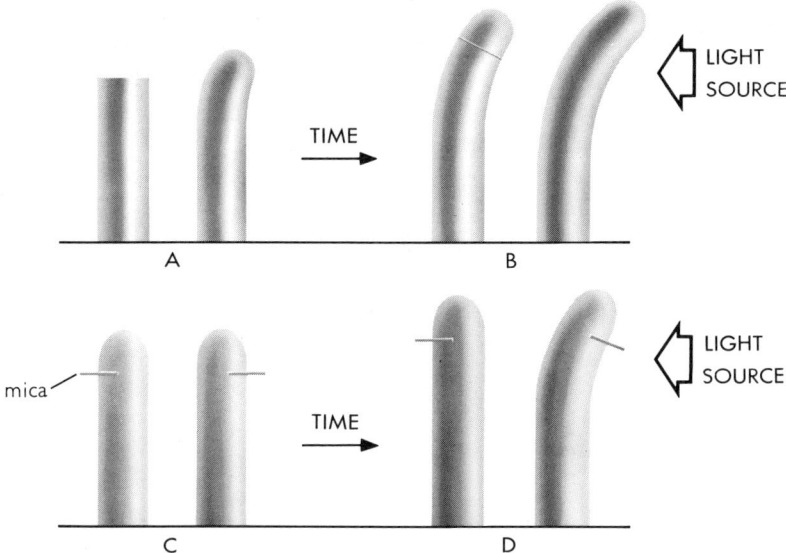

Figure 3.24 Boysen-Jensen's two experiments. (A) and (B) show the first experiment; (C) and (D) show the second.

How did the supposed chemical substance cause the bending towards the light? A year later, in an attempt to obtain information on the question, Boysen-Jensen inserted thin pieces of mica partway through oat coleoptiles and just behind the tips. In designing this experiment, he assumed that the chemical substance from the tip of the plant could not pass through the mica as it evidently had done through the gelatin. When the seedlings were placed so that the mica was on the side towards the light source, the seedlings bent towards it. When they were placed so that the mica was away from the light source, they did not bend. From these results Boysen-Jensen concluded that some substance produced by cells in the coleoptile tip moved down the side of the coleoptile opposite to the light and increased elongation of cells on that side. Greater lengthening of cells on the 'dark' side made the plant bend towards the light (Figure 3.25).

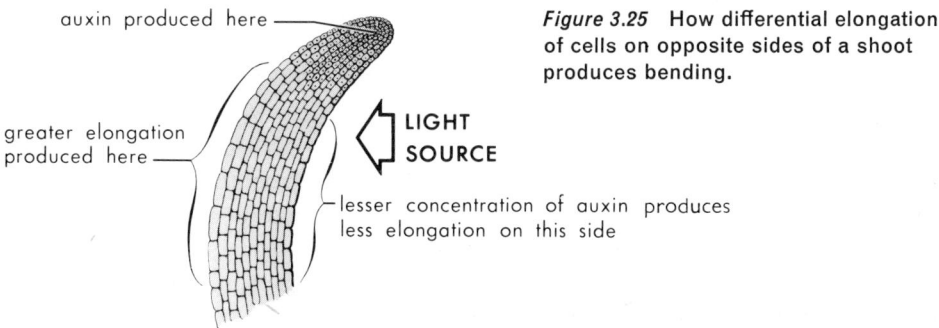

Figure 3.25 How differential elongation of cells on opposite sides of a shoot produces bending.

In 1928 Frits Went worked out techniques for collecting the substance Boysen-Jensen had shown must exist. Tips of oat coleoptiles were cut off and placed on thin layers of agar. Later the agar was cut into blocks. The tips were then removed from the agar and discarded. Each small agar block was placed on the edge of a seedling from which the tip had been removed. Without exposure to light the seedling bent – and always away from the side on which the piece of agar was placed. Evidently the substance in the tip had diffused into the agar, and then from the agar it had diffused into the coleoptile. Further, Went found he could measure the amount of the substance by measuring the angle of bending that an agar piece produced in a seedling.

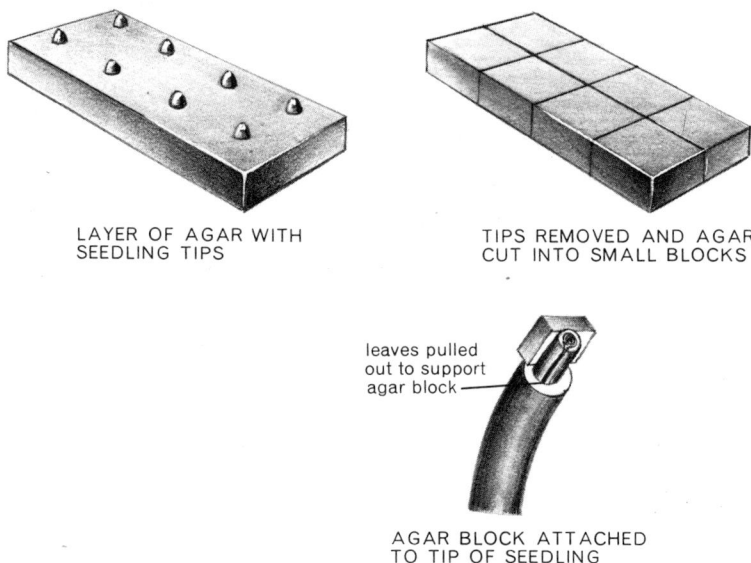

Figure 3.26 Went's method of measuring auxin production.

Because the substance produced in the seedling tip stimulated increased elongation, it has been referred to as a growth substance and named *auxin*, but its exact chemical nature has not yet been determined. However, many known chemical substances have the same effect on the growth of plants. One of these, indoleacetic acid, is effective in extremely small amounts. For example, 0.000 000 5 milligramme applied to one side of an oat seedling will bring about a clearly visible bending. Indoleacetic acid has been found to be present in plants; it is very possible that it is a natural auxin.

Many man-made chemical substances have effects similar to those of indoleacetic acid. One, called '2,4-D', stimulates growth when used in small quantities; but large quantities of it can kill many kinds of plants. Since

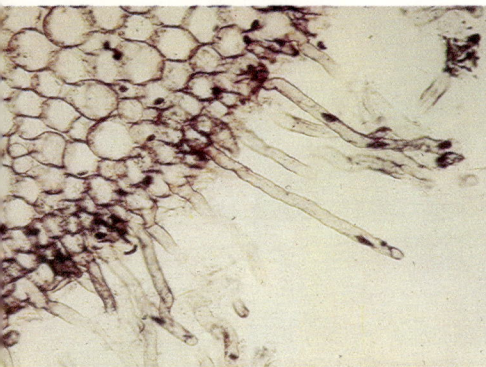
Thin-walled root hairs of *Vicia* (vetch), ×250, through which water enters the plant. What other substances might also enter?

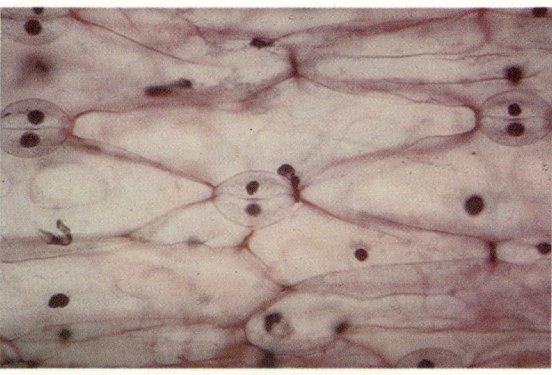
Stomata of box plant, ×420. As shown in the picture, would they allow a free diffusion of gases?

Sieve tubes, ×130. They form the sugar-conducting system of angiosperm plants.

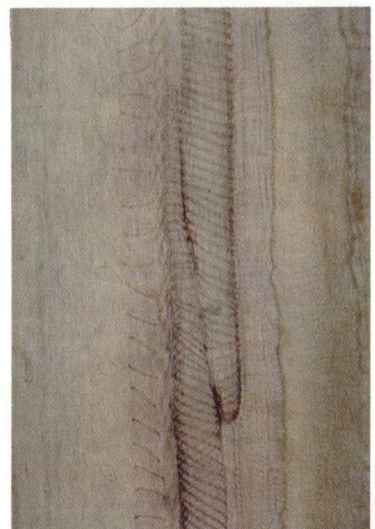
Xylem vessels, ×100, through which water and mineral salts pass up the plant from the roots.

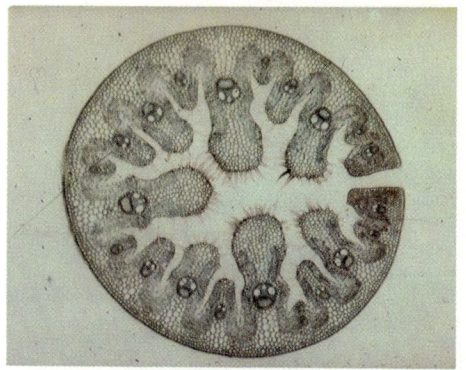
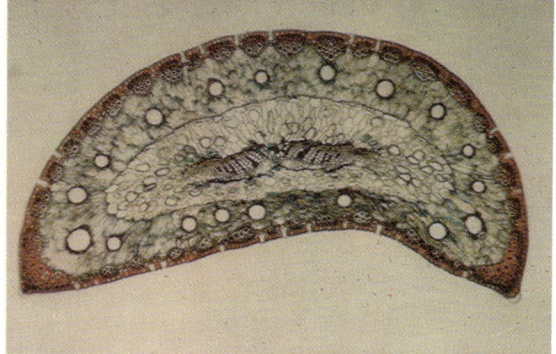
Cross sections of leaves. *Left*: the structure of the marram grass leaf (×25) helps the plant to conserve water. *Right*: a pine needle, ×25. What function do you think is served by its special structure?

Plate VII Some aspects of plant structure.

Plate VIII Ducklings exhibiting the 'following' instinct towards their mother. If a human takes them from the nest as soon as they hatch, then the ducklings will follow that person rather than their true mother.

Plate IX Different kinds of photographic films 'see' the same scene differently, just as do different kinds of animal eyes. Here sweet williams are shown (*left*) somewhat as many mammals may see them, and (*right*) as most insects and primates see them.

2,4-D in the concentrations usually used does not affect members of the grass family (monocotyledons), it is used to control dicotyledonous plants in lawns and in wheat fields. 2,4-D and MCPA, another 'auxin-type growth regulator', are the most widely used pesticides of any kind in Britain; they comprise some two-thirds of the total of all herbicides, insecticides and fungicides applied to our crops.

Figure 3.27 The top row of holly cuttings was treated with beta-indolebutyric acid; the bottom row was not treated. How might this substance related to growth be used commercially?   X 3/7

Further evidence that there is still much to learn about the chemical control of growth in plants is shown by the case of the 'silly seedlings'. A number of years ago, Japanese rice farmers noticed that some individual rice plants sometimes grow gigantically tall and then droop, fall over, and die. Japanese botanists found that these *bakanae* ('silly seedlings') are infected with a fungus. They studied the effects of the *bakanae* disease and discovered that certain substances formed by the fungus – *gibberellins* – bring about the strange growth of the *bakanae*. When treated with gibberellins, many kinds of plants grow to double or triple their normal height; but many species are only slightly affected by such treatment. And it is now known that some tracheophytes as well as fungi produce gibberellins. The study of gibberellins and their effects is a very active field of botanical research.

Looking into Organisms

INVESTIGATION 3.3

RATE OF GROWTH: LEAVES

INTRODUCTION
Within a seed, a plant embryo exists; in most cases much of the embryo consists of a bud. On page 85 it was pointed out that the multiplication of leaf cells takes place chiefly while the leaf is still in a bud, and the expansion of the leaf from the bud is largely a result of the enlargement of cells.

PURPOSE
To study the growth of a leaf, beginning with leaves in the embryonic bud.

MATERIALS AND EQUIPMENT
(for each group)
Broad bean seeds, 18
Beaker, 250 cm³
Fungicide solution
Scalpel
Hand lens
Metric ruler
Seed box
Sand or vermiculite
Graph paper, 1 sheet per pupil

PROCEDURE
1. Select eighteen bean seeds of approximately the same size and place in a beaker.
2. Add fungicide solution to the seeds until the volume of the solution is about twice that of the seeds. Allow to soak for 20 minutes.
3. Pour off the fungicide solution and rinse the seeds thoroughly with water. Fill the beaker with water and leave the seeds in it overnight.
4. After 24 hours take three seeds from the beaker and, using a scalpel, cut carefully through the seed coat of each of the three beans.
5. Remove the seed coats and open the beans.
6. Using a hand lens, find the embryo plant which lies between the two large cotyledons in each seed.
7. Measure the length of the embryo leaves in each seed, and calculate the average length.
8. Enter your results in a table of the form shown below.

Day	Length of Leaves	Average Length

9. Plant the remaining fifteen seeds about 1.5 cm deep and 5 cm apart in sand or vermiculite. Water thoroughly; provide adequate light and a relatively constant temperature; keep the soil damp but not flooded.
10. On Days 3, 6, 10, 13, 17 and 20 after planting, measure the length of the first two leaves of three plants to the nearest millimetre. On Day 3 (and possibly on Day 6 also) you may find it necessary to dig up three germinated seeds, since the plants may not have grown above the surface. If this is necessary, discard these seeds after you have made your measurements.
11. After the plants appear above the 'soil', measure the leaves on the same three plants each measurement day. Make the measurement along the centre vein (midrib) of each leaf, from the apex to the base; do not include the length of the petiole. Average the measurements each day.

STUDYING THE DATA
1. Plot the data graphically. Put time on the horizontal axis and average length of leaves on the other. The rate of growth is indicated by the slope of the graph line.

A. Does the slope change? If so, describe the change.

B. Where did the most rapid growth occur?
C. Are there fluctuations? If so, try to explain them.

SUMMARY

From the examination of this graph, is it possible to deduce any general principle? If not, what additional data do you think would be required before any general statement could be made?

FOR FURTHER INVESTIGATION

1. Obtaining data on growth of individual plants until maturity usually requires a considerable amount of time. Figure 3.28 shows data on the growth of a bamboo, a plant that grows quite rapidly. Draw a graph from these data and compare it with the graph of leaf growth.

2. Is the shape of a growth-rate graph influenced by the kind of measurement recorded? Weight rather than a linear measurement has frequently been used in growth studies. The data in Figure 3.29 were obtained from a field of corn. Every two weeks after the seedlings appeared above ground, several plants were pulled up and weighed. The weights were averaged and recorded.

AGE (in weeks)	AVERAGE HEIGHT (in metres)
1	0.7
2	1.5
3	2.5
4	4.0
5	6.2
6	8.3
7	10.2
8	12.0
9	13.2
10	13.8
11	14.1
12	14.2

Figure 3.28 Bamboo

AGE (in weeks)	AVERAGE WEIGHT (in grammes)
2	21
4	28
6	58
8	76
10	170
12	422
14	706
16	853
18	924
20	966

Figure 3.29 Corn

Draw a graph from the above data and compare it with the other growth-rate graphs.

NON-VASCULAR PLANTS

The great majority of muticellular plants are tracheophytes; but bryophytes, fungi and many of the algae are also multicellular. Their structures differ from those of tracheophytes, but they carry on the same basic functions: absorption of nutrients, transport of dissolved substances, storage of food, growth, and so forth.

Many bryophytes appear to have roots, stems and leaves. Microscopically, however, none of these parts resembles the roots, stems and leaves of tracheophytes. In particular, they lack vascular tissues – xylem and phloem. Because botanists use the terms 'root', 'stem' and 'leaf' to indicate vascular organs, these words should not be used in naming the parts of liverworts or mosses.

More important than the naming of the structures, however, is the effect that the lack of vascular tissues has on the physiology of the plants. A few bryophytes live in water; but most are land plants, getting their water from the soil. Because they lack vascular tissues, the upward transportation of soil water in them is, apparently, not efficient enough to allow growth to heights above 40 cm; at least, this is the maximum height among bryophytes. Even such heights are reached only in environments with a high humidity, where transpiration must be very slow. On the other hand, many mosses are able to go into a dormant state when the water supply is low. Such species survive in some very dry places, as in deserts and small crevices in rocks, where they actively grow only during a few days after each rain.

Fungi, too, have no conducting tissues, but the lack of chlorophyll is a much more distinctive characteristic in the physiology of fungi. Fungi, like animals and many protists, are consumers. They must obtain their energy from food, multicarbon compounds that they secure from the environment. Unlike animals, however, they seldom require such molecules as amino acids from the environment. Like other plants, if supplied with multicarbon compounds and with mineral nutrients, they can usually synthesize all the organic substances they require. During their metabolic activities, many fungi produce substances that are rare or unknown among other organisms – the complex acids of lichen fungi, for example. In recent years biochemists have become very interested in the special physiology of fungi.

Figure 3.30 A clump of dry moss (*left*). The same clump (*right*) two minutes after water was added at its base. What has happened to the moss plants?   X 2

Multicellular algae also lack vascular systems; but because they live in water, this is no hindrance to their growth. Indeed, some of the brown algae reach a length of 45 m, far longer than most middle-latitude deciduous trees are high. Such seaweeds, however, are seldom more than a few centimetres thick, so none of their cells are far from the environmental water and the mineral nutrients it contains.

All algae carry on photosynthesis. Besides containing chlorophyll *a*, many contain chlorophylls *c* and *d* instead of the chlorophyll *b* characteristic of tracheophytes and bryophytes. Apparently this does not cause any great difference in the biochemistry of photosynthesis. However, most groups of algae have a physiological characteristic that is useful in classification – the kind of food they store. Although most plants store food principally as starch, some of the algae store it in the form of other polysaccharides or even oils.

The conspicuous land plants are multicellular, with differentiated tissues and organs. Most of these are tracheophytes; therefore, this chapter has been devoted largely to the structure and physiology of these plants. The structure of leaves is adapted to their principal function of photosynthesis. The structure of roots is adapted to their principal function of absorption. The structure of stems is adapted to their principal function of conduction. In general, the structure of tracheophytes is adapted to life in land environments.

Growth in multicellular plants results from the production of new cells and their subsequent enlargement. The production of new cells occurs only in specialized tissues, a characteristic that helps to distinguish multicellular plants from animals. Studies of responses of plants to environmental factors, such as light, have led to the discovery that plant growth is regulated by chemical means.

Finally, some aspects of the physiology of non-vascular plants have been compared and contrasted with the physiology of vascular plants and of animals.

GUIDE QUESTIONS

1. On what basis can we call a leaf a plant organ?
2. What characteristics of leaf structure (internal and external) seem to be related to leaf function in photosynthesis?
3. What is transpiration?
4. How does wilting of leaves occur?
5. What are the principal functions of roots?
6. Through what root structures does a plant absorb most of its water and nutrients?

7. What evidence indicates that absorption of substances from the soil involves more than simple diffusion?
8. How do stems differ from roots?
9. What are the principal differences between xylem and phloem tissues?
10. Explain the transpiration–tension theory of conduction in your own words.
11. In what ways is the idea of root pressure unsatisfactory as a general explanation for the rise of liquids in stems?
12. How does conduction occur through phloem tissue?
13. Summarize the functions that plant stems perform.
14. What is the function of meristems?
15. How did Boysen-Jensen demonstrate that tissue at the tip of a shoot produces a substance causing elongation of stem cells?
16. In what ways do gibberellins resemble auxin?
17. Mosses never grow very tall. What seems to be the principal reason for this?
18. Metabolically fungi resemble both animals and other plants. How?

PROBLEMS

1. The leaves of water-lilies (tracheophytes) float. The plants are rooted in mud at the bottom of ponds. How might the cellular structure of their roots, stems and leaves differ from cellular arrangement in the roots, stems and leaves of terrestrial tracheophytes?
2. A few species of tracheophytes do not carry on photosynthesis. In what ways might you expect their roots, stems and leaves to differ from those of photosynthetic tracheophytes?
3. Most roots are not exposed to light and contain no chlorophyll. How is the gas exchange between root and environment different from the gas exchange between leaf (in sunlight) and environment?
4. During the growing season farmers spend considerable time cultivating their crops – loosening the soil between plants. What advantages does this have for the crop plants? Investigate the practice called 'dry farming'. How is it related to the physiology of plants?
5. Ten years ago a farmer built a fence 1.5 m high and attached one end of it to a tree that was 7 m high. Now the tree has grown to a height of 14 m. How far above the ground is the attached end of the fence? Explain your answer.
6. The following questions concern lateral growth in woody stems: (a) How is an annual ring formed in the wood of a tree? (b) Within a given biome, how would the annual ring formed in a wet year differ from one formed in a dry year? (c) Sometimes two rings are formed in one year. How might this happen? (d) What is the science of *dendrochronology* and how is it used? (e) What happens to phloem tissue as the trunk of a tree increases in diameter? (f) Would you expect to find annual rings in the bark of a tree?
7. A plant is placed in an atmosphere containing abundant carbon dioxide, but no growth occurs. What are some possible explanations for this?
8. In a middle-latitude biome a pine and an apple tree are growing side by side. Compare the requirements of these two trees for water throughout the year.

SUGGESTED READING

AUDUS, L. J. *Plant Growth Substances*. Hill, 1959.

DAVIES, D. D. *Intermediary Metabolism in Plants*. Cambridge University Press, 1961.

FOGG, G. E. *The Growth of Plants*. Penguin Books, 1963. (Though growth is the focus of attention, all phases of plant physiology are discussed. Somewhat advanced.)

GREULACH, V. A. and J. E. ADAMS. 2nd edn. *Plants: An Introduction to Modern Botany*. John Wiley & Sons, 1967. (Modern treatment of plant physiology, with clear and carefully selected illustrations.)

MEYER, B. S., D. B. ANDERSON and R. H. BOHNING. *Introduction to Plant Physiology*. D. Van Nostrand, 1960.

RICHARDSON, M. *Translocation in Plants*. Edward Arnold (for Institute of Biology), 1968.

STRAFFORD, G. A. *Essentials of Plant Physiology*. Heinemann Educational, 1965.

VAN OVERBEEK, J. *The Lore of Living Plants*. McGraw-Hill, 1964. (An excellent discussion of plant physiology. Contains suggestions for pupil investigations. Fairly easy.)

WILSON, C. L. and W. E. LOOMIS. *Botany*. 3rd edn. Holt, Rinehart & Winston, 1962. Chapters 6–10 and 12. (An excellent discussion of structure and functions of tracheophytes.)

ZIMMERMANN, M. H. 'How Sap Moves in Trees', *Scientific American*, March 1963. Pp. 132–8+.

CHAPTER

4

THE FUNCTIONING ANIMAL

INVESTIGATION 4.1

ANIMAL STRUCTURE AND FUNCTION

INTRODUCTION

What functions are performed by both men and grasshoppers, by both men and earthworms, by both men and jellyfish? Your first reaction may be that these species have very little in common. But they are all animals, and gradually you will think of functions that all animals must perform if they are to survive.

No one species can fully illustrate animal structure and function: man, grasshopper, earthworm, jellyfish – we might learn much from any of these. For a long time frogs have been favourite laboratory animals as they have the following advantages: they are of a convenient size, they are easily obtained, they are easily kept in the laboratory, and they are comparatively inexpensive. Still more important, they are vertebrates – sufficiently like ourselves to throw some light on our own structure and function, yet sufficiently unlike us to provide some important contrasts.

PURPOSE

By direct observation you will investigate the structure and function of a vertebrate.

MATERIALS AND EQUIPMENT
(for each group)

Procedure A
Live frog
Gauze bandage, 60 cm
Aquaria, 2 per class and containing water to depth of 10 cm

Procedure B
Dead frog
Dissecting dish
Pins, 10
Forceps
Hand lens
Scissors

PROCEDURE A. THE LIVING FROG

1. Moisten the top of the table on which the frog is to be placed.
2. Take the frog and place it on the table, tying the bandage round its leg to a table leg or any other fixed object.
3. Sit quietly by the table and allow time for the frog to become accustomed to its surroundings. By avoiding sudden motions you will increase your opportunities for making accurate observations.
4. Compare the general structure of

the frog's body with that of your own. Think of your body as consisting of a head, neck, trunk and four appendages.

A. Are any of these lacking in the frog? If so, which?
B. Consider a cat, cow or lizard. What major division of the body is present in these and many other vertebrates, but is lacking in both the frog and man?

5. Compare the body structure to the left and to the right of the frog's backbone.

C. What kind of symmetry does the frog's body have?
D. What kind of symmetry does your body have?

6. Locate the eyes.

E. In what ways do the frog's eyes differ from yours?

7. Locate the ears. They are situated behind and below the eyes. The eardrum is stretched across the ear opening.

F. How do your ears differ from those of the frog?

8. Examine the skin of the frog.

G. In what ways does the skin of the frog differ from yours?
H. In the human body each of the upper appendages consists of a series of parts called the upper arm, the forearm, the wrist, the hand and the fingers. Each of the lower appendages consists of the thigh, shank, ankle, foot and toes. Are any of these parts lacking in the frog? If so, which?
I. In what ways do the terminal parts (those furthest away from the trunk) of the frog's appendages differ from those of a man?

9. Using the blunt end of a pencil *gently* prod the frog until it jumps.

J. What is the function of each pair of appendages in the jumping process?
K. You can leap somewhat as the frog does but the frog cannot stand erect as you do. By examining the structure of the frog's legs and trunk, what evidence can you give to support the above statement?

10. Locate the frog's nostrils and by observing carefully, watch the frog breathe (ducts lead from the nostrils to the posterior part of the mouth cavity).

11. Without touching the frog, watch the floor of the mouth (upper throat).

L. What happens to the mouth cavity when the floor of the mouth is lowered? Does it get larger or smaller?
M. From where can air have come to fill the mouth cavity?

12. Observe the motion of the nostrils.

N. How does their motion relate to the motion of the floor of the mouth?
O. As the floor of the mouth is raised, where can the air in the mouth cavity go?
P. When you breathe, where does the principal motion occur?
Q. Can you breathe with your mouth open? Can the frog?

13. Remove the bandage from the frog's leg and place the frog in the water at the end of a large aquarium.

R. How are the toes used in swimming?
S. What structure is associated with the toes in swimming?
T. Are these structures present on the fingers?

14. Try to get the frog to float.

U. What is the position of the eyes, ears and nostrils with respect to the surface of the water?

15. Hold the frog under water for two minutes.
V. Do you observe any breathing movements? Try to explain your answer.
W. While the frog is under the water, do you see any eye structure which is lacking in man? If so, describe it.
16. Return the frog to the container provided by the teacher.

PROCEDURE B. THE EXAMINATION OF A DEAD FROG

1. Place the frog on the dissecting dish, ventral side upwards and fasten it to the wax or cork by inserting pins through the ends of the appendages.
2. The skin of the frog is attached quite loosely to the muscles. With the forceps, hold the skin free from the muscles of the ventral body wall and use scissors to make a small crosswise cut through the skin at the midline of the abdomen. See Figure 4.1A.
3. Referring to Figure 4.1B, insert one tip of the scissors into this opening and cut along the midline of the body towards the region of the throat. Keep the lower blade of the scissors as horizontal as possible during cutting.
4. Make another cut along the midline towards the anus.
5. Refer to Figure 4.1C. Cut laterally from the ends of the longitudinal cuts as shown in this figure.
6. Refer to Figure 4.1D. There are now two flaps of skin which can be opened to the side. To open them fully and pin them down you must separate the skin from the body wall in a few places; a sharp scalpel is the best instrument for this job.
7. Open the muscular body wall following the procedure used in opening the skin. The organs of the body cavity lie just inside the body wall, so be sure to lift the body wall from the organs beneath and to insert only the tip of the scissors while cutting.

Figure 4.1 Steps in opening the body cavity of a frog.

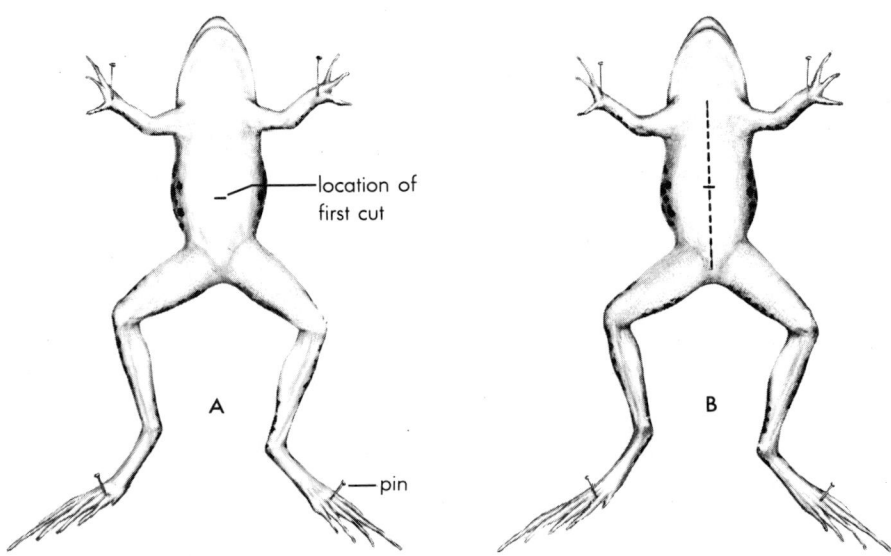

When cutting towards the throat, you will run into the breastbone; be very careful to avoid cutting the organs which lie beneath it.

In opening the body wall laterally, you may remove about 8 mm of breastbone. This may require some effort.

8. Examine the organs of your specimen. How many organs can you identify?
9. On the frog's right side the liver covers the *gall bladder*. Using forceps, raise the liver and find the gall bladder.

A. What colour is the gall bladder?

10. At the posterior end of the stomach where it joins the small intestine there is a narrow constriction, the *pyloric sphincter*. Identify the pyloric sphincter.
11. Identify the pancreas.
12. Remove the stomach and, using scissors, slit it along its outer curvature and spread it open.
13. Examine it with a hand lens and give a description.
14. Free the small intestine from the *mesentery* (the membrane which holds it in place) and discard it.
15. If your specimen is female, remove the eggs and the oviducts (white coiled tubes through which the eggs pass).
16. Push back the mesentery and the remaining organs and look for the kidneys which are attached to the back.

B. What colour are they?

17. Describe their shape.
18. If your frog is male you will find a *testis*, a yellowish bean-shaped organ attached to each kidney. Determine whether or not testes are present.
19. Attached to the anterior end of each kidney you may find clusters of yellowish finger-like structures, the *fat bodies*. These vary in size depending on the time of year. Compare the fat bodies in your frog with those in frogs dissected by other groups.

C. Are the fat bodies usually larger in males or in females?

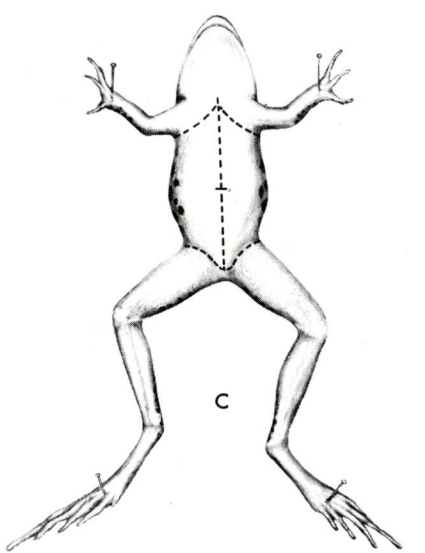

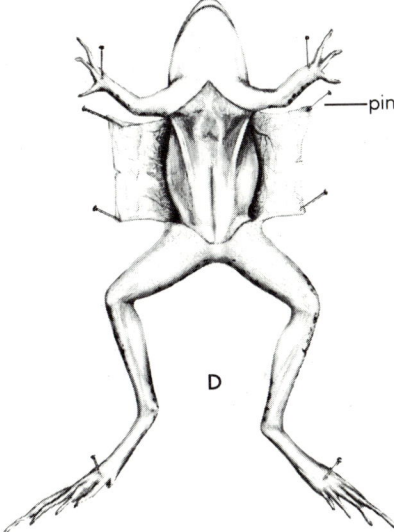

20. Using a hand lens, locate the thin tube which leads from the posterior end of the kidneys.

D. To what does it lead?

21. Dispose of your frog as directed by your teacher.

SUMMARY

On the basis of this investigation and your understanding of your own body, write a brief comparison of the structures and functions of frog and man.

FOR FURTHER INVESTIGATION

1. Divide a group of live frogs into two sets, each containing the same number of individuals. Weigh and mark each frog. Leave one set overnight in a container with a small amount of water; then weigh again. Leave the other set overnight in a container without water; then weigh again. Compare the data from the two sets of frogs. Suggest an explanation.

2. Prepare one of the dead frogs as a skeleton. First, remove as much flesh as possible, using scalpel and forceps. This is a rather difficult task because many of the bones are small and delicate: be careful not to cut through the small ones in the appendages and the thin ones in the head. Second, gently simmer the roughed-out skeleton for about thirty minutes in a little water to which some soap powder has been added. Third, gently scrape the remaining flesh from the bones, using a scalpel and a stiff-bristled toothbrush. Finally, using thin wire, assemble the bones in their natural relationship to each other and attach them to a piece of stiff cardboard.

ACQUIRING ENERGY AND MATERIALS

Animals live almost everywhere: in water, in soil, under logs, in trees, and within other organisms. Accompanying this diversity of environments is an astonishing structural diversity among animals. But there is one striking similarity among all animals – they spend a great deal of time either eating or hunting for food. Our primitive ancestors, too, spent most of their time seeking and consuming food. Today you don't spend much time hunting, but consider how much of your parents' time is spent in earning money to pay the food bill. Eating is the means by which animals acquire energy. Eating is also the means of acquiring materials for the repair of tissues and for growth.

In the general sense, 'food' is the word for things that animals eat, but in this book we have used it in a special sense – to indicate materials from which organisms can release usable energy. Materials that can be used in any manner – for repair, for growth, for regulation of body processes, as well as for energy-release – are nutrients. Thus all foods are nutrients, but not all nutrients are foods.

As they eat, animals obtain, in addition to foods in the narrow sense, minerals (such as iron and calcium compounds), vitamins (used in regulating various body functions) and water. For the release of energy, all animals must also obtain oxygen, which is usually not classified as a nutrient. Acquiring energy and materials, then, is a matter of taking in things from the environment.

NUTRITION

The processes by which animals obtain, distribute and use nutrients are known collectively as *nutrition*. Nutrition can be considered under three headings: (1) ingestion (taking food into a digestive cavity); (2) digestion (the breakdown of large food molecules to small molecules that can pass through cell membranes); and (3) absorption.

Ingestion. A microscopic particle of food might be overlooked by many animals, but to a sponge it is a meal. Sponges have no special organs for food-getting. Indeed, they have no organs at all; their bodies are merely collections of cells. One kind of sponge cell has a flagellum similar to that of *Euglena*. The beating of such flagella keeps a current of water moving through the sponge. When a food particle comes by, one of the cells may engulf it and draw it into a vacuole, just as an *Amoeba* does. This process of taking food into some cavity of the body (*ingestion*) is a characteristic of animals that distinguishes them from plants.

Many other aquatic animals ingest food that is brought to them by water currents. Some, however, actively pursue food. For land animals, mere waiting seldom provides a sufficient supply. An animal must have some means of seizing a food object. If the food consists of active, living organisms, they have to be caught. One way in which predators do this is by poisoning the prey. For example, the tentacles of coelenterates are equipped with stinging

Figure 4.2 Can you see how the tongue of this chameleon is used as an organ of ingestion?   X 1/3

capsules. Each capsule contains a long, spirally coiled, hollow thread with barbs near the base. When some food organism brushes one of the tentacles in passing, the thread is shot out with such force that it pierces the body of the victim, injecting it with a paralysing poison. The stunned or dead animal is then drawn into the 'mouth' by the tentacles.

When a leech finds a victim, it attaches itself by means of a posterior sucker. Then an anterior sucker is applied, a wound is inflicted with a three-toothed jaw, and the blood of the victim is taken in as food. The victim may not suffer serious injury. A leech may remain attached to the same food source for a long time, or it may drop off until another meal is needed.

Among vertebrates, jaws, beaks and teeth are structures that aid ingestion. The jaws of snakes illustrate an adaptation that permits them to swallow prey much larger than their mouth openings: the lower jaw can be completely disengaged from the upper jaw and the two can be moved independently so that food is forced into the throat.

Ingested food enters some sort of cavity within an animal's body – a *digestive cavity*. Digestive cavities are of three main kinds: a temporary, completely enclosed, intracellular cavity (food vacuole); a cavity with one opening; and a tubular cavity with two openings (an *alimentary canal*).

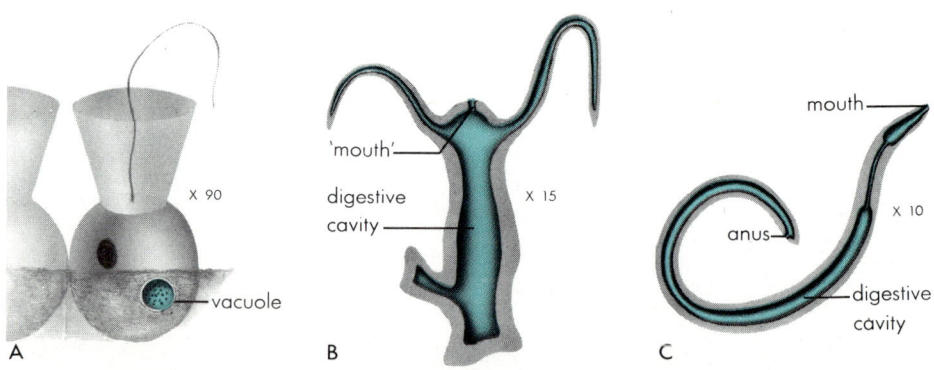

Figure 4.3 Kinds of digestive cavities: (A) *Intracellular* (vacuole) – in a cell of a sponge. (B) *Extracellular* with one opening (sac) – in a *Hydra*. (C) Extracellular with two openings (alimentary canal) – in a roundworm.

Digestion. We have discussed the entry of materials into cells; by and large, only relatively small molecules can pass readily through cell membranes. But most foods that animals ingest are neither small molecules nor even very tiny particles. Even the microscopic particles taken in by sponges are much too large to pass through cell membranes. Until a food is actually within a cell membrane, it cannot be of use to that cell. In almost all cases, then, foods taken in by animals must be broken down into small molecules. The processes by which this breakdown is accomplished are known collectively as *digestion*.

Although most foods must be changed chemically during the course of digestion, chemical reactions proceed very slowly unless food is first reduced to relatively small pieces or particles. This breakdown of large pieces of food into smaller particles is the *physical phase* of digestion. Most mammals have teeth that cut or grind the food, but in many other animals the physical phase of digestion is accomplished by muscular movements of the digestive cavity, known as *peristalsis*. The gizzard of a bird, for example, is a specialized part of the stomach that grinds food into small particles; in some species its effectiveness is increased by bits of sand and small pebbles that the bird swallows while eating. Although the physical phase of digestion is important in most species, in many it is unimportant. For example, a python may swallow a whole young pig and lie quietly for a week while digestion proceeds without a physical phase.

The *chemical phase* of digestion is simply the reverse of the synthetic processes described in the chapter on bioenergetics. The bonds connecting units in large molecules are broken by *hydration cleavage* – the reverse of dehydration synthesis.

In sponges and to a varying degree in coelenterates and flatworms, chemical digestion is *intracellular* – that is, it takes place 'inside' a cell. Because a cell forms a food vacuole by surrounding a food particle with a section of cell membrane, a vacuole is really an enclosed bit of an organism's environment. Enzymes that catalyse the reactions of the chemical phase of digestion are secreted into the food vacuole. As chemical digestion proceeds, the resulting small molecules pass from the vacuole into the cytoplast. Only then is food truly inside the cell.

In most animals, however, digestion is largely or exclusively *extracellular* – enzymes are secreted *from* cells *into* a digestive cavity. Thus a digestive cavity is really only an extension of the environment of the animal – part of the environment more or less surrounded by the body of the organism. A sausage in your stomach is still part of your environment and is not really part of your body. Only when digestion has reduced it to small molecules that can pass through cell membranes does it actually become part of you.

The chemical phase of digestion is basically similar in all animals. However, there is great variation in the form and complexity of digestive systems in which it occurs. In the digestive sac of coelenterates, some of the cells lining the cavity are specialized as enzyme-secreting cells, and some have flagella that move the foods through the cavity; but there is no grouping of cells with a common structure and function into tissues. In the simple digestive tube of a roundworm, digestive enzymes are produced entirely by cells in the lining of the tube, but in most animals with digestive tubes there

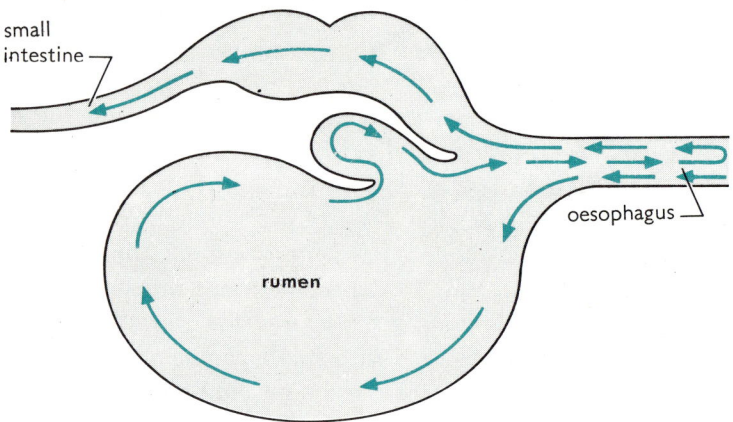

Figure 4.4 The complex stomach of a cow. Food is swallowed as quickly as it is ingested, stored in the rumen, and later brought back into the mouth for chewing. Bacteria in the other parts of the stomach carry on cellulose digestion, for which a cow has no enzymes. What ecological relationship exists between cow and bacteria?

are specialized digestive glands. Many herbivorous vertebrates (cows, rabbits, horses, geese) have special digestive chambers that contain great numbers of micro-organisms which produce enzymes for digesting cellulose. Vertebrates have no such enzymes and so benefit from the presence of these micro-organisms.

Absorption. The rate at which small molecules resulting from digestion can leave the digestive tube to pass into the cells of an animal's body is dependent on the amount of internal surface available. The greater the amount of the internal surface, the higher the rate of transfer of digested substances out of the digestive cavity. Folding is a common method by which the amount of internal surface is increased. In addition to folds, the lining of a part of the digestive tube of a mammal has many minute, finger-like processes known as *villi*. These villi increase the amount of surface area through which small molecules can pass.

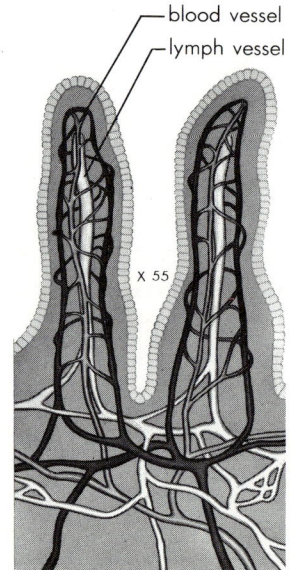

Figure 4.5 Two villi.

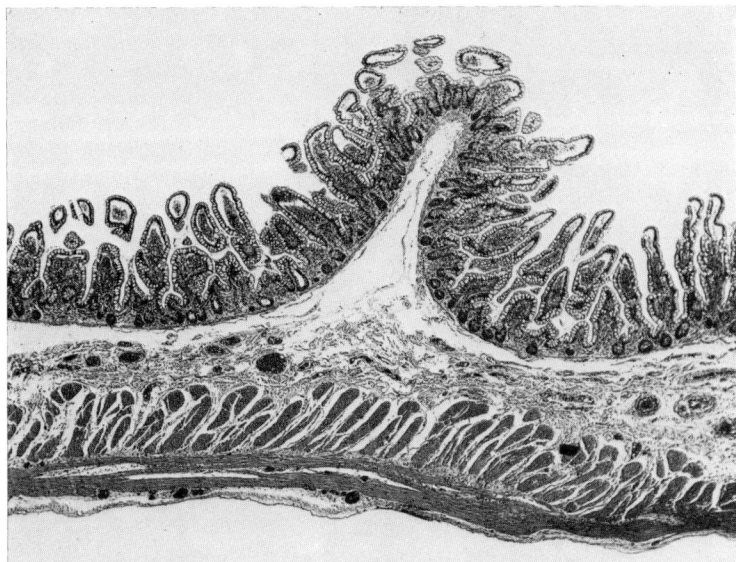

Figure 4.6 Portion of a small intestine. You can see small villi on the surface of the fold on the inner side.   X 20

Digestion in man. So far we have discussed the nature of the digestive process and have looked briefly at some digestive specializations among various animals. Now let us examine in some detail the digestive system of a complex animal. It is convenient to use man – ourselves – as an example.

Digestion begins in the mouth, where the teeth break large pieces of food into smaller pieces. *Saliva*, secreted by three pairs of *salivary glands*, flows into the mouth cavity, where it moistens the food and begins to change it chemically. However, food is usually not in the mouth long enough for much chemical digestion to occur there. The tongue keeps the food in position between the teeth during chewing and then pushes the chewed food to the back of the mouth cavity. There, muscular contractions carry it into the *oesophagus* and thence into the stomach.

In the stomach, muscular contractions knead the food, breaking it up and mixing it with *gastric juice*, secreted by *gastric glands* in the walls of the stomach. Gastric juice contains hydrochloric acid and the enzymes *gastric proteinase* (or *pepsin*), and *rennin*. Gastric juice is mostly water; the contents of the stomach, therefore, soon acquire the consistency of a cream soup. Hydrochloric acid provides the acid conditions required for the action of pepsin, which catalyses the breaking of peptide bonds in some protein molecules, producing large fragments of protein molecules (polypeptides). Rennin, which is found only in mammals, coagulates milk so that it will stay in the stomach for a sufficiently long period to be broken down by other

106   Looking into Organisms

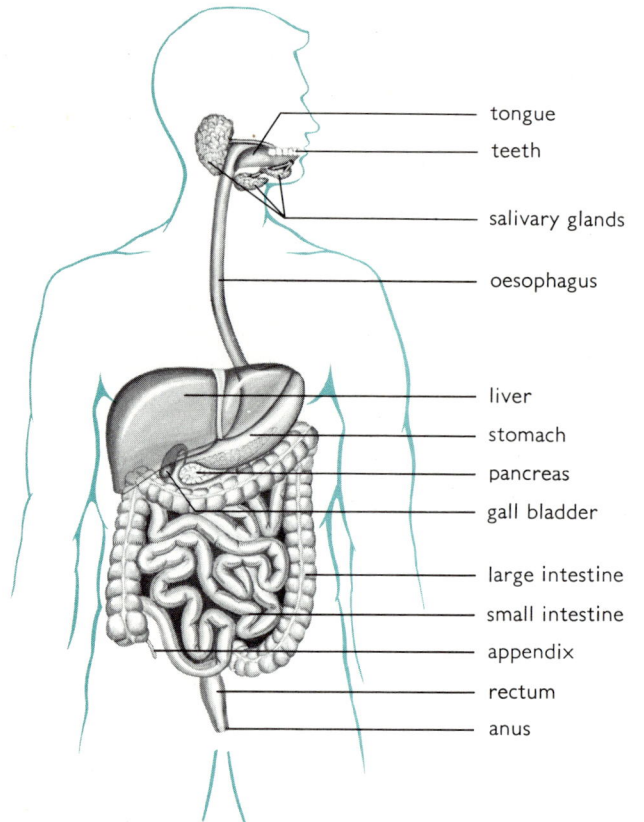

Figure 4.7 Digestive system of man. The *appendix*, attached to the large intestine, is a sac that has no known function in man. The *rectum* is the posterior end of the large intestine.

enzymes. This is especially important in very young mammals which feed entirely on milk. Contraction of the *pyloric sphincter* (a circular layer of muscle in the wall of the digestive tube between the stomach and the small intestine) holds the food mass in the stomach for up to four or five hours.

From time to time the pyloric sphincter relaxes, permitting some of the *chyme* (semi-digested food) to pass from the stomach into the small intestine. In the small intestine three more digestive juices are added to the chyme. These juices are alkaline and therefore neutralize the hydrochloric acid of the chyme. This is important because the enzymes that are active in the small intestine require an approximately neutral medium. The first of these juices is *bile*, which is secreted by the liver and stored in the gall bladder. Human bile contains no digestive enzymes, but bile is important because it neutralizes acid and contains substances that cause large globules of fat to be broken up into fine droplets. This permits the chemical digestion of fats to take place much more rapidly. *Pancreatic juice* contains several enzymes that catalyse the digestion of proteins, fats and carbohydrates. *Trypsin* catalyses the reaction which breaks down proteins into peptides and amino acids; *lipase* catalyses the breakdown of fats to fatty acids and glycerol; and *amylase* assists in the breakdown of starch to maltose. Additional enzymes are added to the small intestine in the *intestinal juice*. There are other peptidases which assist trypsin in the complete breakdown of proteins to amino acids, and *sucrase*, *lactase* and *maltase* which help to break down sucrose, lactose and maltose respectively into glucose and other simple sugars. Most chemical digestion occurs in the small intestine.

In the small intestine also, almost all absorption of nutrients occurs. Through the surface of the villi, amino acids, simple sugars and other nutrients are absorbed by diffusion or active transport into the blood. Some fat molecules are absorbed without being digested; they pass into the lymph vessels of the villi. Most of the fatty acids and glycerol recombine during absorption to form fat, which then passes into the lymph vessels; very small amounts of fatty acids are absorbed into both the lymph vessels and the blood vessels.

Normally, digestion and absorption are completed in four to seven hours, and substances left in the small intestine then pass into the large intestine. There much of the water is absorbed. Undigested foods and indigestible substances, together with mucus, dead cells from the lining of the digestive tube, and bacteria, make up the *faeces*, which leave the digestive tube through the *anus*.

Figure 4.8 Summary of chemical digestion in mammals. Products absorbed are shown in italic type. In what connection were these substances discussed in Chapter 2?

SECRETION	ENZYME	SUBSTANCES ACTED UPON	PRODUCT
saliva	amylase	starch	maltose
gastric juice	gastric proteinase	some protein	polypeptides
pancreatic juice	amylases	starch	maltose
	lipase	fats	*glycerol* and *fatty acids*
	pancreatic proteinases	protein	polypeptides and smaller fragments
	peptidases	polypeptides and smaller fragments	*amino acids*
intestinal juice	disaccharidases	sucrose, maltose, lactose	*simple sugars*
	peptidases	polypeptides	*amino acids*

INVESTIGATION 4.2

THE ACTION OF A DIGESTIVE ENZYME

PURPOSE
Here you will investigate the effects of varying conditions on the action of salivary amylase.

BACKGROUND INFORMATION
In Chapter 2 the discussion of enzymes centred on those involved in energy release and in synthesis. Here you will study an enzyme concerned with digestion. Refer to Figure 4.8 to check on the action of salivary amylase.

MATERIALS AND EQUIPMENT

For Procedure A: establishing the normal action of the enzyme

Unsweetened biscuit
Test-tubes, 4
Thermometer (−10 °C to 110 °C range)
Funnel and support
Sheets of filter paper, 2
Iodine–potassium iodide solution
Benedict's solution
Test-tube holder
Bunsen burner

For Procedure B: varying the conditions of enzyme action

Test-tubes, 7
Glass rod
pH test papers
Beakers, 7
Starch solution
Ring stand
Bunsen burner
Test-tube holder
Benedict's solution
Thermometers (−10 °C to 110 °C), 5
Ice
Hydrochloric acid solution, pH 6 and pH 3
Sodium hydroxide solution, pH 8 and pH 11

PROCEDURE A

1. Watch the teacher's demonstration of the action of maltose on warm Benedict's (or Fehling's) solution. Ensure that you could carry out the procedure.
2. Crush a piece of biscuit (about 1 cm^2), put into a test-tube and add warm water (37 °C) to a depth of about 5 cm.
3. Shake and pour into a filter funnel lined with filter paper. Collect the filtrate (the liquid which seeps through the filter paper) in a test-tube until there is about 1 cm in the tube. Collect a further 2 cm in another test-tube.
4. Test the first portion of filtrate for starch and the second for maltose.
5. If the test for maltose is positive (i.e. maltose is present), take another brand of biscuit and repeat Instructions 2 to 5.
6. Select one pupil and ask him (or her) to salivate and collect the saliva in a test-tube.
7. When a few cm^3 have been obtained, test for maltose. If the test is positive, select another pupil until a negative test is obtained.
8. Give the pupil with the negative test a piece of biscuit (about 9 cm^2) to chew. The biscuit should be one with a negative test for maltose.
9. After chewing for two or three minutes, deposit the mass of biscuit and saliva into a funnel lined with filter paper.
10. Add 5 cm^3 of water (37 °C) and collect about 3 cm^3 of the filtrate in a test-tube.
11. Test the filtrate for maltose.

A. What conclusions can you draw if the test is (*a*) negative, (*b*) positive?

PROCEDURE B

In Procedure A the enzyme action occurred in its normal situation, in the mouth, i.e. *in vivo* (Latin: in a live condition). To test the action of the enzyme under other conditions, we must work *in vitro* (Latin: in glass – i.e. in a test-tube, beaker, etc.).

1. Collect saliva from the pupil who provided it for Procedure A. Seven test-tubes each filled to a depth of 2 cm will be required.
2. Using the pH papers, determine the pH of the collected saliva.
3. Deal with the seven tubes as follows.
Tube 1. Add a few drops of starch solution and shake the tube. Place in a 37 °C water bath for 10 minutes. Remove and test for maltose.
Tube 2. Add a few drops of starch solution, shake and place the test-tube in a beaker of boiling water. Allow it to remain in the boiling water for 10 minutes. Remove and test for maltose.
Tube 3. Add a few drops of starch solution and shake the test-tube. Place it in a beaker containing crushed ice and allow it to remain there for 10 minutes. Remove and test for maltose.
Tube 4. Add a volume of pH 6 hydrochloric acid equal to the volume of saliva. Mix by rolling the tube between the palms of your hands. Add a few drops of starch solution and mix as before. Place the tube in a water bath at 37 °C for 10 minutes. Remove and test for maltose.
Tube 5. As above, using pH 3 hydrochloric acid in place of the pH 6.
Tube 6. As above, this time using the pH 8 sodium hydroxide solution.
Tube 7. As above, using the pH 11 sodium hydroxide.

STUDYING THE DATA

A. Under what conditions of temperature and pH does the enzyme act *in vivo*?
B. Under which of the experimental temperature conditions did the enzyme act *in vitro*?
C. Under which of the experimental pH conditions did the enzyme act *in vitro*?

CONCLUSIONS

A. Use the data to work out a general statement concerning the effect of temperature variation on the action of the enzyme.
B. Use the data to work out a general statement concerning the effect of pH variation on the action of the enzyme.
C. Would you expect intracellular enzymes to be more sensitive or less sensitive to variations in temperature and pH than extracellular enzymes? Give reasons for your answer.

FOR FURTHER INVESTIGATION

In this investigation conditions were varied rather crudely. More refined techniques can be devised to test the effects of smaller differences in the conditions as the amount of colour change in the test solutions is in proportion to the amount of maltose produced. Thus quantitative studies can be made by carefully controlling the amounts of starch added, test solution used, and the time allowed for the reaction.

OBTAINING OXYGEN

For short periods of time animals may release energy by anaerobic methods, but eventually they depend on cellular respiration. Therefore animals must live in environments where oxygen exists, and they must be able to supply a sufficient amount of oxygen to their cells. Likewise, they must be able to rid themselves of carbon dioxide. The exchange of these gases is respiration in the original sense of the word.

In small animals, such as rotifers and many planktonic crustaceans, uptake of oxygen and release of carbon dioxide can occur entirely through the body

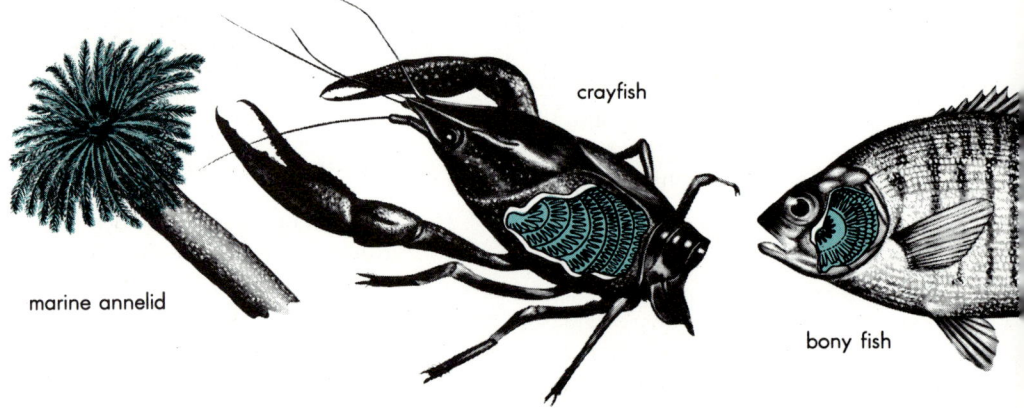

Figure 4.9 Gills in three aquatic animals. The body of the marine annelid is enclosed in a mud tube: only the gills are exposed.

surface. This is because the body surface is large compared with the volume of living material that requires oxygen and produces carbon dioxide. As size increases, the ratio of surface area to volume becomes smaller, though in very flat bodies or in very long cylindrical ones, the change in ratio remains relatively slight. In general, then, larger animals do not have body surfaces large enough to allow a sufficient exchange of gases with their environments. Thus, all but very small or slim animals have organs that increase the surface area through which respiration may occur.

In aquatic animals such organs are usually feathery or plate-like structures called *gills*. These may be waved through the water, or the water may pass over them as the animal moves; dissolved oxygen then diffuses in and carbon dioxide diffuses out through the membranes of the outermost gill cells. Gills are remarkably similar in a wide variety of water animals.

Any surface through which the respiratory gases can diffuse is also a surface through which water can diffuse. Therefore, animals that live on land may lose a great deal of water through their respiratory organs. For this reason terrestrial animals that breathe through gills or through the body surface (slugs, earthworms and salamanders, for example) must live in places where air is moist – that is, where evaporation is slow.

For terrestrial animals that live where the air is dry, an extensive surface is needed within the body where air can be kept moist. Two principal ways of meeting this requirement have evolved. In insects and some other arthropods, a complicated system of air tubes extends to all parts of the body, bringing oxygen directly to most cells. Movements of the body help to move air through the tube system. In air-breathing vertebrates air passes into a pair of sacs so finely partitioned that they have a spongy appearance – the lungs. Through the moist surface of the lungs respiratory gases diffuse.

Again we take man as an example. Movement of the ribs and the diaphragm enlarges the chest cavity, lowering the air pressure in the lungs so

The Functioning Animal 111

Figure 4.10
Movements of breathing in man.

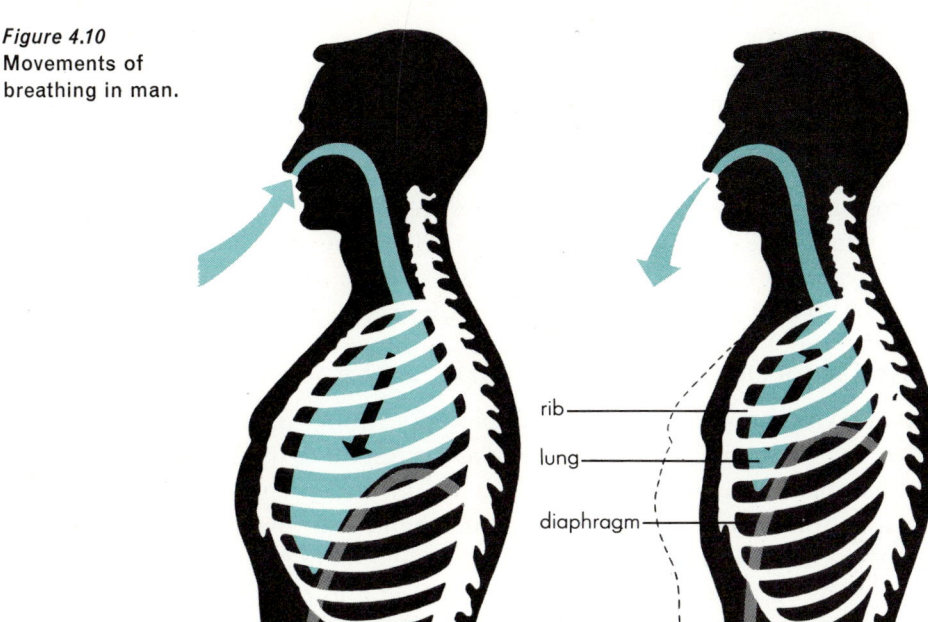

that external air moves inwards. As the air is drawn in through the nostrils and passes through the nasal cavities, it is warmed and moistened. Into the *pharynx* pass both the stream of air from the nasal cavities and food from the mouth. The opening that leads to the lungs is protected by a flap of tissue called the *epiglottis*. It is usually open, admitting air; it closes when food

Figure 4.11 The breathing system of man.

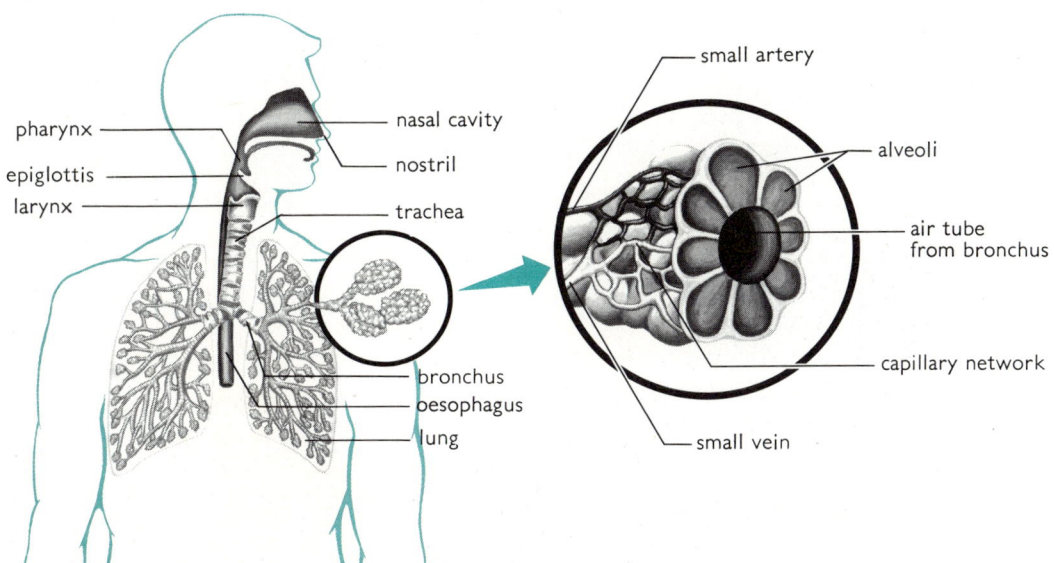

passes by on the way to the oesophagus (not always in time, as you may know from personal experience).

The *trachea* – the air passage that extends through the neck ventral to the oesophagus – divides in the upper chest into two *bronchi*. Each bronchus leads to a lung, where it branches and rebranches, the smallest divisions ending in almost microscopic air sacs, *alveoli*. The enormous number of alveoli provide a very large area of moist surface. The walls of the alveoli are extremely thin and contain a dense network of tiny blood vessels. Respiratory gases diffuse into and out of the blood through the thin membranes.

TRANSPORTING MATERIALS IN THE BODY

In a playful mood one day, a child placed a rubber band tightly around the tip of her cat's tail. Then her attention was turned to other activities, and the rubber band was forgotten. Several weeks later, when the cat's tail was grasped, off came the tip – the rubber band still around it. This incident clearly points to the importance of the circulation of blood. When blood does not reach cells, they are deprived of the food and oxygen it brings to them; also, they are unable to rid themselves of the poisoning wastes that blood takes from them. For such cells, the result is death.

An early milestone in the development of biological science was the discovery of the circulation of the blood. This occurred in the early part of the seventeenth century through the research of William Harvey. As a physician,

Figure 4.12 William Harvey, 1578–1657.

Harvey was interested in the physiology of man; but as a scientist, his curiosity pushed his investigations in many other directions, too. In his book, *On the Motion of the Heart and Blood*, he wrote:

> I have also observed, that almost all animals have truly a heart, not the larger creatures only, and those having red blood but the smaller and seemingly bloodless ones also, such as slugs, snails, scallops, shrimps, crabs, crayfish, and many others; nay even in wasps, hornets and flies. I have with the aid of a magnifying glass, and at the upper part of what is called the tail, both seen the heart pulsating myself, and shown it to many others.

SIMPLER TRANSPORT SYSTEMS

However, Harvey did not know that many animals have much simpler transport systems, lacking not only hearts but even a circulating fluid. The living substance of cells is in constant motion. In a single-celled organism, such movements are an adequate transporting system. They are also adequate in some multicellular organisms. In sponges and coelenterates, for example, almost all cells have some part of their surface exposed to the environment; each cell can obtain its own oxygen and get rid of its own wastes. Though not all cells in these animals take in food, no cell is very far from those that do; so diffusion and active transport are sufficient for the distribution of food materials.

Approximately the same situation occurs in free-living flatworms, but in them the distribution of digested foods is aided by a greatly branched digestive sac that extends to all parts of the body. In roundworms a fluid-filled body cavity surrounds the digestive tube. As the worm wriggles, the fluid is squeezed about from place to place, and in this crude way substances dissolved in it are eventually carried to and from the body cells.

CIRCULATORY SYSTEMS

Usually, an animal that has a body fluid in which substances are transported also has a system of tubes through which the fluid flows. Muscular pumps (usually called hearts) propel the fluid (usually called blood), and the direction of flow is controlled by valves within the tubes. Regardless of detailed anatomical arrangements, the basic function performed by such a *circulatory system* is always the same: At a place where blood flows slowly, in contact with thin membranes, substances move in or out by diffusion or active transport. The blood then moves rather rapidly to another place where it again flows slowly, in contact with thin membranes, and substances again move in or out.

Invertebrate systems. In arthropods and most molluscs blood is pumped through tubes (blood vessels) that empty into body spaces. Through these spaces the blood moves about sluggishly, in close contact with the tissues. Eventually it gets back into another set of tubes, which carry it back to the pumping point. Such an incomplete vascular system is called an *open* circulatory system.

Annelids, on the other hand, have a *closed* circulatory system: blood is enclosed in vessels throughout its course. In an earthworm the system consists of five pairs of hearts and a complicated set of more and more finely branched vessels; these vessels eventually link up again and empty into a large dorsal vessel. This vessel returns the blood to the hearts. Valves along the walls of the vessel keep the blood flowing in one direction throughout the system.

Figure 4.13 Diagrams of fluid transport in four invertebrate animals.

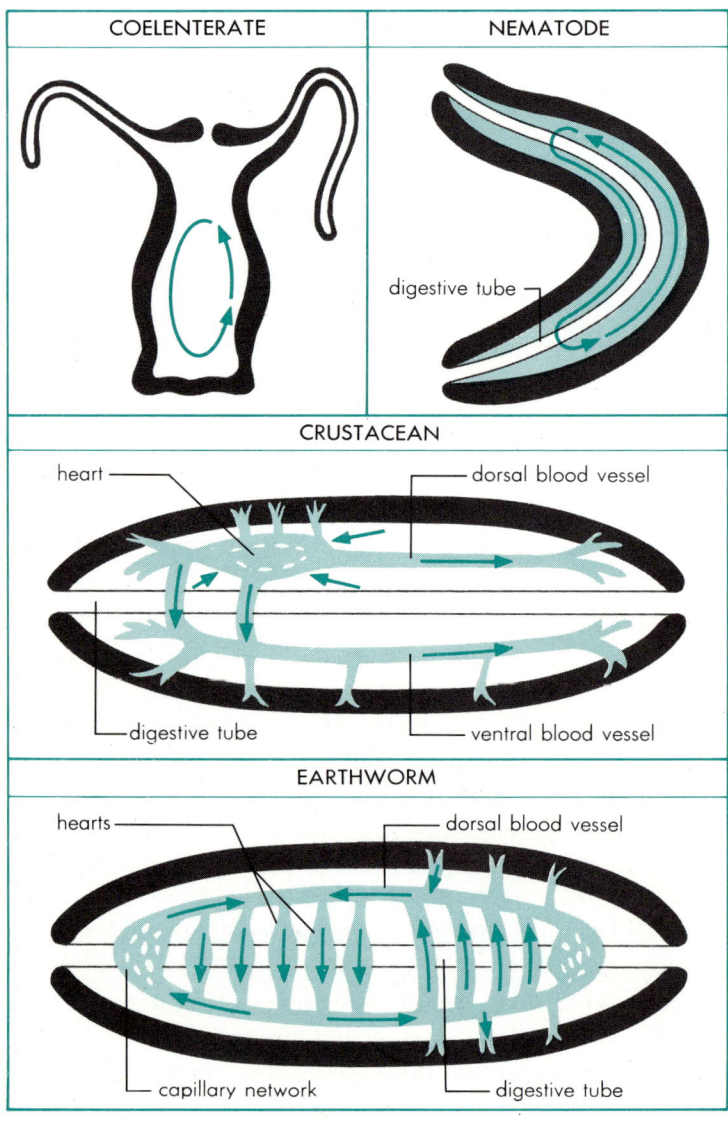

Vertebrate systems. In vertebrates circulation also occurs in a closed system. The vessels of this system are of four kinds. A single, very muscular *heart*, consisting of two or more chambers, keeps blood moving through the systems. *Arteries* have rather thick, muscular walls and carry blood away from the heart. *Veins* have relatively thin walls that contain little muscle tissue; they carry blood towards the heart. *Capillaries* have very thin walls; they connect arteries with veins.

By many ingenious experiments, William Harvey showed that blood leaves a vertebrate heart through arteries and returns to the heart through veins. Therefore, by reasoning he concluded that blood circulates. But he did not know by observation how blood passes from arteries to veins. Harvey lived in the first part of the seventeenth century, before the use of the microscope became widespread. Later in the century Marcello Malpighi first observed capillaries and thus confirmed Harvey's reasoning.

In all mammals and birds the heart is a double pump. Its right and left sides are enclosed in the same wall, but each has its own veins and arteries. In mammals the right side receives blood from almost all parts of the body and sends it to the lungs. The left side receives blood from the lungs and pumps it to all other parts of the body. Each of the pumps has two chambers. An *auricle* receives incoming blood. When the heart muscle relaxes, this blood passes into a *ventricle*. When the heart contracts, the walls of the ventricle give the blood a strong push that sends it out through an artery.

Figure 4.14 Diagrams of circulation in three vertebrate classes. Colour indicates oxygenated blood; grey, deoxygenated blood. A=auricle; V=ventricle.

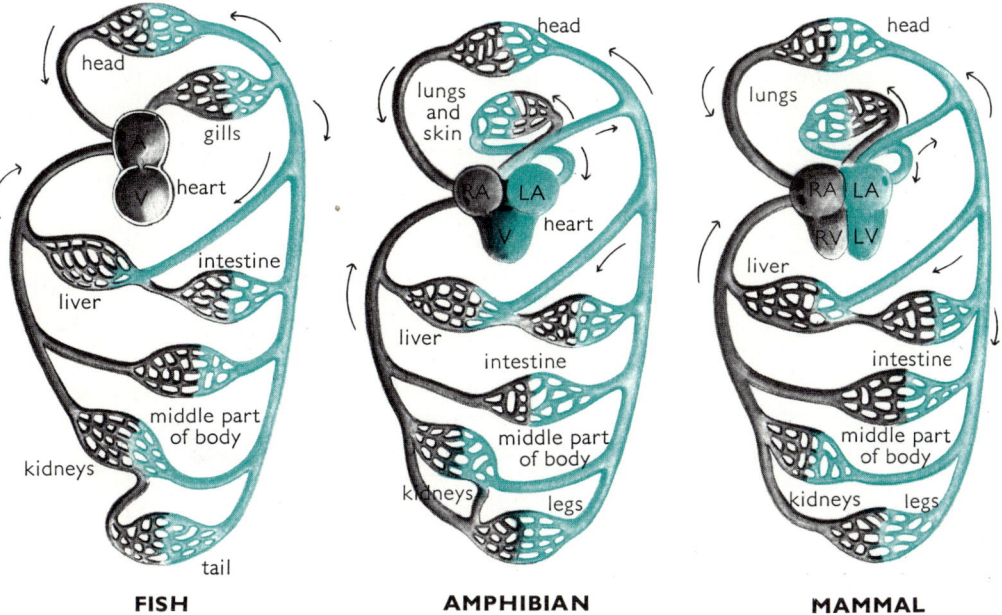

Arteries near the heart contain flaps of tissue that act as valves. When blood is being pushed by contraction of the ventricles, the flaps flatten out and blood flows away from the heart. When the ventricles relax between heartbeats, back pressure of the blood forces the flaps open, preventing the blood from flowing back towards the heart. Such valves are numerous in veins.

The millions of microscopic capillaries have walls only a single cell thick. Through these walls occurs the passage of substances to and from cells – the principal function of blood circulation. As blood flows slowly through the capillaries, substances move from the blood into the cells of the body tissues, and other substances move from the tissues into the blood.

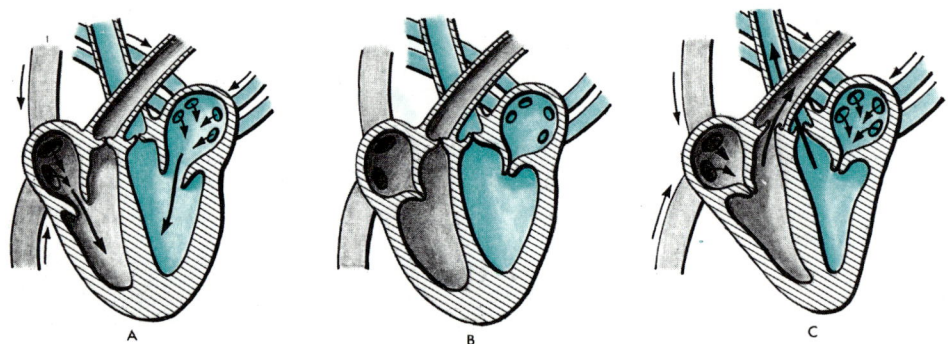

Figure 4.15 Three steps (A, B and C) in the pumping action of a mammalian heart. Why does the blood not flow back into the auricles when the ventricles contract?

BLOOD

In the simpler kinds of marine animals there is little difference between the body fluids and sea water; but in land animals the body fluids are complex mixtures of substances in water, and the environment is a mixture of gases. These two examples are extremes; there are many intermediate degrees of difference between the fluids within animals and the substances in their environments. Such differences are great in fresh-water animals and sometimes rather marked in complex marine animals. In general, blood in organisms with circulatory systems is more or less different from the fluids in the environment.

There is great variation in the blood of different animal groups. Some bloods are red; others are greenish, brownish or colourless. Some contain cells. But all bloods are made up of water in which many substances are dissolved or suspended.

Plasma. When we watch human blood flow from a small wound, it appears to be a uniform red liquid, but if we examine a thin smear of it

Figure 4.16 A centrifuge. Liquids that contain tiny solid particles (as blood does) are placed in the tubes. Rapid whirling separates the particles from the liquid, as shown in Figure *4.17*.

under the microscope, we see many faintly reddish cells; other cells show up when the smear is stained. By means of a centrifuge, these cells can be concentrated and a clear yellowish liquid – *plasma* – obtained.

About 91 per cent of human plasma is water. The rest is made up of substances dissolved or suspended in the water – about 8 per cent proteins, and close to 0.9 per cent minerals, especially compounds of calcium, potassium, sodium and phosphorus. There are also small amounts of amino acids, simple sugars, and wastes from metabolism.

Research during recent years has shown that there is great complexity in blood proteins; among them are the antibodies that result from infection. But many blood proteins are inherited. In general, the more closely related animals are taxonomically, the more blood proteins they have in common. However, even individuals within the same species have some protein differences; it may even be that the blood of each individual has its own unique proteins.

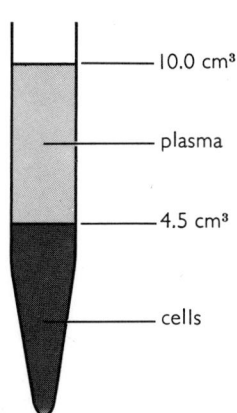

Figure 4.17 Centrifuged human blood. What percentage of the sample was plasma?

Blood cells. Whole blood contains *red cells* (red corpuscles) and *white cells* (white corpuscles). Usually considered with them are *platelets*, which are fragments of cells. The oxygen-carrying ability and colour of blood are primarily due to an iron-containing pigment in the red cells, *haemoglobin*. When oxygen is abundant around a red cell (as it is, for example, in the lung capillaries), it combines with the haemoglobin in the cell, forming *oxyhaemoglobin* (bright red in colour). When oxygen is scarce around a red cell (as it is likely to be in active muscle tissue, for example), the oxygen is released, leaving haemoglobin (a duller red). In the condition called *anaemia* there is either an abnormally low number of red cells or a low haemoglobin content. The activity of an anaemic individual is severely reduced.

ELEMENT	DIAMETER (in μm)	NUMBER (per mm³)	MAIN FUNCTION
 red corpuscles	7–8	4 500 000– 5 500 000	oxygen transport
 white corpuscles	9–12	7 000– 10 000	defence against micro-organisms
platelets	2–4	300 000 (much variation)	blood-clotting

Figure 4.18 A comparison of some characteristics of blood 'elements', a term used by those who wish to emphasize that platelets are only fragments of cells.   all × 1070

Human red cells, which have no nucleus, live 110–120 days; then they are removed from circulation and destroyed in the liver and spleen. The liver salvages iron ions from these cells, and cells in bone marrow use these ions in making new red cells.

White cells, which do have a nucleus, have no haemoglobin and are therefore colourless. Unlike red cells, they do not merely float along in the plasma; a white cell can move about very much like an *Amoeba*, even slipping through the thin walls of capillaries and wandering about among the cells of muscle and other tissues. There are several varieties of white cells, which differ in size, reaction to stains, and function. Primarily, however, white cells serve to destroy invading particles such as pathogenic organisms. They do this by engulfing and digesting the particles much as an *Amoeba* does. Some white cells also seem to aid in the repair of wounds.

Platelets are colourless, usually spherical, and without nuclei. Their lifespan is estimated to be four days.

Clotting. Normally when a vertebrate animal suffers a small wound, the blood at the surface of the wound clots; but if blood is gently drawn into a siliconized vessel, it will not clot. Neither exposure to air nor slowing of the flow is the cause of clotting. The process of clotting illustrates the complexity that research sometimes reveals behind apparently simple biological processes.

Clotting begins with the platelets. Whenever they are exposed to a rough surface – almost any surface other than the smooth lining of the blood vessels – they tend to stick to it and then to break up. As they do so, they release a substance called *thromboplastin*. The thromboplastin acts as an enzyme to bring about a change in *prothrombin*, a protein in the plasma. This reaction, which will not occur unless calcium is present (as it always is in normal blood), converts prothrombin to *thrombin*. Thrombin then acts as an enzyme to convert *fibrinogen*, a soluble blood protein, into *fibrin*, an insoluble substance that forms threads within the plasma. Blood cells are trapped in a network of fibrin threads, thus building up a clot.

LYMPH

Some plasma readily passes through the capillary walls, though little of its protein content does so, and white blood cells may also escape from the closed vascular system. Red cells never pass through the walls of the blood vessels. Thus the fluid that bathes cells, though much like blood, is nearly colourless and is lower in protein content.

Some of this fluid may ooze back into the blood capillaries; the remainder of it collects in another set of vessels, where it is called *lymph*. These vessels join each other, forming larger vessels. Contractions of the muscles that surround the lymph vessels move the lymph along. In the walls of the small intestine, lymph vessels absorb fats; and many of the metabolic wastes of cells pass into the tissue fluid. Thus lymph has a higher fat content and a higher waste content than does blood.

Eventually all lymph vessels join, forming a duct that carries the lymph to the region of the left shoulder; there the lymph is emptied into a vein. Thus the fluids that leave the blood at the capillaries are brought back into the blood again.

Enlargements occur at several points in the lymphatic system. In these enlargements, or *lymph nodes*, the vessels divide into tiny twisted passages; as a result, the lymph flows slowly through the nodes. Here pathogenic organisms and other foreign materials that may have entered the body are attacked by white blood cells. During an infection the lymph nodes may contain so many white blood cells that they become greatly swollen. You may have felt them in your armpits or in your neck during a severe cold.

INVESTIGATION 4.3

A HEART AT WORK

PURPOSE
In this investigation you will study the effects of varying environmental temperature on the heartbeat of a small animal.

BACKGROUND INFORMATION
Crustaceans of the genus *Daphnia* are abundant in small bodies of fresh water. Individuals are just about large enough to be seen with the naked eye in good light, though when magnified even 20 times, many of the internal organs — including the heart — can be seen through the body wall.

MATERIALS AND EQUIPMENT
(for each group)

Daphnia, in a small beaker of aquarium water, 6 to 8
Thermometer (−10 °C to 110 °C)
Dropper
Microscope slide with depression
Stereomicroscope
Stopwatch or watch with a second hand
Large beaker
Crushed ice
Hot water
Graph paper, one sheet per pupil
Hand tally counter
Paper tissues

PROCEDURE
1. Using the dropper, transfer one *Daphnia* to the depression in the slide. Soak up excess water with a piece of paper tissue as, by keeping the amount of water at a minimum, you increase the likelihood that the animal will lie on its side, in which position the heart action can best be seen.
2. Look carefully for the beating of the heart, using the stereomicroscope. Do not confuse its motion with that of the legs which also beat rhythmically.
3. Return the *Daphnia* to the beaker.
4. Read through the remainder of the procedure and formulate an appropriate hypothesis.
5. Check that the temperature of the water in which the *Daphnia* are living is at room temperature. Mount a *Daphnia* as before.
6. One member of the group should be appointed timekeeper, another the observer.
7. The observer should familiarize himself with the hand tally counter and should practise clicking at each heartbeat.

Figure 4.19 Daphnia.   X 100

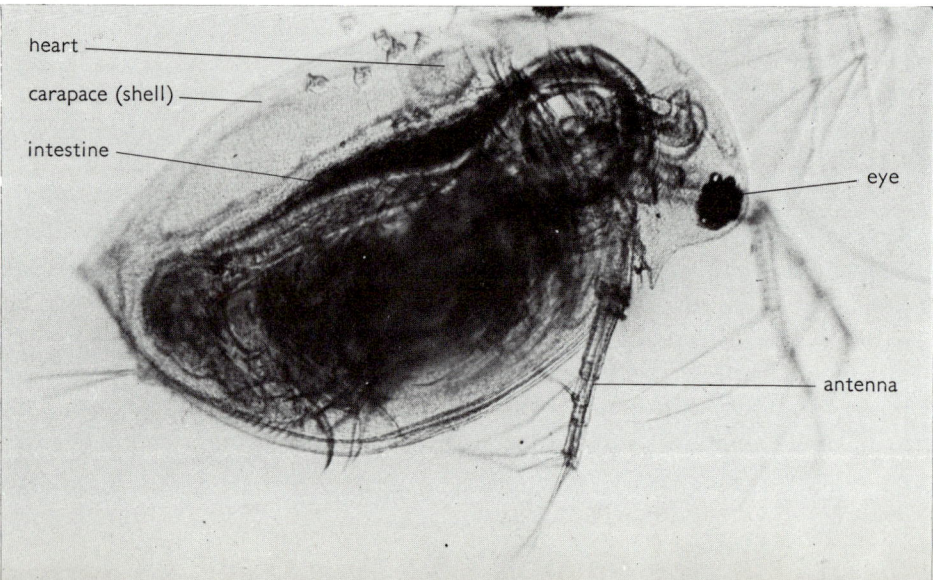

8. When the observer is ready, the timer should start him, and then stop him after 15 seconds. The number of heartbeats recorded should be multiplied by 4 to give the rate per minute. Record your result.
9. Make at least 3 timed counts, allowing each member of the group to take a turn at being an observer or a timer.
10. Return the *Daphnia* to the beaker.
11. Place the beaker of *Daphnia* in a larger beaker containing water and crushed ice. Stir the water in the *Daphnia* beaker gently with a thermometer.
12. When the water temperature reaches the point assigned to your group by your teacher, quickly transfer a *Daphnia* to the slide and make at least 3 counts. Record the counts.
13. While the counts are being made, other members of the group should remove the *Daphnia* beaker from the large beaker, pour out the iced water and replace it with hot water (50 °C–70 °C).
14. Place the *Daphnia* beaker in the hot water and stir gently with a thermometer. By the time the water temperature in the *Daphnia* beaker reaches the second point assigned to your group, counting at the lower temperature should be finished. Transfer a *Daphnia* from the warm water to the slide and make at least 3 counts as quickly as possible. Record your results.
15. Express all results as the number of heartbeats per minute.

STUDYING THE DATA

1. Consider the data obtained from *Daphnia* at room temperature.

A. Why were several counts taken by each team?
B. What factors might account for variability in these data?
C. Compare the variability in the data from all groups with the variability in the data from your own group. How can you account for any differences?
D. Calculate the average rate of heartbeat from the assembled class data. Which is more likely to be reliable, the average obtained by your team or the average obtained by the class? Give reasons for your answer.

2. Assemble the data on heartbeat at different temperatures. If two or more groups obtained data at the same temperature, calculate a general average for that temperature.
3. Graph the data, placing the temperature on the horizontal axis and the heartbeat rate on the vertical axis.

CONCLUSIONS

A. On the basis of your graph make a general statement concerning the effects of variation in environmental temperature on the rate of heartbeat in *Daphnia*.
B. Does your graph support your hypothesis?
C. Would you expect similar effects of temperature on the heartbeat of (*a*) a frog, (*b*) a dog? Give reasons for your answer.

FOR FURTHER INVESTIGATION

1. Young pond snails have thin shells through which their heart can be seen. Make a study of snail heartbeat for comparison with that of *Daphnia*. Try to account for any differences you find.

2. The easily observed heart of *Daphnia* can lead to some understanding of the way in which drugs affect the heartbeat rate. Investigate the effects of ethanol (about 5 per cent), or a tranquillizer (e.g. chloropromazine) and of a stimulant (e.g. dexedrine sulphate) on *Daphnia* heartbeat.

REMOVING MATERIALS FROM THE BODY

Large sea turtles shed tears when they go ashore to lay their eggs. These are neither tears of joy nor tears of sorrow. They have nothing to do with egg-laying and are shed at other times also, but they are most likely to be observed by man when the turtles are ashore. This shedding of tears is merely a way in which salts acquired from sea water are kept from accumulating in the body of the animal. All organisms must constantly release materials into the environment, just as they must constantly take materials in from the environment.

EXCRETION, SECRETION AND ELIMINATION

The process by which waste materials are removed from cells is called *excretion*. If the substance that passes out of the cell is one that is in some way useful to the organism, then the process is called *secretion*. Because carbon dioxide is a metabolic waste formed in every living animal cell, it is an excretion from each cell. Gastric juice, which passes through the membranes of cells that line the stomach, is a secretion because substances in it are useful in digesting food. In these two examples, the distinction between excretion and secretion is clear, but sometimes the distinction is difficult to make.

Both secretion and excretion involve the passage of substances through cell membranes. They may occur by diffusion. Frequently, however, a substance is more abundant in the environment outside a cell than it is within. Then energy is required to 'pump' the substance out of the cell by the process of active transport.

Once a substance has passed out through the cell membrane of an organism, it has been excreted or secreted, but – especially in multicellular organisms – it may not be entirely out of the body of the organism. For example, tears are secreted (or excreted – this is one of the cases where it is difficult to decide) from the cells above the eye into ducts that empty on to the surface of the eyeball. Tears in the tear ducts are no longer in cells, but they are still within the body, at least in the usual sense. The process by which substances are forced out of body cavities – either small ones, such as tear ducts, or large ones, such as the digestive tube – is called *elimination*.

To clarify the usage of the three terms 'excretion', 'secretion' and 'elimination', consider bile. Bile contains substances useful in digestion; it is thus a secretion from cells of the liver. Some of the bile substances, however, have no usefulness – substances derived from the destruction of old red blood cells, for example. These are wastes, so bile is also an excretion. Finally, bile becomes a part of the substances that are eliminated from the digestive tube through the anus.

KINDS OF EXCRETION

Now consider a little more carefully what we mean by 'wastes'. Some products of metabolism are, in one way or another, *toxic* (poisonous) to protoplasm – for example ammonia, which is formed in the breakdown of proteins. Some substances, however, are toxic only if large amounts accumulate in the cells – for example, sodium chloride, which is always present in cells. This salt is always being taken in by diffusion from the environment. Only by continuous excretion can the normal proportion of sodium chloride be maintained in the cells. Even water, which forms such a large proportion of any cell, must be kept in balance between input and output. In general, then, any substance can be called a waste if an organism has too much of it.

In small aquatic animals wastes may simply diffuse out through cell membranes, in the way that respiratory gases are exchanged with the environment. Sponges and coelenterates, though not always small, also excrete waste directly through the body surfaces, since all their cells are close to the water environment. Most animals, however, have special devices for ridding the body of wastes.

Water. By the process of cellular respiration, water is constantly being produced by animal cells. What happens to this water depends on the kind of environment in which the animal lives. Consider a jellyfish living in the sea. Its cells contain a complex mixture of substances in water. Outside the cell membranes is another complex mixture in water, the salty sea. If the concentrations of water molecules in the two mixtures differ, water molecules move from one to the other by diffusion; but in jellyfish, and a great many other marine invertebrates, the concentrations inside and outside are normally almost equal. As fast as metabolic water is produced, it diffuses into the environment.

Now consider a planarian living in a fresh-water stream. There are very few dissolved substances in fresh water; the concentration of water molecules is high. In a planarian's cells the percentage of dissolved substances is high, which means that the water concentration is relatively low. Therefore, water is always diffusing into a planarian's cells. Metabolic water is constantly added to this excess. We might expect that water would accumulate within a planarian's cells, swell against the cell membranes, and eventually burst them. When certain drugs that interfere with the mechanism of active transport are used experimentally on planarians, this is exactly what happens. For fresh-water animals, then, excretion of water is necessary to survival.

The same problem faces us. We take in a great deal of fresh water; and, of course, our cells also produce water by metabolic processes. Though (as land animals) we are always in danger of drying out, we are also in danger of swelling up with excess water, and in the condition called dropsy this actually occurs. All through our lives we and all other land animals walk a very thin tightrope, balanced between having too much water and too little.

A great variety of structures maintain a water balance within the cells of animals. In planarians this function is performed by a system of tubules spread throughout the body. The functional unit of the system is a *flame cell*. Each flame cell, located at the end of a tubule, has a tuft of cilia that projects into the tubule. The waving of the tuft (to early microscopists, this action resembled the flickering of a flame) creates a slight negative pressure, or suction, within the tubule. This tends to draw water from the surrounding tissues and push it along the tubule. The many tubules join and eventually empty into the environment through a pore.

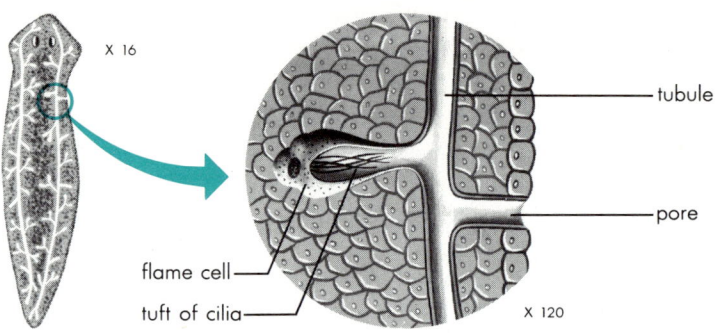

Figure 4.20 Excretory structure in a planarian.

Variations of the flame-cell system are found in some other invertebrates. Most annelids (including earthworms), as well as molluscs and crustaceans, have quite different excretory systems. In these animals the functional unit is a tubule around which there may be a network of blood capillaries. In many cases the tubule connects with the body cavity. Fluid from the body cavity is modified as it passes through the tubule to the outside; more wastes are added and useful materials are absorbed back into the blood or body fluid. In other cases the tubule is blind, so that all substances to be excreted must be transported into it. In vertebrates somewhat similar blind tubules are found in the kidneys.

Nitrogenous wastes. There is considerable evidence that the organs usually called excretory – from the flame cells in flatworms to kidneys in vertebrates – have evolved chiefly as water-regulating devices. They still deal with water, but in most animals they also function in the excretion of nitrogen-bearing wastes.

Amino acids, all of which contain nitrogen, are used by cells to build up proteins. When an animal is growing, rather large quantities of amino acids may be required. But often the amino-acid intake is much greater than requirements. This is especially true of animals that are no longer growing. Moreover, some proteins of an animal's body are constantly being broken down into amino acids. Therefore, a surplus of amino acids usually occurs.

Unlike carbohydrates and fats, amino acids (or proteins formed from them) cannot be stored in large quantities, and they cannot be used for the release of energy until the amino group ($-NH_2$) is removed. In vertebrates the removal of amino groups occurs chiefly in the liver.

The ammonia (NH_3) that results from this process is quite toxic. It is also quite soluble, and if a large supply of water is available, the ammonia can be carried out of the body in solution. In some aquatic animals this is exactly what happens. If a fresh-water fish is placed through a tight-fitting rubber partition so that head and gills are on one side, and tail and the opening from the kidneys are on the other, ammonia accumulates in the water on the 'head side' of the partition. In such fishes, then, nitrogenous wastes are excreted through the gills.

In other vertebrates the kidneys are the main avenue through which nitrogenous wastes are excreted, but the wastes are not in the form of ammonia. In birds and reptiles (and in insects, which also are terrestrial animals) amino groups are incorporated into *uric acid*. This rather complex substance is almost insoluble and can be excreted with the loss of only a small amount of water. In most adult amphibians and mammals, however, the amino groups are converted to *urea* – $CO(NH_2)_2$. Unlike uric acid, urea is soluble. It diffuses into the blood, from which it is removed by the kidneys.

(A) Structural formula   (B) Model

Figure 4.21 Urea. How many molecules of urea must a mammal excrete to rid itself of the same amount of nitrogen as does a fish excreting 100 molecules of ammonia?

Three distinct processes, all of which require the expenditure of energy, occur in a mammalian kidney (Figure 4.22). The first step is filtration of blood. This occurs in a *glomerulus*, a ball of capillary-like blood vessels, surrounded by the expanded end of a tubule. Each kidney contains many thousands of glomeruli. Blood pressure (which represents energy expended by the ventricle in pumping blood) forces some of the fluid of the blood

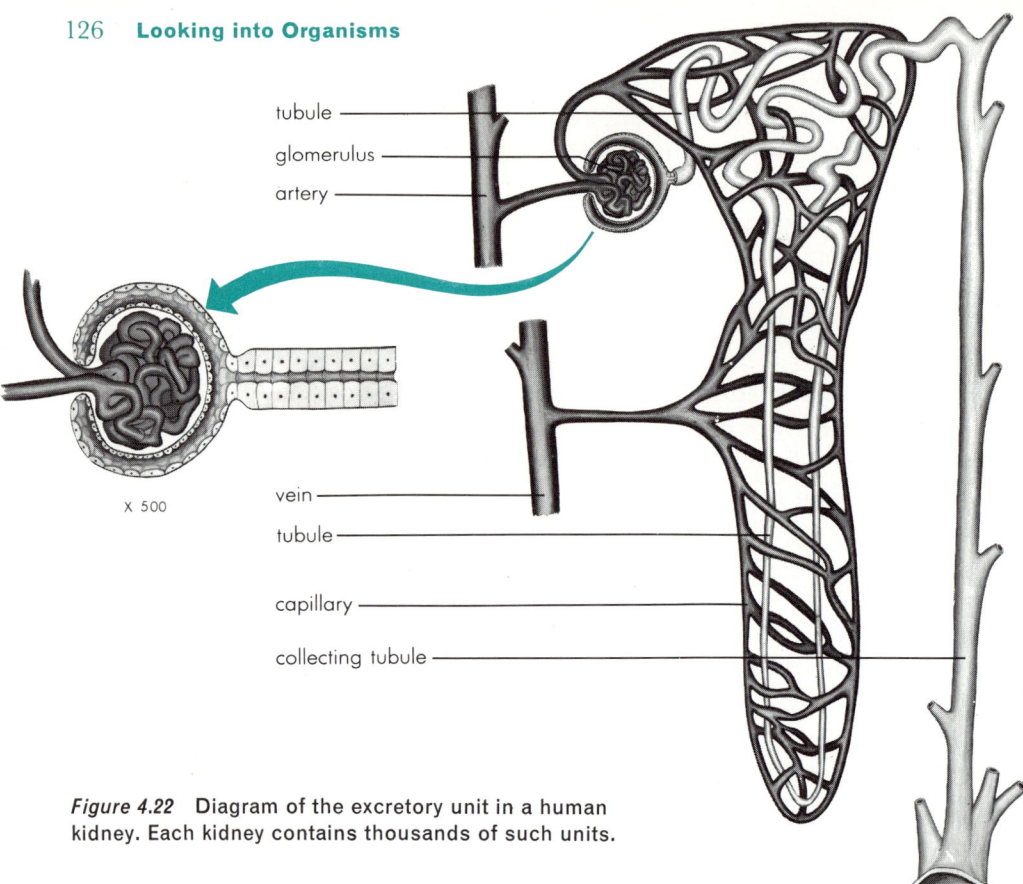

Figure 4.22 Diagram of the excretory unit in a human kidney. Each kidney contains thousands of such units.

through the walls of the blood vessels and through the thin wall of the expended end of the tubule. This fluid (filtrate) contains no blood cells or proteins, but otherwise it has the same composition as blood. As the filtrate moves down the tubule, useful substances – such as sugar, amino acids, water, some salts – are reabsorbed by cells in the wall of the tubules (by active transport). These substances are then transferred to the blood in capillaries that surround the tubule. Urea and some other wastes are left behind in the tubule. Some cells of the tubules are able to transfer certain wastes from the capillary blood into the space of the tubule. Thus as the original filtrate moves along the tubule, it is gradually converted – by removal of useful materials and addition of further waste materials – to *urine*.

Constantly, day and night throughout life, urine trickles from each kidney into a urinary bladder. From time to time the urine is eliminated from the urinary bladder through a *urethra*. It has been estimated that a healthy, normal pair of human kidneys filters some 135–150 litres of fluid every twenty-four hours, while only about 1.5 litres of urine are eliminated from the bladder during the same period. In other words, only about 1 per cent of the fluid filtered by the kidneys is eliminated.

A kidney is, therefore, a homeostatic organ. It regulates, to a considerable extent, the water content of the body by controlling the amount of water recovered by the tubule, and it prevents the level of waste nitrogen, salts, and many other substances in the blood from going above a certain level.

Other substances. Excretion of salts involves not only sodium chloride but also many other salts. These enter from the environment faster than they are needed, especially in vertebrates that live in sea water or on land. In land animals, kidneys are the chief excretory organs for salts as well as for nitrogenous wastes. However, on page 122 we took note of the salt-excreting glands near the eyes of sea turtles; and of course our own tears are slightly salty too. Recently it has been discovered that many sea birds also have salt-excreting glands, but these glands are located in the nostrils rather than near the eyes.

There is, then, no one organ that performs all excretory functions in the body of a vertebrate. In our own bodies, water, small amounts of nitrogenous wastes, and salts are excreted through the sweat glands; the liver excretes the remains of dead red blood cells; and almost all the carbon dioxide produced during the release of energy from cells (along with a considerable amount of water) is excreted through the lungs. Excess substances can reach the environment in several ways; but loss of function in both kidneys is always fatal.

Figure 4.23 Urinary system in man. Adrenal glands are attached to the kidneys but are not a part of this system.

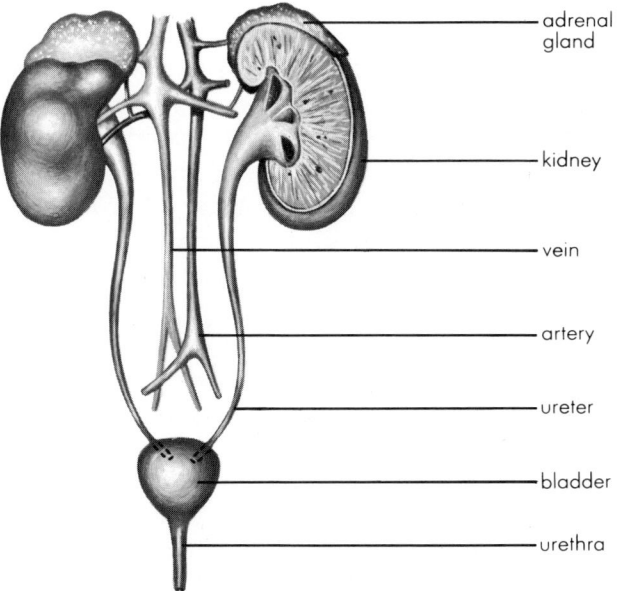

MAINTAINING A STEADY STATE

One of the first ideas that you encountered in this course was the concept of steady state – a never-still, see-saw balance in biological systems held within narrow limits by homeostatic mechanisms.

ENVIRONMENTS: INTERNAL AND EXTERNAL

We can look at the steady state within a multicellular organism in much the same way we looked at the situation outside the individual. To any one cell within a multicellular organism, the other cells of that body are 'outside' – they are part of that cell's environment. In this view, a cell can be likened to an individual, a tissue to a species population, an organ to a community. This analogy can be carried too far, but it can help us to understand some of the things that go on within an organism. The environment of a cell within the body of a multicellular organism is, as the word 'environment' implies, external to the cell, but it is internal to the multicellular organism as a whole. Thus we get the rather paradoxical but useful concept of an *internal environment*.

The environment in which an individual cell of a multicellular organism lives is made up not only of neighbouring cells but also of body fluids. These fluids are to a cell what the sea is to an individual sea animal: the source of its requirements, the place to which its wastes are returned. In fresh-water and land animals the primary function of homeostatic mechanisms is to keep body fluids as favourable and stable an environment for each cell as sea water usually is for each marine organism.

Let us consider an example of homeostasis in an internal environment – the regulation of the glucose content of human blood. After a heavy meal the processes of digestion leave a large amount of glucose in the small intestine. This is absorbed into the blood, but it does not stay there long. Figure 4.14 shows that a vessel (called the *hepatic portal*) carries blood (and glucose) from capillaries of the digestive system directly to capillaries in the liver. Here glucose in excess of 0.1 per cent is removed and changed to the polysaccharide glycogen, which is then stored in the liver cells. If the meal produces a very large amount of glucose (as it may if it contains many carbohydrates), the liver cannot take in all the excess. In this case, glucose is excreted through the kidney.

Now suppose the individual takes part in some kind of exercise, such as rugby or tennis. Muscle cells use a great deal of glucose for energy release at such times. This glucose is drawn from the cells' environment, the body fluids. Reduction of glucose in the body fluids leads to reduction of glucose in the blood. Under these circumstances glycogen in the liver is changed to glucose, which enters the blood. In this manner the liver and the circulatory and excretory systems provide the homeostatic mechanisms that maintain glucose in steady state in the environment of cells.

INTERNAL STEADY STATE

A homeostatic mechanism requires a means of communication. If the activities within a multicellular organism are to be regulated, some means of communication between cells and tissues within the organism must exist. In most animals this communication occurs in two ways: by means of specialized cells of the *nervous system*, and by means of chemicals that travel through body fluids. In some ways the separation of nervous and chemical communication is misleading, but it is at least convenient for beginning our study.

CHEMICAL COORDINATION

That most animals have nervous systems has long been known. Knowledge of the chemical system of coordination, however, has accumulated only within the last century. Just as knowledge of microscopic organisms was dependent on the development of microscopes, so knowledge of chemical systems in organisms has been dependent on the development of chemistry as a science. Today the biochemist plays an important part not only in the study of the activities within cells but also in the study of interrelationships among cells, tissues and organs, and even in the study of interrelationships between individuals and between populations.

Hormones. In all multicellular organisms some cells probably secrete chemical substances that in various ways influence the growth, development, or behaviour of other cells. We discussed one of these – auxin – in the last chapter. In general, such substances are called *hormones*.

As yet very little is known about hormones in most of the animal phyla. They have been studied chiefly in molluscs, arthropods and chordates. The hormones of the invertebrates influence the same kinds of body processes as the hormones of vertebrates, but the chemical structure of invertebrate hormones is not as well known.

Hormones may be secreted by individual cells scattered among other cells of an animal's body, but usually the secreting cells are grouped into tissues and often into distinct organs – glands. Unlike the glands that secrete tears, sweat and saliva, the glands that secrete hormones do not empty into a tubule or duct; their secretions pass directly into the circulatory system and are then carried through the body in the blood. Because the hormones from these *endocrine*, or ductless, glands interact with each other, we can say that there is an endocrine *system*, even though its parts are scattered through an animal's body.

The endocrine glands of vertebrates. With some relatively minor variations, all groups of vertebrates have similar hormones. However, the same hormone may have quite different functions in animals of different vertebrate classes. For example, the hormone that causes the mammary glands of mammals to secrete milk causes hens to incubate their eggs.

Hormones that cause changes in skin colour in certain fishes and amphibians are present in us; but human skin does not contain the special colour cells that would enable us to match the colour of our surroundings. Within any one vertebrate class, however, a particular hormone has approximately the same effects in most species. Therefore, the results of hormonal experiments on rats, guinea pigs and dogs, all of which are mammals, can – with caution – be applied to human physiology. The following discussion applies primarily to mammals.

The *hypothalamus* is in the ventral part of the brain and really is a part of the nervous system. Special nerve cells of the hypothalamus produce *neurohormones* that pass through the blood in special vessels to the *anterior pituitary gland*, which lies just below the brain. These hormones cause the anterior pituitary gland to release hormones that control the rate at which some of the other endocrine glands function. Thus the hypothalamus is a major link between the nervous system and the endocrine system.

All vertebrates have *thyroid* glands. Thyroid hormone regulates the speed of cellular respiration. Too little brings about an increase in weight, since food is stored rather than used in energy release. There are other results, such as slow movement, sleepiness and lowered body temperature. Too much thyroid hormone increases the rate of cellular respiration. Little food is stored and the individual loses weight, but excess energy results in great activity.

Parathyroid glands are found in all vertebrates except fishes, but only in mammals are they embedded in the thyroids. Parathyroid hormone controls the metabolism of calcium, which plays a part in muscle contraction. It is interference with calcium metabolism that brings about death if the parathyroid glands are injured or removed.

The pancreas is a gland with a duct through which a digestive juice is secreted. Embedded in the pancreas are bits of endocrine tissue (the *islands of Langerhans*) that produce *insulin*. This hormone controls the metabolism of glucose, and so lack of insulin results in lack of cellular energy. The unmetabolized glucose is excreted in the urine.

Adrenal glands are found in amphibians, reptiles, birds and mammals. Hormones similar to those produced by these glands are secreted by fishes, but the secreting tissues are not organized into glands. The best-known adrenal hormone is *adrenalin*. Adrenalin raises the blood pressure, speeds up the heartbeat, increases the rate of clotting of the blood, and raises the percentage of glucose in the blood. All these effects increase the chances of survival when an individual is faced with an emergency – particularly one that is likely to result in wounding.

During early development of an individual, the adrenal gland is formed from two different tissues. The part that secretes adrenalin develops from nerve tissue; most of the rest develops from tissue that also gives rise to the reproductive system. Hormones of this latter part of the adrenal gland affect

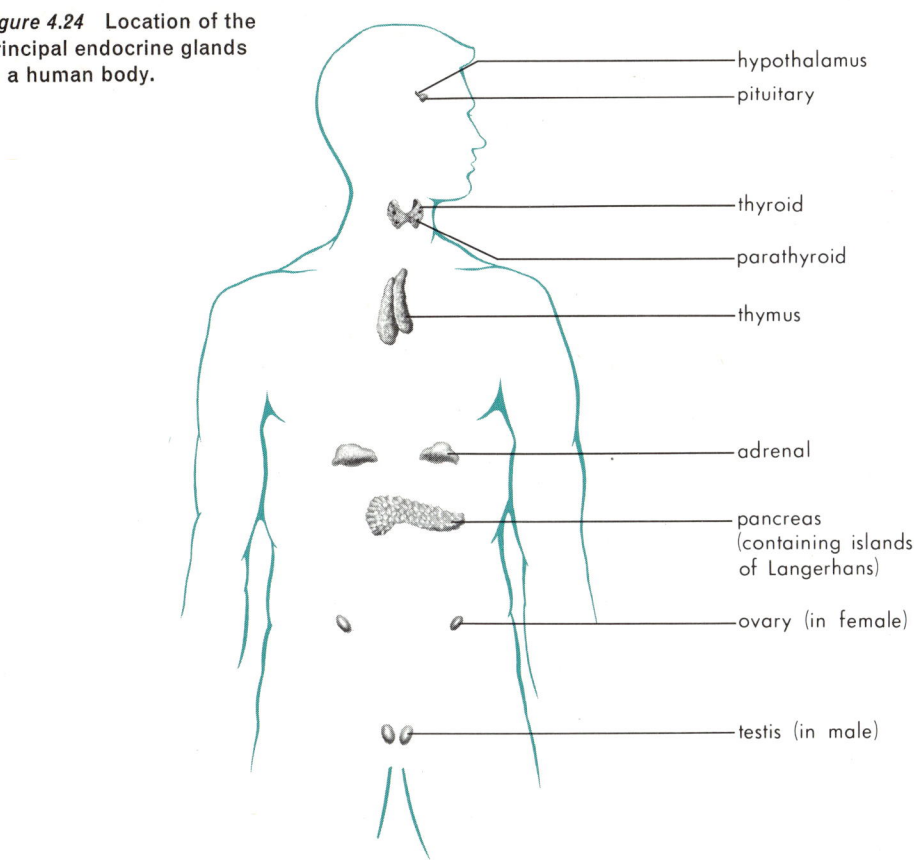

Figure 4.24 Location of the principal endocrine glands in a human body.

many functions, among them the depositing of fats, the synthesis of proteins, the formation of glucose from amino acids, and the excretion of salt. This part of the adrenalin gland is controlled by a pituitary hormone. Obviously, adrenal glands are of vital importance to the biochemistry of an organism.

Ovaries and testes are the organs in which reproductive cells are formed, but embedded in them are endocrine cells. Hormones from these cells control growth, development and reproductive behaviour.

Other kinds of chemical coordination. Biologists differ about the limits of the endocrine system. Sometimes included are small glands in the walls of the intestine, just below the pyloric valve. When food passes through the pyloric valve, these glands produce *secretin* – the first substance to which the word hormone was applied (in 1902). This hormone travels through the bloodstream to the pancreas, where it stimulates the production of pancreatic juice.

No biologist would call carbon dioxide a hormone. It is obviously a waste product – an excretion rather than a secretion. But carbon dioxide in the blood plays a part in the coordination of breathing. Numerous experiments have shown that the movements of the muscles in breathing are regulated by the nervous system – specifically, by a part of the brain that lies near the base of the skull. What determines whether the breathing movements are slow or rapid? Within limits you can voluntarily control your breathing. For a short time you can breathe deeply and quickly – or the reverse, as you may choose. If, however, you hold your breath, the need to start breathing again becomes irresistible. As you hold your breath, the concentration of CO_2 in your blood becomes greater and greater. Eventually the increased concentration of CO_2 stimulates the nerves to resume the breathing motions in the chest. This chemical control of breathing operates whether you are conscious or unconscious.

Many other kinds of substances that cannot be called hormones aid in coordination of physiological processes.

NERVOUS COORDINATION

The control of breathing illustrates again how closely nervous and chemical coordination are associated; the distinction between the two kinds of coordination is mostly a matter of convenience. In general, however, the more rapid adjustments in animals are usually brought about by the nervous system.

Kinds of nervous systems. Sponges have no nervous systems. Indeed, they have nothing that we can call nerve cells. Yet, just as do other organisms without nerve cells (protists and plants), sponges adjust to changes in their environment – they react to *stimuli*.

Coelenterates do have nerve cells, some of which are even specialized to receive only certain kinds of stimuli. The nerve cells are connected in a network that permits local responses as well as some coordinated responses, such as ingestion of food.

Flatworms have nerve networks, too (and even man has such a network, in the walls of the intestines), but a flatworm also possesses a more centralized system. A 'nerve ladder', consisting of two cords with interconnecting branches, extends the length of the body. At the anterior end is a rather large mass of nerve tissue, a *ganglion*, a centre in which nerve impulses are exchanged. Moreover, a flatworm has cells specialized for receiving stimuli. The eye-spots of planarians cannot form images, but they can detect the direction and intensity of light. The flaps that look like ears can sense food at a distance in the water – which gives flatworms a kind of sense of smell.

In annelids the nervous system is well developed. The main nerve cord is on the ventral side of the body. Numerous ganglia occur along the cord, and a large ganglion that really deserves to be called a *brain* is found at the anterior end of the body. Although earthworms have no obvious sense organs, a little experimenting will show that they detect many kinds of stimuli. Other annelids have several specialized sense organs, including eyes.

Molluscs show a great variety of nervous systems – all basically of the annelid type. Arthropod nervous systems are also essentially like those of annelids, but with a greater variety of sense organs.

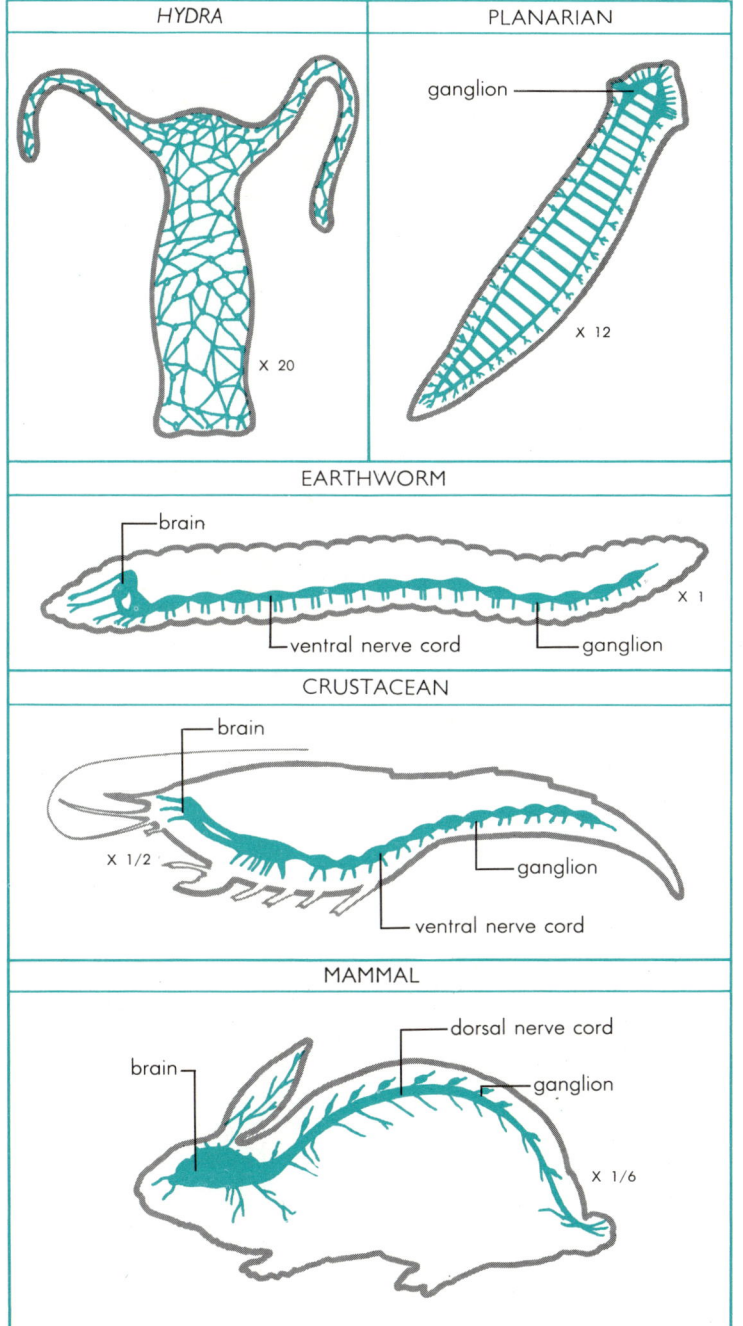

Figure 4.25 Nervous systems in five diverse kinds of animals.

The dorsal, tubular nerve cord is a distinctive characteristic of the chordate phylum. In vertebrate chordates the anterior ganglion – the brain – dominates all the rest of the nervous system.

Nerve cells. The basic structural unit in all nervous systems is a *neuron*, a nerve cell. Functionally a neuron is a conductor of nerve *impulses*.

Let us take neurons of mammals as examples. Three kinds can be distinguished: *Sensory* neurons receive impulses from a *receptor* (such as the part of the eye that reacts to light) and transmit impulses to another neuron. *Motor* neurons carry impulses to an *effector* – that is, to a muscle or a gland. *Associative* neurons transmit impulses from one neuron to another.

Neurons do not occur singly. The nerves that are visible in a dissected vertebrate are bundles of fibres. In man the fibres of some neurons are almost a metre long. The cell bodies of neurons are mostly in the brain, in the spinal cord, or in the ganglia that occur in pairs along the length of the spinal cord.

Just what a nerve impulse is, physiologists do not completely understand. Complex electrical phenomena are involved, but an impulse cannot be regarded as a simple electric current. Impulses are short in duration – usually only a few ten-thousandths of a second long. Information in the nervous system is usually transmitted by bursts of impulses rather than by single impulses. Under natural conditions an impulse can pass in only one direction in a neuron and is confined to one neuron. Neurons do not directly touch

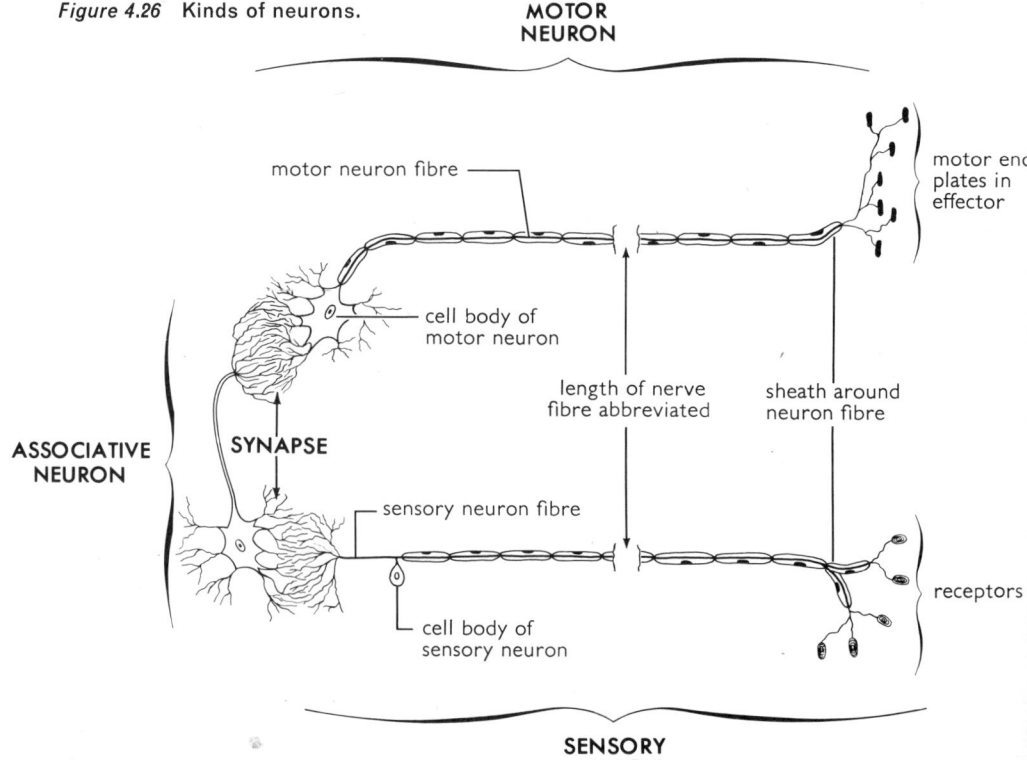

Figure 4.26 Kinds of neurons.

each other. When a sufficiently strong impulse, or rather a burst of impulses, reaches the end of the fibre of a neuron, it releases a chemical substance that induces an impulse in the next neuron. The very narrow space between two neurons through which chemical substance passes is called a *synapse*. Synapses occur also between receptor cells and neurons and between neurons and effector cells. Transmission in a synapse can take place only in one direction. Therefore impulses are conducted only in one direction by all neurons.

Nerves and internal coordination. Much activity in your nervous system occurs without your being aware of it. Though you have limited control over your breathing, you do not ordinarily think about it. The rate of your heartbeat, the movements of your stomach and intestines, the secretion of bile by your liver – these are activities of which you are unaware and which you are unable to control. They are under the control of the *autonomic* nervous system, which in turn is controlled through the hypothalamus. The autonomic system consists of interconnecting neurons that operate, for the most part, independently of the external environment but that coordinate activities in the internal environment.

For example, a steady supply of blood to all tissues is one of the principal requirements for maintaining a favourable internal environment. Suppose that after sitting on the touchlines for the first half, you are put into a rugby game. The sudden muscular activity forces blood into the right auricle of the heart much faster than blood is being pumped out, because (for the moment) the heart continues to beat at the normal rate – the rate it maintained while you were sitting on the bench. The walls of the auricle are stretched by the blood that is (so to speak) dammed up. Within the auricle walls are the tips of sensory neurons. They are stimulated by the stretching, and impulses pass along the fibres to the brain. These impulses induce impulses in motor neurons going to the heart, 'telling it' to speed up its contractions. This description is somewhat simplified. However, it illustrates the basic functional unit of the nervous system, the *reflex*.

Figure 4.27 Diagram of a reflex. The bending of the leg involves neurons in the leg and spinal cord only. Feeling the tap on the knee involves the brain, but this is not necessary for the reaction to occur.

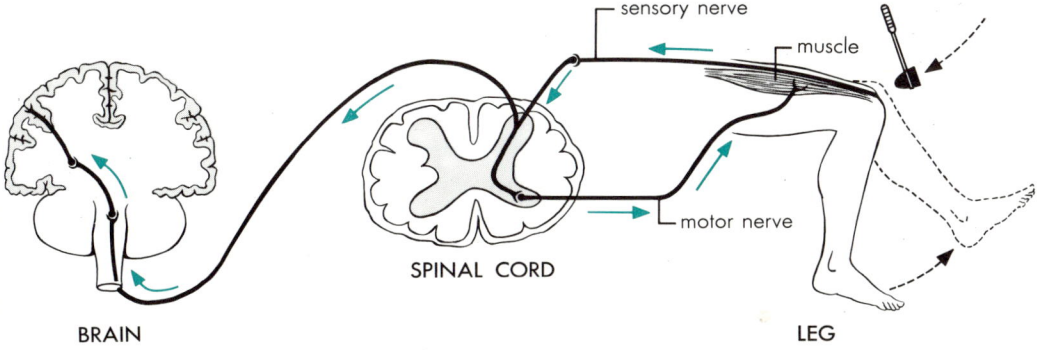

ADJUSTMENT TO THE EXTERNAL ENVIRONMENT

A need for adjustments in the internal environment usually arises from events outside the body – the rugby game that we discussed, for instance. Such events may result in changes throughout the whole organism. Some of these changes may, in turn, influence events in the outside environment. The overlap between internal and external coordination is great, but the distinction simplifies discussion.

SENSES

The rugby player's heart beat faster because he went into the game, but the endings of the sensory nerves were in the walls of the heart – and they could not receive direct stimulation from the rugby game. Usually we do not think of the internal sensory neurons when we speak of the senses; we consider only the sensory endings that receive stimuli from the external environment. The player heard the whistle and the order of the coach. As a whole organism, he reacted to these *stimuli*.

Ability to receive and to react to stimuli from the environment is one of the basic characteristics of living things, but the ability is developed to different degrees in different organisms. In most animals different kinds of stimuli are detected by specialized sensory cells – *receptors*. In man, for example, receptors in the skin of the fingertips are sensitive to pressure but not to light. Receptors in the nose are sensitive to chemical substances but not to light. Only receptors in the eyes are light sensitive, but they are not sensitive to sound waves and other stimuli.

In most animals at least some of the receptors are concentrated in special organs. The principal ones in man are well known – the eyes, the ears, the nose. Other kinds of receptors, such as those sensitive to pressure and heat, are distributed widely in the skin.

Probably no organism can detect all the possible stimuli in its environment. A dog whistle stimulates a dog; but it has no effect on us, because it produces tones that our receptors of sound waves do not detect. Sometimes an inability to detect stimuli – or an ability to detect them and not be affected by them – is to an organism's advantage. How obviously impractical it would be if you were conscious of all the activities and sounds going on around you at this moment! Moreover, probably no organism has specialized receptors for all possible stimuli in the environment. Many cave-dwelling animals have no receptors for light, and we have no receptors for the electromagnetic waves that carry radio and television signals. Lack of sensitivity to light is ordinarily no handicap to cave animals. On the other hand, there are situations where insensitivity might result in a catastrophe. A man may suffer fatal damage from nuclear radiation without being aware of his exposure, for he has no receptors that can detect it.

MOVEMENT

An animal obtains information about its environment through receptors; but the ability to react – to *do* something about a stimulus received through a receptor – depends on ability to move. Movement is one of the most obvious characteristics of animals. Of course, not all animals move rapidly, and some remain through much of their lives as firmly rooted as any plant – oysters and sponges, for example. In looking at movement as part of an organism's ability to react to environment we are not concerned merely with rapid motion or with locomotion. Any motion that helps an individual adjust to stimuli from its environment is important. In animals, motion usually involves specialized cells – muscle tissue.

Muscles. As in so many other matters, sponges are an exception among animals: they have no muscle tissues, although individual cells are capable of movement. The larvae swim by means of cilia, just as many protists do.

In coelenterates some of the cells – especially those in the outer layer – have a degree of muscular specialization, though this is usually combined with other characteristics. As a result, coelenterates can elongate and move their tentacles, and many can expand and contract their bodies. In flatworms many cells are further specialized; they are organized into definite muscle tissues, though locomotion is accomplished largely by cilia. In all other animal phyla, muscle tissues are organized into bundles (muscles) and controlled by nervous systems.

There are two general types of muscle, *striated* and *smooth*. Striated muscle is best developed in arthropods and vertebrates; it moves parts of the

Figure 4.28 Kinds of vertebrate muscle tissue.

A Smooth muscle X 525

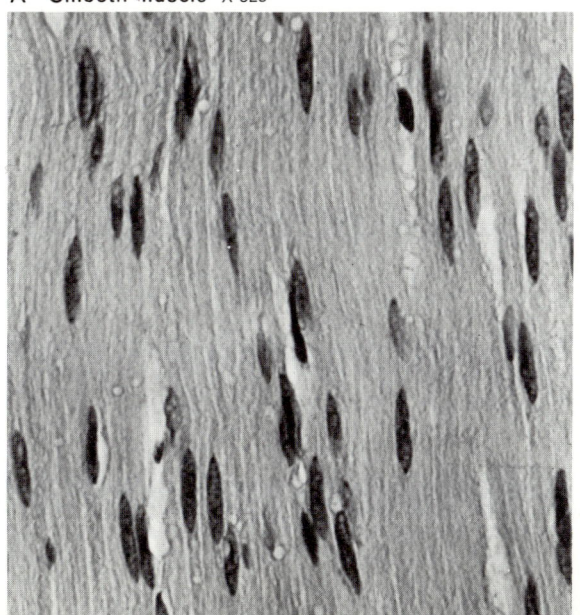

B Striated muscle X 700

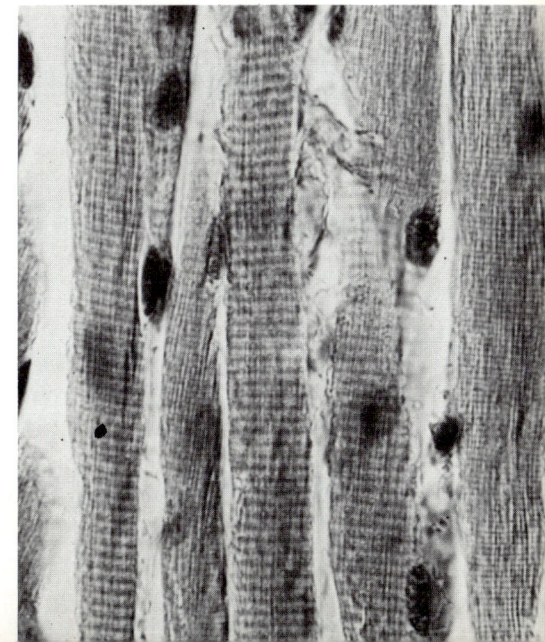

skeleton and, in general, is capable of more rapid contraction than is smooth muscle. In these phyla smooth muscle is found in such places as the walls of blood vessels, of various ducts, and of the digestive tube. Smooth muscle is usually involved in the regulation of the internal environment; striated muscle, on the other hand, is usually involved in adjustments of the organism to the external environment.

The chemistry of muscular contraction is a very active field of biological investigation. In some recent experiments proteins were extracted from muscle and an artificial fibre was made from them. This fibre was placed in a water bath. When ATP was added, the fibre contracted. Moreover, tests showed that the ATP was changed to ADP in the fibre during contraction. This and many other experiments indicate that proteins make up the contraction apparatus of muscles and that the energy for this action comes from ATP.

Even when an animal appears to be at rest, its muscles are not completely relaxed. The muscles of a healthy organism are always in a state of partial contraction called *muscle tone*. This produces the firmness that can be felt even in 'relaxed' muscles.

Skeletons. By contracting, muscles in the body of an earthworm produce movement without the aid of a skeleton. In our own bodies, muscles that have no connection to our bones moves food along the alimentary canal. But much of the movement of animals – especially locomotion – is a result of muscles and skeletons functioning together.

Skeletons have three main functions: support, protection and locomotion. In most animal phyla the first two of these are the most important. The skeleton of a sponge consists of small, more or less rigid parts scattered through the soft, living tissues; it probably serves chiefly to support the sponge. Among coelenterates the stony skeletons built up by corals serve both to support and to protect. These two functions also are obvious in echinoderm skeletons; indeed, the skeletons of echinoderms *hinder* locomotion rather than help it. In molluscs the skeleton (shell) is almost entirely protective, though scallops swim by rapidly opening and closing their shells.

Almost all skeletons adapted for locomotion are found among the arthropods and chordates. Arthropod skeletons are external, with the muscles attached to the inner surfaces. These exoskeletons are composed of chitin, which is rather flexible when thin. In many arthropods calcium compounds, deposited along with the chitin, make the exoskeleton quite hard and strong. It is all one piece, but it is rigid only in sections; thin, flexible chitin joints allow bending.

The chordate skeleton is inside the muscles. It may consist of one or both of two kinds of tissue: cartilage and bone. The hardness of bone is, in part, due to calcium and magnesium compounds. Both cartilage and bone contain cells that secrete these compounds; thus the skeleton can grow as the animal grows. Though the skeleton begins as cartilage, in the majority of vertebrate chordates most of this cartilage is gradually replaced by bone. At your age this process is well advanced but it is never complete – the tip of your nose and the external parts of your ears will never become hard bone.

In vertebrates, endoskeletons serve all three skeletal functions. However, protection, except in such animals as turtles, is seldom as complete as in most arthropod skeletons. In man the chief protective bones are those of the skull, and of the ribs which form a kind of cage around the organs in the chest cavity.

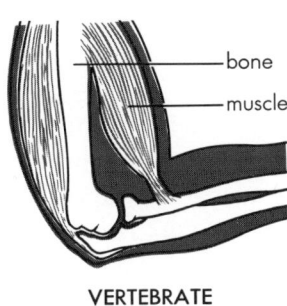 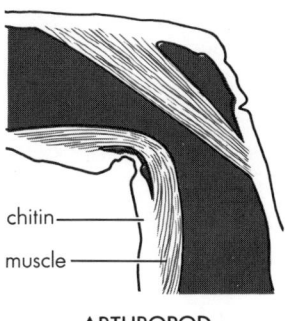

VERTEBRATE   ARTHROPOD

Figure 4.29 Relationship of muscles to skeletons. Why are *two* muscles shown in each example?

Skeletal movement. The parts of a vertebrate or arthropod skeleton act together as levers. Muscles supply the force to move them, and joints act as fulcrums (points around which movement occurs). A muscle attached to a bone is like a rope attached to a wagon: with a rope we can pull a wagon, but we cannot push it. If we want to move the wagon back to its original position, we must attach a rope to the other end and again move it by pulling. Muscles act in the same way – in pairs. While sitting, you can raise and straighten your leg by contracting one set of muscles, and gravity will pull it back to a bent position. If you stand and then wish to bend your knee, you will have to use another set of muscles – muscles with an action opposite to that of the ones you used to straighten the leg. By the contraction of opposing sets of muscles, all skeleton movements are performed.

PHYSIOLOGICAL STEADY STATE AS A WHOLE: AN EXAMPLE

In closing this chapter, we can summarize much of our understanding of animal physiology by considering a case of homeostasis – the regulation of body temperature in 'warm-blooded' animals. The chemical reactions of metabolism – like all chemical reactions – are influenced by changes in temperature; they slow down in low temperatures and speed up in high temperatures. Therefore 'warm-bloodedness' is an advantage because it permits an animal to be active when environmental temperatures are low.

The temperature of the skin and even of tissues some distance beneath the skin fluctuates many degrees in most 'warm-blooded' animals – birds and mammals. It is only internal body temperature that is held constant. This 'deep body temperature' can remain constant only if the rate of heat loss is the same as the rate of heat production. For a control system that can maintain this balance, receptors that respond to changes in temperature are necessary. There are two sets of such detectors. The skin has *thermoreceptors* that detect changes in environmental temperature. Through nerve impulses these receptors give the hypothalamus 'advance notice' that adjustments are necessary if the deep body temperature is to remain unchanged. Within the hypothalamus itself are other thermoreceptors that detect changes in blood temperature. The hypothalamus, with its mixture of nervous and endocrine functions, is the regulator in the homeostasis of temperature control.

What does a 'warm-blooded' animal do when the environmental temperature becomes cooler than the body temperature? The first adjustments are usually those that conserve heat. Impulses pass along neurons of the autonomic nervous system, constricting the small arteries of the skin. This reduces the flow of blood to the skin, which, in turn, reduces the amount of heat lost through the skin. Have you noticed that a person is pale when he is cold? He is conserving heat!

At the same time, other impulses along the autonomic nervous system contract the small muscles that control the position of each hair or feather in the skin of the animal. This erects the individual hairs, thus increasing the amount of 'dead-air space' between them. This in turn improves the insulation provided by fur or feathers. These same nerve impulses occur in your body when you become chilly. But the human body no longer has a dense hair covering, although the little hair muscles are still there. The muscles contract, but all you get is gooseflesh.

If these measures fail to prevent a downward change in deep body temperature, the rate of heat production can be increased. This may be accomplished in an almost undetectable manner by increase of metabolic rate in cells, or it may be accomplished by an involuntary increase in muscle activity – by shivering. This muscle activity itself increases the release of energy from food. Of course, this is always accompanied by a 'loss' of energy in the form of heat. In this case the additional 'lost' energy is useful in maintaining body temperature.

In addition to making these internal adjustments most birds and mammals behave in ways that conserve heat. When it is cold, a cat curls up in a ball and covers its nose with its tail. This reduces the amount of surface exposed to the cold air; it also covers an uninsulated surface (the nose), through which heat loss is very rapid. A bird tucks its legs up under its feathers and puts its head under its wing. Many birds can thus cut their heat losses in half. How many times have you put on a sweater almost without thinking, when the air became cool?

Figure 4.30 What does the position of the cat probably indicate about the environmental temperature?

What happens when the environmental temperature becomes warmer than the body temperature? Then maintenance of a constant body temperature requires a reduction in heat produced, an increase of heat loss, or both. Again impulses on autonomic neurons originating in the hypothalamus activate the mechanisms. The walls of the small arteries in the skin relax and more blood circulates to the skin: thus more heat is lost from the body surface. In some mammals such as men and horses, the activity of the sweat glands increases. This provides more water on the skin surface. Evaporation of water always requires heat; heat for the evaporation of sweat comes from the body. Dogs do not have sweat glands but a dog can increase the rate of heat loss by increasing the flow of air over the moist surfaces of the upper part of the respiratory system – by panting. There are many behaviour patterns that are important in keeping body temperature from going too high.

Heat production through metabolism is reduced by inactivity. In hot weather many mammals and birds are quite inactive during the warmer part of a day. And during that part of a day, most birds and mammals seek the coolness of shade, where heat can be lost fairly rapidly. Water conducts heat much more rapidly than air; also the temperature of natural bodies in water is usually lower than air temperature. Therefore bathing, wading, or standing in water increases heat loss.

Thus many homeostatic mechanisms are involved in maintaining the steady state of body temperatures in 'warm-blooded' animals. We would find equally extensive mechanisms if we were to examine the maintenance of water content of the body, glycogen content of the liver, salt content of the blood, or any other aspect of internal steady state.

INVESTIGATION 4.4

CHEMORECEPTORS IN MAN

PURPOSE
In this investigation you will find out about the physiological characteristics of your chemoreceptors.

BACKGROUND INFORMATION
Chemoreceptors – nerve endings sensitive to chemical substances – are common among animals that have well defined nervous systems. Among arthropods they are often found in the antennae. Among vertebrates they are found mostly in the mouth and nasal passages. Students of human physiology think of chemoreceptors as involving the senses of taste and smell.

The study of chemoreceptors among animals other than men is complicated by a lack of communication. How can we find out just what an animal senses? When studying chemoreceptors in man, we can at least obtain descriptions ('sour', 'sweet', 'bitter', 'spicy', etc.) of particular stimuli. But then there are difficulties in interpreting such reports, so that complete understanding of chemoreceptors – even in man – is not easy.

MATERIALS AND EQUIPMENT
A. *Location of Taste Receptors*
   (*for each pair of pupils*)

Solid watch glass or other small container
Salt solution (10 per cent), 2 cm³
Applicators (toothpicks with small ball of cotton wrapped around one end), 4
Waste jar (1 for every 6 pupils)
Beakers filled with water, 2
Sucrose solution (5 per cent), 2 cm³
Acetic acid solution (1 per cent), 2 cm³
Quinine sulphate solution (0.1 per cent), 2 cm³

B. *Taste Threshold*
   (*for each pupil*)

Small paper cups, 6
Sucrose solutions (0.001, 0.005, 0.01, 0.05, 0.1 and 0.5 per cent), 3 cm³ of each
Salt solutions (0.001, 0.005, 0.01, 0.05, 0.1, and 0.5 per cent), 3 cm³ of each
Beaker filled with water
Dropper
Waste jars
Chalk – 3 colours

C. *Relationship of Smell to Taste*
   (*groups of 3 pupils*)

Blindfold, e.g. handkerchief
Small paper cups, 3 to 6
Solution of orange juice, milk, onion juice, vinegar (2 per cent), sugar, pickle juice

PROCEDURE A. LOCATION OF TASTE RECEPTORS

During Procedure A pupils work in pairs.

Pupil 1: Pour about 2 cm³ of 10 per cent salt solution in a watch glass.

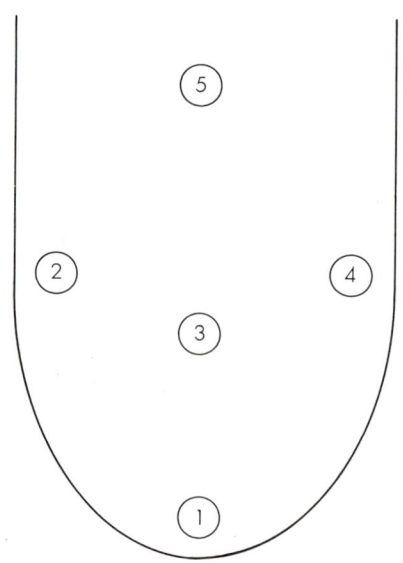

Figure 4.31

Pupil 2: Make a copy of Figure 4.31 and label it *Salt*.

Pupil 1: Dip an applicator into the solution. Drain excess solution from the applicator. Touch the applicator to the tongue of Pupil 2 at the point marked 1 in Figure 4.31.

Pupil 2: At point 1 in your drawing, place a minus sign (—) if you sense no taste of salt, a plus sign (+) if you sense a mild taste of salt, and a double plus (++) if you sense a strong taste of salt.

Pupil 1: As soon as Pupil 2 has recorded his sensation, touch the applicator to his tongue at point 2.

Pupil 2: Record your sensation, using the appropriate symbol. Continue until sensation has been recorded at all five points on the tongue.

Pupil 2: Rinse your mouth with water.

Pupil 1: Break the applicator and discard it. Pour the salt solution from the watch glass into the waste jar. Rinse the watch glass.

Pupil 2: Pour about 2 cm^3 of 5 per cent sucrose solution into the watch glass.

Pupil 1: Make a copy of Figure 4.31. Label it *Sweet*.

Pupil 2: Dip an applicator into the sucrose solution, drain off excess solution, and touch the applicator to the tongue of Pupil 1 at point 1.

Pupil 1: Record your sensation. Continue until sensation has been recorded at all five points.

Pupil 1: Rinse your mouth with water.

Pupil 2: Break the applicator and discard it. Pour the sucrose solution from the watch glass into the waste jar. Rinse the watch glass.

Pupil 1: Pour about 2 cm^3 of 1 per cent acetic acid solution into the watch glass.

Pupil 2: Make another copy of Figure 4.31 and label it *Sour*.

Pupil 1: Dip a new applicator into the acid solution and proceed to test Pupil 2, following the procedure described above.

Following the same procedure for changing solutions and pupils, test the effects of a 0.1 per cent solution of quinine sulphate. The diagram on which the sensation is recorded should be labelled *Bitter*.

PROCEDURE B. TASTE THRESHOLD

Stimuli have different degrees of intensity. The intensity of a stimulus may be so low (weak) that it is not detected by the organism. The degree of intensity that an individual can just barely detect is the *threshold* intensity for that individual. In tests for the taste threshold, intensity is expressed as the percentage of the test substance in a given volume of water.

During Procedure B you will work alone.

1. Mark six paper cups as follows: 0.001, 0.005, 0.01, 0.05, 0.1, and 0.5 per cent.
2. Put 3 cm^3 of the appropriate solutions into each of the cups.
3. Arrange the cups in order of increasing concentration.
4. Using a dropper, transfer 2 drops of the 0.001 per cent solution on to your tongue. In your lab-book write the name of the solution and its concentration and beside this write a plus sign if you can taste the solution and a minus sign if you cannot.
5. Rinse the dropper in water and follow the above procedure for the solution of next higher concentration.
6. When you reach a concentration which you can taste, check by testing the next higher concentration. Stop testing at this point.

PROCEDURE C. RELATIONSHIP OF SMELL TO TASTE

Here you work in groups of three.

1. Number yourselves 1, 2 and 3.
2. Pupil 2, blindfold Pupil 1 (it is important that the pupil being tested is unaware of the identity of

the substance). Pupil 3 should copy out the form shown below into his lab-book. Write the name of the solution in the space under the heading Solution Presented.
3. Pupil 2 should hold Pupil 1's nose while he sips the solution and tries to identify it. Pupil 3 will record his response.
4. Pupil 1 should now sip the same solution without having his nose held and try to identify it. Pupil 3 will record the response.
5. Repeat the procedure, changing round one place, i.e. Pupil 1 becomes Pupil 2, etc.

STUDYING THE DATA

1. On the blackboard make four large diagrams of the tongue (Figure 4.31). Label them *Salt*, *Sweet*, *Sour* and *Bitter*. Assemble from all pupils the data obtained in Procedure A. At each test point on the diagrams, record the total number of minus, plus, and double-plus responses.

A. Which kinds of variability are the results of 'error of observation'?
B. Which are the result of physiological variability?

2. On the blackboard assemble the data obtained in Procedure B. Beside each concentration use two colours of chalk to tally separately the number of male subjects and the number of female subjects for whom that concentration represented the taste threshold. Add the two counts and write the total in a third colour.
   For each kind of solution, calculate the mean (average) threshold concentration for males, for females, and for the entire class.
3. On the blackboard list the solutions used in Procedure C. Tally separately the tastes reported with nose closed and with nose open.

C. Are the kinds of tastes reported with the nose open more varied than those recorded with the nose closed? Less varied? Neither?
D. Are the identifications made with the nose open more accurate than those made with the nose closed? Less accurate? Neither?
E. What assumption is involved in holding the nose closed?

CONCLUSIONS

A. Do the data from Procedure A support the hypothesis that receptors of the four kinds of taste are unequally distributed on the surface of the tongue? Explain your answer.
B. If the data support this hypothesis, where on the tongue is each kind of taste receptor most numerous?
C. Do the data from Procedure B support the hypothesis that the threshold for sweetness is lower than that for saltiness? Higher? Neither?
D. Do the data indicate that the sense of taste in one sex is more acute (i.e. has a lower threshold) than in the other? If so, which sex has the lower threshold for sweetness? For saltiness?

SUBJECT	SOLUTION PRESENTED	NOSE CLOSED		NOSE OPEN	
		Taste	Identity	Taste	Identity

E. On the basis of the data from Procedure C, write a brief statement concerning the relationship of the sense of taste to the sense of smell.

FOR FURTHER INVESTIGATION

1. Smell oil of cloves through one nostril, expiring air through the mouth. Hold the bottle containing the oil about 1.5 cm from the nose. How much time passes before the smell of cloves is no longer detected? This is called 'olfactory fatigue'. Immediately smell oil of peppermint through the same nostril. Is the latter odour detectable?

2. Stick your tongue out and keep it out, during the following procedure. Wipe your tongue dry with a piece of gauze or a paper tissue. Place a few crystals of sugar on the tongue and note the time. How much time passes before the sugar is tasted? Rinse your mouth with water. Again stick your tongue out, but do not dry it before placing sugar crystals on it. How much time passes before the sugar is tasted? Try the same procedure with salt crystals.

3. To test the hearing threshold, use the ticking of a watch as the stimulus and the distance of the watch from the ear as the measure of intensity. The subject should be blindfolded, and the test should be made where other sounds are at a minimum.

According to the classification used in this book, all animals are multicellular organisms. Most have powers of locomotion at some stage in their life histories and none of them carries on photosynthesis. As a result of this last characteristic, food-getting is a fundamental activity in all animals.

We have examined the ways in which animals obtain food and other nutrients and prepare them for absorption into cells. We have also considered the means by which animals acquire oxygen. In most animals, particularly the larger ones and those that do not live in marine environments, there are special systems for distributing nutrients and oxygen to all the cells. With nutrients and oxygen delivered, each cell then releases energy for its own use, including synthesis of its complex molecules. Some cells (as in bone and cartilage) secrete materials useful to the organism as a whole.

In doing these things, an organism produces various waste substances, or it may acquire or produce substances in excess of needs. By the processes of excretion, these waste materials are passed from the bloodstream out into the environment. As a result, steady-state conditions for different materials are maintained within the organism.

Adjustment of the individual organism, through homeostatic mechanisms, to maintain steady-state conditions in a changing environment involves both the nervous and endocrine systems. Coordination of the functions of the various parts of an animal's body is brought about by hormones, which move through the circulatory system (if one is present). Hormones affect such processes as growth, development and reproduction. The more rapid internal adjustments are under the control of the nervous system, though there is a close coordination with the hormonal system in such matters.

To react to the environment, organisms must receive stimuli from it. In most animals, parts of the nervous system are specialized as receptors for such stimuli. Reaction usually involves specialized cells of contraction (muscle cells) or of secretion (gland cells), or both.

GUIDE QUESTIONS
1. Why is eating such an important animal activity?
2. How do the various food-getting devices of animals illustrate structural diversity?
3. What is the function of digestion in maintaining the life of an animal?
4. How is chemical digestion related to the chemical syntheses carried on by cells?
5. In man, where does most of the absorption of digested foods occur?
6. Chyme in the small intestine is semi-liquid, yet faeces are normally semi-solid. Explain.
7. Some salamanders have no lungs. Why is it necessary for them to live in a moist environment?
8. How is air moved into and out of the lungs of mammals?
9. What occurs in the alveoli of lungs?
10. Distinguish between open and closed circulatory systems.
11. What are the differences between arteries, veins and capillaries?
12. How is blood in mammals kept flowing in one direction?
13. What is blood plasma?
14. How does haemoglobin function in transporting oxygen?
15. In what ways are red and white blood cells and platelets distinguished?
16. Draw a diagram to show how blood clots.
17. How does lymph differ from blood?
18. How can bile be considered both a secretion and an excretion?
19. What are the principal kinds of excreted substances?
20. How does a mammalian kidney function?
21. List places in the human body from which excreted substances are eliminated.
22. What is meant by the internal environment of an animal?
23. What are hormones?
24. What are the principal glands of the endocrine system in man?
25. What evidence supports the idea that the endocrine and nervous systems are closely associated?
26. How do sensory neurons differ from motor neurons?
27. How does a synapse function in the transmission of a nerve impulse?
28. What is the autonomic nervous system?
29. What are the principal differences of brain structure in different vertebrate classes?
30. What are the principal kinds of information that vertebrates obtain through their receptors?
31. Distinguish between striated and smooth muscle.
32. How do the skeletons of arthropods and vertebrates function in locomotion?

PROBLEMS
1. How might you proceed experimentally to show that (*a*) secretin causes the pancreas to secrete digestive enzymes, (*b*) *diabetes mellitus* is caused by lack of insulin, and (*c*) hormones secreted by the

pituitary gland affect thyroid and adrenal glands?
2. Antibodies from horse blood can produce some kinds of immunity in man. Insulin from a cow pancreas can be used in treating human diabetes. Why cannot whole blood of horses and cows be transfused to man?
3. We have implied that excretion is a general biological process essential for maintenance of life in all organisms. Yet the process is seldom mentioned in botany textbooks. Explain.
4. Blood transports many substances dissolved in the plasma. It can be shown, however, that in mammals less than 10 per cent of the carbon dioxide in the blood is dissolved in plasma. How is the rest of the CO_2 transported?
5. Describe in detail the route followed by a molecule of oxygen as it moves from the air of your external environment to a mitochondrion in one of your muscle cells.
6. The thyroxin molecule contains four atoms of iodine. What effects would an iodine-free diet have upon a mammal?
7. Haemoglobin acts as a respiratory pigment in animals of several phyla, but there are other such pigments in the animal kingdom. Investigate this matter, considering the following questions: (a) Do all respiratory pigments act in the same way? (b) What are the chemical similarities and differences among respiratory pigments? (c) Do respiratory pigments provide any clues to the evolutionary relationships among animal phyla? (d) Is there any significance in the chemical relationships between haemoglobin and chlorophyll? In the fact that haemoglobin occurs in the nodules formed by *Rhizobium* on the roots of legumes?
8. A temporary reddening of the skin surface is sometimes called a 'flush' and sometimes a 'blush'. The first term is often used in cases of fever; the second is usually used to describe a reaction to some situation in the external environment. Is the body mechanism the same in both cases? If so, how does it operate? If not, what are the differences?
9. You eat a lettuce and cheese sandwich. Describe what happens to the sandwich from the moment you take the first bite until its remains are passed from the anus. First you must decide what classes of substances are in the sandwich.
10. In some cases of slow blood clotting, doctors prescribe calcium compounds. Explain. In other cases they prescribe vitamin K. What part does this vitamin play in the clotting process?
11. Many kinds of combustion, such as that in petrol engines and furnaces, produce carbon monoxide (CO) as well as CO_2. Haemoglobin combines readily with CO, and any haemoglobin molecule to which CO is attached cannot combine with oxygen. What effects would an atmosphere containing CO have on a person? Gather facts on carbon monoxide poisoning and suggest a treatment for it.
12. In mammalian physiology the kidney can be regarded as a principal organ of internal homeostasis. Explain.
13. List the life functions of animals. Then compare the structures by which each is accomplished in a sponge, a planarian, an insect and a mammal. Since all of these animals exist in large numbers, we must conclude that despite such diverse structures they all successfully carry on their life functions. Explain how this can be.
14. Instruments may be classed as those by which man increases his power to *do* things (usually called tools or machines) and those by

which he increases his power to sense things. Contrast the abilities of a prehistoric man (who had only the biological receptors) and of a modern man to receive information from the environment. In what ways are instrumental sensors related to biological receptors?

SUGGESTED READING

BEAUMONT, W. *Experiment and observation on the gastric juice and physiology of digestion* (1833). Dover, 1959.

BEST, C. H. and N. B. TAYLOR. *The Living Body*. 4th edn. Chapman & Hall, 1959. (An authoritative account of the circulatory system.)

BURNET, M. 'The Thymus Gland', *Scientific American*, November 1962. Pp. 50–57.

COMROE, J. H. 'The Lung', *Scientific American*, February 1966. Pp. 56–66.

DODD, I. A. *Programmed Physiology*. Methuen, 1967.

GORDON, A. S. *Blood Cell Physiology* (BSCS Pamphlet 8). George G. Harrap & Co., 1963.

GRAUBARD, M. *Circulation and Respiration: The Evolution of an Idea*. Harcourt, Brace & World, 1964. (A book of quotations from original investigations with a commentary that shows how physiologists came to understand these processes. Fairly advanced.)

HODGSON, E. S. 'Taste Receptors', *Scientific American*, May 1961. Pp. 135–42.

HUNGATE, R. E. *Cellulose in Animal Nutrition* (BSCS Pamphlet 22). George G. Harrap & Co., 1965.

LAKI, K. 'The Clotting of Fibrinogen', *Scientific American*, March 1962. Pp. 60–66.

MONTAGNA, W. 'The Skin', *Scientific American*, April 1961. Pp. 56–63.

OVERMINE, T. G. *Homeostatic Regulation* (BSCS Pamphlet 9). George G. Harrap & Co., 1965.

RASMUSSEN, H. 'The Parathyroid Hormone', *Scientific American*, April 1961. Pp. 56–63.

SCHMIDT-NIELSEN, K. *Animal Physiology*. 2nd edn. Prentice-Hall, 1964. (Concentrated on physiological steady state and the relation of animals to their environment. Lightly written but authoritative. Fairly easy.)

SIMPSON, G. G. and W. S. BECK. *Life: An Introduction to Biology*. Routledge & Kegan Paul, 1965. (Maintenance and coordination in organisms considered as general biological processes. All organisms – plants, animals and protists – are discussed, but man is the focus of attention. Advanced.)

STREHLER, B. L. *Time, Cells and Ageing*. Academic Press, 1965.

SUCKLING, E. E. *Bioelectricity* (BSCS Pamphlet 4). George G. Harrap & Co., 1962.

ZUCKER, M. B. 'Blood Platelets', *Scientific American*, February 1961. Pp. 58–64.

CHAPTER
5

BEHAVIOUR

THE STUDY OF BEHAVIOUR

The piano has been played for many kinds of audiences, but probably only a biologist would think to play the piano for earthworms. Yet at no time during his performance did the inquisitive Charles Darwin feel he was wasting his talent on the worms. He wanted to find out how earthworms behaved when they heard sounds.

Not satisfied with just playing the piano for the earthworms, he blew whistles, shouted, breathed on the worms with a tobacco breath and held red-hot pokers near them. He jumped up and down on the lawn to see if they would retreat into their burrows and fed them cabbage and onion to test their sense of taste. He sprinkled a field with chips of chalk and thirty years later dug up the field to see how deep the earthworms had buried the chalk. He carefully watched worms drag leaves into their burrows, then obtained some foreign tree leaves and some paper triangles to see if earthworms could work out how to manoeuvre these strange objects. For more than half of his lifetime, Darwin observed and was fascinated by the things that earthworms do – by their behaviour.

WHAT IS BEHAVIOUR?

A botanist once startled his students by taking them on a twenty-four hour 'plant watch'. At first the students were reluctant and unexcited about the investigation, because they assumed that plants did not do anything. Before the end of the study, however, they had made so many question-arousing observations that they pleaded to continue their investigation of plant behaviour another day.

In varying degrees, all living organisms – animals, plants and protists – are doing something, are reacting to stimuli from their environment. Not all these reactions are covered by the term 'behaviour'. Indeed, the word is defined in various ways by biologists, but the concept that it covers is not difficult to understand. When light is directed to a green plant, the plant begins to split water molecules in the light phase of photosynthesis. This is a reaction to a stimulus, but it is not behaviour. If the light is directed at the plant from one side, the plant turns its leaves and growing tip towards the light – an easily visible reaction. This is behaviour. A cat lies in the sun; muscles move its latest meal through its intestines. This is not behaviour. A bird chirps nearby. Unless the cat is deaf, the receptors of the cat's ears react with an impulse to the brain, but this is not behaviour. The cat's drooping eyelids open, its ears rise, and its tail twitches. This is behaviour.

Behaviour involves more than the reaction of a cell (unless the individual is a single cell) or of an organ or even of a single organ system. It involves the whole individual and it is directed towards the external environment of the individual. In considering behaviour, we are returning to an external view of the organism. But what an organism as a whole *does* depends upon its internal functions – its physiology. In the past, both physiologists and ecologists (or scientists with an ecological viewpoint) have contributed to the study of behaviour. Today a special science of behaviour is developing.

DIFFICULTIES IN BEHAVIOURAL STUDIES

Observation and experiment. About a million and a half different species of living things are known to biologists; probably the behaviour of no more than 0.1 per cent of these has been carefully observed by them. At first it might seem that the observation of behaviour would be easy. We all observe the behaviour of our pets and of other animals, though few of us notice the behaviour of plants or protists. Now you perhaps realize that merely looking at or watching something is not necessarily scientific observation. Because behaviour is action, observing it is especially difficult. Behaviour often occurs so quickly that it is difficult for the observer to determine just what he has seen; paradoxically, in plants it may occur so slowly that the observer may have difficulty determining whether it has occurred at all. Films have helped to solve these difficulties and, at the same time, have provided a basis for the verification that is essential in science.

Where should behaviour be observed – in the field or in the laboratory? Study in the field can be very difficult. The organisms that the biologist wishes to study may be hard to find. They may be difficult to observe when they are found; they may be difficult to approach and to keep under observation for a long period of time to provide reliable facts. The mere presence of an observer may affect the behaviour of many vertebrate animals.

In the laboratory, organisms can be more easily watched, and the watching can be arranged so that they are unaware of the observer. In the laboratory a biologist can learn much about what an organism *can* do; but behaviour in an artificial laboratory environment is not necessarily the same as behaviour in a natural environment. A laboratory biologist may well remain ignorant of what an organism *will* do as a part of its ecosystem. For some purposes such information is important – important, for example, to an understanding of population changes or to an understanding of a species' niche.

As in other branches of science, a behavioural biologist attempts whenever possible to test hypotheses by making observations under controlled conditions. Experiments may be performed either in laboratory or in field, but in field experiments the control of conditions is usually more difficult.

Figure 5.1 Behavioural study in the laboratory: here a rat is shown in a T maze.

Behavioural scientists called *psychologists* usually do most of their experiments in laboratories, using rather few species of organisms. Laboratory rats are their favourite subjects. Psychologists have a tendency to emphasize the physiological side of behaviour. In the past three decades, biologists with an ecological viewpoint also have turned their attention to behaviour. These *ethologists* usually work in the field, and they have studied a wide array of organisms in natural ecosystems. Not only are their methods different, but also their concepts: they attach more importance to hereditary factors in explaining behaviour than psychologists do. Psychologists and ethologists have sometimes disagreed greatly, but, as has happened before in the history of biology, with increase of knowledge, differences in viewpoint are being reconciled.

Interpretation. All biologists have difficulties in drawing conclusions from their data and especially in fitting their conclusions together with those

Figure 5.2 Behavioural study in the field: recording the voice of an elephant seal.

of other investigators. This is the job of interpreting results, giving meaning to them. Behavioural scientists have some special difficulties.

We may consider a rabbit *hiding* under a blackberry bush. How do we know it is hiding? Perhaps the rabbit is seeking shade or looking for food, or it might just be resting.

Consider a laboratory experiment. We place on the side of a frog's body some substance that we think unpleasant. Immediately the frog moves its hind foot to rub at the spot where the substance was placed. We think the frog does not like the substance and is trying to rub it off, but how do we know that the frog is not trying to rub it *in* because it likes the stuff? The interpretation of this behaviour becomes even more perplexing if we destroy the frog's brain; the frog continues to bring its hind foot up to rub at its side. Without a brain, there can be no question of its 'liking' or 'not liking' the substance.

In observing behaviour, we tend to put ourselves in the organism's place, to think that it sees and feels as we do, to explain behaviour in human terms. We commonly say that a growling dog is 'angry', a singing lark 'happy', a purring cat 'contented', and wide-eyed deer 'frightened' – that the roots of a cactus are 'searching' for water. But we don't know whether other organisms have any of these human emotions. This is *anthropomorphism*, the interpretation of the behaviour of other organisms as if they were human.

The more we think we know about an organism, the more likely we are to interpret its behaviour anthropomorphically. Only a little caution is required to rid ourselves of this way of thinking when studying the behaviour of plants.

It is more difficult to resist anthropomorphism when we start to deal with motile organisms – and very difficult indeed when we study organisms that have obvious sense organs.

Behavioural scientists must constantly beware of anthropomorphic interpretations. This is especially difficult because they must discuss their findings in a human language. Human language is a product of the human brain and therefore reflects human ways of reacting to the environment. To use human language to describe and interpret the behaviour of other species without introducing human viewpoints is probably impossible, but behavioural scientists try to minimize such viewpoints – and as a result their language often seems strange and obscure to non-scientists.

Another difficulty. Take a walk with a dog. You and the dog go along the street or through the woods. You notice certain smells from freshly cut grass, from flowers, from car exhaust; but what a variety of smells there are for the dog, all to be sniffed carefully, all meaning something and yet completely unnoticed by you! You have great difficulty imagining the ability to follow the 'smell trail' of an animal or man that has passed an hour or a day before. People live in a world that is primarily visual. Our perceptual world – what we perceive in our environment – is made up mostly of colours, shapes and movements. Dogs lack colour vision and do not distinguish shapes as well as we do. Dogs hear sounds that we do not; this can be shown with dog whistles, which will call dogs home though we hear nothing.

If it is difficult to understand the perceptual world of a dog, a fellow mammal with which we live closely, how much more difficult it is to understand the world of a bird, lizard, fish, bee, ant, or octopus. Yet, if we are going to understand the behaviour of any organism, we have to know what it perceives in its environment.

Therefore, in studying the behaviour of any organism, it is important to determine what kinds of receptors it has and how sensitive they are. Since man often does not perceive stimuli that affect other organisms, a biologist must frequently depend on instruments that can translate things he cannot perceive into things he can. Flowers that look white to him may have patterns of colour to bees, because bees see by ultraviolet light – light of a wavelength that is invisible to human eyes. He can 'see' what the bee sees only by taking photographs with film sensitive to such wavelengths. Similarly, instruments can translate sounds that men cannot hear into lines on a piece of paper; then the biologist can study the characteristics of the sounds even though he cannot hear them.

LEVELS OF BEHAVIOUR

All organisms exhibit behaviour. *Irritability*, the ability to respond to stimuli, seems to be one of the fundamental characteristics of living substance. This ability allows even the simplest organism to adapt to changes in its environment. But some organisms have differentiated special cells, tissues, or organs in which this fundamental ability is specialized. In general, the greater this differentiation, the more complex the behaviour is. Therefore, one way to study behaviour is to compare different levels of behavioural complexity.

BEHAVIOUR INVOLVING NO NERVOUS SYSTEM

A slime mould engulfs food particles but flows around inorganic particles; that is, it responds differentially to objects in its environment, just as you respond differentially to a doughnut and a rubber band. The protist, however, accomplishes this behaviour without any nerve receptors, brain or muscles. Many protists show such selectivity in response to objects in their environment.

If a ciliate of the genus *Vorticella* is touched lightly, it usually contracts its stalk. If the stimulus is continued, however, the organism seems to become accustomed to it. If a *Vorticella* is repeatedly touched, it responds in a variety of ways: it may bend away; it may reverse the direction in which its cilia are beating; it may contract; it may even swim away. Thus, the behaviour of *Vorticella* is variable.

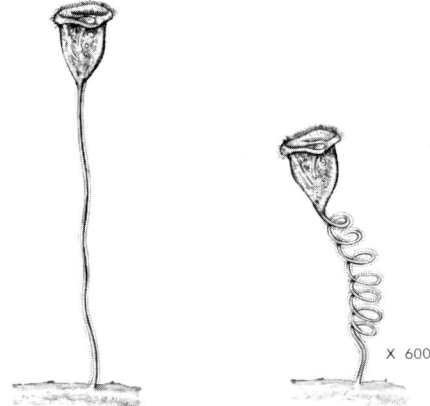

Figure 5.3 *Vorticella*: an individual in feeding position (*left*); same individual after a light touch (*right*).

These protists have no nerve cells or any other cellular differentiation, but they show two characteristics of behaviour – selectivity and variability. Plants also lack nerve cells, but they, too, show some basic behavioural characteristics. In general, however, reactions of protists are rapid and reactions of plants are slow.

Tropisms. In bryophytes and tracheophytes most behaviour is closely associated with growth. We have already studied the behaviour called phototropism. There are many such *tropisms*, but in each of them a plant part turns towards (positive) or away from (negative) a stimulus. The phototropism of stems is positive – the stem turns *towards* the light. The *geotropism* of stems is negative, but the geotropism of roots is positive.

Though tropisms represent a somewhat fixed kind of behaviour, they are not entirely invariable. The responses sometimes vary with differences in the

×1/3

Figure 5.4 Leaves of a plant of the genus *Mimosa* as they normally appear (*left*) and a short time after being touched (*right*). How do you think an organism without muscles can perform this response?

intensity of the stimulus. Bermuda grass is positively phototropic to weak light but negatively phototropic to strong light.

Taxes. Tropisms are responses in sessile organisms. In motile organisms, similar responses are called *taxes* (singular, 'taxis'). In a taxis the whole organism moves towards or away from the source of a stimulus. The kinds of stimuli are quite similar for tropisms and taxes. A *Euglena*, for example, is positively *phototactic*. Near its anterior end is a spot of pigment sensitive to light, a kind of receptor. As *Euglena* swims, its body rotates so that the pigment spot detects the direction of illumination. Somehow this information is transmitted to the flagellum, which then directs the organism towards the light.

A — Reaction to a drop of 0.5% salt solution.

C — Reaction to a piece of filter paper.

Figure 5.5 Behaviour of small populations of *Paramecium* in response to five environmental stimuli. Using the terms in the text, describe the behaviour in each case.

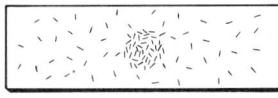

B — Reaction to a drop of weak acetic acid.

D — Reactions to a bubble of air and a bubble of CO_2.

INVESTIGATION 5.1

TROPIC RESPONSES IN PLANTS

PURPOSE

Here you will study the reaction of plants to certain physical environmental stimuli.

MATERIALS AND EQUIPMENT
(for each group)

Part A

Soaked maize grains, 4
Petri dish
Cotton wool
Scissors
Heavy blotting paper
Sellotape
Wax pencil

Part B

Flowerpots, about 8 cm in diameter, 4
Cardboard boxes, at least 5 cm higher than flowerpots, 4
Scissors
Red cellophane
Paste
Blue cellophane
Sellotape
Soil
Radish seeds, 40

Part C

Test-tubes, 25 mm × 200 mm, 4
One-hole stoppers, to fit test-tubes, 4
Shoots of *Zebrina*, about 20 cm long, 4
Melted paraffin wax in a beaker
Small brush
Wax pencil
Ring stand
Burette clamps, 4

PROCEDURE

Part A

1. Read through the instructions for Part A and construct an appropriate hypothesis.
2. Place 4 soaked maize grains in the bottom half of a petri dish. Arrange them cotyledon side down and in the position as shown in Figure 5.6.
3. Fill the spaces between the maize grains with wads of cotton wool to a depth slightly greater than the thickness of the grains.
4. Cut a piece of heavy blotting paper slightly larger than the bottom of the petri dish and fit it snugly over the seeds and cotton wool.
5. Hold the dish on its edge and observe the grains through the bottom. If they do not remain in place, repack with more cotton wool until they do.
6. When the grains are secure, wet the blotting paper thoroughly.
7. Seal the two halves of the dish together with strips of Sellotape.
8. Place the dish on edge in a shady corner of the room and rotate it until one of the grains is at the top.
9. Mark the dish with an 'A' beside this topmost grain and, proceeding clockwise, label the other grains B, C and D.
10. Fasten the dish to the table or

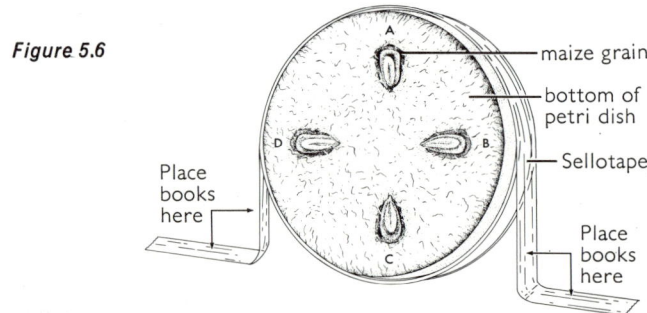

Figure 5.6

bench with a long strip of tape, as shown in Figure 5.6. If further support is required, stack books on top of the tape and against the edges of the dish. Do not change the position of the dish during the course of the experiment.
11. When the grains begin to germinate, make sketches daily for five days showing the direction in which the root and the shoot grow from each grain.

Part B

1. Read through the instructions and construct an appropriate hypothesis.
2. Number four cardboard boxes 1 to 4 and label each with your group symbol.
3. Turn the boxes bottom side up and cut a rectangular hole in one side of each of Boxes 1 to 3. Use the dimensions shown in Figure 5.7.
4. Tape a strip of red cellophane over the hole in Box 1. Tape a strip of blue cellophane over the hole in Box 2.
5. Leave the hole in Box 3 uncovered.
6. Using a pencil, number four flowerpots 1 to 4 and label each with your group symbol.
7. Fill the pots with soil and plant 10 radish seeds in each. The seeds should be planted 0.5 cm deep and 2 cm apart.
8. Press the soil down firmly over the seeds and water the pots.
9. Place the pots in a location which receives strong light but not direct sunlight.
10. Cover each pot with the box bearing its number so that the sides having the holes face the light.
11. Once each day remove the boxes and water the pots. DO NOT MOVE THE POTS AND BE SURE TO PLACE THE BOXES BACK IN THE SAME POSITION AFTER EACH WATERING.
12. When most of the radish seedlings have been above ground for two or three days, record the direction of stem growth in each pot: upright, curved slightly, or curved greatly – and if curved, tell in what direction with respect to the hole in the box.

Part C

1. Read through the instructions and construct an appropriate hypothesis.
2. Fill four test-tubes with water and insert a one-hole stopper firmly into each tube.
3. Remove all leaves within 8 cm of the cut ends of four *Zebrina* shoots.
4. Push the cut end of each shoot

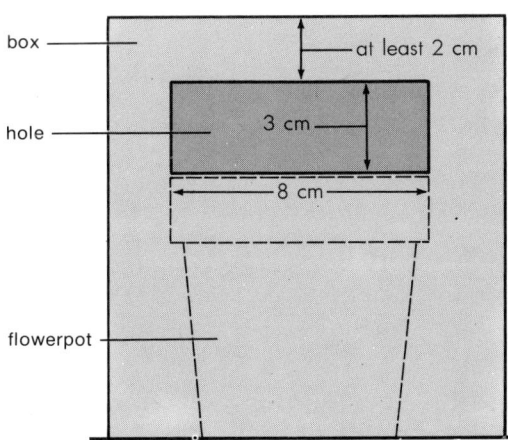

Figure 5.7

through a stopper until about 5 cm of the shoot is in water.
5. Seal the stoppers and shoots by applying melted paraffin wax. (The wax should be no warmer than is necessary to keep it liquid.)
6. Using a wax pencil, label the tubes A, B, C and D.
7. Attach a burette clamp to each tube and fasten them to a ring stand as shown in Figure 5.8.
8. Place the entire assembly in a location that receives bright light from one side.
9. Observe the shoots daily for a week.

STUDYING THE DATA
Part A
A. From which end of the grains did the roots grow?
B. Did the roots of all four grains eventually turn in one direction? If so, what was the direction?
C. From which end of the grain did the shoots grow?
D. Did the shoots of all four grains eventually turn in one direction?
E. To what stimulus did the maize roots seem to be responding?
F. Was the response positive or negative?
G. To what stimulus did the maize shoots seem to be responding?
H. Was the response positive or negative?
I. Has your hypothesis been substantiated?

Part B
A. In which pot were the stems nearest to perpendicular?
B. In which pots were the stems curved?
C. In which pot/pots did most curvature occur?
D. What was the direction of the curvature?
E. Has your hypothesis been substantiated?

Part C
A. Did any shoots grow without bending? If so, which ones?

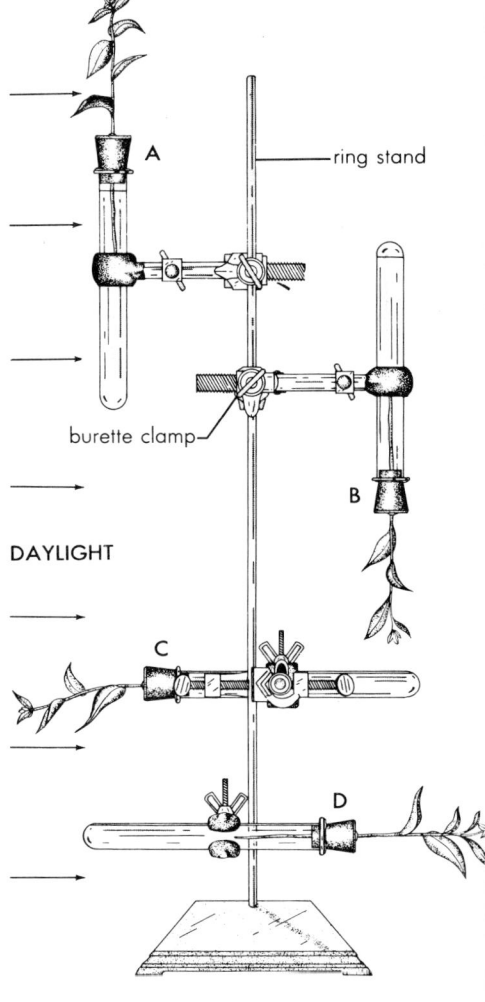

Figure 5.8

B. Did any shoots bend as they grew? If so, which ones and in what direction did they bend?
C. Has your hypothesis been substantiated?

FOR FURTHER INVESTIGATION
Will centrifugal force overcome the response of plant parts to gravity? To test this idea, you may mount the set-up used in Part A on a clinostat (your teacher will explain how this machine works).

BEHAVIOUR INVOLVING NERVOUS SYSTEMS

Except for sponges, all animals have differentiated nerve cells. All organisms that have nerve cells also have differentiated muscle cells – usually organized into tissues or systems that have specialized ability to contract and so bring about movement. The combination of specialized nerve and muscle cells so greatly supplements the responses possible through general irritability and hormones that some biologists restrict use of the term 'behaviour' to animals that possess such cells.

INNATE BEHAVIOUR

When a male moth emerges from its cocoon, it flies unhesitatingly towards the source of the odour produced by a female of its species. The first time that a squirrel encounters a nut, it attempts to bury it – even if it has never seen another squirrel do so, and if the nut is lying on the floor of a cage rather than on the ground. Young spiders without any previous experience weave webs as well constructed as those of older spiders.

These are examples of unlearned, *innate*, behaviour; they are actions that seem to be inherited just as structures are inherited. Behaviour that is brought forth by a particular stimulus in almost all individuals of a species, even in those without any previous experience, is usually considered innate. In tests of such behaviour, animals are reared in isolation; whatever these animals do, they do without following another animal's example. With mammals there is always at least some chance of learning from the mother; thus it is difficult to determine what part of their learning is innate.

Some innate behaviour is simply a matter of reflex (page 135), but the behaviour of the newly-emerged male moth is more complex than a reflex, because many muscles must work in coordination to produce flight. This behaviour must be called a taxis, though it is certainly more complex than the taxes in protists.

The behaviour of the squirrel with a nut is still more complex; certain muscles must be used in digging, others in putting the nut into a hole, and others in covering it. Moreover, these actions must be performed in the correct sequence. The construction of a spider's web requires even more complex behaviour. Yet evidence shows that all these are innate behaviours. They have been called *instincts* or *fixed-action patterns*. The first term is older, but some behavioural scientists think that it is no longer useful because too many false ideas have grown up around it. The second term is misleading because the behaviour is not entirely 'fixed'; that is, invariable. All behaviour depends on an organism as well as a stimulus. A sick squirrel or one that is merely tired may pay no attention to a nut, and spiders to which certain drugs have been given weave very poor webs.

Much behaviour, especially behaviour of invertebrates, can be classed as instinctive. This, of course, does not *explain* the behaviour. It is necessary for physiologists to explore the nervous and hormonal mechanisms that operate such behaviour. Psychologists analyse such behaviour by experimental interruptions of the action sequence making up an instinctive behaviour.

Figure 5.9 Any light tap on the side of the nest causes nestlings of many birds to react in the way shown here. This behaviour seems to be innate.

X 2/3

Many ethologists have been interested in the stimuli that start the chains of physiological reactions in fixed-action patterns. They have found that the stimulus for a complex behaviour pattern is often very simple. Such a stimulus – called a *releaser* – acts like a key that unlocks the whole physiological sequence. Like a key, a releaser is specific; only a particular releaser stimulus starts a particular behaviour pattern. For example, herring-gull chicks become very disturbed when a hawk flies over them; but the releaser is not the actual hawk. Experimentally, the chicks became disturbed even when shown a moving piece of cardboard cut in the shape of a hawk. When birds were shown a cardboard hawk model moving over them tail first, they exhibited no disturbance reaction. Evidently the tail-first shape was not the right 'key' to initiate disturbance behaviour.

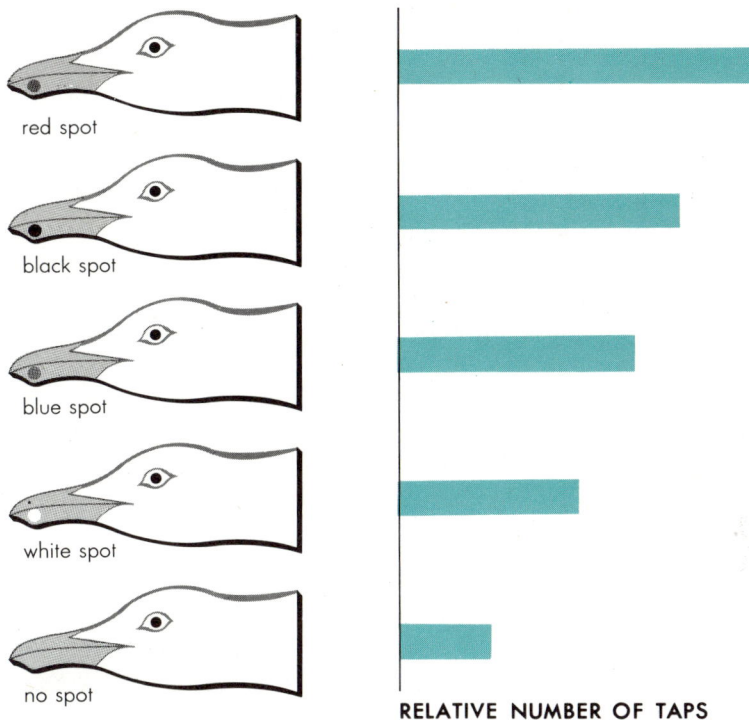

Figure 5.10 Herring-gull nestlings tap at a red spot on the bill of the parent; the parent then feeds them. An ethologist presented different cardboard models (*left*) to the newly hatched chicks and recorded the the result (*right*). Can you draw any conclusion about this behaviour?

LEARNED BEHAVIOUR

The nut-burying behaviour of squirrels seems to be innate; so, too, is nut opening. A young squirrel opens a nut satisfactorily; but as the squirrel becomes older and more experienced, its efficiency at opening nuts increases greatly. Chaffinches reared from hatching in sound-proof rooms develop a song pattern basically like that of wild chaffinches. However, the songs never develop all of the notes of the wild song unless the birds are allowed to hear the wild song. Evidently the song pattern is innate, but something is added to the innate behaviour during the life of the birds. Both squirrels and birds *learn* behaviour patterns.

What is learning? This is not easy to describe precisely. Learning depends on the experiences of an individual, and it usually brings about a lasting change in behaviour. We must say that learning brings about a 'lasting' rather than a 'permanent' change in behaviour, because forgetting occurs in learned behaviour – as every pupil knows. Some kinds of lasting changes in behaviour occur simply as a part of an organism's development. For example, when a tadpole's legs develop and its tail disappears, the change in behaviour (from tail swimming to leg swimming) is clearly associated with a change in structure. In other cases it is extremely difficult to determine whether changes in behaviour depend on learning or merely on structural development. Is not experience, practice – that is, learning – necessary before a child can climb stairs? An experiment was tried with identical twins – twins with exactly the same heredity, in whom the rate of development should be the same. At an early age one twin was allowed much practice on stairs; the other was kept on flat surfaces and given no experience with stairs. Yet, when the second was finally allowed to climb stairs, his performance was about as good as that of his experienced twin.

Figure 5.11 During the nesting season a male robin raises his head and puffs out his red breast whenever he encounters another male. Here an ethologist has placed a tuft of red feathers in a tree. Without anthropomorphism, can you explain the reaction of the bird?

Do all animals learn? So far, in all experiments with sponges, coelenterates and echinoderms, it seems possible to explain their behaviour without assuming that learning has occurred, but in flatworms there is no doubt that a simple kind of learning does occur. Unlike the other animals mentioned, a flatworm has an anterior end and a posterior end, with a bilaterally symmetrical nervous system and an anterior ganglion (Figure 4.25). There may be something about such a structural development that favours the learning process. At least, animals of other phyla in which learning occurs also have central controlling ganglia.

A flatworm does not learn very easily, nor does it learn very much. There is a wide variation in the abilities of different animals to learn. Many kinds of beetles, if put on a table-top, will crawl to the edge and fall off; and no matter how many times this happens, they never learn about the edge of the table. At the other extreme is the case of a young pilot whale that was captured a few years ago by collectors employed by a large aquarium in the

U.S.A. When finally they got the whale into a tank, it attempted to dive, struck its snout on the bottom and thereafter refused to leave the surface. One experience was enough.

Imprinting. Most learning requires more than a single experience. In the 1930s, however, Konrad Lorenz discovered a kind of learning in birds that depends on just one experience – but that experience must come shortly after hatching. Geese follow the first moving object they see after hatching. Normally this is their mother, but geese hatched in an incubator followed Dr. Lorenz. Afterwards they behaved towards him as though he were the female goose. He was *imprinted* in the experience of the goslings as 'mother'.

The 'imprinting' object corresponds to the influence of a releaser, but differs in that the particular stimulus is not recognized innately – it must be learned. Much experimentation has shown that in many cases, the first moving object that a young bird or fish sees releases many reactions that are normally released by the presence of a parent. This is particularly true if the object also gives appropriate sounds – quacking, in the case of ducks, for instance. If imprinting can be called learning, it is a very simple kind, closely related to innate behaviour.

Conditioning. Imprinting was discovered by an ethologist. Conditioning was discovered much earlier by a physiologist. Ivan P. Pavlov was interested in the physiology of mammalian nervous systems. He began to study the reflex involved in the production of saliva in dogs and soon found that the odour or sight of meat was sufficient to start salivation. Pavlov wondered whether other stimuli would produce the salivation response. Just before presenting meat to a dog, he rang a bell. This procedure was repeated many times with the same dog. Before long the dog was beginning to secrete saliva as soon as the bell was rung, before the meat was presented. Eventually Pavlov found that the dog could be made to salivate merely by the ringing of the bell, entirely without the stimulus of the meat. This kind of learning – the transfer of a reflex response from one stimulus to another – is called *conditioning*.

Pavlov extended his research in many directions. He showed that the substitute stimulus must come *before* the original stimulus if the response is to be transferred. He also showed that the shorter the time interval between the two stimuli, the quicker the reaction becomes associated with the substitute stimulus. Later biologists have extended Pavlov's principles to other animals, including man.

Trial-and-error learning. In conditioning, the learner is a passive subject. More complicated kinds of learning require movement by the learner. All animals make many kinds of movements. Learning begins when an animal associates certain movements with favourable or unfavourable results. Thus, experimentally, *trial-and-error* learning involves either 'rewards' or 'punishments', or both.

B. F. Skinner has devised a box for investigating trial-and-error learning. A bar in the box releases a pellet of food when pressed. A hungry rat, placed in the box, moves about at random and sooner or later strikes the bar. Before long most rats associate pressing the bar with the reward of food. This device has been used to investigate many questions about learning; for example: What happens if the food pellet is not released after the rat has learned to obtain it by pressing the bar? What happens if the pellet is released sometimes but not always?

With any animal that is capable of locomotion, learning can be studied by means of a maze. Basically, a maze is a route with one or more choices of turns leading to a goal that is favourable or unfavourable to the animal. The simplest form is the T maze (see Figure 5.1). How can we know that learning has occurred in a maze? With a T maze we expect that by chance 50 per cent of the turns will be to the right and 50 per cent to the left. If, after several trials, the animal turns to the right (where food is located) 90 per cent of the time and to the left only 10 per cent of the time, we might conclude that it has learned. In more complicated mazes, time may be used as a basis for conclusions. At first, an animal explores blind alleys; as it 'learns' the maze, fewer and fewer trips are made down the blind alleys, and the time to reach the 'reward' is reduced.

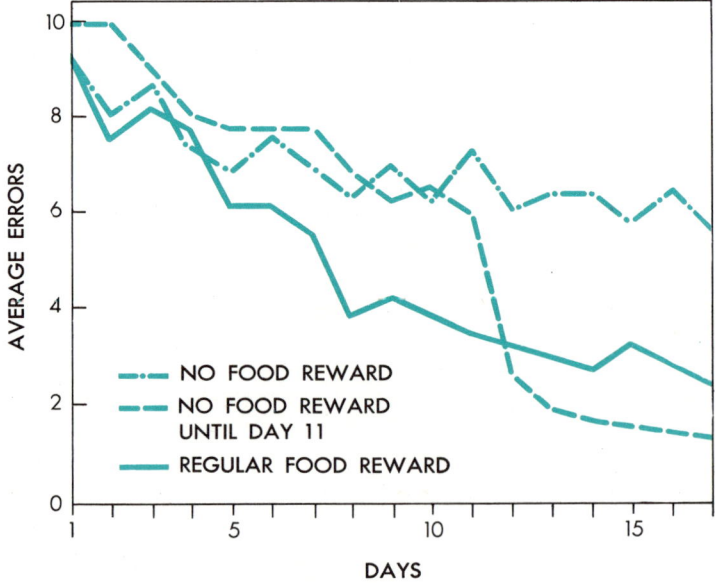

Figure 5.12 A learning experiment. Three groups of rats were tested daily in a maze. The route through the maze forked 14 times, and none of the choices could be repeated. The number of errors in choice was counted for each rat, and an average obtained for each group. How do you interpret the results?

REASONING

It is difficult to describe what we mean by 'reasoning'. The process involves situations in which specific stimuli are lacking and trial and error has a very minor part. Perhaps reasoning is best described in an example. In Figure 5.13 the dog cannot quite reach the food by going directly towards it. First it must go back around stake B. Given enough time, almost any active animal accomplishes the task by trial and error. In this way dogs learn quickly. The test of reasoning hinges not on how *quickly* the animal learns by trial and error but on what the animal does on the *first* exposure to the problem.

Put in the dog's place, what would you do? You would immediately 'size up the situation', walk back around stake B, and reach the food. Chimpanzees and most monkeys do the same thing. This behaviour is often described as resulting from *insight*. Many primates apparently do not see A, B, C and the rope as separate items but as parts of a whole situation – the 'meaning' is in the situation, not in the items.

Figure 5.13 A problem.

In another kind of experiment, an animal is allowed to watch the experimenter place food under one of two identical cups. After a delay, the animal is released to find the food. (Of course, odour must be controlled in such an experiment.) Animals such as rats, cats and dogs fix their attention on the cup covering the food and go directly to it. If their attention is temporarily diverted, however, they do no better than would be expected on the basis of chance. Most primates, however, do not seem to fix their attention on the cup under which the food is placed. Indeed, even if they are removed from the situation and then brought back later, they still go immediately to the

166 Looking into Organisms

Figure 5.14 Another problem – and its solution by a primate. How would you describe this behaviour?

correct cup. Does the non-human primate mind form some lasting image, such as 'food under right-hand cup'? If so, this behaviour closely approaches the language-based behaviour of man.

Non-primates apparently do not have insight. Some, such as dogs, learn quickly, and even an octopus can learn to go around barriers. Often observations of wild animals reveal behaviour that seems to demonstrate insight, but of course such behaviour may be merely the result of past experience.

Behaviour 167

Figure 5.15 Porpoises learn many things very easily. Is this what we mean by 'intelligence'?

INVESTIGATION 5.2

BEHAVIOUR OF AN INVERTEBRATE ANIMAL

PURPOSE
In this investigation you will observe the reactions of wood-lice to different stimuli and use one kind of stimulus to test the animals' learning ability.

BACKGROUND INFORMATION
Wood-lice are terrestrial crustaceans, relatives of crabs and shrimp. Because they breathe by means of specialized gills and have no way of preventing

evaporation of water from their bodies, they must live in habitats where relative humidity remains fairly high. Wood-lice can be found where such conditions exist, e.g. under logs and rocks and in damp leaf litter.

MATERIALS AND EQUIPMENT
(for groups of 4)

Part A
  Container with a plastic lid
  Mixture of moist soil and leaf litter
  Sponge, a cube of sides 2 cm
  Carrot or potato
  Wood-lice, 10–12
  Small nail
  Glass or metal tray, about 20 cm × 30 cm
  Blotting paper, about 20 cm × 15 cm
  Laboratory desk lamps, 4
  Masking tape

Part B
  Specimen tubes with plastic lids, 4
  Mixture of moist soil and leaf litter
  Paper tissue
  Carrot or potato
  Glass-marking pencil
  Wood-lice, 4
  Box, about 10 cm × 15 cm × 2 cm, all plastic or with plastic cover
  Cardboard, about 12 cm × 12 cm
  Scissors
  Roll of masking tape
  Forceps

PROCEDURE

Part A
1. Set up a habitat for the wood-lice as follows.
    (*a*) Place moist soil and leaf litter in a container with a plastic lid to two-thirds its depth.
    (*b*) Place a few dead leaves on the surface and add a small piece of moistened sponge.
    (*c*) Add a slice of carrot or potato (about 5 cm × 2 cm × 1 cm).
    (*d*) Place your wood-lice in the container and cover with the plastic lid into which 6 to 8 air holes have been punched.
    The animals can be kept in this container indefinitely if the sponge is kept moist and the carrot or potato slice is changed every few days.
2. In subdued light, place all the wood-lice in the centre of a large tray, and observe group behaviour.

A. Do the animals tend to remain together? If not, do they wander about aimlessly or do they move in one direction?

3. Remove the animals gently and place some moist blotting paper at one end of the tray so that one half of the bottom is dry and the other half is covered with moist paper.
4. Place all the wood-lice at the centre of the dry end of the tray and observe them for several minutes.

B. What percentage of the animals remain on the dry half of the tray?
C. If some move to the moist end, do they climb on top of the blotter or move underneath it?

5. If some animals move underneath the blotter, wait for about five minutes and then remove the blotter and observe the animals.

D. Do they tend to be uniformly distributed or are they clustered in groups? Make a note of any other behaviour which you observe.

6. Set up two lamps of equal intensity 50 cm apart.
7. Place a wood-louse equidistant from the two lamps and about 20 cm from an imaginary line joining the two lamps. The animal should be facing this imaginary line.

E. If the animal moves, sketch its route in relation to the lamps.

8. Repeat this several times, sketching the route each time.
9. Cover the animal's right eye with a piece of masking tape and repeat the procedure. Again sketch the route taken in several trials.

F. Is there any consistent difference in

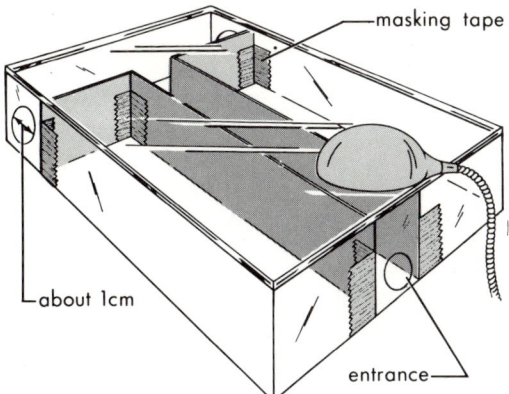

Figure 5.16

the routes taken under the two different conditions?

G. To what stimulus is the animal reacting?

Part B

1. Mark four specimen tubes A to D and add your group symbol to each. Perforate the lid of each tube.
2. Half fill each with moist soil and leaf litter, add a spiralled strip of moist paper and a small piece of potato or carrot.
3. Place one wood-louse into each tube and replace the lid.
4. Using a transparent plastic-topped cardboard or plastic box, prepare a T maze as shown in Figure 5.16.
5. Use pieces of cardboard for the inner walls, holding them in place with masking tape.
6. Cut one hole in the box wall at the base of the T and one at the end of each arm.
7. Place a lamp in the position shown but do not turn it on.
8. Place Animal A into the maze through the hole in the base of the T and cover the hole with masking tape.
9. Turn on the lamp.

A. How does the animal react?

10. When the animal reaches the cross-arm of the T it will usually turn in one direction or the other. Note the direction.
11. When the wood-louse reaches the end of the arm, remove it immediately and repeat the 'test run'. Make a total of five 'test runs', recording the direction of turn each time.
12. Return the animal to its tube.
13. Repeat for Animals B, C and D.
14. Begin with Animal A and make five more 'trial runs'. Test Animals B, C and D also.
15. After 24 hours, repeat the procedure (i.e. Instructions 8 to 14).
16. You will now have the results of 20 trials with each wood-louse. Tabulate the results for each animal and record on the vial as follows.
    (a) L for a consistent left turner.
    (b) R for a consistent right turner.
    (c) E for an animal which turns in either direction without consistency.
17. You are now ready to train your animals. Select the L and R animals for the training procedure. Do not use the animals classified E.
18. Select one animal, either an R or an L.
19. Place a lamp at the end of the arm down which it consistently turned. Do not turn the lamp on.
20. Place the animal in the maze as before and when it reaches the T junction, turn on the lamp.

B. What is the animal's reaction?
21. Remove the wood-louse and return it to its tube.
22. Carry out this procedure with each of the L and R animals, shifting the location of the light so that it is always at the end of the arm down which the animal consistently turned during 'trial runs'.
23. Go back to the first animal and repeat the sequence of testing until each wood-louse has been given ten runs.
24. Repeat the whole training procedure each day for at least three days.
25. After the training has been completed, test each animal in the maze *once without using a light*.
26. Record the direction turned in each case.

STUDYING THE DATA

Part A
A. Can the behaviour of your animals with respect to moisture be related to survival? If so, how?
B. Can the behaviour of your animals, with respect to light, be related to survival? If so, how?
C. Review the discussion of levels of behaviour. Which term best fits the behaviour which you have observed?

What additional information would increase your confidence in your decision?

Part B
A. What kind of learning was the procedure used in this investigation designed to produce?
B. Did you obtain any evidence of learning in the animals which you used? If so, what was the evidence?
C. If you obtained evidence of learning in the species, did all individuals learn equally well?
D. Do you think that individual differences in ability to learn would have any effect on a population of wood-lice?

FOR FURTHER INVESTIGATION
A biologist investigating tolerances of organisms to factors in their environment (e.g. temperature, humidity) has difficulty separating the effects of one factor from the effects of another. In Part A of this investigation the same problem is encountered with respect to stimuli. Criticize the procedure used and try to design a procedure that would better separate the effects of the stimuli involved.

SOME PATTERNS OF ANIMAL BEHAVIOUR

We have been discussing behaviour from the viewpoint of its mechanisms – how it is started and how it is performed. To many biologists, another viewpoint is more important: how behaviour functions in the survival of individuals and of species. From this viewpoint, the kinds of behaviour are so varied that they are difficult to classify. There is behaviour associated with adjustment to factors in the abiotic environment – heat, humidity, salinity, for example. There is behaviour associated with food-getting, with escape from enemies, with reproduction. None of these kinds of behaviour has been fully studied for any species; the study of behaviour is a young science.

Rather than attempt a brief glance at many parts of behavioural science, we will restrict the rest of this chapter to a somewhat longer consideration of a few. We will proceed from an aspect of behaviour in which attention is primarily upon the reactions of an individual organism, to an aspect in which attention is primarily upon interactions among a group of individuals.

PERIODICITY IN BEHAVIOUR

Almost everyone has observed that many activities of plants and animals do not occur continuously, but often at similar times in each twenty-four-hour day. Many birds sing most near the time of sunrise. Flowers of some species of plant open in the morning and close at night; those of other species open in the evening. Most species of moths fly by night and rest by day; most butterflies behave in the opposite way.

Most people assume that these daily cycles in activities are the direct result of day and night. To some extent this is quite true, but experimentation has shown that it is not entirely true. In 1729 a French scientist took plants deep into a mine. He discovered that for several days (while the plants were still healthy) the leaf movements were very similar to those under natural conditions of day and night. These observations strongly indicated that something within the plant, not something in the environment, was prompting these movements to take place.

As too often happens in biology, scientists of the time failed to recognize the importance of these observations. It was not until more than two hundred years later that a German botanist, Erwin Bünning, on the basis of his own investigations and those of others, was able to support them convincingly. He showed that in many organisms – not only plants but animals and protists also – some behaviour occurred periodically without regard to changes of light and dark, a kind of innate rhythm of behaviour.

Figure 5.18 shows the record of activity of a chaffinch when kept in a

Figure 5.17 Chaffinch. X 1

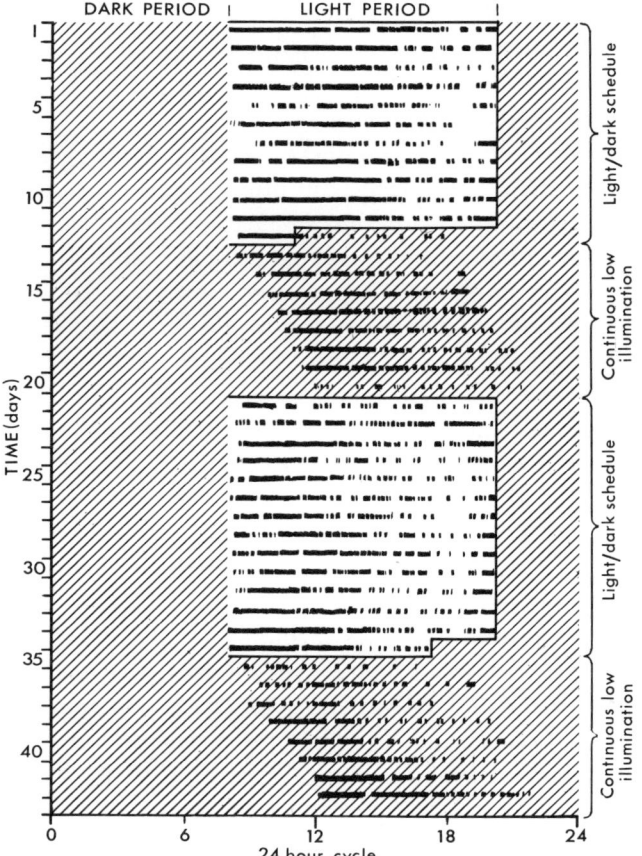

Figure 5.18 The activity rhythm of a chaffinch kept on a light/dark schedule of illumination alternating with conditions of constant low illumination (*after Aschoff and Wever*).

sound-proof chamber under conditions of constant temperature but with differing schedules of light. The bird's activity was measured by microswitches below each perch, and these were activated by the movements of the bird. Under conditions of low illumination in each twenty-four-hour period (a natural day), the onset of activity of the chaffinch began half an hour later than the day before. The chaffinch therefore had a periodicity in activity behaviour of 24.5 hours. Similar demonstrations have been made with a large variety of organisms and a large variety of activities – for example: leaf movements in plants; cell division in some protists; change in human body temperatures; times of activities in mammals and insects; changes in metabolic rates in some tissues. Almost all these periodicities of behaviour turn out to be only approximately twenty-four hours long. They are therefore now referred to as *circadian rhythms*.

Circadian rhythms are innate. But under environmental conditions that provide a light–dark cycle, the rhythms conform to the cycle – the innate mechanism is modified by stimuli from the environment. Thus, under a twenty-four-hour light–dark cycle, the activity rhythm of a chaffinch becomes a precise twenty-four-hour rhythm. This rhythm can adjust to other light–dark cycles. But there are limits; the rhythm cannot conform to a cycle consisting of nine hours of light and nine hours of darkness.

Although details differ in different species, most organisms can readjust circadian periodicities to a new light–dark cycle in a few days. In this era of jet aeroplane travel, the problem of adjustment is quite important to man. Consider a traveller who flies by jet aeroplane from London to New York. At first his circadian rhythms – his 'biological clock' – tend to retain London time. When he appears at a meeting in New York at 3 p.m., his 'biological clock' is still very close to 8 p.m. London time, and he is likely to be extremely hungry during the meeting. Therefore, persons attending important meetings at places many degrees of longitude distant frequently have to arrive several days in advance in order to permit their 'biological clocks' to reset.

TERRITORIALITY

It is spring in England. A male chaffinch is perching on a low tree. He sings. Again and again he sings. Another male appears. Immediately the first male leaves the tree and flies to the tree in which the second sits. If the second does not leave, the first approaches more closely and there may be a brief fight. Almost invariably the second bird loses the fight and leaves. The first bird then goes back to his perch and resumes singing.

By repeated observation we begin to see that the singing occurs only when a second male bird approaches within certain limits, that often a second male avoids the presence of the conspicuous singing male, and that the presence of a female does not stimulate the same behaviour from the first male.

Chaffinches are partial migrants, and in winter they flock together, the females often in one flock and the males in another. The males may roost side by side without disturbing one another. There is little or no singing.

In 1920 Eliot Howard published a book in which he described his observations of birds nesting in his garden and orchard. By carefully watching the movements of individual birds, Howard discovered that each male tended to remain within a limited area that was strongly defended against intrusions by other birds of the same species. He interpreted the constant singing of the newly arrived males in the spring as a way of warning other males that particular areas – territories – were already occupied.

Since 1920 many studies of *territoriality* have been made. Most of the studies were made on birds, and one of the problems that arose was: How can we explain the different behaviour in summer and winter? By years of experiment with captive birds and years of investigation with others, some progress has been made towards understanding this problem.

Consider a male chaffinch in late winter; the days are becoming longer. The lengthening hours of daylight somehow affect the bird's hypothalamus. This, in turn, somehow causes the anterior pituitary to begin issuing the hormones that cause gradual growth and development of the testes. At the same time the hypothalamus stimulates the production of other hormones. These increase the bird's appetite and he takes in more food than is required for his daily activities. The excess food is stored as fat. The combination of these (and perhaps other) hormonal activities brings about local nocturnal flights. When the reserve of fat is used up, the bird interrupts his migrations and restores it.

By the time the male has reached a suitable breeding place, his testes are producing male sex hormones. One effect of these hormones – together with the sight of the breeding area – is to cause territorial behaviour. The response of the bird to another male is completely different from his response a few weeks earlier in the wintering or migratory flock.

As the year proceeds, the days cease to lengthen. The internal mechanism that responded to the lengthening days of spring is insensitive to the long days of June and the shortening days that follow. The hypothalamus no longer causes the anterior pituitary to release hormones affecting the testes. The testes thus shrink in size and discontinue the production of male sex hormones. Without the effect of male sex hormones on the central nervous system, the territorial reaction to other males disappears. Males abandon their territories and assemble in flocks with females and young, or with other males.

Territorial behaviour appears to have value for the survival of organisms. Animals placed in unfamiliar surroundings have little chance of avoiding predators; but a territory becomes a familiar area. After the territories are established, usually there is little actual fighting. Hence individuals have more time and energy to devote to other aspects of daily life. In the kind of territoriality represented by chaffinches, the conspicuous singing by male birds may increase the chance that unmated females will locate mates. In this kind of territory, also, an area is reserved from which food may be gathered to feed the young. Thus territorial behaviour may restrict the size of a breeding population to the number of pairs whose young can be supported by the available food supply.

Figure 5.19 In herring gulls, only the immediate vicinity of the nest is 'defended'. This territorial dispute does not affect birds nesting only a few metres away.

The territory described for chaffinches is only one of many kinds now recognized; some are places for mating, some are for nesting, some are for feeding, and others are for various combinations of these activities. The essential fact about a territory is that it is defended – most often by males, sometimes by females, sometimes by mated pairs, and sometimes even by a whole flock.

The study of territoriality is a meeting point for many kinds of biologists. Both nervous and endocrine systems are involved in the physiology of territorial behaviour; the interactions of individuals are of interest to ethologists; and the function of territoriality in community structure and in the homeostasis of ecosystems greatly concerns ecologists. It is not surprising that Howard's concept, developed from study of birds in his garden, has now spread far and wide. Territorial behaviour of one kind or another has been found among mammals, reptiles, amphibians, fish, and even some invertebrate animals.

INVESTIGATION 5.3

SOCIAL BEHAVIOUR IN FISH

INTRODUCTION
In man, much behaviour is social – that is, it involves reactions between different individuals of the same species. Human social behaviour is difficult to study not only because it is complex but also because much of it is expressed in words rather than in actions. In addition, the student of human social behaviour, being human himself, may easily confuse his own reactions with the reactions of the group he is studying; or he may unconsciously allow his emotions and attitudes to influence his observations.

Much can be learned about social behaviour – some of it perhaps relevant to human societies – through observation of, and experimentation with, other species. Of course, there are difficulties in observing, describing and interpreting the behaviour of other species, too. The temptation to anthropomorphize is great, but may be less so with some organisms than with others. Perhaps such a danger is easier to guard against when fishes rather than mammals or birds are studied.

PURPOSE
In this investigation a number of simple experiments with two species of fish should enable you to draw some conclusions about simple social behaviour.

MATERIALS AND EQUIPMENT
(for each group)

Glass jars, 1 litre capacity, 5
Glass jar, 4 litres capacity
Wax pencil
Pieces of cardboard about 30 cm square, 5
Aquarium water, 5 litres maintained at 24 °C
Male *Corydoras*, 4
Male *Betta*, 2
Mirror
Smooth sheet of cardboard 20 cm × 10 cm
Scissors
Paint, several colours
Paint brushes

PROCEDURE
1. Arrange the six jars in a row on a table that does not receive direct sunlight, placing the large jar at one end.
2. Number the jars 1 to 6, beginning

with the large jar. The numbers should be small and near the tops of the jars.
3. Place a piece of cardboard between the jars so that fishes in adjacent jars will not be able to see each other.
4. Pour aquarium water into the jars until each is about half full.
5. Into each of the first four jars place a male *Corydoras*. Place a male *Betta* into each of the remaining two jars.
6. Allow a day or two for the fishes to become accustomed to their surroundings before trying the following experiments.

Experiment A
1. Remove the cardboard from between Jars 5 and 6 (containing the two *Betta*), thus allowing the two fishes to see each other.
2. In your lab-book record the behaviour of each fish; note especially the use of the fins, tail, mouth and gill covers.
3. After observing the behaviour – called a *display* – replace the cardboard between the jars.

Experiment B
1. Remove the cardboard from between Jars 1 and 2 (two *Corydoras*).
2. In your lab-book record the behaviour of each fish as accurately and in as much detail as possible.
3. Replace the cardboard.

Experiment C
1. Fifteen minutes after Experiment A is completed, press the mirror against the side of Jar 6 (*Betta*).
2. In your lab-book record the behaviour of the fish.

Experiment D
1. Fifteen minutes after the completion of Experiment B, press the mirror against the side of Jar 3 (*Corydoras*).
2. In your lab-book record the behaviour of the fish.

Experiment E
1. Remove the cardboard from between Jars 4 and 5 (*Corydoras* and *Betta*).
2. Using your notes from Experiments A and B as a basis for comparison, record the behaviour of each fish.

Experiment F
1. During the next one or two days, cut three fish models in the shape of *Betta* and two in the shape of *Corydoras*. Paint them as follows:
   (a) One of the *Betta* models to resemble the *Betta*.
   (b) One of the *Betta* models to resemble the coloration of *Corydoras*.
   (c) Paint the third *Betta* model a selection of other colours.
   (d) Paint one of the *Corydoras* to resemble the coloration of *Betta*.
   (e) Paint the other *Corydoras* model a selection of other colours.
2. Allowing about six minutes between trials, place each painted model, one at a time, against Jars 5 and 6.
3. Record the behaviour of the fish during each trial.

Experiment G
1. When the fish have been in the jars for one week, remove the *Corydoras* from Jar 4 and place it in Jar 1.
2. Note the behaviour of each fish – the original occupant and the 'newcomer'.
3. Now remove the *Corydoras* from Jar 3 and place it in Jar 1. Note the behaviour of the three fish.
4. Allow the three fish to live together for one week. Observe them occasionally during this time. Note whether they tend to band together or to go their separate ways. Note also any reactions to accidental collisions.

Experiment H
1. When the three *Corydoras* have been

together for one week, remove a fish from Jar 1 and place it in one of the empty jars.
2. Next day return it to Jar 1.
3. Note the behaviour of the two fish that remained in Jar 1; note also the behaviour of the 'returnee'.
4. Now remove the fish from Jar 2 and place it with the three in Jar 1.
5. Note the behaviour of the fish already in Jar 1, comparing their reactions to this 'stranger' with their reactions to the 'returnee'.

SUMMARY AND CONCLUSIONS

The experiments in this investigation are designed to elicit reactions that provide data for understanding the behavioural relationships between individual fish. To accomplish this, each separate observation must be linked with the others. Study your notes and attempt to write a summary ending with one or more conclusions concerning social behaviour among fish. Your conclusions must, of course, be consistent with your observations.

The following questions are intended to guide your thinking: they need not be answered specifically.

A. Why was the exercise performed with male fish only?
B. Do males of all fish species react in the same way to other males of their species?
C. Do males react to males of another species in the same way that they react to males of their own species?
D. By what means – shape, colour, movement, other means – does a male *Betta* recognize another male?
E. Is *Corydoras* individualistic, or do the individuals tend to associate in groups?
F. Do *Corydoras* recognize other *Corydoras* as individuals?

FOR FURTHER INVESTIGATION

Techniques similar to those described can be used with other kinds of aquarium fish. With some modifications, these techniques can also be used to investigate some aspects of the behaviour of cage birds.

Carry out further experiments with other fish or birds.

COMMUNICATION

We discussed territoriality mostly in connection with the endocrine and nervous mechanisms that bring it about – from a physiological viewpoint. But territoriality is meaningless unless it is also viewed as a kind of interaction between individuals – from an ethological viewpoint. In anthropomorphic terms, a singing male bird is 'telling' other males that he 'claims' the area around him; he is 'telling' females that the area is available for nesting. Communication between individuals is part of territorial behaviour.

Any activity on the part of one organism that causes a reaction in another organism can be regarded as communication. In this broad and basic sense, communication must occur in all ecological relationships – among plants and protists as well as among animals. Most biologists tend to use the term in a narrower sense, though they do not always agree on the limits. In this discussion, communication is restricted to animals.

To be of value for communication, each kind of stimulus must have a 'meaning'. A biologist can find out what the meaning is only by observing what organisms do when the stimulus is given. A male chaffinch sings; other males avoid the vicinity of the singer; many females may approach the vicinity of the singer. In this case the stimulus has one meaning for the males, another for the females. Apparently it has no meaning for the cows that are grazing nearby because they show no signs of reacting to it. Many men have reacted to the singing of birds by writing poetry – but most biologists would probably not regard this as communication between bird and poet.

Anything that can be sensed by another organism – any type of stimulus – may serve for communication. Scents, sights and sounds are the most commonly used stimuli. Scent is used as a means of communication, particularly by mammals and insects. By leaving their scents at various places, some mammals mark the limits of their territories. An ant lays down a 'trail' of formic acid from a food supply direct to its ant-hill. The formic acid seems to mean 'go this way'. If the formic acid is destroyed, the ants are no longer able to go directly to the food but scurry round and round until they apparently find it again by chance.

Man, having a poor sense of smell, makes little use of communication by scent, but he uses sight – visual communication – extensively. So do other animals in which sight is present. Usually visual stimuli consist of movements. Often the movements are made more conspicuous by some structure of the body. A startled roe deer communicates its alarm to the rest of the herd by leaping away, displaying white patches on the rump. The giver of a visual stimulus need not necessarily have good vision, because communication may

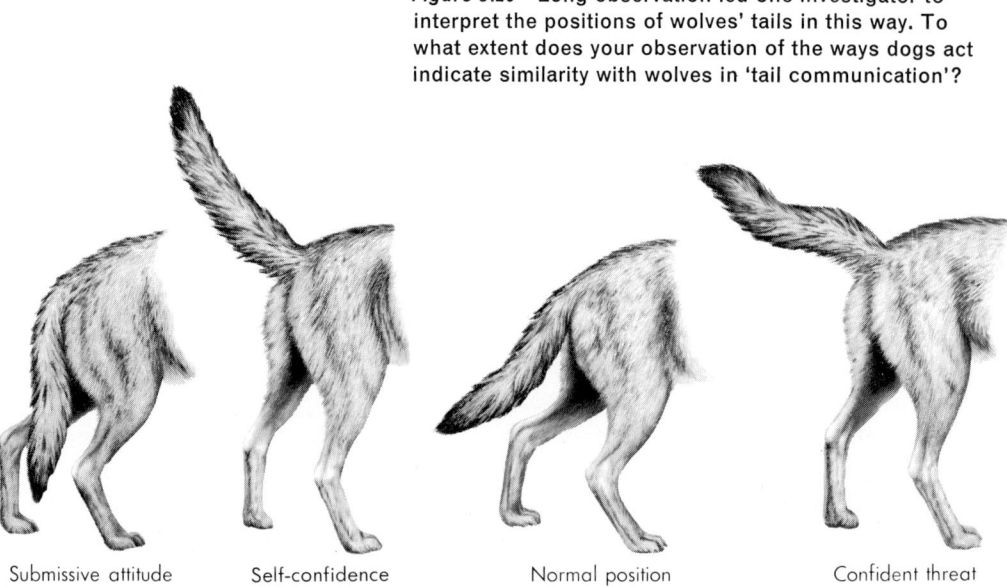

Figure 5.20 Long observation led one investigator to interpret the positions of wolves' tails in this way. To what extent does your observation of the ways dogs act indicate similarity with wolves in 'tail communication'?

Submissive attitude   Self-confidence   Normal position   Confident threat

Figure 5.21 The emperor moth has false eyes on its wings.

be interspecific – directed towards another species. Some caterpillars have spots that superficially resemble large eyes. The true eyes of a caterpillar are small and probably cannot see the spots on another caterpillar's back, but a food-seeking bird may be 'frightened' sufficiently by the large 'eyes' to allow the caterpillar to escape. One observer recorded that a bird fell backwards off a twig when suddenly confronted with such a caterpillar. Some adult moths, for example the emperor moth *Saturnia pavonia*, have eye markings on the wings. Can you suggest a possible function for this adaptation?

To most people communication by means of sounds means language. Some biologists refer to 'animal language', but many psychologists doubt that any organism besides man has a means of communication comparable to human language. We have sounds, such as 'ouch!', that communicate meaning in much the same way as do the sounds of other animals; but is an M.P.'s speech in the Houses of Parliament only a series of such sounds? Whatever your answer to that question may be, animals do make a great variety of sounds that result in observable behaviour in other animals – sound communication.

SOCIAL BEHAVIOUR

Any interaction among individuals of the same species could be called 'social' behaviour; but such a definition is so broad that it has little meaning. The meeting of two cuckoos on the boundary of their territories, even if it results in a show of hostility, is not usually considered social behaviour. Social behaviour requires the formation of groups of individuals that are maintained more than momentarily. Oysters form groups, often very close groups; and, once formed, the grouping lasts for life; but this is not usually considered social behaviour either.

Sometimes a food supply brings together many animals. When fruit is ripening on a cherry tree, large numbers of birds come together in the tree. Communication occurs; one bird may interact with another, and the grouping may last for several days. This is a simple kind of grouping, but it contains the basic requirements of a social organization.

Of course, a grouping of birds in a fruit tree may be composed of several species. This is not of great importance to many investigations of animal social behaviour; but in the remainder of this discussion, we shall deal with groupings containing individuals of a single species.

Figure 5.22 A school of mackerel. Can you think of any ways in which this behaviour might be an advantage to the fish? X 1/14

Fish schools. A school of fish represents a fairly simple aggregation. Schooling fish tend to have sleek bodies that glitter as they move. The school's organization and movements are controlled in part by such visual stimuli releasers; fish that cannot see do not school. A school is usually made up of fish not only of the same species but also of the same size. At any particular instant, all individuals in the school swim in one direction and as a compact group. Pressure receptors along the sides of the fish may receive stimuli that tend to keep each fish at a certain distance from the others.

Part of this behaviour involves fixed-action patterns, but learning is also definitely involved. Contacts between very young fish increase their ability to swim together in one direction. Older fish, when separated from each other over a period of time, tend to 'forget' how to school.

Insect societies. When they look at social behaviour in other animals, most people probably have human behaviour in mind. They are looking for something more organized, more complex than schools of fishes or flocks of birds, or even herds of reindeer and other mammals. When they look through the animal kingdom for something comparable to human societies, most people find the greatest similarities in the social behaviour of certain insects.

Among ants, bees and termites, large numbers of individuals carry on many diverse special tasks and seem to work closely together for the good of the group. The more we study these insects, the more similarities we find to human societies. Within a group, we find individuals that specialize in different kinds of work: food collectors, fighters, 'baby-sitters', nurses. Some species cultivate fungi. Some species wage war and make slaves. Some species construct complicated housing projects.

One can easily see the anthropomorphism in the previous paragraph. Psychologists and ethologists do not look upon social behaviour in this way. Repeated experiments show that the highly organized invertebrate societies are based entirely on innate behaviour.

Primate societies. One of the outstanding developments in biology during the last decade has been the large increase in the study of animals usually placed in the same taxonomic order with man – the primates. This has involved all parts of primate biology, but it has been especially great in the study of behaviour. It has been carried to an unusual degree by coordination of laboratory and field investigations.

In between laboratory and field have been studies of captive colonies. In one such colony of Japanese macaque monkeys, a female found that she could clean the dirty potatoes they were being fed by washing them in a stream. Within a few years, all except the baby monkeys and a few old ones were

Figure 5.23 Laboratory study of primate mother–offspring relationships. Presented with several mother substitutes, this infant monkey clings to an object that is soft and warm and gives milk.

Figure 5.24 Social behaviour in animals such as these vervet monkeys is easily studied by ethologists.

washing potatoes. These same monkeys were also fed wheat, which was spread about on a sandy beach for them. At first the monkeys painstakingly picked up each grain of wheat in their fingers. Then a few monkeys began picking up handfuls of sand and wheat, running into the shallow water, and letting the water wash away the sand from the grain. Again, within a few years, a quarter of the monkeys were using this learnt and much more efficient technique for obtaining their food. Although similar observations have occasionally been made in other social groups of birds and mammals, in primates a valuable kind of behaviour discovered by one individual is especially likely to be learned by its companions.

One of the earlier field studies was made by C. R. Carpenter, who spent almost a year observing howler monkeys on Barro Colorado Island. This island is a forested hill that became isolated when Gatun Lake was formed in the course of the construction of the Panama Canal. Howlers are the largest American monkeys (in body weight) and the noisiest. Cries of howler monkeys can be heard many kilometres away. Their choruses regularly greet the dawn, and they howl at any intruder into their forests.

Carpenter was especially interested in the social organization of the howlers. He found that there were about 400 howlers on the island, organized into 23 clans. Clans varied in size from 4 to 35 individuals, with an average of 17 or 18 individuals – 3 adult males, 7 adult females, and young.

The clans were strictly territorial, each staying within a clearly defined area. When two clans came near each other along a territorial border, vigorous howling started – a vocal battle that continued until one band or the other retreated. There were a few solitary 'bachelor' males. These, when they tried to join a clan, were shouted off – though Carpenter watched one 'bachelor' who, after persistent attempts over several weeks, was finally accepted into a clan.

Carpenter could not find that the clans had leaders. A male was usually in the lead when a clan moved, but sometimes it would be one male, sometimes another. Moreover, the males seemed to show no jealousy over the females, and no instances of fighting within a clan were observed. Among other kinds of monkeys, particularly the Indian rhesus monkeys and the African baboons, there is evidence that one of the males is the recognized leader.

Carpenter also studied gibbons in Thailand. He found them to be organized into *monogamous* families: each group consisted of one adult male, one female, and one or two young. Gibbons are not monkeys, but apes. Recently, excellent field studies have been made of other apes, particularly chimpanzees and gorillas. In these species groupings seem large, not of single families. Even though these apes are the living things most similar to man, it is clear that man and apes have had separate evolutionary histories for a long time. Ape behaviour, then, does not necessarily shed direct light on the origin of human societies. Nevertheless, go to the primate house in a zoo and watch what occurs on the other side of the bars. You will find that not only biologists are interested in primate behaviour.

INVESTIGATION 5.4

PERCEPTUAL WORLDS

INTRODUCTION

In studying animal behaviour, biologists often use complicated and expensive apparatus; but much can be learned by merely watching – noting what an animal does and under what circumstances it does it. Refer to Investigation 5.2 to see how experimental evidence can be obtained using very simple apparatus.

Whether well equipped or not, the student of animal behaviour needs first of all to know something about the stimuli that an animal under study can perceive, i.e. something about its 'view' of the world. You have already investigated some aspects of the perceptual worlds of two animals (Investigation 5.2).

PURPOSE

Here you will try to find out all you can, within the limits of time available, about the perceptual world of one particular kind of animal.

PROCEDURE

1. Arrange yourselves into groups and from the list of animals provided by your teacher, select a species for study.
2. Become generally familiar with your animal. Consider such matters as reaction to: (*a*) light (intensity and colour), (*b*) sound, (*c*) touch, (*d*) chemical substances (smell and taste).

    Consider the animal's ability to see.

Consider the animal's awareness of the biotic environment (organisms of its own species and of others).

Consider how you will determine whether or not an observed event is brought about by a particular factor in the environment.

3. Make your plans for studying the perceptual world of your animal, bearing in mind its size, natural habitat and senses. Remember that the best understanding of normal behaviour can be gained when the animal is disturbed as little as possible.

4. Draw up a short list of materials and equipment and have it reviewed by your teacher.
5. Make your investigation.
6. Prepare a group report on the perceptual world of the animal studied, indicating how each piece of information was obtained.

STUDYING THE DATA

Circulate the reports obtained and, in discussion, decide which group has obtained the most scientifically valid information.

The ability to react to stimuli from the environment is a characteristic of all living things. Such reactions, behaviour in a broad sense, enable individual organisms to adjust to changes in their environment. Behaviour can be studied from the point of view of the anatomical and physiological processes that make it possible. It can also be studied from the viewpoint of its function in the life of the organism. Though physiology and ecology must both be kept in mind for any complete understanding of behaviour, these two approaches have usually characterized separate groups of biologists.

The behaviour of organisms that lack nervous systems is rather limited. The nervous and muscular systems of animals allow a much wider variety of responses; but this variety introduces difficulties into the study of animal behaviour. Because the activities of animals sometimes resemble human behaviour, it is difficult to resist the tendency to interpret their behaviour in human terms. We are inclined to see human senses, human emotions and human thought patterns in animals; thus, we often misinterpret even when we observe carefully.

The behaviour of animals can be conveniently divided into innate behaviour and learned behaviour, though in practice it is often difficult to distinguish the two. Both innate and learned behaviour frequently involve endocrine mechanisms as well as the nervous systems. Reflexes, taxes and instincts are innate. All animals show innate behaviour to a greater or lesser degree, but the more highly developed the nervous system, the less important such behaviour tends to be. Some degree of learning seems to be possible in every animal having a nervous system with a central controlling ganglion. Reasoning seems to be confined to the larger primates.

Many kinds of animal behaviour can be grouped in many ways. We have considered four aspects of animal behaviour: periodicity, territoriality, communication and societies.

GUIDE QUESTIONS

1. What is behaviour?
2. How, in general, do behaviour studies by ethologists differ from behaviour studies by psychologists.
3. Why is anthropomorphism a danger in interpreting the behaviour of animals?
4. What other difficulties does the behavioural scientist encounter?
5. Is excitability related to behaviour?
6. How does a tropism differ from a taxis?
7. What do we mean when we say that a kind of behaviour is innate?
8. What is a 'releaser'?
9. What evidence is there that much behaviour is the result of both fixed-action patterns and learning?
10. What difficulties are involved in defining 'learning'?
11. Why does imprinting differ from other types of learning?
12. What is conditioning?
13. How is trial-and-error learning studied?
14. How does insight differ from learning?
15. What functions may territorial behaviour serve in the ecology of an organism?
16. What kind of stimuli most often serves for communication between animals?
17. How can a biologist determine the 'meaning' of a communication stimulus?
18. What factors are usually present in behaviour that is called 'social'?
19. What kinds of behaviour can be recognized in the schooling of fish?
20. Why do behavioural biologists regard insect societies as only superficially like human societies?

PROBLEMS

1. A human infant clutches at anything that touches its hands, and the strength of its grasp is great enough to support its weight. This grasping reaction appears to be innate. Would you call it a reflex or an instinct? Explain. What adaptive value might this behaviour have had in the past? Do you think it has any adaptive value now?
2. The following are examples of behaviours that have been called instinctive: (*a*) the web-building of spiders; (*b*) the nest-building of birds; (*c*) the comb-building of bees; (*d*) the dam-building of beavers. Suggest ways in which it might be possible to obtain evidence showing to what extent these activities are innate and to what extent they are learned.
3. Prepare a list of animals arranged in order of the care given the young – from least to most. You should have a variety of phyla and classes represented on your list. List the same animals in order of numbers of young produced – from most to least. Explain any relationships you can find between the two lists.
4. In embryonic mammals movements of the diaphragm and muscles attached to the ribs do not occur. At birth, however, these movements begin immediately. Does the young mammal *learn* this behaviour, or are there other ways to explain it? Relate this problem to the distinction between innate and learned behaviour.
5. The behaviour of an animal results from a complex interaction between the environment and the physiology of the animal. Find out what is known about the relationship of environmental factors to the migratory behaviour of birds. What environmental factors influence this behaviour? How do they act on the physiology of the birds? How do physiological changes bring about changes in behaviour. How do changes in behaviour affect the physiology of the birds?
6. Can an understanding of animal behaviour have any value in understanding human behaviour?

7. Biologists have found evidence of organization in even the simplest groupings of animals – for example, in herds of domestic cattle. What is a social hierarchy? How is it formed? How is it maintained? What is the effect on the hierarchy of introducing new individuals to the group? What effect do hormones have on hierarchy behaviour?

SUGGESTED READING

BEST, J. B. 'Protopsychology', *Scientific American*, February 1963. Pp. 54–62.

BROWN, F. A., Jr. *Biological Clocks* (BSCS Pamphlet 2). George G. Harrap & Co., 1962.

CARR, A. *Guideposts of Animal Navigation* (BSCS Pamphlet 1). George G. Harrap & Co., 1962.

CARTHY, J. D. *The Study of Behaviour*. Edward Arnold, 1967. (Gives a useful synthesis of some of the important aspects of the subject.)

CHANCE, M. R. A. and C. J. JOLLY. *Social Groups of Monkeys, Apes and Men*. Cape, 1970.

COLLIAS, N. E. *Animal Language* (BSCS Pamphlet 20). George G. Harrap & Co., 1964.

DILGER, W. C. 'The Behaviour of Lovebirds', *Scientific American*, January 1962. Pp. 88–98.

FARNER, D. S. *Photoperiodism in Animals* (BSCS Pamphlet 15). George G. Harrap & Co., 1964.

HARLOW, H. F. and M. K. HARLOW. 'Social Deprivation in Monkeys', *Scientific American*, November 1962. Pp. 136–46.

HOWARD, E. *Territory in Bird Life*. Fontana, 1964.

LACK, D. *The Life of the Robin*. Revised edn. Penguin, 1953.

LORENZ, K. Z. *King Solomon's Ring*. Methuen, 1952. (Excellent scientific research lies behind this book, but the material is not presented in textbook style. Easy.)

MANNING, A. *An Introduction to Animal Behaviour*. Arnold, 1967. Chapter 2: The Development of Behaviour.

MEYERRIECKS, A. J. *Courtship in Animals* (BSCS Pamphlet 3). George G. Harrap & Co., 1962. (An easily read account of animal courtship, from insects to mammals.)

NEAL, E. *The Badger*. Collins, 1969.

PALMER, J. D. 'How a Bird Tells the Time of Day', *Natural History*, March 1966. Pp. 48–53.

SAVORY, T. H. *Instinctive Living*. Pergamon Press, 1959. (An interesting account of invertebrate behaviour.)

SHAW, E. 'The Schooling of Fishes', *Scientific American*, June 1962. Pp. 128–34.

SIMPSON, G. G. and W. S. BECK. *Life: An Introduction to Biology*. 2nd edn. Routledge & Kegan Paul, 1965. Chapter 14. (Considers behaviour from a wide viewpoint. Somewhat advanced.)

SUDD, J. H. *An Introduction to the Behaviour of Ants*. Arnold, 1970.

TINBERGEN, N. and EDITORS of *Life*. *Animal Behaviour*. New York: Time Inc., Book Division, 1965. (A well-illustrated consideration of many aspects of behaviour.)

——. *The Study of Instinct*. Oxford University Press, 1951.

——. 'The curious behaviour of the stickleback', *Scientific American*, December 1952.

INDEX

Italic page references indicate illustrations in text (chart, diagram, graph, map or picture). Plate numbers refer to colour plates.

Absorption of materials: in plants, 74; in animal digestion, 104, 107
Acetic acid, 38, *38*, 44
Acetyl coenzyme A, 38, 39
Active transport: in cells, 14; drugs and, 123; in kidney tubules, 126; of mineral nutrients from soil to roots of plants, 73–4; through phloem cells, 83; in primitive organisms, 113; through villi, 107
Adenine, *47*
Adenosine diphosphate (ADP), 36, *37*, *47*, 54, 138
Adenosine monophosphate, *47*, 47
Adenosine triphosphate (ATP), 36, *37*, 41, 46, 53–6, *55*, *56*, 138
ADP. *See* Adenosine diphosphate
Adrenal glands, *127*, 130–1, *131*
Adrenalin, 130
Aerobic respiration, 41
Ageing, 24–5
Algae: lack of vascular systems, 93
Alimentary canal, of *Hydra*, roundworm and sponge, *102*
Alveoli, *111*, 112
Amino acids, 45–6, *45*, 107, 117, 124–5, 131
Ammonia, 123, 125
Amoeba, food intake, 101
AMP. *See* Adenosine monophosphate
Amphibians: blood circulation of, *115*; territorial behaviour in, 175
Amylase, 106, *107*
Anaemia, 118
Anaerobic respiration, 41. *See also* fermentation
Animal behaviour: communication, 177–9; perceptual worlds, 183–4; periodicity in, 171–3; social behaviour, 179–83; social behaviour in fish, 175–7; territoriality, 173–5
Animal mitosis, 16–18, *17*
Animals: absorption of materials by, 104; cell division in,

16–18; digestion, 102–4; as food seekers and consumers, 100; ingestion, 101–2; nutrition, 101–9; respiration, 109–12; structure and function, 96–100
Annelids: circulatory system in, 114; excretory system of, 124; nervous system in, 132
Anterior pituitary gland, 130, 173
Antibodies, 117
Anthropomorphism, 152
Ants, 178, 181
Anus, 107, 122
Apes, social organization of, 183
Arnon, Daniel, 49
Arteries, 115, 116
Arthropods: chemoreceptors in, 142; circulatory system in, 113–14; muscles of, 137–8; nervous systems in, 133; skeleton of, 138, 139, *139*
Associative neurons, 134
ATP. *See* Adenosine triphosphate
Auricle, 115, 135
Autonomic nervous system, 135, 140
Auxin, role in elongation of cells in phototropism, 87, 88, *88*

Baboon, 183
Bacteria, *5*, 107
Banyan tree, 77
Bark, 78, 86
Bases, of nucleic acids, 47
Bees, social behaviour in, 181
Beetles, absence of learning in, 162
Behaviour, 149–86; communication, 177–9; difficulties in behavioural studies, 150–3; innate, 159–60; involving nervous systems, 159–66; involving no nervous system, 154–8; learned, 161–4, 167–70; levels of, 153–70; patterns of animal behaviour, *151*, 170–84; periodicity in, 171–3; reasoning, 165–6; social, 179–83; territoriality, 173–5

Bermuda grass, phototropism in, 155
Betta, 175–7
Bile, 106, 122
Biochemical reactions, study of, 33–4
Bioenergetics, 29–60
Biological clock, 173
Birds: digestive processes in, 103; heart action in, 115–16; heat conservation in, 140
Blackberry bushes, transpiration in, 67–8
Black bread mould (*Rhizopus nigricans*), 15, *15*
Bladder, *127*
Blade (leaf), 64, *64*
Blood: clotting of, 119; discovery of circulatory system, 112–13; filtration by kidneys, 125–7; plasma, 116–17; platelets, 118; red and white cells, *5*, 118; variations in, 116
Blue-green algae: cell division in, 16; chlorophyll in, 50; distribution of DNA in, 47; structure of grana, 50. *See also* Green algae, Brown algae
Body fluids, 116, 123, 124, 127, 128
Body temperature, regulation of in 'warm blooded' animals, 140–1
Bone, 138, 139
Bony fish, gills of, *110*
Boysen-Jensen, Peter, 86, 87
Brain, in annelids, 132; dominance in vertebrate nervous systems, 134
Breathing, 34; co-ordination of, 131–2; movements in man, 110–12, *111*
Bronchi, 112
Brown, Robert, 18
Brown algae, chlorophyll in, 50; growth of, 93
Bryophytes, chlorophyll in, 50; limits on upward transport of soil water, 92
Buds, 77, 78, *78*
Bünning, Erwin, 171
Burström, Hans, 74

Cactus: spines as modified leaves, 64; storage function of stems, 84
Calvin, Melvin, 55
Cambium tissue, 78, 85–6, *85*
Capillaries, 115, 116, 118, 119
Carbohydrates: digestion of, 106; synthesis of, 43–4, 49
Carbon-14, 57–8
Carbon dioxide: in cellular respiration, 37–40; in photosynthesis, 48, 49, 53, 55–6; role in co-ordination of breathing, 131–2; as waste, 122, 127
Carnauba wax, 45
Carotenes, 4, Plate IV
Carpenter, C. R., 182–3
Carrot, 76
Cartilage, *23*, 139
Cat, 140, *141*
Catalysis, 33
Cell ageing and death, 24–5
Cell differentiation, 21–4, 84
Cell division: meristems, 84–6; mitosis in animals, 16–19; mitosis in plants, 19–21
Cell duplication, 15. *See also* Cell division
Cell membranes, 5–6, *6*, 9, 12
Cell physiology, 9–10; metabolism, 9; transport in cells, 9–10. *See also* Energy releasing processes
Cell structure: components of, 3–7; diversity in, *5*, 7–8; in mitosis, 16–21, *17*
Cell theory, 2–3
Cellular respiration, 34–40, *37*, 109, 123, 130
Cellulose, 44
Cell walls, 7
Centrifuge, *117*
Centromere, 16, *17*
Centrosomes, 4, 16, *18*
Chaffinch, *171*; behaviour of, 161, 172, *172*, 173–5
Chameleon, *101*
Cheese-making, role of bacteria in, 41
Chemical co-ordination: endocrine glands, 129–31, *131*; hormones, 129; other substances that aid co-ordination, 131
Chemical digestion, 103–4, *107*
Chemoreceptors, in man, 142–5
Chest cavity, 110–11, 139

Chitins, 138, *139*
Chlorophyll, 4, Plates IV, VI; kinds of, 50; pattern of energy absorption, Plates III, V; role in photosynthesis, 65
Chlorophyll a, b, c, and d, 50, 93, Plate III
Chloroplasts, 4, 49–50, *49*, 57
Chordates, skeletons of, 138–9, *139*
Chromatids, 16, *17*, *18*
Chromatography, 50–2, Plate IV
Chromosomes, action during mitosis, 16, *17*, *17*
Chyme, 106
Cilia, in flame cells, 124
Circadian rhythms, 172–3
Circulatory systems: Harvey's discovery of, 112–13, 115; in invertebrates, 113–14; in vertebrates, 115–16, *115*
Citric acid, 38, *39*
Closed circulatory systems, 114, 119
Clostridium tetani, 41
Clotting of blood, 119, 130
Coelenterates: absence of learning in, 162; digestion in, 103; excretion of wastes in, 123; fluid transport in, *114*; intracellular digestion in, 103; means of catching prey, 101–2; muscular specialization in, 137; responses to stimuli, 132; skeletons of, 138; transport systems in, 113
Coenzyme A, 38
Cohesion of molecules, 82
Coleoptiles, 86–8
Communication, between animals, 177–9
Companion cells, 80, *80*
Conditioning, 163
Conduction of liquids, as principal function of stems, 80–3
Connective tissue, *23*
Contraction, in muscle, 138
Co-ordination, chemical and nervous, 129–35
Coral, 138
Cork, Hooke's study of, 1–2, *1*
Cortex (root), 74
Corydoras, 175–7
Cows, digestive system of, *104*
Cristae, 5
Crustaceans: excretory system of, 124; fluid transport in,

114; learning in, 167–70; nervous system in, *133*; oxygen uptake in, 109–10
Cuticle, 67
Cyclosis, 15
Cytoplast, 4, 6, 15, 18, 40, 68, 80, 103

Dahlia, 76
Daphnia, 120–1, *120*
'Dark reactions', in photosynthesis, 55–6
Darwin, Charles: study of earthworms, 149; study of phototropism, 86
Darwin, Francis, 86
Deciduous twig, 77–8, *78*
De Humani Corporis Fabrica, 1
Dehydration synthesis: of sucrose, 44; of fatty acids, 45
Deoxyribose nucleic acid (DNA), 47
Diatoms, chlorophyll in, 50
Dicolyledon, stem of, *75*, 78
Differential permeability, 12
Differentiation. *See* Cell differentiation
Diffusion, 9–10, *13*, through membranes, 12–14; of minerals from soil water into root hairs, 73; in primitive organisms, 113; random movement of molecules, 10, Plate I; through villi, 104; of water from leaves to air, 66–7
Digestion: in animals, 102–4; in man, 105–7, *107*
Digestive cavity: as extension of animal's environment, 103; kinds of, 102, *102*
Disaccharides, 44
Dixon, H. H., 82
DNA. *See* Deoxyribose nuclei acid
Dogs, behaviour in, 163, 165
Dropsy, 123
Dutrochet, Henri, 2

Earthworms: breathing in, 110; circulatory system of, 114; Darwin's studies of, 149; excretory system of, 124; fluid transport in, *114*; nervous system in, 132, *133*
Echinoderms: absence of learning in, 162; skeletons of, 138
Effectors, 134, *134*

Electron carriers, 39–40, 53, 54
Elements, needed by plants, 73–4
Elimination of wastes, 122
Elodea, 85
Emperor moth, 179, *179*
Endocrine glands, 129, *131*, 175
Endoplasmic reticulum, 6, *6*
Endoskeleton, 139
Energy releasing processes, 32–3; catalysis and enzymes, 33; cellular respiration, 34–41, *40*; energy units, 32; fermentation, 40–3
Energy transfer compounds, 35–6
Environment, internal and external, 128
Enzymes, 33, 44, *107*; of digestion, 104, 105–9, *107*; of respiration, 40
Epidermis, in leaves, 65, 67, of root hairs, 74
Epiglottis, 111, *111*
Equatorial plate, 16–17
Ethanol, 41
Ethologists, 151
Euglena: food intake, 101; phototaxis in, 155
Excretion, 122–7; of nitrogenous wastes, 124–7; of salts, 127; of water, 123–4
Exoskeleton, 138
External environment, adjustment to, 136
'Eyes', of potato, 77
Eye-spot, 132

Faeces, 107
Fats: deposition of, 131; digestion of, 106, 107; in lymph, 119; synthesis of, 44, 45
Fatty acids, 44, 107
Fermentation, 40–3, *41*
Fibrin, 119
Fibrinogen, 119
Fibrous root system, 72, *72*, 76, *76*
Fibrovascular bundles, 79, *79*
Fish: blood circulation of, *115*; schooling in, 180, *180*; social behaviour in, 175–7; territorial behaviour in, 175
Fixed-action patterns, 159
Flame cells, 124, *124*
Flatworms: intracellular digestion in, 103; learning in, 162; muscular specializa-tion in, 137; nervous systems in, 132; transport systems in, 113
Food production, in stems, 83
Formic acid, 178
Frog, dissection of, 96–100, 98–9
Fructose, 44
Fungi: and gibberellins, 89; lack of chlorophyll, 92

Galactose, 44
Ganglion, 132
Gastric juice, 105, 122
Gastric glands, 105
Gastric proteinase (pepsin), 105
Geotropism, 154
Gibberellins, 89
Gibbons, 183
Gills, 110, *110*, 125
Gizzard, digestive function of, 103
Glands, 129–31
Glomerulus, 125
Glow-worms, 35
Glucose, 35, *35*; metabolism of, 128, 130, Plate II; regulation of, 128, 130, 131; role in energy release in cells, 37–41
Glycerol (glycerine), 44, 107
Glycine, 45
Glycogen, 128
Glycolysis, 37–9
Grana, 49
Grape stem, pith from, 23
Grass leaf: epidermis, 66; meristem, 85
Green algae, chlorophyll in, 50. See also Algae, Blue-green algae, Brown algae
Growth, in animals and plants: chemical control of, 86–9, 131; meristems in plants, 84–6
Guard cells, 66–7; action of, 67

Haemoglobin, 118
Harvey, William, 112–13, *112*, 115
Heart: action of, *116*; effects of temperature change on heartbeat, 120–1; function in circulation of blood, 115, 135
Heartwood, 78
Heat regulation, 140–1
Hepatic portal, 128
Herring gulls: nestling behaviour, 160, *161*; territoriality, *174*
Hill, Robin, 49
Homeostasis: chemical co-ordination, 129–32; in an internal environment, 128–9; nervous co-ordination, 132–5; regulation of body temperature in 'warm blooded' animals, 140–1
Hooke, Robert, studies of cork, 1–2, *1*
Hormones, 129–31, 173–4
Horse chestnut leaf, *64*
Howard, Eliot, 173, 175
Howler monkeys, social organization of, 182–3
Hydra: digestive cavity of, *102*; nervous system of, *133*
Hydration cleavage, 103
Hydrochloric acid, 105, 106
Hydrogen peroxide, 33–4
Hypothalamus, 130, *131*, 135, 140, 173

Imprinting, 163
Indoleacetic acid, effect on growth of plants, 88
Indolebutyric acid, 89
Ingen-Housz, Jan, 48
Ingestion of food, 101–2
Innate behaviour, 159–60; periodicity, 172
Insects, oxygen intake in, 110; social behaviour in, 180–1
Insight, as factor in animal behaviour, 165
Instinctive behaviour, 159, Plate VIII
Insulin, 130
Internal environment, nervous co-ordination of, 135
Invertebrates: circulatory systems in, 113–14; investigation of learning ability, 167–70; territorial behaviour in, 175
Irritability, as fundamental characteristic of living substance, 153–4
Islands of Langerhans, 130, *131*

Japanese monkeys, 181–2
Jellyfish, 123
Joule, 32

Kamen, Martin, 53
Kidneys, *127*; function of, 125–7, 128

Kinetochore, 16
Krebs cycle, 37–40, *37*

Lactase, 107
Lactic acid, 41
Lactose, 44, 107
Lamarck, Jean Baptiste de, 2
Langerhans, islands of, 130, *131*
Larynx, *111*
Lateral buds, 77, *78*
Learned behaviour: in animals, 161–4; conditioning, 163; imprinting, 163; in an invertebrate, 167–70; reasoning, 165–6; trial-and-error learning, 163–4
Learning, 161–6
Leaves: cellular structure of, 65, 68, *75*; diversity among, 64; investigation of rate of growth in, 90–1; separation of pigments of, 50–2; three-dimensional diagram, *75*; water loss in, 66–8
Leeches, ingestion of food, 102
Leeuwenhoek, Antony van, discovery of microscopic life, 1
Lenticels, 78, *78*
Life, in cells, 12, 29
Light energy, 48, 53
Light reactions, in photosynthesis, 53–5
Light sensitivity, 136
Lilac leaf epidermis, *66*
Lipase, 107
Lipids, 45, 49, 67
Liver, 127, 128
Liverworts, 92
Lockjaw, 41
Lorenz, Konrad, 163
Lungs, 110, 112, 127
Lymph, 119; nodes, 119; vessels, *104*, 107

Macaque monkeys, 181–2
Mackerel, *180*
Maize: stem tissues of, 79; transpiration in, 68
Malpighi, Marcello, 1, 115
Maltase, 107
Maltose, 44, 107
Mammals: blood circulation of, *115*; digestion in, 103; endocrine glands of, 130–1; excretion of, 125–7; heart action in, 115–16; *116*; nervous system in, *133*; territorial behaviour in, *175*; types of neurons in, 134–5. See also Man
Man: breathing movement in, *111*; breathing system in, *111*; chemoreceptors of, 142–5; digestion in, 105–7; respiration in, 110–12
Marine annelid, gills in, *110*
Mass spectrometer, 53
Mayer, Julius Robert, 48
Maze behaviour, 164
Meristems, 84–6, *85*
Mesophyll: action of guard cells and stomata, 66–7, *67*; role in 'transpiration tension', 66–7; theory of rise of liquids in plant stems, 82; site of chloroplasts and photosynthesis, 65, *65*
Metabolism, 9, 117, 123
Migration, 174
Mimosa, reaction to touch, *155*
Mineral nutrients: in blood, 117; from soil, 73–4; in sea water, 93
Mitochondria, 4, *5*, 18, 40
Mitosis: in animals, 16–18; in meristems, 84
Molecular theory, 9
Molluscs: circulatory system of, 113; excretory system of, 124; nervous system of, 132–3; skeletons of, 138
Mosses, survival in dry places, 92, *92*
Motor neurons, 134, *134*
Mountain ash leaf, *64*
Mucus, 107
Multicellular organisms: basic structural characteristics of, 21–2; continuity of cells in, 24
Muscle tissue (in vertebrates), 137–8, *137*
Muscle tone, 138

NADPH, 53–6
Nematodes, fluid transport in, *114*
Nerve cells. *See* Neurons
Nerve cord, 134
Nerve impulses, 134
Nervous co-ordination: kinds of nervous systems, 132–4, *133*; nerves and internal co-ordination, 135
Nervous system, 129; kinds of, 132–4, *133*
Neurohormones, 130
Neurons (nerve cells), 23, 134

Nitrogenous wastes, excretion of, 124–7
Non-vascular plants, 91–3; algae, 93; bryophytes, 92; fungi, 92; lichens, 92
Nucleic acids, and synthesis of, 47
Nucleolus, 4, 18
Nucleus, 3, *4*, 16, 18, 47
Nucleotides, 47, *47*
Nutrients, of plants, 73–4
Nutrition, 101–7; absorption, 104; digestion, 102–4; ingestion, 101–2

Oesophagus, *104*, 105, *106*, 112
Oils, 93
On the Motion of the Heart and Blood, 113
Open circulatory systems, 113–14
Organelles, 4
Organs, 22
Organ system, 22, 24
Ovaries, 131, *131*
Oxaloacetic acid, 38, *39*
Oxidation, 34
Oxygen: in cellular respiration, 39–40, 109; in photosynthesis, 48, 49, 53; isotopes, 53
Oxyhaemoglobin, 118

Pancreas, 130, *131*
Pancreatic juice, 106
Paramecium: diffusion into, 13–14; reactions to five environmental stimuli, *155*; structure of, *3*, *5*
Parathyroid glands, 130, *131*
Pathogens, 118, 119
Pavlov, Ivan P., studies of conditioning, 163
Pepsin, 105
Peptides, 106
Perceptual worlds: differences in, 153; investigation of, 183–4
Periodicity, in animal behaviour, 171–3
Peristalsis, 103
Petiole, 64
Pharynx, *111*, *111*
Phase-contrast microscopy, 3
Phloem: formation of, 78–9, 86; movement of liquids from leaves to roots, 83; sieve tubes and companion cells, 80, *80*

Index 191

Phosphate, 47, *47*
Phosphoglyceraldehyde, 56
Photosynthesis, 48–59, *56*, 66; in algae, 93; biochemistry of, 52–8; and carbon dioxide intake, 48; 'dark reactions' in, 55–6, *56*; early experiments on, 48–9; leaves as organs of, 63; 'light reactions' in, 53–5, *54*, *55*; and mesophyll, 65, *65*; methods of investigation, 57–8; plastids in, 4; rate of, 58–9; in stems, 83; and stomata, 70–1
Phototropism, 86–8, 154, 155
Physical digestion, 103
Physiological activity, investigation of chemical and energy changes involved in, 30–2
Pilot whale, learning in, 162–3
Pinocytosis, 14–15
Pith, *23*, 78
Pituitary glands, 130, *131*
Planarians: excretion of wastes in, 123, 124, *124*; function of eye-spots in, 132; nervous system in, 132, *133*
Plants: chemical control of growth in, 86–9; meristems of, 84–6; mitosis and cell division in, 19–21; and rate of growth, 90–1; tropic responses in, 156–8. *See also* Non-vascular plants, Vascular plants
Plasma, 116–17, *117*, 119
Plastids, 4
Platelets, 118, *118*, 119
Polypeptide, 46
Polysaccharides, 44, 93
Porpoises, learning in, *167*
Predators, as poisoners of prey, 101–2
Priestley, Joseph, 48
Primates, behaviour in, 165–6, *166*, *181*, 181–3, *182*
Privet plant, *65*
Proteins, 45–6; digestion of, 105, 106–7; in blood, 117; synthesis of, 46
Prothrombin, 119
Psychologists, 151
Pump, heart as, 115–16, 125, 135
Pyloric valve, 106
Pyruvic acid, 38, *38*, 41
Pythons, chemical digestion of prey in, 103

Rabbit, nervous system in, *133*
Radish seedling, 72–3, *73*
Random movement of molecules, 10
Reasoning, as factor in animal behaviour, 165–6
Receptors, 134, *134*, 136
Red algae, chlorophyll in, 50
Red blood cells (corpuscles), 5, 16, 118, *118*
Reflex, 135, *135*, 159, 163
Releaser, 160
Rennin, 105
Reptiles, territorial behaviour in, 175
Respiration: in animals, 109–12; in plants, 57. *See also* Cellular respiration
Rhesus monkeys, recognition of leaders, 183
Rhizopus nigricans, 15, *15*
Ribose, 47
Ribose nucleic acid (RNA), 47
Ribosomes, 6
Ribulose diphosphate, 56
RNA. See Ribose nucleic acid
Robin, *162*
Root caps, 75, 84
Root hairs, and absorption of water and mineral nutrients in plants, 73–4, *74*, Plate VII
Root pressure, 83
Roots: absorption function, 72–4; anchorage function, 72; kinds of, *72*; storage function, 76, *76*; three-dimensional diagram, *75*
Rose leaf, *64*
Rotifers, 109
Roundworms: digestive cavity, *102*, 103; transport system, 113
Ruben, Samuel, 53
Rumen, *104*

Salamanders, breathing in, 110
Salivary amylase, investigation of effects of varying conditions, 108–9
Salivary glands, 105, 129
Salivation, in dogs, 163
Salts, excretion of, 127, 131; transport in stems, 80
Sap, 74, 80–1
Sapwood, 78
Saussure, Nicolas de, 48
Scale scars, 78, *78*
Scallops, 138
Schleiden, Matthias, 2

Schooling fish, 180, *180*
Schwann, Theodor, 2
Secretin, 131
Secretion, 122
Sedum leaf epidermis, *66*
Senebier, Jean, 48
Sense organs, 132, 133
Sensory neurons, 134, *134*, 135, 136
Sieve cells, 83
Sieve tubes, 80, *80*, Plate VII
Sight (perception), interpretation of, 153, Plate IX
'Silly seedlings', 89
Simple sugars, 43, 117
Skeletons: function of, 138–9; movement of, 139
Skinner, B. F., 164
Slime moulds, differential response in, 154
Slugs, breathing in, 110
Small intestine, and digestion, *105*, *106*, 106–7
Smell, relation to taste, 143–5
Smooth muscle tissue, 137–8, *137*
Snakes: and ingestion of food, 102, digestion, 103
Social behaviour in animals: in fish, 175–7; in fish schools, 180, *180*; in insect societies, 180–1; in primate societies, 181–3
Sodium chloride, diffusion and excretion of, 123
Soil nutrients, 73–4
Specificity, of enzymes, 33
Spindle, 16, 17, 18
Sponges: digestive cavity in, *102*; excretion of wastes by, 123; ingestion of food by, 101; intracellular digestion in, 103; lack of muscle tissue in, 137; reaction to stimuli in, 132; skeleton of, 138; transport systems in, 113
Squirrels, behaviour of, 159, 161
Staining of cells, 2
Starch, 44, 74, 93, 107
Steady state: chemical co-ordination, 129–32; in an internal environment, 128–9; nervous co-ordination, 132–5; physiological, 139–41; temperature, 139–41
Stems: conduction of liquids, 80–3; distinction between root and shoot system, 76–7; growth in, 85; macroscopic structure, 77–8; microscopic

structure, 78–80; photosynthetic and storage functions, 83–4; three-dimensional diagram, 75
Stimuli, 136, 178
Stomach, digestion in, 105–6
Stomata, 65, 66, 66–7, *67*; and photosynthesis, 70–1; role in gas exchange and transpiration, 66–7, Plate VII
Storage roots, 74, 76, *76*
Storage stems, 84, *84*
Striated muscle tissue, 137–8, *137*
Structural formula, 35
Sucrase, 107
Sucrose, 43–4, 107
Sugar-beet, storage in stems, 84
Sunflower, stem of, *79*
Swallows, nesting behaviour of, *160*
Sweat glands, 127, 129
Sycamore, leaves of, *64*
Synapses, 135
Syntheses, 43–7; and carbohydrates, 43–4; and fats, 44–5; and nucleic acids, 47; and proteins, 45–6

Taproot system, 72, 76, *76*
Taste, relation of smell to, 143–5
Taste receptors, location of, 142–3
Taste threshold, 143
Taxes, 155, 159
Tears, 122
Temperature regulation, 140–1
Tensile strength, of a column of water, 82
Terminal bud, 77, *78*
Termites, social behaviour in, 181
Territoriality, 173–5
Testes, 131, *131*, 173, 174
Thermoreceptors, 140
Thrombin, 119
Thromboplastin, 119

Thymus gland, *131*
Thyroid glands, 130, *131*
Tissues, and diversity in, 22, 23
T maze, *151*, 164
Toxic substances, 123
Trachea, 112
Tracheids, 79, *80*
Tracheophytes: chlorophyll in, 50; the first, 63; roots of, 72
Transpiration, 67–9, Plate VII
'Transpiration tension' theory, 82
Transport of materials: active transport, 14; in blood, 116–19; in cells, 9–10; circulatory systems, 113–16; cyclosis, 15; diffusion, 9–14; effect of temperature change on heartbeat, 120–1; Harvey's discovery of circulation of blood, 112–13; lymph, 119; pinocytosis, 14–15; simpler transport systems, 113
Tree trunks, 78, *79*
Trial-and-error learning, 163–4
Tripeptide, 46, *46*
Trisaccharides, 44
Tropic responses in plants, 156–8.
Tropisms, 154–5. *See also* Phototropism
Trypsin, 106–7

Unlearned behaviour, 159–60
Urea, 125, *125*
Ureter, *127*
Urethra, 126, *127*
Uric acid, 125
Urinary system, human, *127*
Urine, 126, 130

Vacuoles, 7; in root-hair cells, 73
Valves: in blood vessels, 114; in heart, 116

Vascular plants: growth 84–91; leaves, 63–71; roots' 72–6; stems, 76–84
Veins: in leaves, 66, 81; in plants, 75, 81; in vertebrates, 115
Ventricle, 115
Vertebrates: breathing in, 110–12; circulatory systems in, 115–16, *115*; digestion in, 103; nervous systems of, 134; muscles of, 137–8; skeletons of, 139, *139*; structures that aid ingestion in, 102
Vervet monkeys, *182*
Vesalius, Andreas, 1
Vessels, and transport of sap, 79–80, *80*
Villi, 104, *104*
Vorticella, behaviour of, 154, *154*

'Warm blooded' animals, 139–40
Waste materials, 123
Water: loss in leaves, 66–8; in soil, 73; storage in stems, 84; as waste, 123
Weed control, use of chemical substances for, 88–9
Weismann, August, 24
Went, Frits, 88
White blood cells (corpuscles), 5, 118, *118*
Wilting, in leaves, 68
Wood-lice, 167–70
Wood rays, 78
Wood tissue, 22
Woody twig, dormant, *78*

Xanthophylls (yellow pigments), 4, 54, Plate IV
Xylem: formation of, 78, 85–6; tracheids and vessels, 79, Plate VII; as vehicle of movement of water from roots to leaves, 81

Year's growth, in twigs, *78*
Yeast, 41